THE FURIES

THE FURIES

☆

JOHN JAKES

THE KENT CHRONICLES
VOLUME FOUR

NELSON DOUBLEDAY, Inc.
Garden City, New York

Produced by Lyle Kenyon Engel

Printed in the United States of America

For my son John Michael

CONTENTS

"Mr. President, I wish to speak today, not as a Massachusetts man, nor as a Northern man, but as an American . . .

"It is not to be denied that we live in the midst of strong agitations, and are surrounded by very considerable dangers to our institutions and government. The imprisoned winds are let loose. The East, the North, and the stormy South combine to throw the whole sea into commotion, to toss its billows to the sky, and disclose its profoundest depths. I speak today for the preservation of the Union . . .

"I hear with distress and anguish the word 'secession,' especially when it falls from the lips of those who are patriotic, and known to the country, and known all over the world, for their political services. Secession! Peaceable secession! Sir, your eyes and mine are never destined to see that miracle . . .

"I will not state what might produce the disruption of the Union; but, Sir, I see as plainly as I see the sun in heaven what that disruption itself must produce; I see that it must produce war."

March 7, 1850   Daniel Webster,
                                                to the United States Senate,
                                                in support of Henry Clay's
                                                compromise bills
                                                on slavery.

THE FURIES

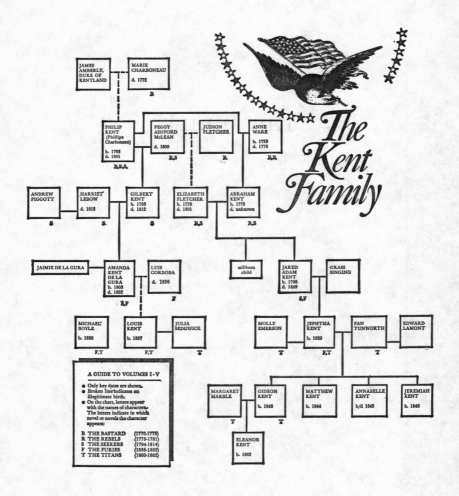

The Kent Family

JAMES AMBERLY, DUKE OF KENTLAND

MARIE CHARBONEAU
d. 1772
B

PHILIP KENT (Phillipe Charboneau)
b. 1753
d. 1801
B,R,S

PEGGY ASHFORD McLEAN
d. 1800
R,S

JUDSON FLETCHER
R

ANNE WARE
b. 1753
d. 1775
B,R

ANDREW PIGGOTT
S

HARRIET LEBOW
d. 1813
S

GILBERT KENT
b. 1783
d. 1812
S

ELIZABETH FLETCHER
b. 1775
d. 1801
R,S

ABRAHAM KENT
b. 1775
d. unknown
R,S

JAIMIE DE LA GURA

AMANDA KENT DE LA GURA
b. 1803
d. 1852
S,F

LUIS CORDOBA
d. 1836
F

stillborn child

JARED ADAM KENT
b. 1798
d. 1849
S,F

GRASS SINGING

MICHAEL BOYLE
b. 1830
F,T

LOUIS KENT
b. 1837
F,T

JULIA SEDGWICK
T

MOLLY EMERSON
T

JEPHTHA KENT
b. 1820
F,T

FAN TUNWORTH
T

EDWARD LAMONT

MARGARET MARBLE
T

GIDEON KENT
b. 1843
T

MATTHEW KENT
b. 1844
T

ANNABELLE KENT
b/d 1845

JEREMIAH KENT
b. 1846

ELEANOR KENT
b. 1862

A GUIDE TO VOLUMES I–V

- Only key dates are shown.
- Broken line indicates an illegitimate birth.
- On the chart, letters appear with the names of characters. The letters indicate in which novel or novels the character appears:

B THE BASTARD   (1770-1775)
R THE REBELS   (1775-1781)
S THE SEEKERS   (1794-1814)
F THE FURIES   (1836-1852)
T THE TITANS   (1860-1862)

Author's Introduction
to this Special Edition

WHEN the first volume of The Kent Chronicles appeared in October, 1974, its publication could have been likened to the dropping of a small pebble into a huge pond. Few people connected with the project, I think—and certainly not the author—believed there would be more than a modest ripple created by THE BASTARD and its successors.

But in one of those genuinely unplanned and unplannable miracles which occur now and then—miracles which help make the publishing business a sort of Monte Carlo of words, ink, and paper—the ripple effect grew larger with each succeeding book. Within a relatively short time, many readers began to adopt the Kents as their second family—just as I had.

It seems to me there are two main reasons why this happened:

Although readers are often told by pundits that there's something slightly shameful about enjoying an old-fashioned *story*, those same readers, bless them, continue to ignore the message. Any writer has to be grateful for that.

But the gratitude is doubled because the Kent saga is not only the continuing tale of a family, but the story of our country's beginning and growth. That story can't be re-told too often; especially in these times when we often founder in pessimism, forgetting that Americans have overcome enormous obstacles in the past, and steadfastly continued to perfect a form of government which, with all its faults, remains a beacon of hope for the world.

I've received many a letter complaining about the dullness of history as it seems to be taught in school. The letters often ask rhetorically why the colorful, human side of that history seldom appears in conventional texts. I've never quite figured out a satisfactory answer for the question. But this series, in its own way, is an attempt to help remedy the apparent deficiency.

It's been interesting to travel around the country, talk with readers, and watch another developing aspect of "the ripple effect." In the beginning—and this is a completely subjective, unscientific analysis!—the series seemed to attract mainly those people who liked historical novels and couldn't find a sufficient quantity of new ones; in other words, the first readers were dedicated readers.

Of late, though, I've begun to encounter a different kind of Kent fan. Typically, he or she will start a conversation by saying, "I don't usually read books, but—" Or, "I only read a couple of books a year, but—" That too adds to a writer's satisfaction, which, contrary to popular belief, isn't really derived from gloating over sales figures, but from knowing a given book has touched an individual human being on a one-to-one basis.

So if the series has attracted readers who might not normally have turned its pages even a year ago, so much the better.

Many people have repeatedly asked for more permanent versions of the novels. Consequently this special edition fills a genuine need, and its publication provides just one more opportunity for men and women to watch the unfolding drama of America through the eyes of the Kents—a family, by the way, that I never intended to be made up entirely of successful, flawless paragons. Real families are seldom like that.

My thanks, then, to the publishers of this edition for their willingness to present the times, triumphs and travails of the Kents—and the canvas of our common past—to yet another segment of the American reading public.

JOHN JAKES

July, 1976

BOOK ONE
Turn Loose Your Wolf

CHAPTER 1

The Chapel

SHE AWOKE LATE IN the night. At first she thought she was resting in her room, on the second floor of the adobe building local custom dignified with the name Gura's Hotel. It was a hotel, of sorts. But the small, well-kept establishment on Soledad Street served customers other than those who wanted a meal, a glass of *aguardiente* or a bed to be used for sleeping—

For a few drowsy, delicious moments she believed she was back there. Safe. Secure—

Her mind cleared. Reality shattered the comforting illusion. Gura's Hotel might only be a few hundred yards west of where she lay in the darkness, one torn blanket affording poor protection from the chill of the moonless night. But much more than distance cut her off from all that the hotel represented.

She was cut off by the four-foot-thick walls of the roofless chapel of the mission of San Antonio de Valero. She was cut off by the trenches among the cottonwoods—*los alamos*—that lined the water ditches outside. She was cut off by the heavily guarded plank bridges over the San Antonio River. She was cut off by an enemy force estimated to number between four and five thousand men.

Yet something other than the physical presence of an army was fundamentally responsible for her separation from the hotel. No one had forced her to come to the mission some said was nicknamed for the cottonwoods, and others for a garrison of soldiers from Coahuila that had been stationed here early in the century. Her own choice had isolated her.

In those lonely seconds just after full consciousness returned, the woman whose name was Amanda Kent de la Gura almost regretted her decision. She lay on the hard-packed ground, her head against a stone—the only kind of pillow available—and admitted to herself that she was afraid.

She had been in difficult, even dangerous circumstances before. She had been afraid before. But always, there had been at least a faint hope of survival. Only the most foolishly optimistic of the hundred and eighty-odd men walled up in the mission believed there was a chance of escape.

Turned on her side, her best dress of black silk tucked between her legs for warmth, Amanda stared into the darkness. In memory she saw the flag that had been raised from the tower of San Fernando Church on Bexar's main plaza. The flag was red, with no decoration or device to signify its origin. To the men and the handful of women who took refuge in the mission when the enemy arrived, however, the meaning of the flag was clear. It meant the enemy general would give no quarter in battle.

Amanda's mood of gloom persisted. Only with a deliberate effort of will did she turn her thoughts elsewhere. Pessimism accomplished nothing. Since she couldn't sleep, she ought to get up and look in on her friend the colonel—

But she didn't move immediately. She listened. She was disturbed by the silence. What had become of the night noises to which she and the others had grown accustomed during the past twelve—no, thirteen days?

She yawned. That was it, thirteen. It must be Sunday morning by now. Sunday, the sixth of March, 1836. The first companies of enemy troops had clattered into San Antonio de Bexar on the twenty-third. Counting the extra day for a leap year, today would mark the thirteenth day of the siege—

She couldn't remember when the night had been so still.

There was no *crump-crump* of Mexican artillery pieces hammering away at the walls. No wild, intimidating yells from the troops slowly closing an armed ring around the mission. No sudden, terrifying eruptions of music as the enemy general's massed regimental bands struck up a brassy serenade in the middle of the night, to keep the defenders awake; strain their nerves. The general knew that tired men were more susceptible to fear—and less accurate with their firearms—than rested ones—

None of those tactics had worked, though. If anything, the resolve of the garrison had stiffened as the days passed; stiffened even when it became apparent that Buck Travis' appeals for help, sent by mounted messengers who dashed out through the enemy lines after dark, would not be answered.

Colonel Fannin supposedly had three hundred men at Goliad, a little over ninety miles away. Three hundred men might make the difference. But now everyone understood that Fannin wasn't coming. He hesitated to risk his troops against such a huge Mexican force. That message had been brought back by one of Travis' couriers, the courtly southerner Jim Bonham. He had risked his life to return alone when he could have stayed safely at Goliad after delivering Travis' plea to Fannin.

Oh, Buck Travis still talked of relief columns from Brazoria. Perhaps from San Felipe. But there really was no Texas army—nor any organization to this rebellion as yet. All Travis could honestly hope for—all any of them could hope for—was to hold the mission as long as possible; make it an example of the will of the Anglo-Americans to resist the Mexican tyrant. No one could get out any longer, not even under cover of darkness. The Mexican trenches and artillery emplacements had been advanced too close to the walls.

But why was this night, of all nights, so silent—?

She pushed the soiled blanket away from her legs. The quiet unnerved her. She wished Crockett would take up his fiddle as he'd done on several evenings when Mexican grape and canister whistled and crashed against the walls. Crockett's lively fiddling, counterpointed by the wild wail of John McGregor's bagpipes, would have been welcome. It would have lifted her spirits as it had before—

But I'd settle for just a cup of coffee, she thought, standing; stretching; brushing the dust from the black silk skirt spotted with beige patches of dried mud. She was weary of corn and beef and peppered beans served up without coffee. She and the dozen other women—Mexicans, mostly—cooked for the garrison. Although the women did their best, the men complained about the lack of a hot drink to wash down the meals. Amanda didn't blame them.

She folded the blanket, laid it on the ground and turned toward the east wall of the chapel. There, on a platform reached by a long ramp of earth and timber, she glimpsed the dim shapes of the twelve-pounders—three of the mission's fourteen cannons. She thought she saw a couple of men slumped over the guns, sleeping. Worn out. If only there'd been a little coffee to help everyone stay awake—!

Suddenly she wondered whether the enemy general knew they had none. Perhaps he did, and was gambling that a night of quiet would cause the defenders to fall into exhausted slumber. Did that mean a surprise attack was imminent—?

As she pondered the worrisome possibility, her right hand strayed to her left wrist. Unconsciously, she touched the fraying bracelet of ship's rope,

its once-bright lacquering of tar dulled by time. The bracelet was a link to
a past that now seemed wholly unreal.

But it *had* been real, hadn't it? There *was* a great house in a splendid
eastern city. And ample meals. And clean bedding. And a tawny-haired
cousin with whom she'd fled when her mother was killed and the family
printing house burned—

Her fingers closed on the bracelet. God, she wished she were out of this
place. She felt guilty admitting that, but it was true. The probability of
death had become an inescapable reality. Too much to bear—

With an annoyed shake of her head, she overcame her gloom a second
time. Such feelings were not only unworthy, they were wasteful of precious energy. She could still see to her good friend's welfare, even if she
could do nothing about the fact that, very soon now, she might die—

Along with every other Anglo-American walled up within the mission
that those in Bexar, Anglo and Mexican alike, referred to as the Alamo.

ii

A huge mound of stones blocked the center of the chapel's dirt floor.
The rubble was left from last year, when the Alamo had been occupied by
soldiers under the command of General Martin Perfecto de Cos, the elegant brother-in-law of the President of the Republic of Mexico. Cos and
his men had been driven out by Texans—and the President himself had
mustered a new army, marching north from Saltillo to punish those who
had dared to fight his troops and resist his repressive laws.

A short twelve years earlier, a newly independent Mexico had welcomed American immigrants to its Texas territory. Under special legislation of 1824 and '25, *empresarios* such as the Austins, father and son, were
encouraged to purchase land at favorable prices; to recruit settlers and
bring them to the new Mexican state. The Americans all promised to become Catholics, but the government seldom bothered to enforce the vow
once it was made. One of the most popular men in all Texas was a genial
padre named Muldoon, who frankly didn't care whether the immigrants
ever set foot in his church. To be a "Muldoon Catholic" was perfectly satisfactory to the Mexican government—

Indeed, the government's generosity to foreigners had very little to do
with winning souls to the Mother Church. It had a great deal to do with
the general feistiness for which Americans—particularly those on the west-

ern frontiers of the nation—were famous. The Anglos were intended to serve as a buffer between the marauding Texas Indian tribes and the more heavily settled Mexican states below the Rio Grande.

The Americans who came with the *empresarios* were hardy people. They defended their land, cultivated it, and thrived under the easy benevolence of the republican government. More and more Anglos arrived every year—

Until a series of political upheavals brought Mexico's current President to power.

Fearful of Andrew Jackson's well-known hunger for territory, and aware that the number of Americans in Texas was growing daily, the new President had instituted a series of harsh laws, including one in 1830 that prohibited further immigration. Another struck at the heart of the state's agricultural system, abolishing the sale and use of black slaves.

Friction resulted; then outright hostility. When Stephen Austin visited Mexico City in 1834, intending to press Texan claims about infringement of liberties, the President jailed him. From that time on, relations between the capital and its northern province worsened—

Erupting at last into open warfare.

The preceding June, a little army of Texans had swooped down on the port of Anahuac and driven out the officer responsible for enforcing newly imposed customs duties that made exporting of crops and importing of essential commodities all but impossible for the settlers. Anahuac marked the start of the armed struggle led by the Texas War Party, of which Buck Travis was a leading member. Now most of the Americans in Texas —about thirty thousand in all—were openly talking about, or waging, a rebellion—just as their forebears had done sixty years earlier, to protest the taxes and repressive policies of the English king who had ruled the continent's eastern seaboard.

When the Texans had driven General Cos from the Alamo in December, he had retreated back across the Rio Grande. Not a Mexican soldier was left in the entire state—until the President himself, stripped of his last pretense of friendliness, had led his new army and its horde of camp followers north to Bexar.

The President's arrival split families, as their members took sides. His presence sent a good portion of Bexar's population into frantic flight, their belongings piled in carts. The President secured the half-deserted town that had formerly held about four thousand people. He raised the red flag on the church. Those Texans determined to resist had already retreated to the Alamo. So began the siege, the President steadily advancing his fortifications at night, his goal to ultimately storm the mission on the east side of the winding San Antonio River—

All of the resulting turmoil and uncertainty seemed summed up for Amanda in the rubble pile she now circled with quick, precise steps. Moving briskly required effort. She was tired. She felt unclean. She wished she had a brush for her lusterless hair.

And coffee.

But somehow, as she walked on, a hardness that had been forged within her by years of risk-filled living reasserted itself. She wanted to survive this siege. But failing that, she could at least end her life in a way she could be proud of—

I don't want to die here, she said to herself. *I've come so close to death so many times, I thought I'd earned a reprieve for a few years. But if this is the end, I ought to face it the way my own grandfather did when he fought against the British king—*

Her grandfather had survived the American rebellion and died of natural causes in 1801, two years before her own birth. Yet because her father, Gilbert, had told her so much about grandfather Philip—whose rather stern portrait she remembered from the library of the house in the east—he remained a very real presence. So real that she often thought of him as if he still lived and breathed:

I wouldn't want him to be ashamed of how I die. I would never want him to be ashamed that I belong to the Kent family.

That she was probably the family's last surviving member was perhaps the saddest part.

iii

The Alamo chapel dated from the 1750s. Franciscan friars from Spain had built it, as part of a doomed effort to win Christian converts among the predatory Indian tribes. Unfortunately, the tribe the fathers chose as their chief target was notorious for a lack of belief in higher powers. Of all the Indians Amanda was familiar with, the Comanches came the closest to uniform atheism.

The chapel was located on the southeast corner of the sprawling complex of stone and adobe buildings that had grown to cover almost three acres. Invisible beyond the chapel's stout doors was the two-story long barracks, which ran roughly northeast to southwest. The barracks formed one wall of the great open rectangle known as the Alamo main plaza.

On the plaza's ramparts and in the rooms below, the defenders were awaiting the inevitable final assault by several thousand Mexican foot and cavalry. Some said there were a hundred and eighty-two men in the mission. Others put the number at one more than that. It included thirty-two who had ridden in from Gonzales knowing there was almost no chance of escape.

On Friday, Lieutenant Colonel William Barret Travis had called them all together in the main plaza and given permission for any man who wished to leave to do so. Only one had accepted the offer.

Strangely, hardly anyone called the man a coward. Perhaps it was because gnarled little Louis Rose was a friend of Colonel Bowie's. Or perhaps it was because he had long ago proved himself in combat. Rose had fought with Napoleon in Russia before taking ship to the Americas. He was no longer young, he explained, and he'd faced death too often. Once more would be pushing his luck too far.

Clearly the little soldier had no innate loyalty to the cause that held the rest of them together. Travis told him to collect his belongings and go over the wall while there was still time. By first light, Rose had vanished.

Amanda paused to glance into the sacristy, one of the few rooms adjoining the chapel that still had a roof. The sacristy, where most of the women and children slept, was dark and still.

She moved on, her expression pensive. How would the President treat the wives and youngsters after the battle? That the rebels would lose the battle hardly seemed in doubt any longer. Almost miraculously, not a man had been seriously injured during the thirteen-day siege. But things would be entirely different when the enemy launched a direct attack on the walls. The Mexicans had rifles with bayonets and, presumably, ample ammunition. The personal armament of the Americans consisted of squirrel guns, pistols, tomahawks and knives. And powder and shot were running low inside the mission. Some of the Alamo cannons had fired rocks and hacked-up horseshoes in the past couple of days—

Given all that, the Americans remained in reasonably good spirits. They managed to act contemptuous of Santa Anna's nightly artillery bombardment, and made bawdy jests about the midnight band music. It struck her that, with Louis Rose gone, there wasn't one man who could truly be called a professional soldier.

She knew of four lawyers among the hundred and eighty. There was a physician—Dr. Pollard, who attended Bowie. Bill Garnett, only twenty-four, was an ordained Baptist minister. Micajah Autry, one of the Tennesseans whom Crockett had brought in, wrote passable poetry. There were several men from England and Ireland; even another Rose—first name James—who claimed he was ex-President Madison's nephew. Most had been lured to the southwest by the promise of new land; a second chance. In the border states, it was said, many a man simply shut his cabin door, carved or chalked G.T.T.—Gone to Texas—on it, and walked away.

Some of the more recent arrivals, though, had come in direct response to appeals by the Texans for help in resisting the Mexican dictator. Crockett was one of those. He'd marched into Bexar in February, with a dozen sharpshooters tramping along behind him. There was not only the promise of a fight here, he said, but maybe a new start afterward—and that he needed. His anti-Jacksonian politics had caused his defeat in his most recent run for Congress. In a fury, Crockett had told his constituents, "You can go to hell—I'm going to Texas." In the Alamo, he joked about getting the worst end of the bargain.

She saw him now as she approached the entrance to the baptistry at the chapel's southwest corner. A lean man, Crockett was seated on a stool beside the cot where Bowie lay, his pneumonia-wasted face lit by a lantern on the floor. The tail of Crockett's coon cap hung down over the back of his sweat-blackened hide shirt. His shoulders moved, but Amanda couldn't see what he was doing.

Bowie didn't hear her approach. His bleary eyes were fixed on Crockett's hands, which finally became visible to Amanda from the doorway. The Tennessean was ramming a charge into one of the relatively new percussion-cap pistols. Another, matching pistol lay in Bowie's lap, alongside the nine-inch hilted knife that had given the big, sandy-haired Colonel of Volunteers the reputation as a dangerous man, a killer. Jim Bowie hardly fitted that description now, she thought sadly.

Crockett turned. So did Bowie's black slave, Sam, who squatted in a corner, his young face showing strain. In a moment Crockett stood up. Like Bowie, he was exceptionally tall. Not bad-looking, in a raw-boned way. He pretended to be a rustic, but Amanda had talked to him often enough to know that he was widely read, and had constantly worked at educating himself during most of his fifty years. The tales about his prowess as a frontiersman—spread throughout the United States in campaign biographies—had been craftily designed, often by Crockett himself, to help him win his races for Congress.

Now Crockett touched the muzzle of the pistol to his cap. "Miz de la Gura. You're up early."

She stepped into the light, the once-elegant black silk dress rustling. "I seem to have gotten used to going to sleep to band music, Colonel," she smiled.

"Know what you mean." Crockett smiled too, but uneasily.

The lantern light revealed Amanda as a fairly tall woman, five feet seven, with a full, well-proportioned figure. She'd lost about ten pounds in the preceding two weeks, and it showed in hollows in her cheeks, and half-circles beneath her large, dark eyes. Her nose was a trifle too prominent for perfect beauty. But men still found her immensely attractive. She knew it, and in the past she'd occasionally capitalized on the fact.

Outside, in the chapel, a child began to fret, as though caught in a nightmare. Amanda identified the voice as belonging to Angelina Dickinson, eighteen months. The child's mother, Susannah, was married to Captain Almeron Dickinson, in charge of the garrison's artillery. Almeron was undoubtedly up with the chapel cannon. His eighteen-year-old wife was the only other Anglo woman in the mission. The rest were wives or sweethearts of the Mexicans such as gunner Gregorio Esparza who had sided with the Americans against Santa Anna.

Bowie's big fingers shook as he tried to pick up the pistol Crockett had laid beside its mate and the knife. He acknowledged Amanda's presence with a blink of his eyes, then a labored question:

"How are you, Mandy?"

"Well enough, Jim. You?"

"Passable."

"Has Dr. Pollard looked at him tonight?" Amanda asked Crockett.

The Tennessean shook his head. "I think he's catching a few winks like the rest of the boys."

Sam, the black, said in a tense voice, "Santy Anny—he pretty quiet this evening."

Amanda nodded. Crockett said, "Too blasted quiet."

The Dickinson girl's fretful crying faded. No doubt Angelina was sleeping wrapped in rags and her father's Masonic apron—the warmest covering available. Bowie's sunken eyes remained fixed on Amanda as she spoke to Crockett again:

"There must be a reason for the silence, Colonel. Do you think the troops are moving closer to the walls?"

"Can't be certain with those clouds hiding the moon." Crockett dug a

nail against an upper gum, then spat out a bit of meat. "I'd expect so,
however." He inclined his head toward the man on the cot. "I reckon Jim
feels the same way. He sent Sam to find me, so I could load his pistols."

"You—" Her voice shook now. "—you think it may be tonight—?"

Crockett shrugged. Gone was the ready grin that had buoyed the spirits
of the defenders so often. He said:

"There's a good chance. If I was Santy Anny, I'd expect everybody to
catch up on their rest when it was quiet—which is exactly what's happened. Even Colonel Travis is asleep."

"Tha's right," Sam nodded. "I seen Joe a while ago. He tol' me the
colonel was sleepin' like the dead."

Amanda looked at Bowie again, not certain that he was recognizing her
any longer. She thought about the strange partnerships that fate often arranged. No two men could be more dissimilar than James Bowie and
William Barret Travis—

Amanda was a long-time friend of the massive, forty-year-old Bowie. He
was a Catholic, with a checkered history of dueling, slave-running and
land speculation. Grief had brought him to Gura's Hotel often these past
couple of years.

Bowie had originally shared command at the Alamo with Travis. Suffering the first symptoms of pneumonia, he'd kept on working—until his ribs
were crushed in an accident that happened while he was helping to raise a
cannon to the plaza wall. Since then he'd been lying here in the chapel,
with command of the garrison completely in Travis' hands.

Neither man liked the other very much. They had height in common,
and sandy hair, but little else. Travis was nominally a colonel of the lately
formed Texas cavalry. Bowie led the volunteers. Most of the men at the
garrison preferred him to the ambitious Baptist lawyer from San Felipe de
Austin—

It was said that Travis had come to Texas after murdering a man in Al-
abama for trifling with his wife. Perhaps his wife hadn't been altogether
unwilling, since Travis had left her behind and had lately been courting
another young woman. He was envious of Bowie's popularity with the
rank and file, and scornful of his rival's fondness for alcohol. Yet a
common love of Texas, and a common plight, had finally destroyed the
barriers between them. When the accident put Bowie out of action,
he ordered the men under his direct command to follow the twenty-seven-
year-old Travis without question.

Crockett started out. "I expect I'd better get back to the wall and see to loading Old Betsy." He touched Amanda's sleeve. The sleeve's puffy leg-of-mutton shoulder was a tatter now.

Looking at her, he added, "You know, Miz de la Gura, you're to be admired for staying here. But you should have gotten out while there was a chance. Or never come in."

She shook her head. "I've heard that from Jim too. But he needed someone to look after him—Dr. Pollard has a gun to handle. Jim and I are friends. His father-in-law helped me straighten out some deed problems when I opened the hotel with the money my husband left."

The father-in-law she referred to was Juan Martin Veramendi, who had been vice-governor of Texas and one of Bexar's leading citizens. Bowie had wed Veramendi's lovely yellow-haired daughter Ursula.

She, her father, her mother and the two children of her marriage had all perished in 1833 while Bowie was off in Mississippi, attending to some business. The family had been stricken at the Veramendi resort home down in Monclova by one of the tendrils of the cholera epidemic that had been spreading worldwide out of Asia for the past ten years. The same disease had carried off Amanda's husband a year earlier.

Bowie had never recovered from the loss of his loved ones. Even the physical charms of Henriette, one of the three girls who inhabited second-floor rooms at Gura's Hotel, failed to comfort him for long. More and more frequently during recent months, Bowie had taken to dropping by Gura's solely to drink and talk with Amanda. But he downed four glasses of *aguardiente,* the powerful cane-based liquor, for every sip she took. There weren't enough women, enough words or enough alcohol in the world to mitigate his pain—

Amanda's three girls were gone now. She'd urged them to leave Bexar when the Mexican army was reported on its way. Two of the girls, mixed-blood Mexican-Comanche wenches, had probably returned to their tribes. Henriette had headed for Nacogdoches under the protection of a middle-aged customer who sold Bibles.

The Tennessee frontiersman clucked his tongue:

"Well, I guess there's nothing any of us can do about escaping now. I do sort of wish old Santy Anny would hurry up and come on. I'm tired of being hemmed in by walls. Never liked the feeling. I'd sure like to get a look at him, too. He sounds like a pompous little piece of shit—oh, I beg your pardon—"

Amanda smiled. "No need to apologize, Colonel. I've heard every cussword in the book, and then some. And you're right about the President. They say he is pompous. But clever, too."

"Just can't believe that," Crockett returned. "A man can't have his head on straight if he goes around calling himself the Napoleon of the West."

"Perhaps with justification. He's managed to stay on the winning side through all those changes of government, remember. People are afraid of him. For one thing, they say he's tall—several inches taller than I am, which is unusual for a Mexican. He cuts a commanding figure—"

"That may be. But I think Señor Napoleon's going to get more than he bargained for when he tries to take this place. What's so damn—so blasted infuriating is that we could hold out for months if we had supplies and a thousand men!"

Bowie's hoarse voice rasped from the cot:

"We'll give 'em a run with what we've got, we—"

He started coughing, his face convulsed with pain.

Amanda darted to the stool Crockett had vacated. Sam crawled forward on his knees, likewise alarmed by his master's coughing. From the doorway, Crockett said:

"Yes, we sure will. There's only one thing I'm really sorry about. I wish I'd got here soon enough to grab me a piece of ground and farm it a while. I'm about old enough to settle down, and I'd like to see if this land's as almighty fertile as you people say—"

Amanda laid her palm on Bowie's sweaty left hand. The coughing stopped. The lines in his face smoothed. His blue-gray eyes sought her face, as if hunting relief from his pain. Under his plain linsey shirt, he was wrapped in bandages, Dr. Pollard's only means of repairing the damage done to his ribs when the cannon fell from its tackle.

A moment later Bowie glanced at Crockett:

"You can bet it is. Mandy, tell him what your husband used to say about the soil in Texas—"

Half-turning to Crockett, she forced a smile:

"He said it was supposed to be so rich, you could plant a crowbar at night and by morning the ground would sprout ten-penny nails."

The words were heavy, humorless. Bowie's illness had made him forget that Amanda's husband had usually repeated the remark with great cynicism. Crockett, though, knew almost nothing about her history. He laughed.

"My kind of country," he said, re-settling his cap. "Pity it doesn't belong to the United States. I heard once in Washington that President

Jefferson thought he bought Texas as part of the Purchase. But Spain said no. Well, I guess that doesn't make much difference now—"

"No," Bowie breathed, "all we can do is follow your advice, Davy." He paraphrased a frequent remark of Crockett's: "Be sure we're right, then go ahead."

That widened Crockett's smile all the more. "Yep," he said. Then he touched his coon cap. "Miz de la Gura—good morning to you."

Silently, the tall frontiersman melted into the shadows of the chapel. Out there, two of the Mexican women had wakened and were talking softly. One was Señora Esparza. Ironically, her husband Gregorio, the gunner, had a brother, a sergeant, in the besieging army.

"Davy's correct about one thing," Bowie said. "I think an attack's due most any time."

"That scares me, Jim."

"And me," he admitted. His left arm lifted, fingertips brushing against the sun-browned, work-toughened flesh of her hand. "You've been a good friend, Mandy. The best anyone could want—"

It almost broke her heart to hear how weak his voice had become; to see his huge, muscular body so feeble and wasted. She clasped his hand in both of hers:

"I only wish I'd been able to bring Ursula back to you. And the children. They were good people. So was your father-in-law. He was kind and friendly even though most of the *respectable* citizens of Bexar wouldn't deign to walk on the same side of Main Plaza with me."

"Well, you weren't—" Bowie realized he was speaking in past tense; corrected with a pained smile: "—aren't in the most respectable of professions."

That roused her wrath:

"I made sure the hotel was never a public nuisance! That the girls were honest—and examined by a doctor once a month. I ran a straighter place than the owners of the cantina! Their liquor was watered, their cards were marked—"

"Yes, Mandy, I know that and you know that. But to most other people, Gura's was still a whorehouse. Period."

She looked crestfallen. "I don't claim I've lived a perfect life. Sometimes, just to survive, I've done things I'm not proud of. But at least I've never concealed them. Which is more than you can say for a man like *el presidente*. Santa Anna twists whichever way the wind blows—"

A little more animation showed on Bowie's face. "Here we are jabbering like a couple of old folks. Looking back. As if everything's over."

"It is, Jim." She fingered one of his pistols. "Isn't that why you asked Colonel Crockett to load your guns?"

Bowie didn't reply. She thought he'd fallen asleep. Then, with a little wrench of his shoulders, he stirred. He asked her to help prop him against the wall at the head of the cot. As she did, she caught a glimpse of Sam staring at his master. The black saw death in Bowie's face. Death for all of them, perhaps. But the tears in Sam's eyes were not for himself.

"Forty—" Bowie yawned. "Forty's plenty long enough for a man to live. But you're young, Mandy."

"Thanks for the compliment, but it's not true. Thirty-three is getting on. Like Colonel Crockett, I really have only one regret. I wish one of my children had survived."

"I forget how many there were—"

"Two."

"Ah, that's right. I don't know why I can never remember."

"Probably because they were both born before Jaimie and I ever met you." She stared at the lantern's flame, seeing the past. "The boy was stillborn. The girl lived six weeks. When she died, it broke Jaimie's spirit. He didn't want to work the farm any more. It was almost as if our failure to have children put a curse on everything else he was doing. Blighted it—made it unbearable—" She smiled in a melancholy way. "I knew it was partly an excuse but I never said anything. It was time we tried something else. Jaimie and I weren't good farmers—"

She realized Bowie had closed his eyes. Alarmed, Sam said:

"Is he all right?"

"He's just dozing, Sam. You rest too. I'll watch him."

In the ensuing silence, her mind began to drift. Away from the chapel. Away from the trap that had closed around them all. Even though much of the past had been sad, remembering it soothed her now; drained away some of her tension. She thought fondly of her husband, Jaimie de la Gura, and of her weary thankfulness when he had decided to abandon the thirty acres near the Brazos that the two of them had worked for several years, to provide a livelihood for the family that never became a reality—

They had worked that land to exhaustion. But Jaimie lacked the instinctive kinship with the earth that seemed to be a requirement for raising cash crops at a profit. Jaimie's neighbors could produce forty to eighty bushels of corn for every acre they owned. He was fortunate if his fields yielded twenty.

In their last two years on the farm, the life had become hateful to both of them; the two-room, dog-run cabin more and more disagreeable. Even now Amanda grew queasy when she recalled the smell of the swine Jaimie tried to raise and fatten for market. Her idea of hell was a limbo without purposeful sight or sound—with nothing to torture the lost soul but the smell of pigs.

A year before the birth and death of their daughter, they had discussed trying to plant the prime cash crop, cotton. But working cotton fields required plenty of laborers. Jaimie might have been able to negotiate a loan to buy a few slaves. But he was against the system in principle. As a boy in New Orleans, he'd sided with his mother when conscience drove her to complain about the original source of the de la Gura money—West Indian blacks brought illegally through the bayous in defiance of the law of 1807 banning the importation of slaves from Africa.

Jaimie's mother had been a devout Catholic. Slavery violated Christianity as she understood and practiced it. She had filled her son's mind with her beliefs—and he carried some of that youthful indoctrination with him until he died.

Whenever he and his Brazos neighbors discussed the slavery question, Jaimie liked to remind them that President Jefferson, though a slaveholder himself, had prophesied a "revolution of the wheel of fortune" for blacks. He could quote a couple of lines from the President's *Notes on the State of Virginia*—lines that reflected Jefferson's mortal fear of a coming apocalypse—

"Indeed I tremble for my country when I reflect that God is just: that His justice cannot sleep forever."

So cotton was out of the question for the de la Guras.

The whole miserable enterprise came to an end when they buried their daughter. With the money they got from the sale of their land, they had negotiated for a house in the growing riverside settlement of Bexar.

Soon after, Jaimie had set out for New Orleans to buy some needed furnishings, to visit the cemetery where his parents were buried and to order merchandise for a store he intended to open. But in New Orleans, cholera had struck him down—and his diseased body had been hastily dumped into a grave there, so it wouldn't infect anyone else. Amanda learned of the death by means of a letter from a public official.

What grieved her almost as much as the loss of her husband was the guilt she felt about that journey to New Orleans. Jaimie didn't want to live in Bexar, let alone operate a mercantile establishment. He had been driven to it by his need to escape from all the bad memories the farm represented. He had chosen Bexar for her—knowing full well that the confinement of a town didn't suit him and never would. He had lived outdoors—hunted and trapped in the north along the Missouri river—for much of his adult life, and he knew he'd be no better selling calico than he had been at raising corn.

After Jaimie's death, Amanda wanted nothing to do with storekeeping. But she had to find some way to earn a living. She knew she had some skill in the domestic areas that were the assigned provinces of women, and she decided that the natural place to apply that skill was in managing a decent hotel—which Bexar lacked.

So, late in 1832, she had sold her house, bought an available adobe building on Soledad Street, borrowed heavily from a wealthy Mexican friend of the Veramendis to buy some beds and chairs and washstands and have the place refurbished—and by early in 1833, the first, rather spartan version of Gura's Hotel was open. She had barely been able to meet expenses during the early months.

The young sons of the town's better Mexican families began frequenting her public bar in preference to the cantina. She poured an honest drink. But the young gentlemen complained about Bexar's lack of feminine companionship. The two overweight prostitutes who occupied a filthy crib behind the cantina weren't fit to touch, let alone kiss. The young gentlemen didn't mind stains on their reputations from visiting such women, but they didn't want pox sores in the bargain.

Listening to that sort of thing night after night, Amanda had an inspiration. She soon added the desired service—with appropriate decorum and discipline—to the back rooms of her second floor. After that, her ledger showed a substantial profit every thirty days. She paid off the loan by year's end, and began purchasing some better items of furniture.

She saw nothing overwhelmingly immoral in converting part of Gura's Hotel into a brothel. She had spent her adolescence and young womanhood among the Teton Sioux, and had come to regard sexual activity not as a great many white people did—unavoidable but somehow unclean—but as the Indians saw it: of almost inestimable importance because of its connection with the creation of life. Anything so important could only be engaged in one way—joyously.

The Sioux were not a promiscuous people. Quite the opposite. Adultery, though never formally punished, was frowned upon. The virtue of young women was protected with elaborate rituals of courtship—though Amanda had never been so protected. When she had been sold to a young man of the tribe, she had already lost her virginity. Because of that—and because of her white skin—the rules didn't apply.

Gradually, she came to understand and share the happy duality of the Sioux attitude toward sex. The physical act of love was regarded with mystical reverence—and this produced an earthy appreciation of the act itself. Sex was not a sin but a celebration; a wondrous and necessary part of a fulfilled life.

What a far cry from the views of those white women who whispered about the subject with revulsion. Amanda felt sorry for such warped creatures. The Sioux, both male and female, had a much healthier attitude.

To the Indian philosophy of love she had added her own: a man and woman taking comfort from each other was not half so immoral as the casual taking of human life, a common occurrence on the frontier—and one with precious little moral stigma attached. Witness her friend Bowie's respectability.

She did recognize that charging for the services of her girls injected a certain commercial taint. But which was more reprehensible? Selling a man a jug of popskull that dulled his senses and, over the long run, could ruin his health? Or selling him an hour's pleasure and peace in the arms of a woman?

Perhaps the pious would declare that an *honest brothel* was an impossible concept. But an honest brothel was what she had tried to run.

The puritanical segments of Bexar's population couldn't approve, let alone understand, such an attitude, of course. Although she prospered, she was only tolerated, never accepted, by the best families. Until his death, Veramendi remained one of her few influential friends. Another, surprisingly enough, was the parish priest, a thoughtful, tolerant man named Don Refugio, who had considerable respect for the religious convictions of most Indians—Comanches excepted—and found them in some ways more "Christian" than many of his flock.

But the ostracism she'd suffered seemed trivial in the light of what she was facing now. Her gaze was almost unconsciously drawn to the symbols of the coming struggle: the pistols in the drowsing Bowie's lap. The pistols and the infamous knife—

Copies of Bowie's knife were in demand all across Texas. Even in the States, people said. The inch-and-a-half wide blade had a wickedly honed false edge that permitted a backstroke during a duel. There was also a concave scoop where the back curved to meet the edge at the point.

The prototype had been given Jim Bowie by his brother Rezin in 1827. Bowie had often laughed about the various legends that had sprung up concerning the original knife and its successors—

That each had been forged with a piece of meteorite thrown into the cauldron of molten metal.

That he was in league with the Devil, who had provided the knife's inspired, lethal design in return for a claim against Bowie's soul. There was almost no limit to the wild stories that were circulated.

Bowie had once remarked to Amanda that it was the man more than the weapon that determined the outcome of a fight. But he also admitted he was flattered when others assigned supernatural properties to the knife—

Abruptly, Bowie's eyes fluttered open. He blinked; brushed at the stubble sprouting on his chin. When he spoke, it was evident that he had no awareness of having slept for a short time:

"Still say, Mandy—" He coughed. "—what Crockett said. You should have stayed outside. Maybe the Mexicans would have left you alone."

"What do you think I am, Colonel?" she teased. "A turncoat? I may run a whorehouse, but that doesn't mean I lack principles!"

Bowie laughed. Amanda smiled too, then continued more seriously:

"I knew what I had to do when Buck Travis gave his little speech at the fandango on George Washington's birthday. He said Americans down here had to stand up for liberty. My grandfather did just that back in Boston, sixty years ago."

"Travis is wrong."

"What do you mean, wrong?"

"Wrong about the issue. It's dictatorship."

"You're not making sense. What's the difference?"

"We're fighting because Santa Anna centralized all the power of the government in Mexico City. Overturned the constitution of 1824. Dissolved the state legislatures—"

"That's tyranny, Jim—and the other side of the coin is liberty."

"Depends on what you mean by the word. I mean the rights we were guaranteed in twenty-four. I don't mean independence from Mexico."

Finally she understood. "Well, Sam Houston and the others at Washington—" She meant Washington-on-the-Brazos, the provincial capital that had been established after the outbreak of hostilities. "—may have different ideas by the time they've finished their deliberations. Santa Anna will never give in to demands that the constitution of twenty-four be put back into effect. Coming here with his army is proof of that. So maybe it *is* time for another declaration of independence."

"So we can join the United States?"

"Or become an independent republic."

"Well—" Bowie sighed, closing his eyes a moment. "—however it works out, we won't know."

Behind her, Amanda heard Sam's sudden intake of breath. Occasionally during the thirteen days of the siege she had witnessed similar reactions from others at the Alamo, as the possible finality of their position struck home.

"We had to make the stand, Jim," she said. "It was that or surrender. Or run."

"I know. But sometimes it seems downright idiotic to die in a broken-down church. This place is of damn little military importance and every-one knows it."

"Yes, but as Colonel Travis says, it's how we fight, not where, that counts most. If General Santa Anna pays highly for a victory, he'll think twice before he tries to win another."

A moan from the chapel made her start. Only Angelina Dickinson, she realized. She knotted her hands in her lap. The lantern light glinted on her dark hair as she gazed at Bowie.

"I'm sounding a lot braver than I really am, Jim."

"But you still came into the mission."

"Because of you. Your illness. And—well, there's no getting around it, and I don't mean to sound overly sentimental. But I *am* an American, just like most of the settlers in this part of the country. I've kept track of what's happened these past couple of years. I happen to think the settlers are right, asking for reinstatement of the constitution they lived under when they first came out here. If it comes to fighting, and I have to choose sides, why would I choose any side but my own?"

A moment's silence. Bowie closed his weak hand around hers:

"You're a strong woman, Mandy. Some would just give up and let it go at that."

She smiled. "The people in my family may get scared to death, but one thing they *don't* do is give up easily—"

She heard the slave Sam, mumbling fearfully to himself. She tried to offer some words for his benefit:

"But I really think that red flag must be a bluff."

"Wouldn't count on it."

"Aren't there any rules in warfare? I mean about sparing non-combatants? The nigras? The children—?"

"'Course there are. Santa Anna knows the military customs. But he won't offer terms. There's been an open rebellion. His country stands to lose all of Texas. He means to prevent that—*and* punish us. Hard. If some innocent people are hurt, he'll shrug and look the other way. That's the kind of unprincipled son of a bitch he is—"

A series of loud sounds brought Bowie's drowsy eyes fully open. Sam yelped in alarm. Amanda jumped up, ran to the door of the baptistry—

Out in the darkened chapel, a woman was wailing. Boots hammered on the ramp leading up to the cannon platform. She heard Almeron Dickinson shout:

"They're coming! From all quarters. The foot—the cavalry too. *They're coming*—!"

iv

At last Amanda heard it for herself: the low, tumultuous drumming of men—a great many men—running over hard ground beyond the walls. The noise flooded into the roofless chapel from all directions.

On the gun platform, Captain Dickinson was cursing someone; demanding that he wake up, pronto. Amanda realized her original guess had been correct—silence to allow the defenders to doze off must have been part of Santa Anna's strategy. Dickinson's oaths and yells proved the Texans were less than ready for the assault—

A squirrel gun banged from the other side of the closed chapel doors. Then, above the steadily increasing pound of running feet, a bugle pierced the night. It was joined by another, then by all the brass in the Mexican regimental bands.

The bugles and the fast-cadenced drums were playing an unfamiliar tune. Yet the wild, almost savage music started Amanda trembling as she stood in the baptistry door.

Abruptly, the sky over the chapel burst alight. By the reddish glow of the Mexican rockets, Amanda watched men scurrying into position along the cannon rampart. The wild, pealing music grew louder. Behind her, Bowie said:

"I know that call they're playing. It's the *deguello*."

Struck by the rawness of his voice, Amanda spun. Bowie's emaciated hands closed around the butts of his pistols.

"Comes from an old Spanish word, *degollar*—" He licked his lips. "It means to slit the throat. There'll be no terms. No mercy—"

Grimacing, he wrenched his shoulders higher against the wall, then gestured with the pistol in his right hand:

"Go back to the other women and the children, Mandy. Maybe you'll have a chance that way."

"Jim, I won't leave—"

The cocks of his pistols rasped as he thumbed them back.

"Yes, you will. I'm one of those they want most."

He waved a gun, a furious arc in the air:

"You *get out*—you hear me?"

"Better do what he say, Miz Mandy," Sam told her. "I look after the colonel from here on—"

Amanda whispered to Bowie, "God keep you, Jim."

"And you. Now *get!*"

She whirled and rushed into the darkness of the chapel. The rockets sprayed fire across the heavens. Long matches were glowing on the gun rampart. The night resounded with the sudden blast of cannons, the howls of the Mexican foot rushing toward the walls—and the drums and bugles blaring that melody which meant no quarter.

CHAPTER 2

The Massacre

AMANDA HAD SELDOM BEEN dissatisfied with the sex conferred on her by the accident of birth. Occasionally, she'd even found her femininity to be a decided advantage. But she didn't feel that way as she huddled in the sacristy, surrounded by frightened women and children. This morning, she wished she were a man.

The dimness of the room seemed to heighten her sense of helplessness. She would have preferred to be in the main plaza, where the fighting was taking place. But a few moments after she'd left Bowie, Travis had sent a man to the chapel with explicit orders. The women and children were to stay hidden.

The noise of the battle had already become an uninterrupted, unnerving din. Beyond the door of the sacristy, men ran back and forth between the cannon ramp and the powder magazine, a room in the north wall. On the gun platform, Susannah Dickinson's husband bawled, "Fire in the hole!" every minute or so, and one of the twelve-pounders roared, filling the chapel with a brief glare of ruddy light. From the main plaza, there was a continual crash of musketry, screams and curses in English and Spanish—and the boom of Mexican artillery bombarding the walls.

Surrounded by her four children—three boys and a girl—Señora Esparza prayed aloud in her own tongue. Most of the other women were quiet, too terrified to speak or move.

All at once little Angelina Dickinson began to struggle in Susannah's arms. Amanda stopped her pacing, held out her hands to the child's mother:

"Let me take her a while."

Her face pale and streaked with dirt, Susannah Dickinson lifted the little girl. Amanda bent from the waist, picking Angelina up and closing her in a soothing embrace. The roofless chapel glared red again. Seated on a stone, Susannah began to sway, twisting her hands in her lap as she fought hysteria.

The child pushed against Amanda's shoulder, whimpering. Amanda said softly:

"Be still, Angelina. Put your head down. Close your eyes."

But the words had small effect. Only the strength of Amanda's arms kept the little girl from wrenching away.

Amanda concentrated on holding Angelina, and murmuring to her. Somehow that relieved her own anxiety and frustration. The yelling and the gunfire grew steadily louder—

How long had it been going on? Half an hour? An hour? She was losing track. The sacristy had grown stifling. The odor of human sweat mingled with the reek of burned powder.

Angelina finally realized Amanda wouldn't release her. Her body went limp against Amanda's breast. Amanda squeezed the child's waist reassuringly, felt the small head droop to rest on her shoulder. The sound of firing lessened suddenly.

A lean shadow loped past the doorway. Susannah jumped up, ran forward:

"Almeron—?"

"Don't come out!" Dickinson warned. "I'm going to the barracks to see what's happening—"

A moment later, Amanda and the others heard the squeak of hinges. The great chapel doors had not yet been barred from within.

Susannah Dickinson turned back to Amanda. She ran a hand over her daughter's hair, her voice panicky:

"We've lost everything. Even if the men can hold out, we've lost our homes, our—"

"Don't talk like that!" Amanda exclaimed. "We're still alive. Nothing else matters."

She wished she believed it. She was falling prey to the same despair that made Susannah tremble. Everything *was* gone. Her reasonably settled life in Bexar was over. God alone knew what would become of them—

Renewed firing, more shouts brought Amanda's head up. One of the Mexican women cried out as someone lurched through the door. Amanda recognized the Fuqua boy, one of those who had ridden in from Gonzales. He was only sixteen. He'd been hit in the face by a musket ball.

The left side of the boy's jaw was a glistening ruin of blood and bone.

Weaving on his feet, he tried to speak to Susannah. His mouth produced only grotesque gurgling noises.

The harder the boy tried to speak, the more pathetic his attempts became. His lips kept moving, blood oozing from one corner—

"Galba, what is it?" Susannah Dickinson pleaded. "What are you trying to say?"

The boy's jaws worked frantically. He grunted like an animal. Blood ran down to the point of his chin. All at once his eyes filled with tears.

"I can't understand you!" Susannah cried.

Obviously in great pain, Galba Fuqua clamped hands on his lower jaw, as if he hoped to force the ruined bones to articulate properly. The result was the same as before—gibberish. With a sob and an angry shake of his head, he fled back into the smoke that now filled the chapel.

Amanda and Dickinson's wife exchanged glances, both stricken silent by the boy's suffering. Then Amanda looked out at the sky above the chapel walls. Light was brightening behind the smoke. Dawn—

The Mexican cannon rumbled again. Shrieks and shots and throaty Spanish yells came from every direction. How many assault columns had the Mexicans hurled against the mission? From the sound of it, many more than one.

Haggard and out of breath, Almeron Dickinson appeared. He swiped the back of his hand across his powder-blackened face as his wife ran to his side.

"Great God, Sue—" he panted. "The—the Mexicans are inside the walls!" Señora Esparza covered her face.

"Travis is dead on the north rampart," Dickinson went on. "They're coming over with ladders—climbing over their own dead—hundreds of them—my God, there's no stopping them, Sue—*get back inside and stay there!*"

He shoved her, hard. Then he spun and vanished in the smoke. Moments later, one of the twelve-pounders thundered.

Several Mexican women besides Señora Esparza had understood Dickinson's English. Two of them were on their knees, hands clasped in prayer. Susannah walked slowly back to Amanda, took her daughter from the other woman. Silent tears shone on Susannah's face.

Susannah was clearly ashamed of her inability to contain her fear. Amanda glanced away, staring down at her own filthy, work-toughened hands. No matter how she struggled to fix her mind on something else, one thought asserted itself—

The Mexicans were *inside the walls.*

The shouts and gunfire in the main plaza seemed closer than ever. Bugles blared. Amanda closed her eyes, recognizing the notes of the *deguello—*

No quarter.

ii

The Alamo plaza fell first, then the individual rooms of the long barracks where some of the remaining defenders had barricaded themselves. The chapel doors, barred at last, shook and splintered under heavy cannon fire. Finally they crashed open.

The smoky chapel filled with Mexican infantry. The soldiers wore blue cotton jackets with shoulder-knots of blue and green, dirt-stained white trousers and white cross-belts. Their headgear—tall felt shakos with pompoms—showed their commander's preoccupation with things Napoleonic.

Daylight had come, though the thick smoke weakened and diffused the brilliant sun. Some of the running infantrymen were little more than blurs. But Amanda could still see the bayonets jutting from their muskets—

Hunched over, a man hurled himself into the sacristy. Weeping, Sam hunted a familiar face. He stumbled forward, clutching Amanda's arm:

"The colonel's dead, Miz Mandy—"

"Oh, God, Sam, no!"

"A whole bunch come after him soon's they busted the doors. He killed about half a dozen 'fore they grabbed his knife away. I begged 'em to kill me too but they jus' laughed—"

The crying slave grew incoherent. On the verge of tears herself, Amanda ran a hand back and forth over Sam's black hair. She felt him trembling against her arm. She spoke as calmly as she could:

"Sam? Sam, you must answer me. Do you know what's happened in the plaza and the barracks?"

"Dead, they—all dead. Colonel Crockett wen' down with ten, maybe twenty on top of him. Santy Anny's soldiers, they gone crazy. After our boys fall, the soldiers jus' stand there shootin' at the bodies. Shootin' dead men an' cuttin' them with the bayonets—I swear I never seen anything like—like—oh, Jesus, Miz Mandy, Jesus—"

He flung his arms around Amanda's neck and buried his wet face against her shoulder.

At Amanda's side, Susannah whispered, "Almeron's dead. I know he's dead."

"Stop that! We can't be sure about—"

"But there's no more cannonfire. Don't you hear? The cannons haven't fired for at least a minute. *Almeron's dead—!*"

Screaming it, she flung herself toward the door. Amanda wrenched away from the grieving slave, dashed after the younger woman, caught her and pulled her back from the entrance. As she did, she glimpsed a ghastly sight. Above the milling Mexican infantrymen, bodies were sprawled across the silent twelve-pounders on the rampart. She thought she recognized Jim Bonham. And Señora Esparza's husband. She didn't see Dickinson.

She pushed the half-hysterical Susannah back into the center of the sacristy, then glanced outside again. A man came lurching down the ramp from the platform, his clothing tattered, his skin blackened by powder. In his right fist Major Evans clutched a flaring torch.

Amanda put a hand to her throat. She knew what Evans intended to do with the torch.

Ignite the remaining powder. Blow them all up—

He never had a chance. Before he reached the bottom of the ramp, kneeling Mexican infantrymen fired a volley. Evans literally flew upward, smashed by balls that pierced his forehead, blew out one eye, opened bloody holes in his belly before he fell.

Several soldiers charged the corpse. A moment later, Evans' body was being tossed in the air, jabbed and kept aloft by dozens of bayonets. The Mexicans cried one word over and over:

"*Diablo! Diablo!*"

Devil was one of their favorite epithets for Texans. Now they were yelling it as a joke. But Evans wasn't the only victim of the barbarity. A quick glance toward the bapistry showed Amanda another group engaged in the same sport. She pressed her knuckles against her mouth; averted her head.

The body being lifted and stabbed was Jim Bowie's—

Wild with grief, Susannah Dickinson tried to rush by. Amanda grabbed her:

"You mustn't, Susannah! Stay here. Don't let them see you—"

What a pathetic plea, she thought then. As she manhandled the younger woman back into the sacristy for a second time, she knew discovery was inevitable.

iii

The musket-fire boomed and echoed in the dim, cramped room. A fatalistic calm had settled over the women and children. Señora Esparza stared into space. The eldest of her three sons, a handsome twelve-year-old named Enrique, gazed fiercely at the ceiling, his lips forming words no one could hear. Amanda understood the meaning, though. Very few times in her life had she seen such hatred on a human face.

Unbelievably, the soldiers were still riddling the corpses on the gun platform. Through rifts in the smoke, Amanda saw bodies jump and jerk as the balls struck. The crazed behavior of the Mexicans told her a good deal about the fury of the battle in the plaza. Only incredible losses could explain the savagery of the attackers.

Another bent figure came darting out of the smoke. How Jake Walker, a gunner from Tennessee, had thus far escaped death Amanda couldn't imagine. Then she saw that he had been hit. He seemed to be looking for someone. Suddenly, he rushed forward:

"Miz Dickinson—if they let you live, you got to get a message to my wife. You got to tell her—"

"Jake, not so loud!" Amanda warned.

Too late, Walker whipped his head around. He realized his shout had attracted attention. Soldiers converged on the sacristy door, muskets raised.

Amanda flung herself at Susannah and Walker, hoping to thrust them out of the way. Walker took a step backward. Amanda drove Susannah to the ground, tumbling on top of her.

Walker gaped at the hostile faces in the doorway. He yelled something, raised his hands in front of his face—

The muskets exploded. Walker shrieked as a ball struck him in the throat. He fell, blood gushing down over his chest.

On hands and knees beside the gasping Susannah, Amanda watched a boy belonging to one of the Mexican women clamber to his feet. Tugging a blanket around his shoulders as if he were cold, the boy started to speak. A soldier aimed and shot the boy through the stomach.

The mother moaned and fainted as the boy struck the ground. Enraged,

Amanda jumped up, running at the soldiers, shouting at them in the Spanish she knew so well:

"God damn you for a pack of animals—!"

Muskets were leveled again. She ducked as two went off. Susannah cried out—and Angelina too. The little girl clutched her right leg where the ball had hit.

A soldier slammed the butt of his musket against Amanda's forehead. She sprawled, hitting hard. As she struggled to take a breath, half a dozen soldiers crowded into the sacristy and surrounded Jake Walker. As they'd done with Evans and Bowie, they lifted the body on their bayonets and tossed it. Amanda gagged, averting her head. She felt warm blood from the corpse spatter her face—

Then, abruptly, she heard a new voice, loud and deep. Something whacked against skin. A soldier squealed.

Amanda pushed up from the ground, gained her feet. She was still short of breath; blinking from the thick smoke beginning to fill the room. Her head ached suddenly. She expected a bayonet stroke any instant—

It never came. A man she couldn't immediately identify was flailing the soldiers with the flat of his saber. They fell back, muskets raised to parry the blows.

Her vision cleared a little. The man using his sword to drive the infantrymen into the chapel was a hatless officer in a red-faced blue coat stained with blood and dirt.

"His Excellency gave no orders for slaughtering women, you whoresons!" he shouted. "Get out! Leave these people alone!"

The officer's fury sent the soldiers milling into the smoke. When they were all gone, he touched Jake Walker's corpse with the toe of one boot, getting blood on the leather. His mouth twisted in disgust.

Amanda stood panting and rubbing her watering eyes. Finally she got a clear look at the officer. He was in his thirties; stout. His skin was swarthy, his hair black and wavy. His glance shifted from Walker to the dead boy tangled in the blanket. Looking pained, he tapped the flat of his sword against his trousers and turned his attention to the surviving women and children:

"I assume that most of you speak Spanish? I am here to help you—"

Still sickened by the brutality she'd witnessed, Amanda stepped forward. The officer pivoted. His round face might have been a merry face in different circumstances. Now it showed surprise as Amanda bent her head and spat on the officer's boots.

One of the women groaned, obviously afraid that Amanda's defiance would produce more violence. The officer's jaw whitened. But he didn't raise his sword.

He glanced down at the spittle glistening on his reddened boot. Then back at Amanda:

"I will overlook your disrespect, señorita—" He'd glanced at Amanda's left hand and seen no ring; she had put it away permanently after Jaimie died. "—because I understand how you were driven to it by the excesses of our men. Sequestered in here, you undoubtedly have no idea of what they have been through. Indeed—"

A bitter amusement shone in his dark eyes. He had an almost boyish countenance, Amanda decided. But the essentially benign features had been hardened by weather, and by war. The officer was clearly no coward, but neither did he seem to be cruel. She began to hope she and the others might survive.

The officer shrugged in a tired way, continuing, "—indeed I doubt whether the army can withstand another such victory." The last word was tainted with sarcasm.

"I am Major Cordoba," he went on. "I must inform you that you are the prisoners of His Excellency General Antonio Lopez de Santa Anna, President of the Republic of Mexico." He pointed his saber at Angelina Dickinson. The little girl was leaning against her kneeling mother, crying and clutching her bloodied skirt to her wounded leg. "I shall attempt to secure a litter for the child—"

Still with a bitter edge to her voice, Amanda said, "Don't trick us, Major. If we're going to be taken somewhere and shot, I for one would just as soon get it over with right here."

Cordoba's lips compressed. He was angry. "Señorita—"

"My name is de la Gura. Señora de la Gura."

Amanda's insolent tone made Cordoba color even more:

"Señora, then! You are foolish if you refuse to entrust yourself to me. I have been sent specifically—"

"How can we trust men who shoot children?" Amanda retorted, pointing at the fallen boy.

"The boy's death is regrettable, but—"

"*Regrettable?* It's inhuman!"

Wilting under her glare, Cordoba muttered, "Yes, granted—granted!" Louder then: "But it is impossible to control men who have just concluded an engagement such as this. I repeat—you have no idea of what our troops suffered at the hands of your people."

There was grudging respect in Cordoba's last statement. Amanda's anger cooled a little. The man did seem intelligent—decent, even. That couldn't be said of most of the soldiers.

"Major?" Susannah Dickinson said in English. "My husband was on the gun platform. I—I assume he's dead, but—"

"Please," Cordoba interrupted in Spanish. "It would be easier if you would speak in my language."

"I don't know it very well," Susannah replied, her voice shaky. Amanda hurried to her side and cradled an arm around her shoulder. Clinging to her mother and crying softly, little Angelina looked ready to swoon with pain.

"Ask your question," Amanda said to Susannah. "I'll translate for him."

"Will I have a chance to look for my husband's body? I'd like to see him decently buried."

Cordoba glanced at Amanda. She put the query into Spanish. When she concluded, Cordoba shook his head:

"His Excellency has instructed that only our soldiers are to be buried. Unfortunately, the señora's husband is considered a traitor to the republic. Therefore—"

"For God's sake spare us your lectures, Major!"

"I was only attempting to explain why the señora's husband would be denied burial. I am afraid it will also be denied to yours."

"My husband died four years ago."

"I see."

Cordoba eyed her speculatively while she told Susannah what he had said. Almeron Dickinson's wife closed her eyes and shook her head, looking more defeated than ever.

Cordoba tried to be conciliatory: "For your own safety, I beg you all to remain here while I see about the litter. We will escort you out of the mission and back to Bexar as soon as possible. I suggest that as we depart, you do not look too closely at the sights in the main plaza. For the sake of your own sensibilities—"

The sentence trailed off into awkward silence. All at once Amanda felt completely drained of anger. She was exhausted, and desperate to get out of this death-choked place—

Cordoba started to leave. It was Señora Esparza who stopped him this time:

"We will look our fill. Butcher."

"Please, señora!—you and I are not enemies. We are people of the same nation—"

"No. I am a Texan, like my husband Gregorio. I hate your Santa Anna just as he did. When my children and I go out, we will see what your dictator has done—and remember it until another time. Then we will repay you."

Cordoba smiled in a humorless way. "I don't doubt His Excellency worries about that very thing. That's why he is in such desperate haste to put an end to the rebellion."

The major vanished into the sunlit smoke. A few seconds later, Amanda heard him summoning men—cursing in the process.

Cordoba's command of obscenities made her wonder about him. Was his apparent concern for the welfare of the non-combatants only a pretense? Or was the bluster, the cursing, the false part? She supposed it didn't really make much difference so long as Angelina received prompt attention, and no one else was hurt.

Another burst of musket-fire drew her attention to the chapel. The Mexicans were still mutilating the dead. Laughing, even singing, in celebration of the slaughter—

Amanda's face hardened. As Señora Esparza had said, it would be a long time before the people of Texas forgot the dreadful dawn just past.

iv

In the final assault on the Alamo, Santa Anna's army had pounded the walls with cannons, then scaled them with ladders and pushed the defenders back in hand-to-hand combat to last-ditch positions in rooms in the long barracks. But even Major Cordoba's warning hadn't adequately prepared Amanda for what she saw as armed soldiers escorted the survivors into the main plaza.

The plaza was literally a field of corpses; hundreds of them. For every American, there seemed to be ten of the enemy. There was a stench of blood and powder that the morning sun couldn't burn out of the air. The faces and limbs of the dead were black with flies.

Several of the women began crying again. One of the Esparza children vomited. Amanda dug her nails into her palms and swallowed sourness in her throat. It was apparent that the Texans had given ground a foot at a time. The soldiers who had reached the chapel had done so over small mountains of bodies.

Amanda recognized almost all of the Texan dead. She had cooked for the men, joked with them—and now she saw them lying in grotesque postures, lifeless hands clenched around pistols and knives. She fought to keep from weeping herself.

By the time the captives and their guards were a quarter of the way to the open gate, Amanda's shoes gave off a squishing sound. She glanced down, sickened. So much blood had been spilled, the hard ground couldn't absorb it all. She had stepped in a sticky red pool of it.

Mexican soldiers searched for souvenirs among the heaped bodies. But near the wall, she noted an unusually large mound of corpses that the human scavengers seemed to be avoiding. Most of the dead appeared to be Mexicans, but she recognized one American among them. He lay on his back, his face a patchwork of bayonet-cuts. At least two dozen other wounds had torn his hunting shirt and trousers.

Pacing at her side as he had since they left the chapel, Cordoba noticed her stare:

"That man in the fur cap—is he the one called Crockett?"

"Yes."

"I'm told it took a score or more to bring him down."

"That doesn't surprise me."

"You can see the soldiers fear to go near him even now—"

The sight of Crockett's stabbed body unleashed new rage within her. It found a ready target in Cordoba's continuing presence:

"I don't need your personal attention, Major. In fact I resent it."

"Understandably," Cordoba nodded. His brown eyes kept moving back and forth from one group of soldiers to another. Some of the soldiers watched the prisoners with sullen fury. "However, you must accept it until we are safely outside. I want no incidents—"

"What sort of incidents?"

"Non-combatants are to be spared—that was His Excellency's order. But it won't be obeyed voluntarily. I really think you still fail to understand the importance of this engagement, señora."

"What do you mean?"

"Just this. Your General Houston has boasted too often that, with five hundred men, the province of Texas could be liberated from Mexico. His Excellency had to win this battle—at any price. To do so, he inflamed the passions of his men—"

Cordoba inclined his head toward a pair of soldiers busily plying knives. One soldier was sawing through the bone of a Texan's ring finger in order to claim an emerald signet. His sweaty-faced companion had a different purpose. While Amanda watched, the soldier whacked off the ear of a dead man she recognized as one of Crockett's twelve from Tennessee. With a gruff shout, the soldier displayed the souvenir to other Mexicans nearby. They laughed and applauded. Grinning, the soldier tucked the ear into his pocket.

"—indeed, señora, the very spirit with which your people resisted only heightened the desire for revenge. That's why looting must be permitted. And why the faces are being cleaned—"

He pointed to other soldiers using rags to wipe the dirt from the fallen, Mexican and American alike.

Amanda shook her head, not understanding. Cordoba explained in a somber voice:

"His Excellency wishes no mistakes made about the identity of each body. As I informed you, our soldiers will be buried. Your people will be burned."

"Scum," she breathed. "Murdering scum, that's all you are—"

"Alas, señora, war is seldom an ethical business."

"There could have been terms! Honorable surrender—"

"No. An example was needed. Besides, would your people have accepted terms?"

She pushed back a stray lock of dirty hair from her forehead, unable to reply. Thank God the gate was only a short distance away. Susannah Dickinson, accompanying the litter on which her daughter rested, had already reached the body-strewn ground between the mission and the river. Two black men were just following her out the gate. One was Sam, who had come from the sacristy. The other was Travis' slave, Joe, captured in the long barracks. Both men were crying.

"Well, señora?" Cordoba prodded. "*Would* the Texans have accepted terms of any kind?"

She turned her head, gazing at the disheveled major. He was still something of an enigma. He had the erect bearing and outward flintiness of a professional. Yet there was a certain softness in his eyes that suggested another, more elusive man behind the façade. For the first time she noticed his tunic. It bulged noticeably; his belly was growing fat. And he looked tired.

Less angry, she answered:

"I doubt it. When Anglos get pushed too far, they usually fight back. There's a saying they use when someone threatens them—"

"A saying? What is it?"

"Turn loose your wolf."

"In other words—do what you will?"

"Do what you will—but you'll regret it."

Cordoba sighed. "That was obviously the case here. However—"

Stumbling, Amanda uttered a little cry. The major caught her arm. One of the enlisted men walking with the captives noticed Cordoba's quick reaction, and smirked.

Cordoba glared. The soldier blinked and swallowed, intimidated by the fury of the major's eyes.

Amanda carefully disengaged her arm from Cordoba's hand. He refused to look at her, staring instead at her cordage bracelet. His round face was still flushed.

By all rights she ought to hate him. Yet she couldn't bring herself to it.

"Where are you taking us?" she asked finally.

"You and the Señora Dickinson are going to His Excellency. The Mexican women and children will be set free."

A ripple of dread chased along Amanda's spine. "And Susannah and I won't be?"

"I can't say. His Excellency received reports of noncombatants in the mission, and I was instructed to bring them to him for his personal disposition."

"Where is he?"

"I am not certain of that either."

"Maybe I'll be lucky. Maybe he got killed."

"General Santa Anna? Never. Do you imagine he would lead an assault in person—?" Was there faint contempt in his voice? If so, it was quickly hidden: "You may find yourself reasonably well treated, however. His Excellency has a certain fondness for attractive women."

Amanda realized he meant it as a compliment. But this hardly seemed a suitable time or place. She didn't bother to respond. Cordoba then said:

"You do know His Excellency took a wife in Bexar—?"

Startled, Amanda shook her head.

"It was the night we bridged the river. One of the general's aides discovered a most charming young woman—and her mother—living just over there."

Amanda's eyes followed his pointing hand. She recognized the house he was indicating.

"Would the young woman's name be Señorita Armendariz?"

"That's it, I believe. Quite a beauty."

"I have a different word for her." The Armendariz girl and her mother were two of those who had refused to speak to Amanda on the streets of Bexar. Señora Armendariz had even urged the *alcalde* to close Gura's Hotel. "I'm not surprised that little bitch advanced herself with the general—"

Cordoba almost smiled: "Alas, I don't believe he had marriage in mind. But the señorita's mother insisted."

"Who married them? Don Refugio?"

"The parish priest? No, I'm afraid he would have considered such a ceremony—shall we say—irregular? The 'priest' was actually one of Colonel Miñion's aides. A lad who's quite an actor. His Excellency is already blessed with a wife in Mexico City."

"You mean Santa Anna deceived the girl?"

"*And* her mother. Evidently his desire got the better of him."

"You don't sound as if you approve."

Expressionless suddenly, Cordoba shrugged. "Whatever my personal feelings concerning His Excellency, I am a soldier. I serve him without question."

"Is that right?" Amanda studied him as they approached the gate. "Would you have served him without question if you'd been assigned another kind of duty? If you'd been required to kill Texans?"

"I would have obeyed orders."

"If they included wholesale brutality?"

"I see no purpose to such a discussion," Cordoba said quickly. "It's purely theoretical."

But Amanda realized she'd touched a sensitive spot. Her earlier suspicion was confirmed. It was Cordoba's curse to be afflicted with a conscience.

"Then answer a question that isn't. What do you honestly think Santa Anna will do with Susannah and me?"

"Señora, it is impossible for me to guess. He might be in an expansive mood as a result of the victory. He might parole you at once."

Amanda halted in the gateway, turning to gaze back at the dead in the plaza.

"Major, how many men did you lose this morning?"

"Ten for every one of yours—at minimum. By the end of the third charge against the walls, for example, the Tolucca battalion under General Morales had little more than a hundred men remaining. Its original strength was almost eight hundred and fifty."

"I doubt His Excellency will be in a mood to forgive that kind of loss."

As if to confirm her fear, Cordoba didn't answer.

v

The stench of the dead and wounded was even worse outside the Alamo than it had been within. Bodies of Mexican soldiers lay along the base of the wall. Here and there the wreckage of scaling ladders testified to the difficulty of breaching the mission defenses.

Details of men were already moving across the shell-scarred ground, dragging corpses toward the bank of the San Antonio. Overhead, buzzards were gathering.

As she walked, Amanda was conscious of Major Cordoba dropping behind. She didn't see the frankly admiring way he continued to watch her. She was pondering what might befall her in the next few hours. Surely it couldn't be any worse than the horror just concluded. Surely—

Something about the light interrupted the thought. She studied the angle of the sun and realized it couldn't be much later than eight o'clock. The day had hardly begun. Sunday. God's day. And so many had died—

But His Excellency was wrong if he believed cruelty would destroy the Texans' will to resist. As Señora Esparza had promised, it would probably have the opposite effect. It did on her.

She turned again, gazing past Cordoba to the mission's shot-pitted walls. The tricolor and eagle of Centralist Mexico had been raised above the long barracks. Hate welled within Amanda at the sight of the flag flapping in the sun.

Tired as she was, the hate would give her strength; sustain her through whatever might come before this day ended. She wouldn't grovel in front of the self-styled Napoleon of the West, that much she promised herself.

Shoulders lifting a little, she trudged on toward the river. Her shoes left faint red traces on the hard ground.

CHAPTER 3

The Bargain

AMANDA CROSSED THE San Antonio on one of the plank bridges erected by the Mexicans. It seemed to her that she was returning not to a familiar town, but to one that was alien . . . alien and not a little frightening.

Northward, the low hills were covered with tents and wagon parks. Units of cavalry and infantry were re-assembling noisily, raising huge clouds of dust.

Cordoba's men soon encountered difficulty moving ahead toward the Main Plaza. The narrow streets of Bexar, so drowsy and pleasant only a few months ago, swarmed with soldiers and poorly dressed Mexican women. Many of the women were dragging children whose clothing was equally dirty and ragged.

The women were hurrying in the opposite direction, toward the mission. Band music drifted from the river now—music celebrating the victory. The women jeered at the captives. Amanda was glad Susannah couldn't understand Spanish.

Some stones were flung. One struck Señora Esparza. Cordoba drew his sword and ordered his men to close up around the prisoners. After that, the *soldaderas*—the camp followers—had to content themselves with verbal attacks.

Despite her determination not to succumb to despair, Amanda found her spirits sinking with every step. Her mouth felt parched. Her head hurt. Her arms and legs ached. She wished for the peace and privacy of the tiny walled garden behind the hotel. There, whenever she was lonely or depressed, she had always found solace in simple physical labor. She yearned for the garden now. She imagined the sight of her tomato vines bursting with heavy red fruit in the mellow Texas sunlight. She savored the remembered aroma of strings of onions and yellow and red peppers drying in the shadow of the wall—

Gone. It was all gone. The sense of defeat swept through her like a poison. It seemed that every time she put her life back onto a stable course, something disrupted it. That had been the case for almost as long as she could remember—

She thought of her mother, dying in the street outside the Kent house in Boston. She thought of the terrible morning in Tennessee, when the man who claimed to be a preacher had beaten her cousin Jared, then raped her and carried her off to St. Louis, where he sold her to trappers traveling up the Missouri. She thought of her first night in the tepee of the young Sioux warrior who had bought her from the trappers—

She had endured all of it, calling on an inner strength bequeathed to her in some mystical chemistry of birth by her frail father, Gilbert Kent. She had endured hunger and pain and near-paralyzing fear, buoyed by her will to survive. In an hour, a month, or a year, she told herself, she would find an end to the suffering. And so she had—

But there always seemed to be more waiting.

Grief had nearly destroyed her after Jaimie's death. She had fought with it like an enemy who wanted her life. She had fought, and she'd won another reprieve. Opened the hotel. Fussed over the three girls. Taken comfort from the feel of the garden earth against her hands whenever doubt and sadness threatened her—

And now, because she'd decided she had no choice but to go into the mission, she was forced to begin still one more time—as a stranger in a town of enemies. She wondered whether she could do it.

She noticed a party of officers approaching on foot. Among them was a stout, mustachioed civilian wearing flared trousers, a tight-fitting velvet jacket and a sombrero. The *alcalde*, Don Francisco Ruiz.

Though never her close friend, Don Francisco had always been cordial. He realized that Gura's Hotel fulfilled a need in Bexar, and he had resisted pressure from the Armendariz family and others when they wanted it closed. Don Francisco glanced at Amanda as he passed. One of the officers said something to him and he looked away quickly, without so much as a nod of greeting.

There had been shame in his eyes, Amanda thought. But the shame wasn't powerful enough to make him speak to her. The *alcalde* understood very well who controlled Bexar now. Later, she learned that he had been sent to the mission by Santa Anna himself. He was to search through the bodies of the Texans and confirm to His Excellency that William Travis, David Crockett and James Bowie were indeed dead.

Don Francisco's rebuff brought tears to Amanda's eyes. She was ashamed of herself, yet she couldn't hold the tears back. A *soldadera*—a young, coarse-faced woman with immense breasts and a large mole near the point of her chin—saw her crying, snatched up a stone and lobbed it between two soldiers.

The stone struck Amanda's forehead. The pain jolted her from her self-pity. Eyes flashing, she closed her hands into fists and started after the Mexican girl.

Cordoba was quicker. He brandished his sword and cursed. The young woman laughed and hurried on as soldiers kept Amanda from pursuing her.

The major reached for Amanda's arm. "Are you all right, señora?"

She avoided his hand. "Yes. And I told you before—I don't need any help from you."

Cordoba stared at her for a moment. "Don't be too sure."

Furious, she gathered her skirt in both hands and walked on. In an instant, her eyes were dry.

She'd show him how strong she was. She'd show them all.

ii

The prisoners were taken to the spacious, airy house of Bexar's second-ranking political official, *jefe* Don Ramon Musquiz. Servants carried Angelina Dickinson to a bedroom while the others—Amanda, Susannah and the two blacks—were led to the don's comfortable office overlooking an ornamental garden.

Susannah grew distraught when she wasn't permitted to accompany her daughter. But Cordoba assured her the child was not seriously hurt. After absenting himself briefly, he returned to say that Santa Anna's personal doctor had already been summoned to dress the little girl's wound.

Susannah's dirty, bedraggled appearance showed Amanda what she herself must look like. She sank into a chair, her attention caught by the paper-littered desk. She had been in Musquiz's office before. She recognized a number of articles that didn't belong there: an ornate silver tea service; a liquor decanter with a fat silver stopper; a silver spittoon.

A sandaled servant, an elderly Mexican, entered with a tray. On the

tray were cups, a wine bottle and a plate of hardtack. The servant knew
Amanda. But, like Don Francisco, he thought it prudent not to acknowledge the fact. He concentrated on putting the tray on the desk without
disturbing the papers.

Avoiding Amanda's eyes, the old man addressed Cordoba:

"His Excellency is inspecting the mission. He will return shortly. He
ordered that the prisoners were to be given refreshments."

"How kind of him," Susannah said in a bitter voice. "Is it our last
meal?"

"Very good, thank you," Cordoba said to the servant. As the old man
left quietly, Amanda rose and walked to the younger woman.

"A little wine might make you feel better, Susannah."

"Nothing will make me feel better." Almeron Dickinson's widow
clenched her hands. "Nothing. Nothing."

Major Cordoba acted embarrassed. The four soldiers who had accompanied him into the office appeared to be engrossed by *el jefe*'s fig tree just
outside.

Amanda realized she was incredibly hungry. She saw no reason to refrain from eating the enemy's food. She picked up the plate and walked to
the two blacks to serve them.

Sam took a piece of hardtack. Joe shook his head, still looking utterly
miserable. Amanda returned to the desk. She poured half a cup of wine,
drank it, then picked up two pieces of hardtack and sat down again.

The office was cool and still. With an annoyed expression, Cordoba
began wiping the buttons of his uniform with his cuff. He polished off
some of the dirt, but not enough, apparently, to satisfy himself. He kept
frowning.

Amanda finished the first piece of hardtack. She was raising the second
to her lips when she remembered something. Cordoba saw her wry, sad
smile; gave her a quizzical look.

She held up the hardtack, explaining:

"Jim Bowie said there'd be an attack sooner than we expected. He
heard that the bakeries in the border towns were working night and day,
making this. He said only an army would require that much hardtack."

"If you had that kind of advance warning, señora, why were there not
more men in the mission?"

"Travis thought Jim was crazy. He said your army would never march
in the winter. Not until the grass grew and the horses could forage. Jim
told him we were fighting Mexicans, not Comanches. Travis laughed it

off. If he'd listened to Jim, he might have sent for reinforcements sooner—"

She stopped, following Cordoba's tense glance toward the corridor. Boots clicked out there. She heard men speaking. Then one of the soldiers in the office pointed toward the garden wall:

"They've started burning them."

Amanda looked. A black plume of smoke was climbing into the sky. Her hand closed, crumbling the hardtack—

A party of several officers and one civilian appeared at the far end of the hall. One of the men was noticeably taller than the others. He was perhaps forty years old, and not bad looking. His uniform overflowed with silver frogging, buttons, epaulettes.

Moving briskly, the man led the others toward the office doorway. Just as he entered, he touched his middle, belched, then winced. Amanda's last question about the man's identity vanished. Santa Anna was known to suffer perpetual dysentery.

Cordoba snapped to attention; saluted:

"These are the prisoners, Excellency."

General Antonio Lopez de Santa Anna nodded. "Very good. Take your ease, Major."

But Cordoba remained rigid. The general turned to the civilian member of the group, a willowy fellow carrying a sheet of foolscap.

"Read me the first line again, Ramon."

The secretary cleared his throat. " 'Victory belongs to the army, which at this very moment, eight o'clock A.M., achieved a complete triumph that will render its memory imperishable—' "

Santa Anna touched the paper. "Amend that. A complete and glorious triumph." The secretary's head bobbed. "Have it inscribed and return it to me for signature. I want it dispatched to the minister of war in Mexico City by noon, understand?"

"Perfectly, Excellency." The secretary bowed and hurried out.

Santa Anna turned next to a suave officer who was appraising Amanda's figure with insolent directness.

"Colonel Almonte!"

The officer jerked to attention. "Excellency?"

"I believe we should arrange a victory review in the plaza before the day's over. I will give a short oration. See to it, please. Make certain all the town officials are present."

Almonte saluted, pivoted smartly and left the room.

The general returned his attention to his captives, studying them with an affable expression. The past few seconds had already confirmed what Amanda had heard about the dictator's enormous vanity. And she knew too much about his rapid shifts in allegiance on his climb to power to be lulled by his smile.

iii

Santa Anna slipped into the chair behind the desk. He opened a drawer and took out a gold snuff box. A charnel stench drifted in from the garden. The Texan dead, burning—

From the box Santa Anna removed a pinch of white powder. He placed the powder in one nostril and inhaled. Then he handed the box to another of the officers:

"Ask Doctor Reyes to refill that for me." As the officer hurried out, Santa Anna smiled even more broadly at the two women and the blacks. "It has been an eventful twenty-four hours. A bit of opium powder is marvelous for relieving tiredness, I find."

None of the prisoners offered a comment. Frowning, Santa Anna said to Cordoba:

"You will identify these people, please."

One by one, Cordoba supplied the names of the four, beginning with the blacks and ending with Susannah:

"Señora Dickinson is not fluent in our language, Excellency. But Señora de la Gura can translate."

"De la Gura," Santa Anna repeated. "That isn't an Anglo name."

"My husband was Spanish."

"Spanish—*Excellency*," one of the officers said, taking a step forward. Santa Anna waved him back, trying to soften Amanda's frostiness with another smile:

"Spanish—do you mean Mexican?"

"I mean what I said. My husband was born in New Orleans."

"He was an American citizen, then?"

"After the Purchase, yes."

Santa Anna frowned at the obvious pride in Amanda's voice. He tented his fingers; scrutinized her in silence; finally said:

"It's unfortunate for you that I chose not to divide the survivors simply by consulting a list. With that name, you might have been lost and forgotten among the Mexican women Major Cordoba found in the mission."

His eyes were much less friendly now. But Amanda refused to turn away from the intimidating stare. The general abruptly switched back to cordiality:

"There is an excellent establishment in Bexar bearing the name Gura, I recall."

"The hotel I own," Amanda said.

"The hotel you *formerly* owned. It has been taken over as a billet for my senior staff. That should not be a great loss, however. You could have lost your life. So I presume you will be suitably thankful when I permit you—all of you—to leave Bexar unharmed."

Sam gasped loudly. Susannah looked at Amanda, who told her:

"He says we aren't to be killed."

"Angelina too?"

"I presume so." She repeated the question for Santa Anna.

"Of course, of course! I looked in on the child just before I stepped in here. A delightful creature. Lovely! Reyes, my personal physician, assured me she would be fit to travel within a day or two."

Again Amanda translated. Susannah looked blank:

"Travel? Travel where?"

"She wants to know where we're supposed to go," Amanda said.

"Why, back to your own people!" Santa Anna said, speaking to Susannah in Spanish. "I thought briefly of sending you to Mexico City, as proof of our victory. But I've concluded it would be more useful for you to go to Gonzales. I'll send an escort—my own orderly, Benjamin. He was an Anglo—although a slave—before he joined my service. When you're once again among your own—"

"What do you mean, her own?" Amanda fumed. "Her husband died at the mission. Murdered by your men!"

Santa Anna sat forward suddenly, losing his relaxed manner. "Murder is a very ugly word, señora."

"But it fits."

"No. Those who died were casualties of war. By their traitorous behavior, they arranged their own executions. It was no doing of mine."

Amanda laughed then, so loudly and contemptuously that the officer who had reproved her before drew his sword.

Standing by Susannah's chair, Cordoba tried to warn Amanda with his eyes. She ignored it:

"No doing of yours? Who raised the no quarter flag from the church, may I ask? Who gave the command for the playing of the *deguello?*"

"God, what hypocrites you Anglos are!" Santa Anna snarled. "You cavil at the harshness of war while your white brethren in the United States—and here in Texas until I put a stop to it!—trade in human flesh without a qualm of conscience. Blood of Jesus, woman, don't prattle to me about inhumanity!"

Santa Anna's slashing gesture stunned Amanda to silence. Before she could accuse him of taking refuge behind an issue entirely unrelated to the battle, he barked at Cordoba:

"You will please assume the duties of translator, Major. I dislike this woman's contentious attitude. Especially since I have generously decided to permit the noncombatants to go free."

Seething, Amanda exclaimed, "You'll forgive me, Your Excellency, but I'm suspicious of this sudden outpouring of compassion—"

"Excellency—" The officer who had drawn his sword stormed around the desk. "I suggest that kindness is wasted on this American slut."

"Kindness *and* rational argument, it seems."

"Then let my dragoons have her."

Santa Anna pursed his lips. "A possibility. A distinct possibility—"

"If you're going to kill me, do it and be done!" Amanda raged. "I've had enough of Mexican mercy for one morn—"

"*Amanda!*" Susannah Dickinson cried. "For God's sake be civil to him! I don't know what you're saying, but you're going to make everything worse. Almeron's dead, Angelina's hurt—" Suddenly she began to weep. "I want to live. I want to get out of this place. *I want to live—*"

Amanda held back an angry remark. She had no right to endanger Almeron Dickinson's widow or the blacks because of her own hostility.

Presently the color that had rushed to Santa Anna's cheeks faded. He rose, moving out from behind the desk:

"What did she say, Major? I caught a little of it, but not everything."

Cordoba repeated the sense of Susannah's plea. Santa Anna nodded; said to Susannah:

"I am glad you show some appreciation of the realities of the situation, señora—" He paused, allowing Cordoba time to translate. "Your people were foolish to oppose the Centralist regime. I trust that when you leave Bexar—supplied with food, blankets and money—you will lose no time in communicating to your fellow Texans that resistance is futile. I am more determined than ever to see the rebellion crushed now that the so-called Council at Washington has taken its ill-advised step—"

Cordoba cleared his throat. "I don't believe any of those in the mission knew about the declaration, Excellency."

"Ah, yes, you're probably right." He turned toward the blacks, his tone caustic:

"You are now citizens of the independent Republic of Texas. Not free citizens, of course. I'm sure freedom will be reserved for those with white skins."

The slaves gaped. Amanda asked, "When did it happen?"

"The declaration? Just four days ago. Señor Burnet has been named president, and Señor Houston is general of the army—if there is one."

Amanda was speechless again. The news was both sad and surprising. The sadness came from realizing that none of the men who had died at the Alamo had known they were fighting for a newly independent country.

"I find Houston's appointment particularly amusing," Santa Anna said. "The poor sot the Indians call Big Drunk commanding a few farmers and storekeepers as ill-trained as he is—"

Amanda managed to speak: "Sixty years ago, another army just like that won a war for independence—"

"True, señora. But I shall not make the same mistakes the British king did—nor be so gentlemanly to those I oppose." He stalked toward the blacks. "When you rejoin your people, tell them their so-called republic will be gone in three months. Tell them what you saw here. Tell them what they can expect if they continue to fight—" The deep voice grew louder. "That is the only price I'll extract for your freedom—that you spread my message. Resistance will be crushed without pity. The sensible course is immediate surrender."

Cordoba finished translating for Susannah. She stared at Santa Anna, then slowly bowed her head.

The general glanced to the blacks again. Their uneasy eyes showed him they understood what he wanted—and, like Susannah, agreed to it. Santa Anna smiled with genuine pleasure. The word of his military might would be spread through the little Texas settlements, to demoralize the government that had emerged at last from the wrangling and factionalism prevalent for months at Washington-on-the-Brazos.

Santa Anna approached Amanda:

"And you, señora? If you are set free, will you tell your people that surrender is the only way to avoid annihilation?"

"That's the last thing I'll do—Excellency. I will tell them how you ordered a massacre—"

"*Don't!*" Susannah cried, understanding Amanda's fierce expression all too clearly. "He's only asking us to report the truth. We can't win against them—why do you want to pretend we can?"

For a moment, Amanda wavered. Susannah might be right—

For most of her adult life, she had put survival foremost on her list of priorities. Was she foolish to change those priorities now?

No, she decided, thinking of Crockett's slashed body. Of the boy in the blanket shot down in the sacristy. Of Bowie's bayoneted corpse. *No*—

She couldn't scorn Susannah or the two slaves for their desire to live. She knew Susannah probably believed the Texans could never hold out against the Mexican army. Amanda wasn't sure they could either. But in spite of that, the price Santa Anna was asking for survival was higher than she wanted to pay.

Trying to keep her voice steady, she said, "Take the general's offer, Susannah. I can't. If I go to Gonzales—" There was a catch in her throat; her stomach churned as the smell of the burning bodies worsened. "—if I go there, I'll tell everyone His Excellency deserves to be shown exactly the same mercy he showed at the Alamo. I'll tell them it's better to die for an American republic than surrender to a Mexican killer—"

Santa Anna was livid. "I do not speak English well, señora. But I understand a little of it. You will regret what you have just said." He lost control. "*By God, you will—!*"

He pounded a fist on the desk, overturning the creamer of the tea service. Thick droplets fell from the edge of the desk, striking the inlaid floor with a loud *plop-plop*.

The officer who had mentioned turning Amanda over to the dragoons started to repeat the suggestion. Before he'd spoken half a sentence, she was struck just under her left breast—viciously—by a man's fist.

She spun, raising her arms to protect herself. With shock and disbelief, she saw the contorted face of her attacker.

It was Cordoba.

iv

"You've said enough, you ignorant whore!" Cordoba yelled, drawing his hand back to hit her again.

Susannah Dickinson tried to rush to Amanda's assistance. Two of the enlisted men seized her and wrenched her back as Cordoba slammed his fist into Amanda's stomach, then flung her to the floor.

The room darkened; distorted. She pressed her hands against the wood, trying to rise—trying to comprehend the inexplicable change that had come over the major. He was flushed; breathing hard as he bent his leg backward at the knee, then kicked her in the belly.

Amanda cried out. The room began to swing back and forth. Cordoba's voice sounded faint but furious:

"Let me take her and discipline her, Excellency."

"Better she be shot outright," another of the officers said.

Cordoba again: "No, no, Colonel—if you please! I'll see that she suffers for her insolence. Much more than she'd suffer if you killed her."

Santa Anna: "I find your request a bit unusual, Major. You said nothing during her outbursts—"

"My astonishment—my anger—robbed me of suitable words, Excellency."

"Nor are you known for your temper—"

"Except when my commander is insulted, Excellency."

"Well, that's the proper attitude, certainly."

"Then let me have her!"

Amanda tried to sit up. She was too weak and dizzy. She fell back, her black silk dress tangled around her legs. She'd thought Cordoba possessed some small degree of honor. Like Santa Anna's generosity, that honor had been revealed as a sham. Over the ringing in her ears, she heard him pressing his request:

"—I promise you I'll work her till she drops, Excellency. I lost my serving-woman on the march from Saltillo. *Telele* killed her—the fever from bad water. So if you'll put her in my keeping, I'll teach her to respect Centralist authority—"

Several of the officers muttered about Cordoba's proposal—whether for or against it, Amanda couldn't be sure. Finally, she heard Santa Anna shout for silence. The voices cut off abruptly. The dictator sounded amused again:

"Very well, Major, you may have her. See that she fully enjoys the perquisites of her new station—and that she comes to regret her refusal of my clemency. But mark this—!"

He struck the desk again. The sound was loud as a shot.

"Under *no* circumstances is the offer to be repeated. By you or any

other officer. She will not go free now or ever. Of course, if she finds the
work of a camp woman too difficult—if she should sicken and die—that's
your affair. No questions will be asked."

The room seemed cloaked in darkness. Amanda let it sweep into her
mind, blotting out Santa Anna's soft, satisfied chuckle.

v

A fly buzzed. There was a sensation of intense heat.

She opened her eyes.

Above her, she saw an expanse of light. After a moment she realized
she was lying on hard ground, gazing up at the sloping side of an officer's
marquee, one of dozens that dotted the flat land and the hillsides around
Bexar. The sun was broiling down on the other side of the canvas, lighting it to brilliance.

She still ached from the punishing Cordoba had given her. Slowly, she
rolled her head to the side and saw a mussed cot. A rickety table. A washstand holding a razor case, brushes, a dented copper basin—

Then, in the periphery of her vision, she noticed boots. Boots marked
with dried blood and dirt. One of the boots was resting on a small wooden
box. Hands were drawing a cloth back and forth across the stained
leather—

She turned her head a bit more. Cordoba took his foot off the box,
dropped the cloth. He stood staring down at her, his uniform blouse unbuttoned. Black hair curled above a sweat-grayed singlet.

The inside of the marquee was broiling. She drew in a breath of the
unpleasant air. It was ripe with the smells of horse droppings, the burning
dead, male sweat. Cordoba continued to watch, his expression a blank.

She gathered her strength, attempted to sit up. The effort pierced her
side with a pain that made her wince and cry out softly.

"You stupid, intemperate woman!" Cordoba exclaimed, grabbing her
wrists and pulling her to her feet. As soon as she was upright, he let go.
She sat down hard on the cot, gasping.

Rage still colored the major's cheeks. But it was a different kind of rage
than he'd displayed in front of the general. Puzzlingly different—

Cordoba strode forward. Outside, several mounted men clattered by,
laughing and joking in Spanish. She raised her hand to strike him. Cordoba caught her wrist; pushed her arm down:

"Listen to me! I have very little time before I must attend that wretched review—"

The officer's fingers were hard, like a vise. Behind the mild countenance that had turned so hateful in the Musquiz house, there was unsuspected strength—a strength he exerted to keep her immobilized on the cot as he said:

"Do you know that you nearly got yourself sentenced to a firing squad? Or worse?"

"Let me go, God damn you!"

"No! Not until you hear me out! You made His Excellency furious. He was ready to order you shot—or to turn you over to those dragoons Colonel Fialpa mentioned. In the latter case, a hundred men would have taken you. Then you'd have been thrown to the *soldaderas*. To die—if you were lucky."

She laughed at him, a raw, raging sound:

"Don't start telling me how generous *you* are, Major!"

"I had to mistreat you, don't you understand that? I knew of no other way to get you out of there!"

"You're telling me what you did was—was a *sham?*"

"Yes! Completely!"

"Well, it was too damned realistic!"

"For that, I am truly sorry. It was the only way—" He loosened his grip. "If you promise not to run, I'll release you."

She debated; finally sighed and nodded:

"All right—though I still don't quite believe what you're saying."

He let go.

"God—" She massaged her belly. "You hurt me."

He shrugged. "A trifle."

"You call broken ribs a trifle?"

"Compared to the ministrations of the dragoons, yes. Besides, I don't believe any of your ribs are broken. While you were unconscious, I looked at —that is, ah—I examined—never mind! Take my word, you'll survive."

He stood back, rubbing his reddened cheek. It was beginning to show a sweaty growth of beard. As the red faded, he said:

"Let's get down to the issue, Señora de la Gura. It's quite simple, really. You can stay with me and I'll treat you decently—with a few public demonstrations of cruelty to impress my fellow officers, naturally. Or I can turn you back to Santa Anna and you can take your chances. You lost your opportunity for freedom when you provoked His Excellency. So I trust you understand the choice is no longer liberty or the lack of it, but whether you want to live with me or die with someone else."

Wearily, Amanda gazed at him. She saw an emotion in his eyes that almost made her laugh out loud. He looked as earnest and hopeful as a small boy. She didn't laugh because she couldn't quite bring herself to humiliate him.

After pondering his offer a while, she said, "I realize you're trying to help me, Major. But I'd feel like a traitor staying with you."

"A traitor to whom?"

"To my own people."

"*Ah!*" He gestured sharply. "Better to be alive—with hope—than dead with none. His Excellency predicts total victory soon, but I am not so certain. Especially now that you Anglos are fighting for a country you have declared to be your own."

"I'm not fighting for anything, Major. I'm a prisoner."

"There is always the chance you could be rescued."

"Highly unlikely, I think. I just don't understand your concern for my welfare. What kind of man are you?"

"A man whose *soldadera* died, and who needs—"

"That's not what I mean and you know it."

"What else can I tell you?" he exclaimed, his skin growing pink again. "My life is commonplace—quite unextraordinary. I'm a professional soldier with a duty to perform—and with little fondness for the style of my commander."

"Now we're getting somewhere. You don't like Santa Anna?"

Still flushed, he sat down on the small box. It creaked under his weight but, staring at his hands, he seemed not to notice.

"That is understating the case, señora." After a cautious glance at the tent entrance, he went on, "His Excellency demands the best for himself. The tastiest food. The choicest wine. Snowy linen, polished silver—my God, the man has a passion for silver such as I've never seen before—!"

Fascinated, Amanda watched the major growing angry again.

"You may be sure His Excellency was comfortable on the long march from Saltillo. He slept under fur robes, with a brazier burning in his marquee, when the blizzards struck the hills of Coahuila and the men had no tents and no fires. He pretended not to see the wretched Mayans from the Yucatán battalion lying like bundles of rags at the roadside—dying because they couldn't withstand the northern cold. We were short of provisions from the beginning, so His Excellency cut rations to half—for everyone except himself. Can you imagine how I liked ordering my men to fall out and search for their suppers? *Search?* They ate mesquite nuts—have you ever tasted them?"

"Yes. Bitter."

"Compared to our usual fare, they were a banquet, I can assure you! We lost men by the hundreds—both from desertion and—you'll forgive me —diarrhea. In his haste to mete out punishment, His Excellency also overlooked the small matter of providing enough doctors, medicines and ambulance wagons—but of course he made sure his personal physician was always close by! My God, you wouldn't believe the chicanery the man condones! You can imagine how our wounded need blankets and bedding today. But every stitch in Bexar has been appropriated by His Excellency's brother-in-law, Colonel Dromundo. It's available—to any hurt or dying man who can pay Dromundo's price—"

Glumly, Cordoba shook his head. "They would slit my throat if I said any of this in public. But His Excellency General Santa Anna is fighting for his personal power, not for Mexico."

"Then why do you obey him?"

"Because, for better or worse, he *is* Mexico—at the moment. Don't make any mistake, señora. Despite my dislike of him, I'll honor my promise. You won't go free. And if you try to escape, I won't stand in the way of your punishment. Beyond that, I guarantee you good treatment. My wants are minimal. Decent meals. Clean laundry. My boots polished—I hate a dirty uniform. It's unprofessional."

Amanda thought it over. She was still undecided when Cordoba jumped up. "Believe me, señora, I'm offering you a better bargain than you'd get from most in this encampment!"

He was probably right. And becoming a camp follower was no worse than some of the other things she'd done to stay alive.

"All right, Major," she said. "I accept."

He clapped his hands, delighted as a child:

"Wonderful! Now the first thing you must learn is how to say my first name correctly—"

"Major."

"What is it?"

"There's one subject you overlooked."

"Yes?"

She patted the cot.

He turned red again. "I make no demands there, señora. Clean small-clothes and a hot meal at night will satisfy me."

"Then you're one of a kind."

He shrugged, almost scarlet. "I am what I am."

"Don't you like women?"

He looked at her steadily.

"Some women."

She honestly didn't know what to make of Cordoba. At the moment, he resembled a shy boy more than a man. At least he didn't frighten her any longer, and to be free of fear even for a little while was welcome.

He cleared his throat. "Uh—señora—my name—"

"Oh yes, I'm sorry. Tell me what it is."

"It is Luis."

"Luis," she repeated.

"Good, that's just right—"

Still flushed, he pulled out a cheap pocket watch, then began buttoning his uniform blouse hastily.

"I don't think you'll find me too unpleasant. I am not a violent man. I am a narrow one, I regret to say. All my adult life has been spent in the army. I've had no time for other pursuits—nor any interest in them. But you know something? The older I grow—the more I see of the politicians who direct any army—the more I wonder whether I should have done something else with my life. Campaigning's no pleasure under a man like His Excellency."

As he finished dressing, he added in an apologetic way, "I trust you won't attempt to escape while I'm gone."

"No, I won't." She stretched; wriggled her shoulders, thankful that the aches were lessening.

"You'll have many an opportunity in the weeks ahead. You won't be guarded, or even watched very much—"

"Major, you saved my life."

He waved. A shade too quickly, she thought. "For purely practical purposes, I assure you."

"Even so, I owe you something for that. And I made a bargain. I'll live up to it."

"I do think I should station a corporal's guard outside for a few days. For the sake of appearance—"

"Go ahead if you want. I'm going to lie down for a little. Then I'll tidy up the bed, and try to find some branches to sweep this place out."

"Please, señora—just rest. You have seen horrible sights today. There is no need to busy yourself so soon."

"Yes there is," she said softly. "If I work, maybe I'll forget what I saw."

His eyes met hers, large and melancholy.

"Do you honestly think that's possible, señora?"

"No. But God forgive me, I wish it were."

"So do I."

They stood a moment longer, staring at one another. Then Luis Cordoba snatched up his shako and batted dust off the pompom. After a last look at the bedraggled woman in the center of the sunlit marquee, he touched respectful fingers to his brow and went out.

CHAPTER 4

The Camp Follower

THE ARMY MOVED EASTWARD, and Amanda with it. Cordoba brought her word of terrified Texans fleeing ahead of the Mexican force. The major said Sam Houston himself had ordered the retreat, fearing more slaughter of the kind that had taken place at the Alamo. Susannah Dickinson and the two blacks had evidently reached Gonzales with an account of the massacre.

The weather was rainy and miserable. Trudging in mud beside the wagon carrying Major Cordoba's marquee and equipment, Amanda saw frequent signs that the spirit of resistance had been broken. Homesteads, abandoned and torched, billowed black clouds into the gray sky. Herds of cattle broke the horizon-line and trembled the earth, set free as their owners piled belongings on muleback, left their small ranches and hurried east.

The village of Gonzales was still smoldering when Santa Anna rode in at the head of his host. Amanda walked wide-eyed through the dirt streets, listening to the talk of the *soldaderas.* Houston had insisted on burning Gonzales so there would be no shelter for Santa Anna's troops, the woman said.

But a few rickety buildings survived. In the doorway of one, an old blind woman, an American, listened to the clatter of the army passing, clutched a mangy white cat to her breast and wept.

Amanda was some distance down the street when she heard a shot. She looked back. The doorway was empty. One of the *soldaderas,* surrounded by laughing friends, was waving a pistol—

"General Urrea has taken Colonel Fannin at Goliad," Cordoba told her two days after Palm Sunday. Amanda already felt bad enough without hearing that. Her period had come. She was miserable from the stickiness and chafing of the rags tied beneath her dress.

"Fannin was the one who should have come to the aid of the mission, wasn't he?"

Amanda nodded in a dull way.

"They say he had four hundred men when he was captured. Palm Sunday morning, they all thought they were being paroled. A detachment of Urrea's troops took them to a woods near the village. Urrea had other men hidden among the trees. Fannin and his four hundred were shot to death." There was no satisfaction in Cordoba's voice when he said it.

Amanda lost track of the days. Rain fell intermittently, sometimes a shower, sometimes a torrent. The drenched plains took on a wearying sameness. The Texans were still reported in wild flight. Santa Anna was in high spirits, confident he'd catch the rebel leaders before they reached the sanctuary of American soil beyond the Sabine.

March became April, but Amanda was hardly aware of it. Constant bad news only compounded the weariness produced by the hard routine of the march.

She rose before dawn every day, stiff from sleeping on blankets laid at the foot of Cordoba's cot. Her first chore was to go outside to the communal cook fire, jostle a place among the other camp followers and begin brewing the major's coffee.

At first she had been crowded away from the fire. Taunted with obscene remarks. Even threatened. A couple of incidents in which she'd used her nails, her teeth and her fists to defend herself put an end to the harassment. The other *soldaderas* never spoke to her directly. But they allowed her room to work.

After breakfast, she was expected to help Cordoba's orderly strike the marquee and pack it for transportation in the baggage wagon. All day she followed the wagon on foot, breaking the routine occasionally by dropping back to the wagons of the civilian sutlers.

With money Cordoba had given her, she bargained for food. She refused the tainted meat always offered first, and demanded fresh. She swore and gestured and haggled until the inflated price came down to a satisfactory level. Here, at least, her experience on a farm and at the hotel made her the equal of most of the other women—and superior to some. Quite a few of the *soldaderas* were young girls, unlettered and ignorant of the fact that the sutlers routinely tried to sell spoiled food at ten times its worth.

She did get a rest every afternoon. War or no war, the Mexicans demanded a siesta. But as soon as the army camped for the night, work began again.

She prepared the major's evening meal. And whenever there was a stream nearby, she carried his laundry there, washing it with yellow soap that left her hands raw. She slapped the clothes damp dry on stones, Indian fashion.

Illness was still rampant in the army. So once a week, she insisted on plunging the major's wash into a kettle of boiling water. She boiled his drinking water as well. Although these unusual procedures elicited more laughter from the camp women, Cordoba remained healthy while many of his fellow officers succumbed to dysentery.

She spent a considerable amount of time polishing boots and uniform buttons. Cordoba was almost fanatic about a neat appearance—a reaction, she suspected, to the sloth and disorder prevalent in the camp. Cordoba's gleaming leather and metal were an expression of his outrage—and one of the few aspects of a chaotic world that he could control absolutely.

There was one part of the *soldaderas'* routine in which Amanda refused to participate, though. Every night, the women worked together to dig open trenches. Whenever they had to relieve themselves, they squatted over the trenches like so many hens, chatting amiably with their skirts hiked above their waists and their bottoms clearly in view.

Perhaps because of her city upbringing, Amanda couldn't expose herself that way. She had to seek the privacy of a grove of trees, or at least some shrubs. Occasionally, the lack of such foliage near the campsite kept her in excruciating pain while she waited for darkness.

The other women laughed about her fastidiousness, just as they laughed about her cooking of the clothes. One *soldadera* in particular seemed not just scornful, but hostile. This was the coarse-faced young woman with the mole; the girl Amanda had encountered in the street the morning after the massacre.

Now and again Amanda would run into the girl at the sutler's or along a creek at laundry time, and the girl would be sure Amanda heard some particularly filthy reference to her parentage, or her relationship with Cordoba.

Each time, Amanda met the girl's ugly gaze squarely—almost daring her to lay hands on her. But she didn't. Amanda asked a few questions of Cordoba's men and learned that the girl lived with a captain of the artillery. For a woman belonging to a man of lesser rank to attack the *soldadera* of a senior officer was a violation of the camp's rough protocol; and it was that which kept the girl's hostility from degenerating into the physical. But Amanda was sure the ranks of their respective men fueled the girl's fury; she was probably jealous of an Anglo woman enjoying the favors of a major.

If the girl only knew! Amanda thought. During their first weeks together, Cordoba didn't so much as touch her.

She had frankly expected him to order her into his bed, despite what he'd said that first day. But he treated her with punctilious politeness. He complimented her often, praising the flour biscuits she baked, or the whiteness of his dress shirts:

"I swear to heaven, no man ever had a better *soldadera*. You take to this life as if you were born to it."

"I wasn't, and I don't like it."

"Nevertheless, you're extremely skilled."

She shrugged. "All it takes is making up your mind."

In response to his puzzled frown, she elaborated:

"I didn't have a lot of schooling, Luis. And what I did have, I didn't care for very much. But when I was growing up, I managed to learn something that's as important as what they teach in classrooms."

"What is that?"

"I can do almost anything I want if I want to do it badly enough."

"Such confidence!"

"I'm not trying to brag—the same thing's true of most people. They just don't want to put forth the effort, that's all. When I was young, I lived for a while with a tribe of the Sioux—"

His mouth dropped open. "With *Indians?*"

"Yes."

"You continually astonish me, Amanda. Do go on."

"I was the property of one of the dog soldiers—the warriors who police the buffalo hunts. To satisfy the man I lived with—and keep him from hurting me—I had to learn how to make love like a grown woman—when I wasn't much more than twelve years old. I had to learn to broil the meat of a buffalo hump the way he liked it. I'd never cooked anything in my life—but I learned because it was necessary. And because I didn't want to seem weaker than the Sioux women, I learned every game they played— and practiced until I was better than they were. The man I stayed with was so proud of me, he ordered his first wife out of his tepee forever. And whenever white traders came to the village, he put guards over me and kept me hidden. He was afraid I might be stolen away—"

"I trust you were appropriately flattered."

"Yes—but maybe not for the reason you think. Not because of vanity. His attitude showed me I'd done what I set out to do. Survive. Even thrive. The man I was living with was killed, and I left the Sioux. But before I went, the old chief—the father of my man—told me he'd never seen a Sioux girl who could play the double-ball game—handle the rawhide and the sticks—as well as I did. He couldn't give a higher compliment to any woman. The point is, I don't think learning the game took special talent. Just the will to do it."

"I think you underestimate your abilities."

"Will counts for a lot in this world, Luis. I'll trade money or education for will anytime."

Cordoba was silent. There was a look akin to awe on his swarthy face.

His reticence about sex continued to bother her. At night, he seldom glanced her way as she brushed her hair and prepared for bed. She slept in the same black silk dress she wore all during the day. Could that be part of the trouble? she wondered. The dress, clean but ragged now, struck her as decidedly unfeminine.

One warm evening in the first week of April, she was awake long after Cordoba had fallen asleep on the cot. She moved her head from side to side, uttering a small sigh once in a while. There was a tightness in her body that she couldn't deny.

Jaimie de la Gura had been dead a long time. And there had only been a very few men since then; an occasional customer of Gura's Hotel to whom she took a fancy. The last one, a wandering trader bound for Taos, had slept in her arms more than half a year ago.

She alone was responsible for the unsatisfied hunger, she knew. It was ironic—the brothel madam who could no longer give herself casually. She had given herself that way early in her life, when it was necessary to use her good looks and her sex for survival. But after Jaimie, she changed. Without a basic liking for the partner, she was unwilling—even though her body made its need manifest in aches and sleeplessness.

The need this particular night grew almost unbearable. She finally rose on one elbow; whispered softly in the darkness:

"Luis?"

The major answered with an exhausted snore. She stretched out again, uncomfortable and unhappy. She had come to like Cordoba. But beyond that, his lack of interest made her feel there must be something wrong with her.

True, she was dirty and unkempt most of the time. That didn't seem to make any difference to other men in the army, though. They rutted with women who smelled like a sty.

Cordoba stirred. Said something in his sleep. She propped herself on her elbow again, listening.

The major was mumbling a name. Her heart beat a little faster in the hope that it might be hers—

A moment later, she was ashamed of the foolish conceit. She slid her hands down her belly, pressing her palms against herself. She couldn't go to the cot and waken him now. She knew it would have made him miserable afterward.

In torment, she lay still. It was an hour or more before she fell asleep and dreamed erotic dreams that left her grumpy in the morning.

ii

The army marched into San Felipe on the Brazos on the seventh of April. Once more the Texans were gone, though Cordoba said scouts had sighted Houston and three or four hundred men downriver at Thompson's Ferry.

That the tiny Texas army had recently been in San Felipe was evident when Amanda went down to the Brazos in the red twilight. Carrying Cordoba's laundry, she passed two pirogues with their bottoms staved in. The prow of a third poked up from reeds near the shore. Houston had destroyed any craft the Mexicans might use to cross the rain-swollen river.

Up and down the bank, chattering *soldaderas* kneaded and pounded their men's clothing. As Amanda walked by a group of four, she noticed the girl with the mole. Kneeling in the mud, the young woman stared at her.

Amanda hurried on. She heard the girl and her companions talking. Suddenly she yelped, stumbling as a stone struck the back of her head.

She dropped Cordoba's shirts and underdrawers in the mud; turned; saw the girl wiping her hands on her blouse.

The girl hoisted her skirt and began tucking it into the rope belt she wore, unconcerned about revealing her grimy thighs and black tangle above. One of the older *soldaderas* caught her arm:

"Ah, let the white slut alone, Manuela. She behaves herself—"

"Which is more than can be said for your friend!" Amanda called, rubbing her scalp, then bending to retrieve the laundry.

Head lowered, Manuela started walking toward her. Amanda wondered why the young woman looked even more haggard than usual.

"I'm sick of seeing her parade herself," Manuela said to her companions. "She thinks she's a queen, living with a major—"

Only a step away now, Manuela reached out and twisted a lock of Amanda's hair around a stubby finger. She breathed out the smell of wine as she went on:

"But she's an ice queen, this one. I have a friend who belongs to a sergeant in one of Cordoba's platoons—"

Amanda said, "Let go," then pulled back. But Manuela held the lock of hair. Amanda winced.

"—and I hear Cordoba's marquee is silent all night long. Never any sounds of pleasure. Just the ice queen farting in her sleep."

Amanda's cheeks darkened as she realized she'd been spied on. She supposed she should have expected it.

Manuela kept winding the strand of hair tighter around her finger:

"Probably the major regrets taking an Anglo into his tent. Anglos are as weak between the legs as they are in their bellies—"

Amanda wrenched suddenly, tearing away. Manuela stepped back with a curse. Then she squatted, fingers digging in the mud until they closed on a pointed stone.

A barking dog and half a dozen ragged boys from San Felipe came running along the sunset-reddened bank, drawn by the promise of a fight. Amanda's stomach flipflopped. Manuela meant to do her physical harm—

"You'd better get her away," Amanda warned the other three women. "I don't want a quarrel. But if she pushes it—"

"Yes? What will you do?" Manuela demanded. She spat. "Nothing!"

"She lost her captain three days ago," one of the older women blurted. "He was knifed in an argument over cards—"

Amanda understood the reason for the girl's haggard look. But that didn't lessen her fear. Manuela held out the rock, showing Amanda the point:

"After I finish with this, the major will need another companion."

"I don't think so."

"I do. He may be surprised when I come back in your place. But I don't think he'll be disappointed. I think he'll welcome a woman who knows how to spread herself properly."

Amanda's racing mind sorted the ways she might deal with the situation. Appealing to logic wouldn't work. Manuela obviously had a gut hatred of Texans. And now the loss of her captain had removed any reason for restraint.

The boys had stopped nearby, smirking and nudging one another in anticipation. Manuela shuffled forward again, her bare feet squishing in the mud:

"The fact of it is, I need a man. I'm sure you won't mind surrendering yours since you bring him no happiness—"

Determined to try to bluff her way out, Amanda said, "Unless you want to get hurt, leave me alone."

"Perhaps if you beg me, Anglo."

"*Beg!* The hell I will, you—" Unthinkingly, she resorted to the kind of slur she would never have used when she was calm: "—you greaser bitch."

Manuela licked her lower lip. "I am going to make you hurt for that, Anglo."

"All right." Amanda nodded. "Turn your wolf loose."

"What?"

"I mean go ahead and fight. You'll wish you hadn't."

Briefly started, Manuela laughed with false bravado:

"Eh, the ice queen shows a little fire! What are you going to use to fight me?" She ground her heel on one of Cordoba's shirts. "Dirty laundry?"

Before Amanda was quite prepared, the girl rushed her. The point of the stone slashed toward Amanda's eye.

Amanda lunged aside, lost her footing in the mud. As she fell to her knees, the stone raked her temple. A second later she felt the trickle of warm blood above her eyebrow.

Snarling obscenities, Manuela jumped around behind her. She seized Amanda's hair with one hand, used the other to smash the stone against her scalp. Amanda pitched forward, gasping. Manuela stepped on the back of her neck, driving her face into the mud.

Sputtering and fighting for air, Amanda rolled aside frantically as the young girl started to kneel on her stomach. Mud clogged her eyes, her nostrils. But somehow she avoided the next swipe of the rock and kept rolling —straight into the shallows of the river.

Manuela stormed after her, kicking up droplets that glowed red in the sunset. The dog was barking loudly. The boys clapped and encouraged Manuela, who struck for Amanda's head again.

Amanda grabbed Manuela's forearm with both hands, jerked it to her mouth and bit. Manuela squealed. Amanda shoved her backward. The stone almost slipped from the younger woman's grasp, but she caught it.

Soaked and moving slowly because of it, Amanda still managed to get behind the girl and use her own tactic—a yank of the hair. But Manuela was strong; strong enough to slither free and spin, hacking at Amanda's face with the rock.

Amanda dodged again, laced her hands together, kicked Manuela's leg. The girl doubled over. Amanda's locked hands came down on Manuela's exposed neck with terrific force.

Crying out in real pain, Manuela sprawled face first in the shallows. The stone flew from her fingers, splashed and disappeared under the water. Amanda thought about calling a halt. But if she did, she'd never be safe in the encampment. She had to defeat the Mexican girl completely; decisively—

She gazed around for a weapon. Something Manuela had said came to mind. She darted for the bank, grabbed one of Cordoba's shirts, dipped it in the water and lashed Manuela's cheek.

Floundering in the shallows, Manuela cried out. She tried to grab Amanda's leg. Amanda whipped the girl's face again. Again. Her eyes were red with the glare of the sunset as she struck—

She laid ten, twelve, fifteen strokes on Manuela's face, neck and shoulders. When the shirt showed blood, she stopped. Whimpering, Manuela crawled away in the water—

Amanda was shaking. She stumbled up the bank. The boys and Manuela's companions stared at her in amazement.

She wiped her brow with a soaked sleeve, then stared at the blood from the cut over her eye. She dropped the shirt she'd used as a whip, retrieved the rest of Cordoba's laundry. Manuela was still on her knees in the water, shaking her head in a groggy way. Amanda hooked a toe beneath the bloody, ruined garment, and kicked it toward Manuela's three companions:

"Clean her up. And tell her the major has a lot of other shirts."

Walking as steadily as she could, she moved on down the bank in the stillness.

iii

"God above, what happened to you?" Cordoba exclaimed when she entered the marquee sometime later, the clean laundry bundled under one arm.

She put the laundry on the washstand, her hand none too steady. "Nothing," she said. "I'm all right."

Cordoba was bare-chested. The black hair below his throat showed glints of sweat in the light of the hanging lantern. At the waist of his trousers, his stomach bulged. He laid a palm over the roll of fat, as if ashamed to have her see.

She sank down on the cot. "I'm afraid I lost one of your best shirts, though."

Cordoba seemed not to hear. "How did you cut your forehead?"

"It isn't important."

"I insist that you answer." She didn't. "At least let me find some alcohol—"

"No, I only need to rest a minute."

"Damn you, woman! Tell me who hurt you and I'll see him flogged!"

If she hadn't been so spent, she would have laughed. The major looked furious.

"Not *he*," she said. "It was one of the *soldaderas*. She won't bother me again." Her generous mouth curved in a wry smile. "She had designs on you. She lost her own man, and—well, let's just say she wasn't thinking very clearly."

She lay back. Closed her eyes. She sensed Cordoba crouching down beside her.

"I still want to know the woman's name. I intend to see her punished."

"It's not necessary, Luis—I took care of it."

"You might have been killed!"

"I wasn't."

She studied him. His deep-set eyes seemed unusually dark in the shadows beneath his brows. Teasing, she added:

"Maybe you would have preferred her. She claimed she could please a man better than I do."

Cordoba gathered both her hands in his. She felt the weight of his forearm against her left breast. She was touched by the almost child-like tenderness of his expression:

"You have pleased me more than any woman I have ever known, Amanda. You have made this filthy campaign bearable. Brought me comfort just with your presence. You know I'm poor at talking like a romantic —I am a soldier. I'm trying to say you are the dearest—"

Swallowing, he stopped. The familiar redness tinted his cheeks again.

She smiled. "But I don't seem very good at giving a man what he wants most from a *soldadera*—" She was only partly teasing now. His closeness—the warmth and hardness of his arm—stirred something in her that was part passion, part hunger for reassurance. "I've really wondered why you never touch me."

"Because—" His eyes brimmed with pain. "Because I have a wife."

He bowed his head.

She reached her right hand across her breast; ran the palm down the faint stubble on his face.

"I know that, Luis."

He jerked back. "You *know*—?"

"Well, I guessed. One night, in your sleep, you spoke a woman's name several times. I decided it was the name of a sweetheart or, more likely, your wife."

Each word cost him effort: "I have wanted you very much, Amanda. But I dared not ask—"

"Always so honorable—" Gently, she touched his forehead. "That's a terrible burden to bear in a dishonorable world."

"I told you before—I can't help what I am. I know I must go home to my wife in the capital one day—"

"That could be a long time in the future."

He said nothing.

"Do you have children?"

"Alas, no."

"Well, I wouldn't want you to do anything that would make you feel ashamed later—"

"Stop!" he exclaimed. "It's only on your account that I've held back. You're a beautiful woman—and a decent one. If you were just a camp whore, I'd have taken you and thought nothing of it. Well—almost nothing. You deserve better. I could never dishonor you with lies. False promises—"

"I don't need promises, Luis. I just need you."

Again he averted his head:

"Sometimes I wish I'd never seen you. But I did. And I have come to—to love you with all my being. More than I have ever loved any woman." He raised his head. "Any woman."

"If that's how you feel, nothing else is necessary. Blow out the lamp and lie down with me—"

She saw the dawning wonder in his eyes. Wonder mingled with suffering. He was still agonized by what he had revealed about himself. She tried to relieve his conscience with a light tone:

"It is about time you treated me as a proper camp follower! Besides, I'm too sore to sleep on the ground one more night."

Slowly, slowly, a smile forced itself across his mouth. A tentative smile that turned to joy as he reached upward for the lantern.

iv

In the darkness, he cursed, then apologized. He'd tangled his feet in his breeches as he pulled them off.

He lowered himself beside her on the narrow cot, touching her cheek almost hesitantly. She circled his neck with her arms, turning her head to the proper angle for a kiss.

When their lips touched, much of Cordoba's restraint disappeared. He pressed his mouth hard against hers. She felt his yearning in the sudden clasp of his arms beneath her back—

He murmured her name over and over as they embraced. He spoke lovely, courtly Spanish as he caressed her body. She sighed with pleasure when his hands closed on her bare breasts.

A moment later, she maneuvered beneath him, guiding him and laughing when he gasped at her boldness. He entered her gently, although his breathing roared loud as a storm in her ear. When she urged him to speed, he complied, and with each quickening movement of his body, she understood again that this was no weak man, only one who was tender and humane in a world that sometimes derided those virtues. With the straining of her own flesh, the movement of her hands, the press of her mouth, she tried to show him that she admired and prized what he was.

He was quicker than she, bursting into apologies afterward. She stilled them with a kiss, then drew him into the curve of her arm. Holding him close, she murmured that, before the night ended, there would be another time. A better one—

"Oh," he said, alarmed, "I don't know if that's possible for me—"

"It is. You'll see."

She caught the sound of a boot scraping in the dirt street outside. Another eavesdropper?

She felt sorry for him, whoever he was. Skulking in the April dark, he could only hear the sounds of lovemaking. He would never imagine the sense of completion and peace and—yes, admit it—affection that warmed her soul after long, long months of privation.

v

After that night, Manuela never bothered her again. An even happier result was the change in her relationship with Cordoba.

Before, the conversations had been largely superficial: the events of the day's march; the suspected position of Sam Houston's little army; the latest example of incompetence or dishonesty on the senior staff. But once they had shared each other's embraces, she and the major wanted to share the whole sum of themselves as well—their hopes and histories; their dreams and disappointments.

As the army worked its way south toward Thompson's Ferry, their evening lovemaking usually ended not in langorous slumber but in quiet conversation. Nights when they were both too tired, conversation sufficed.

The only subject Cordoba wouldn't discuss was his wife. Otherwise, he held nothing back. What he had said about himself was true: his background—his world—was limited to soldiering.

He had been born in Veracruz, the fourth of his father's children, and the only son. He was a young subaltern in the army when the political upheavals began in the 1820s. His father, a prosperous importer, remained loyal to Spain. After much painful deliberation, Luis Cordoba put himself on the side of independence, helping to overthrow the Spanish government, then that of the professed revolutionary Iturbide, who had turned on his separatist followers and maneuvered himself into the role of emperor.

Iturbide had been deposed in 1823. A year later, a revised, democratic Mexican constitution began luring the Anglo-American *empresarios* to

Texas. Through it all, Cordoba said, he had remained loyal to Mexico first and the army second:

"When the separatist movement developed, I had the highest of hopes. I thought that, at last, I could fight for something other than simple military victory. For principle. Over the years I've learned how easily principle can be crushed by those with ambition. Now I'm virtually back where I started—obeying orders. Hoping to win if there's an engagement. Not daring to look too deeply into why we're fighting. A man can die in many ways, you know. Death in battle is perhaps the most final, but the least grievous. It's much worse to struggle for a cause, then perceive that you've struggled for nothing. I felt that way—cheated; dead—when His Excellency jettisoned the constitution."

"There's no hope of unseating Santa Anna?"

"Next to none. He's firmly entrenched. God—what a poltroon he is! In its short history, your country has been fortunate to escape his kind, Amanda."

"Oh, we've had our share of poltroons, I think—" She shook her head. "I get such an odd feeling when you speak about the United States."

"Odd? What do you mean?"

"It *is* my country. Yet sometimes it doesn't seem so any longer. My grandfather did fight in the Revolution—"

"Did he! And survived?"

"Yes, though he was wounded. He limped for the rest of his life."

"The Americans have a positive passion for rebellion! Even more so than those of us south of the Rio Grande, I think."

"That isn't always a good thing, Luis. Do you know that when we fought Britain again, twenty-five years ago, several of the northern states wanted to secede because they hated the war? And four years ago—I remember being shocked when I read it in the papers—South Carolina nearly left the union because of Nullification."

"I don't know the term."

"It means a state placing itself above the law of the country. South Carolina didn't like one of the government's tariffs. So the state legislature nullified it. Said it didn't apply to South Carolina. Old Hickory—"

"The president, Jackson?"

"Yes. He said it did, because no state could declare itself separate from the union. He promised to send in troops if South Carolina continued to disagree. The state gave in. I suppose that was proper. I remember hearing my father say that once the country was formed, no one could tear it apart. I didn't understand—I imagined huge ditches in the earth. Now I know what he meant—and how serious the question is."

"Your country is still divided on at least one great issue."

"You mean slavery?"

He nodded.

"That's where our passion for rebellion as you call it could prove our undoing," she said in a somber way. "There are people in the east—mainly in New York and Boston—who call themselves abolitionists. They want to do away with slavery completely. The south can't afford that. There's trouble coming—you can tell even by reading the papers out here."

Boston, Amanda revealed, was the city in which she'd grown up. She had lived in a splendid house owned by Gilbert Kent, her father, a well-to-do printer of books and newspapers.

Gilbert Kent had died at a relatively young age, leaving Amanda in the care of her pretentious and somewhat unstable mother, Harriet. Gilbert's widow had made a poor choice of a second husband—a wastrel named Piggott. He had succeeded in gambling away most of the family's assets, including the printing house, Kent and Son.

"The loss was probably no accident, I learned later. My cousin Jared—the son of my father's half-brother Abraham—served in the navy in the 1812 war. There was an officer aboard Jared's ship—Stovall, his name was—who fancied boys and men in preference to women—"

Cordoba snorted in disgust.

"Jared got in a scrape with Stovall. Injured Stovall's face—scarred it. Permanently. The man never forgot. After the war, he came to Boston in secret. He was the one to whom my stepfather lost Kent's."

"You think this Stovall planned it? Maneuvered your stepfather into a game and cheated him?"

"I'm almost certain of it. Anyway, my cousin had a terrible temper in those days. He set fire to the printing house and shot and killed Stovall's general manager, a man called Waltham—Walpole—something like that."

"In heaven's name, why take vengeance on some flunky?" Cordoba exclaimed.

"Jared didn't intend to—he was aiming for Stovall."

"And so those tragic circumstances marked the end of the family business?"

"I've no way of knowing. Books are fairly scarce out here—especially among poor people. Now and then I've asked questions. No luck. Besides, if the firm burned to the ground, it might not have been rebuilt at all. But

I never heard that Stovall had any connection with publishing. His family operated an iron works of some kind."

"How about the fellow himself? Is he living?"

"There again, I've been too busy staying alive to look into it—and I'm not trying to be clever saying that. It's God's truth. I haven't had the money—or the necessary eastern contacts—for making an inquiry. I know our family employed a Boston law firm, but the name is another of those details that's completely slipped away from me. Sometimes, I think I'm much better off leaving the whole question alone. I'm afraid that if I learned Stovall was still alive, I'd spend all my energy on schemes to repay him."

"You have a deep hatred of him, obviously—"

"Without ever having set eyes on him. If he hadn't lured my stepfather into a gambling game with the firm at stake, my mother might have lived. She died the same day Jared burned Kent's and shot the general manager."

"How did she die?"

"She was run down by a dray right in front of our house on Beacon Street. Everyone called that an accident too, but my mother's second husband caused it. My mother had a fight with Piggott. He told her he'd lost the printing house. She rushed out, intending to go straight to the firm. She stumbled on the curb—the drayman couldn't stop in time—"

Amanda paused, re-living the scene in her mind. Cordoba whispered a word of sympathy. She let a shudder work itself out, then went on:

"That same night, Jared crept back to Beacon Street and told me what had happened. That he'd set fire to the firm because he couldn't stand the thought of someone like Stovall taking over what the Kents had worked so hard to build."

"This Jared sounds like a headstrong sort. Did he have no one to discipline him?"

"No. My mother tried, but she and Jared despised one another."

"What became of his parents?"

"Abraham, his father, tried to homestead in Ohio. Jared's mother was killed there. By Indians. Abraham gave up and came home. A few months later, he disappeared completely. I remember very little about him except that he was a noisy, quarrelsome man. His loud voice frightened me. He was drunk most of the time, I think—anyway, the night the printing house burned, Jared convinced me that we had to leave Boston together. We had no one except each other, and he was afraid of being arrested for murder. We started for New Orleans. I can't remember much about the early part of the trip, except that it was winter. We were always half frozen and half starved. We met a few kind people. I recall one little girl named Sarah, in Kentucky—her mother and father were farmers. They treated us well and helped Jared recover from a sickness. We didn't get far after we left Knob Creek, though. Only to Tennessee—"

From the pain of the past, she summoned the rest of it: her rape and abduction by the bogus preacher, Blackthorn, who sold her in St. Louis to a trader named Maas. He in turn sold her to a warrior of the Teton Sioux, a young, not unhandsome man whose Indian name translated to Plenty Coups:

"Some of this you've already heard—"

Cordoba grinned. "How you were experienced with men at age twelve, for example? I'm certainly fortunate to have the benefit of all that training—"

She pinched him. "I didn't ask for it, Luis! I was pretty well filled out by the time I was twelve—"

He rolled his tongue in his cheek. "That is not hard to imagine."

"Oh, be serious! Do you want to hear this or don't you?"

"I do. Please continue."

"Being a woman was the only weapon I had when I was sold to the Sioux. If I hadn't used it, I would have been treated a lot worse by Plenty Coups."

"How long did you stay with the Indians?"

"Eight—no, closer to nine years. Like you, I never had any children. For some reason, Plenty Coups couldn't."

"I'd say you were lucky to survive such an experience."

"I've told you before, it wasn't all luck."

"Ah, yes. The old chief's compliment when you left—"

"Determination was only part of it. Something else helped me get through those years—and the ones since. Somehow I've always been blessed with almost perfect health. I never realized how precious that was —how rare among women especially—until I saw all the sick squaws in Plenty Coups' village. Work and childbirth and white men's diseases killed more of them than I can remember—"

She told him the rest on succeeding evenings: how Plenty Coups had been injured in a fall from his horse as he rode in to strike a huge bull buffalo with his coup stick during a hunt. Three weeks later—just about the time, they figured out, that Iturbide had been at the height of his power as Emperor Augustin I of Mexico—she was a widow.

A month after Plenty Coups' death, a party representing John Astor's American Fur Company had visited the tribe.

"Jaimie de la Gura, my husband, was one of those men. The American and French winterers and the Delawares who worked with them called him Spanish Jim. He was very handsome—"

Cordoba pulled a face. "More handsome than I?"

"Just about the same." She leaned up to kiss his lips.

"You told His Excellency your husband came from New Orleans—"

"That's right. His father was quite well off. Ran an elegant coffee house. But that was when he was older. Civilized, you might say. There was a wild streak in the de la Gura family. Jaimie's father came by most of his money running slaves with the Lafitte brothers. He wanted Jaimie to enter the clergy or perhaps study law. Jaimie wouldn't do either. He didn't like town living very much. He ran away up the Mississippi when he was eighteen, went to work for a fur trader in St. Louis, and traveled west from there—"

"To find you in the Sioux village."

"Yes. I was allowed to be seen by white men after Plenty Coups died. Jaimie took a liking to me. He asked me to go with him—and he was willing to pay the old chief in trade goods for my freedom. My life with the tribe had come to a kind of ending, so I said I'd go. Jaimie was ten years older than I was. A good man."

"And obviously one of impeccable taste."

She laughed. "We were married in St. Louis. We spent our honeymoon in a real hotel, with solid walls, and beds with the most marvelous sheets and blankets—I'd forgotten what that sort of existence was like. Jaimie still didn't care for it, though. And he was too independent to work for one employer very long. He didn't keep on as a trapper because he felt the life was too hard for a woman. We went south. He worked at odd jobs—we covered a lot of territory before he finally decided we should come to Texas and try farming."

She described the events that had led to Jaimie's death and her subsequent venture with the hotel:

"So you can see I've done a good many things in thirty-three years, Luis—some of which I'm a little ashamed to talk about."

He brushed his mouth against her cheek, as if to dismiss her concern. Then he shifted his position so she could lie more comfortably. He asked:

"This Jaimie—did you really love him?"

"I think so. He was kind to me. I never felt any great outpourings of emotion when he was alive. But I liked him—I enjoyed being with him— at least until things went sour for us. I mourned a long time when he died. If that's love, then yes, I loved him."

The major touched the rope bracelet. "Did he give you this?"

"No, my cousin Jared did. He made it from cordage on the *Constitution,* the frigate he served on during the war."

"Do you know where your cousin is now?"

She shook her head. "That day in Tennessee was the last I ever saw of him. He may be dead. He might have gone back to Boston, though I doubt it—"

"You sound sad when you speak of this Bos—" He had trouble pronouncing it. "Bos-ton. Do you miss it?"

"I miss never being hungry, or cold, or worried about tomorrow. I sometimes feel Boston's where I belong."

"Because of the comforts?"

"No, that's not it. My father came of a very independent, idealistic family. I can still see him in the front sitting room one night when I was little. He was speaking to Jared. I can't recall the exact words, but I understood his meaning, and it made a great impression. My father said anyone who belonged to the Kent family had a duty in this world. A duty to give, not just take—"

Lost in the reverie, she closed her eyes. The images in her mind—a flickering hearth; her cousin's tawny hair and blue eyes; her father's sallow face and frail body beside the mantel; a long, polished muzzle-loader; a gleaming sword; a small green bottle—were incredibly vivid:

"I can hear his voice to this day. And see the things above the mantelpiece. A little bottle of dried East India tea my grandfather collected when the colonists dumped the shipment in Boston harbor. There's a sword my grandfather got from the French general, Lafayette—and a Virginia rifle—"

She opened her eyes.

"Those things were important to my father. I remember him saying they had to be preserved, as tokens of what the Kents stood for. I have no idea what's become of them—"

"Would you like to go back and try to discover that?"

"Yes, I would. Everyone has one special dream they cherish, I suppose— a dream that doesn't stand a chance of being fulfilled. Going back to find those things is mine." Her smile was rueful. "I expect they were sold for junk years ago."

"If you have such a consuming desire, I would have expected you return to Bos-ton long before this. You've had opportunities—"

"After Jaimie died?"

"Exactly."

"I thought of it. But there's a funny kind of pride involved, Luis. I think I told you the Kents were once a wealthy family. I promised myself I'd never go back unless I could be worthy of the name."

"You mean go back as a rich woman?"

"At least well off. So I could properly face anyone who might remember the family. Especially that son of a bitch Stovall or his heirs—" She paused a moment. "You probably think I'm crazy."

"To be truthful, I should prefer to say unrealistic."

She snuggled against the muscle of his naked arm. "I admit it."

"Then again, perhaps I'm the one who is unrealistic. I listen to you, and I can believe you *will* go back one day."

"I don't think I'd be a very good caretaker of those things my father prized. The Kents are supposed to be people who contribute, remember? I've done nothing much but keep myself alive—"

"Nonsense, Amanda! You're a generous, loving woman. An honorable woman! You made that clear when you faced His Excellency—"

She laughed softly. "I love you for saying things like that. But I'm afraid it's your heart talking, not your head."

"It's the truth!"

"Oh, Luis, we won't really find out what we are until it's too late to do anything about it. The Sioux believe the only honest verdict on a human life comes when it's all over."

"Are you saying that trying to live honorably is useless? I can't accept that."

"I can't either—but I do believe the Sioux are right when they claim we see ourselves imperfectly. Untruthfully. And only someone else can judge us—"

Quietly, Cordoba asked, "Do you mean God?"

"The name isn't important, is it? The Mandan Sioux, for instance, believe that when you die, a great vine sprouts from the ground near your body. A vine that's invisible to everyone else. The vine leads straight up to the sky—to paradise. Your spirit rises and begins to climb. About halfway up is the critical point. Either you go all the way unmolested—or great hands reach down from paradise and break the vine, and your spirit falls

back to earth, denied heaven because you lived an unworthy life."
Amused, she added, "Can you guess who those hands belong to?"

"Why, to whoever those Mandan call their God."

"No, to an agent of the high spirit. An intermediary."

"An Indian Christ?"

Merrily, Amanda said, "A very formidable woman."

"A *woman?* That's blasphemous!"

"I think it's delightful. I must say your attitude's typical of men, Luis."

They laughed again, and then he returned to the original thread of the
conversation:

"Well, I can't worry about the afterlife—I have enough problems with
the present."

"And no dreams?"

There was a long moment of silence. Then:

"None that will come true. You, though—you have your Bos-ton. Hold
onto that, Amanda. You may still see your home before that remarkable
vine appears. You have the will—" He began to stroke her hair. "Right
now, though, your home is here. If only for a short time."

"I sometimes wish it could be for a long time, Luis."

He pulled her closer.

"I wish that constantly, Amanda. Constantly."

When she fell asleep against him, his cheeks were wet.

vi

On the eleventh of April, Santa Anna's troops captured a flatboat at
Thompson's Ferry. They began crossing the Brazos the following day.

On the fourteenth, an apparition appeared on the river—a smoke-billow-
ing monster that chugged and rumbled. Great revolving paddle-wheels
propelled the boat through the water. There wasn't a human being anywhere on deck.

Infantrymen lining the banks grew terrified at the sight—though a few
had enough presence of mind to unlimber their muskets and fire at the
boxy pilot house, where dim figures crouched over a wheel. Amanda,
watching with a group of terrified *soldaderas*, tried to calm them:

"That's no demon. It's a boat driven by an engine."

"*Engine—?*"

Round, frightened eyes signaled a total lack of comprehension.

"Well, just take my word for it—there aren't any imps in the boat's belly. Just a machine that moves a shaft and drives the wheels by means of steam."

"Steam—!"

She gave up. They didn't grasp any of it.

Amanda herself had never seen a steamboat before. But she had read about them in Texas newspapers. She knew they were changing the nation in which she'd been born; speeding the pace of its river commerce and drawing the frontiers closer to the cities. Fascinated, she watched the steamboat churn by—

As its stern came into view, she noticed bright red lettering:

YELLOW STONE

Only the night before, Cordoba had told her Houston was using a small steam vessel of that name to ferry his fleeing army across the Brazos. Now, apparently, the retreat was complete—

A handful of the more courageous officers rallied some men and rushed to a point of land where the river narrowed. Using ropes, they tried to snare the steamboat's smokestacks as she chugged by. Pistol shots from the pilot house scattered the would-be ropers. *Yellow Stone* was soon gone around a bend. Amanda stood staring after it, somehow saddened by the sight.

She turned away from the bank, still gripped by wonder and melancholy. That marvelous boat without oars or tow-ropes represented the world in which she'd been born. Unbidden, dim pictures slipped through her mind—

The cozy glow of a fire in a grate.

Ice skaters gliding in a white landscape.

While church bells pealed, she rode in a carriage, finely dressed; recognized as Gilbert Kent's daughter—

With a fierce shake of her head, she returned to reality. Nothing remained of the steamboat but traces of smoke in the sky. Her convictions about the power of her own will seemed pathetic all at once. Her dream of seeing Boston again was just as insubstantial as the vanishing smoke.

vii

Late that same day, dispatch riders sped to Santa Anna's marquee with news that the president of the Republic of Texas, Señor Burnet, could be caught at the settlement of Harrisburg, a scant thirty miles away. Before dark, His Excellency had a picked force moving forward: seven hundred infantry; fifty dragoons; a six-pound cannon, the necessary wagons and, of course, the *soldaderas*. Cordoba's men—and Amanda—were with the special detachment.

The forced march was grueling. The advance party of dragoons reached Harrisburg the following midnight.

No Burnet. The Texas government, such as it was, had fled again.

And where was Houston? Somewhere up the Brazos? No one was sure.

The Mexican citizens of Harrisburg wanted to be helpful, but they lacked information. The Texans who foolishly stayed behind—including three Anglo printers still churning out English-language newspapers— suffered arrest and maintained stoic silence under interrogation. Santa Anna torched the town and sent his cavalry eastward on a probing expedition.

Again riders brought back news that whetted the general's appetite for a final slaughter of the only "army" that stood between him and total conquest of the rebellious province. Houston and his men had been sighted. Moving east—to the sanctuary of the land beyond the Trinity River. To reach it, they would have to cross the San Jacinto, probably at Lynch's Ferry.

Once more the army moved with all speed. For Amanda the march was a nightmare blur of walking, sweating, going without meals, fording flooded creeks, struggling to help free mired wagons—

On April the eighteenth, the Mexicans made rendezvous with their cavalry in the town of New Washington on Galveston Bay. His Excellency granted his men a night's rest while dragoon scouts combed the countryside that was cut by river channels and bayous. On the morning of the twentieth, the scouts galloped back into camp at eight o'clock.

Within an hour, the drums were beating the signal to advance.

viii

As the marquee came down, Amanda noticed how pale Cordoba looked. She asked him why.

"Because—" He swore. The belt that held his saber had to be loosened another notch before it would fit around him. "—because His Excellency is feeling so splendid. Houston has been sighted less than eight miles from here. But I spoke with the dragoons myself. Houston and his men are facing us, not Lynch's Ferry."

She shook her head. "I don't understand what's wrong with that."

"Why, nothing!—except that we have been operating from one assumption all along. The assumption that Houston is in wild retreat before us. I wonder. If he's retreating, why has he stopped?"

Cordoba drew his saber; quickly sketched a crude map on the ground.

"Even His Excellency seems to have forgotten that we are now separated from the main body of the army. In our eagerness to pursue the Texans, we have left Sesma with a thousand of our best at Thompson's Ferry—"

He stabbed the sword at the ground.

"Urrea at Matagorda—"

Another stab.

"—and God knows what's become of Filisola and his two thousand!"

Stab.

Swift strokes obliterated the map and markings as the bugles and drums sounded. The first of the baggage wagons began to roll.

"I wouldn't presume to advise His Excellency, of course," Cordoba said sourly. "I only pose the question—are we chasing frightened men? Or being lured by clever ones? Are we the pursuers or the pursued? I don't like the smell one bit!"

He moved to Amanda. Swept an arm around her and buried his mouth against the curve of her throat:

"Whatever happens, you remain with the women and the wagons. I don't want anything to harm you."

Then he was gone through the dust behind a cantering squad of dragoons.

She should have drawn comfort from Cordoba's concern. Instead, she felt afraid.

Not for herself.

For him.

CHAPTER 5

The Corn of San Jacinto

A MOSQUITO TICKLED Amanda's neck. She reached up quickly and squashed it. One of the *soldaderas* sitting near her in the simmering shade of the baggage wagon opened her eyes.

The woman saw nothing of importance. She closed her eyes again. Perspiration trickled down Amanda's nose. She wiped it away.

The whole camp was taking siesta; Santa Anna had insisted. Because of the heat, the general had left his carpeted marquee of striped silk. She could see him stretched out beneath the great oak tree that crowned the hilltop, his hands folded on his belly.

The oak stood approximately in the center of the campsite chosen last evening. Around the sleeping general, officers sat talking quietly or studying maps. Few were as relaxed as their leader.

Major Luis Cordoba was standing up, staring toward the forward section of the encampment. There, infantrymen in mud-stained white fatigue suits dozed against a semi-circular barricade of packing boxes, pack saddles and other gear. The makeshift breastwork was located just where the hilltop began to slope down to a broad expanse of wild grass.

What time was it? Amanda guessed three o'clock. Dawn on this twenty-first of April had been clear and beautiful. But the temperature had risen steadily. Now the air steamed.

At nine that morning, General Cos had appeared with an extra five hundred cavalrymen. They too were resting, at the extreme rear of the camp. The horses cropped grass while the men napped in whatever shade was available.

Restless, Amanda pushed up from where she'd been sitting. She walked to the end of the wagon. She saw Cordoba glance her way, but the distance was too great for her to read his expression. She assumed he was worried.

His Excellency didn't seem worried. His relaxed slumber was a marked contrast to his fury at sunset yesterday—

Early on the twentieth, the Mexicans had located Houston's force with very little trouble—almost confirming Cordoba's fears. The Texans—reportedly numbering only about half of Santa Anna's fifteen hundred—had gone to ground in a forest of oak trees festooned with Spanish moss. All during the afternoon, they had refused to come out and fight.

Instead, riflemen sniped at the Mexican lines from the gloom of the wood, and two six-pounders fired rounds of fragmented horseshoes. Santa Anna's sole six-pounder replied occasionally, with little effect.

Late in the day, a Texas cavalry unit had probed the Mexican position, only to be driven back—without losses. Santa Anna's curses roared through the encampment until night fell. When Amanda and the major went to bed in his marquee after dark, he told her that, tomorrow, His Excellency intended to take the initiative—

If so, when? The afternoon was already waning.

From the end of the wagon, she gazed at the barricade. Some of the infantrymen were asleep. Others were nervously checking the mechanisms of their antique muskets. Amanda fanned herself, dizzy all at once. She shut her eyes; drew deep breaths of the stale air—

The dizziness passed. She still felt uneasy. Her loyalty really belonged to those unseen men hiding in the wood along Buffalo Bayou. Yet she was deeply concerned for Cordoba, too.

The forest where the Texans hid rose at the far end of a great meadow. Santa Anna had chosen to camp on the hilltop because of its commanding view of the wood and the meadow. From the barricade, his marksmen could rake the meadow's lush grass, which in many places grew taller than full-grown wheat.

Studying the meadow now, Amanda realized something was wrong. The air around her was still. But the grass stirred as if blown by a gentle wind—

She blinked. Were men moving out there?

With one hand on the wagon, she stood on tiptoe for a better view. Along the barricade a number of soldiers had risen and were watching the unusual motion of the grass.

She glanced to the oak. Santa Anna's staff showed increased activity. Men were running back and forth between the tree and the barricade. One was Cordoba, racing toward the oak and brandishing a spyglass.

With a yawn, Santa Anna roused. Beyond him, she saw movement where the cavalrymen had been dozing only a moment ago. Dragoons hurried to their horses, hazy figures against a distant growth of trees. The trees screened a swamp that drained into the little San Jacinto River, which ran down from the north to intersect Buffalo Bayou.

Just as she turned her attention back to the meadow, the notes of a Mexican bugle split the drowsy air. All the men behind the barricade scrambled up, readying their muskets. At a place where the meadow grass wasn't so high, Amanda glimpsed other men advancing with rifles, and a rider jogging on a white horse.

The riflemen quickly left the highest grass behind. While the Mexicans took siesta, the Texans had begun their advance—perhaps counting on the inactivity in the enemy camp. They moved steadily toward the base of the hill, spreading out in a wide semicircle. The horseman in the center of the line grew more visible moment by moment. He towered in the saddle—

It was Sam Houston. The man the Cherokees of eastern Tennessee had christened Raven.

Amanda had met Houston before, in Bexar. On his last visit, he'd spent an hour in the public bar of Gura's Hotel. He was a strapping Scotch-Irishman, with good manners and obvious education. Yet Amanda found there was something primitive about him, and he seemed to defy easy classification.

He indulged his temper as readily as he did his intellect. He spoke of reading Julius Caesar for relaxation, but he was so fond of a particular cussword that some Mexicans called him—and thus any Texan—*Señor God-damn*. In the meadow, his height and the milky whiteness of his horse Saracen identified him beyond all doubt.

An officer at the barricade bawled a command. Muskets lifted, cracked and spurted smoke and orange fire. The volley sent the Texans diving for cover.

Houston wheeled his horse aside, bending low over its neck. The infantrymen reloaded, began firing again. Now the whole camp was in motion. Men raced to join those already in place behind the improvised rampart. The *soldaderas* screeched in alarm and rushed to protect their belongings—

Amanda remained at the end of the wagon, watching. Acrid smoke drifting along the barricade obscured her view for a few moments. Then she saw the meadow again. Houston's men were still moving forward, that long, sweeping arc closing on the base of the hill. Incredibly, the Texans had yet to fire a single shot.

She heard music. The *tap-tap* of a drum, then a fife. The Texans were advancing to the melody of a popular romantic ballad, *Come to the Bower.*

Noise in the Mexican camp soon overpowered the music. Men shouted orders. Hoofs thudded and gear creaked as the cavalry milled at the rear of the hill. In the confusion, Amanda lost sight of Cordoba.

Running, the first Texans reached the base of the hill. The infantrymen fired steadily. And still no shots from the attackers—

Even as Amanda realized this, a volley thundered from the bottom of the hill. On the barricade, a white-suited soldier spun around and fell. From somewhere behind the advancing line, the Texans' two six-pounders boomed.

The fire was brutally accurate. Amanda ducked behind the corner of the wagon as geysers of earth erupted just in front of the breastwork. When she looked again, she saw that a gap had been blasted in the center of the barricade.

Behind her, *soldaderas* wailed and ran in every direction. Through the thickening smoke, she glimpsed Santa Anna berating an orderly. The man sprinted off—for what purpose, she couldn't guess.

Then she heard another sound from the unseen slope of the hill. A raw, animal sound. For a moment, the sound made no sense—

When it did, she shuddered. The Texans were screaming as they climbed the hillside. Shooting and screaming—

"Remember Goliad!"

"—the Alamo—"

"Remember the Alamo!"

The first Texans reached the gap in the barricade and stormed through, firing rifles and pistols point blank at the few defenders brave enough to remain near the opening. Bearded and dirty, the Texans spread out, clubbing men down with rifle butts and attacking them with knives and tomahawks.

A steady stream of Texans poured through the gap. Others came jumping over the barricade. Houston rode through the opening, mounted on a bay horse now. Evidently the white one had been shot from under him. He fired pistols from both hands.

Amanda spun around. All across the camp, an incredible scene of panic was unfolding. Mexicans streamed away from the barricade. Groups of terrified soldiers surged back and forth, leaderless—then began to run. Not toward the barricade. The other way.

Clouds of smoke and dust blew across the hilltop. The dragoons were moving too. Not toward the barricade. Away.

Under the oak, Santa Anna clambered onto a black horse whose rein was held by the orderly she'd seen before. Sword still sheathed, His Excellency went galloping off toward the rear of the hill.

A Texan ball blasted the corner of the wagon. Amanda leaped back, her cheek stabbed by flying splinters. The fife and drum could no longer be heard at all. The Texans were howling too loudly.

They fanned out across the hilltop, almost crazed. They shot and cut and killed—

"*Remember Goliad!*"

"*REMEMBER THE ALAMO!*"

She saw Houston's bay stumble and fall, blood spurting from its belly. Houston dragged himself from under the horse, then doubled as a ball tore into his boot. But he recovered quickly. He shot a Mexican cavalryman out of the saddle. When the Mexican hit the ground, Houston tore the man's pennoned lance from his hands and stabbed it into his throat. In seconds, Houston was mounted on the cavalryman's horse, shoulders hunched and blood welling from the top of his right boot—

The frightened screams of the Mexicans blended with the howling of the Texans. The last of the Mexican infantry broke from the barricade, flung down their weapons and ran toward the rear. Amanda saw a boy hardly out of adolescence twist and raise his hands defensively as two lanky Texans caught up with him.

The boy shrieked, "Me no Alamo! *Me no Alam—*" One of the Texans disemboweled him with two slashes of a bowie.

The Mexicans ran—but not fast enough. They died by the tens and twenties, shot down, clubbed down, kicked and stepped on. Everywhere, Amanda heard the same hysterical plea—

"Me no Alamo! *Me no Alamo!*"

There were a few who didn't try to save themselves that way. One Amanda caught sight of suddenly was Luis Cordoba. With a small group of enlisted men, he was attempting a pathetic defense near the oak.

The major was surrounded by seven or eight men, most struggling to reload their muskets as a band of Texans charged them. Saber drawn, Cordoba shouted for the soldiers to load more quickly. Two pitched over, killed by pistol shots. Amanda started to run toward the tree, dodging between bearded Americans. One leveled his rifle at her, checking his fire only when he saw her white skin.

Amanda had already flung herself on the ground in anticipation of the shot. She buried her head on her arms as other Texans behind her volleyed at a troop of retreating cavalry. When she looked up again, she saw that Cordoba and three other survivors were fighting hand to hand with twice as many opponents.

A rifle butt felled one Mexican soldier. The other two threw down their pieces and dashed around the tree. With all the noise, Amanda couldn't hear what they cried. But she knew—

"*Me no Alamo!*"

His uniform ripped and bloody, Luis Cordoba stood his ground. He raised his saber for a defensive stroke. Amanda lurched to her feet, nearly bowled over again as Houston rode past, shouting commands.

She raced through a litter of Mexican bodies, holding up her black silk skirt and crying Cordoba's name. The Texans backed him toward the oak; crowded around; wrenched the saber from his hand. Blood smeared his forehead. His eyes were huge and fearful suddenly—

A Texan thrust a pistol to within six inches of Cordoba's face and pulled the trigger. The major slammed back against the tree, his mouth gushing blood. Amanda screamed, "*Luis!*" as he sank from sight, the back of his head leaving blood and gray matter on the bark.

Someone grabbed her, flung her aside—"Get out of the way, you Spanish slut!" Two young Texans raced by as she struck the ground, the wind knocked out of her.

Her mind burned with an image of Cordoba dying, the victim of a code of honor that hadn't permitted him to run or beg for mercy—even though he was more entitled to mercy than most of those shrilling, "Me no Alamo!"

With her cheek in the dirt, she wept for him in the brief seconds of incredible noise—hoofs, shrieks, shots—before she fainted.

ii

The battle of San Jacinto lasted no more than twenty minutes. The pursuit and capture of the demoralized Mexicans lasted well into the night. Though most of the senior officers were either caught or surrendered voluntarily, Santa Anna got away.

Amanda was carried to a large tent erected for the use of the Texas army's surgeon, a mild, kindly man named Ewing. She was put on a cot among those occupied by wounded men, some of whom complained about the presence of a woman until Ewing ordered them to be quiet.

Ewing gave her brandy and a chance to tell her story. When he heard it, he promised he'd arrange for her to repeat it to Houston himself after the general awoke from the heavy sleep into which Ewing had drugged him. Houston had lost a good deal of blood as a result of the wound in his right leg.

Next morning, while most of the Texans were sleeping off their raucous celebration of the victory, Sam Houston propped himself under the oak where Santa Anna had rested and Cordoba had died. He began penciling dispatches to President Burnet hiding somewhere on Galveston Island, and to President Jackson in the east. He was still working when a detachment returned with yet another captive—a rather tall Mexican wearing a dirty blue smock, leather cap and slippers of red felt.

The man claimed to be a private who had run away. He said he'd stolen the smock and cap from a slave cabin in the neighborhood. He had been discovered hiding in the sedge grass along Vince's Bayou. He had wanted to swim across, but didn't know how.

What made the prisoner of more than passing interest was his cultivated speech, unusual among ordinary line soldiers. The man was telling his story as the detachment rode into camp. Suddenly some soldiers imprisoned in a rope corral exclaimed, "El presidente!"

Very shortly, the prisoner stood in front of Houston. With a preening smile, the Napoleon of the West admitted his identity and shrugged off the failure of his ruse.

The Texans shouted for a lynch rope. Houston ordered them silent. When Santa Anna requested opium to calm his nerves, Houston had it brought from the fallen marquee. By noon, the marquee was set up again. Inside, the dictator got to work writing orders that called for the total evacuation of all Mexican troops north of the Rio Grande.

Amanda heard the story from Doctor Ewing late in the day. He'd come into the tent where she was resting. After describing Santa Anna's capture, he said Houston might have a few minutes to receive her before supper. The general was anxious to see his old acquaintance who had been at the Alamo, then been held captive by the Mexicans, Ewing told her.

Amanda nodded in acknowledgement, wishing she didn't feel so dispirited. She should have been happy. Her good friend Bowie and all the others butchered at Bexar had been avenged. The Texans had won a splendid victory against a force twice as large as theirs. And done it with incredibly small losses—six killed, two dozen wounded.

The enemy toll was more than six hundred dead and something like twelve hundred captured. Cordoba's prophecy had been right. Houston was a better strategist than Santa Anna had ever suspected—

Cordoba. She couldn't get him out of her mind. That was the problem.

She forced herself to pay attention to Ewing; agreed with his comment that it seemed a little unfair for Santa Anna to be paroled and allowed to return to Mexico City. But Houston was adamant, Ewing said. Though the new republic of Texas had won its independence with savage fighting, it would now conduct its affairs honorably.

Honor. Amanda's mouth pursed in a bitter way. Honor had earned Luis Cordoba his grave.

Puzzled by her dour mood, Ewing said, "I would think you'd show a little more pleasure, Señora de la Gura. You were rescued. Your own side carried the day—"

"Don't misunderstand, doctor. I'm glad Santa Anna was beaten. He deserves much worse than he's getting. But you see—" She gazed at his silhouette against the red sun visible outside the tent. "—nothing is ever clear cut. The Mexican officer who kept me was a fine man. A brave one. He didn't run away yesterday. He didn't cower and pretend he had no part in the Alamo killings—though the truth is, he didn't. But he was still shot down. And Santa Anna's alive. I'm sorry it wasn't the other way around."

Doctor Ewing didn't know what to say. Looking uncomfortable, he tugged out a fobbed watch:

"We'd better go. The general said five sharp."

As she started out, a young man with a bandaged leg glared at her from an adjoining cot:

"You a Texican, woman?"

"Yes."

"Well, I heard what you said. I'll be blasted if I can see how you'd grieve for one of those fucking greasers. I just can't understand that at all."

"No," Amanda said, "I suppose you can't. I don't suppose anyone can."

Her face stark, she followed Ewing into the late afternoon heat.

iii

Amanda expected the interview with General Sam Houston to be difficult. As she walked with Doctor Ewing toward the oak, she saw groups of Texans at cook fires glance her way. Some pointed; scowled; made derogatory comments. She tried to ignore them. Tried to walk with her head up and her expression composed. But it took great effort.

Sam Houston saw her coming. He sat up a little straighter on the blankets spread at the base of the tree. His bootless right leg was swathed in bandages from foot to mid-calf. On either side of him, several packing boxes formed an improvised office. She saw an inkstand, pencils, books, foolscap writing paper—

And a number of Texans loitering on the tree's far side. The side on which Cordoba had fallen. Thank God she wouldn't have to stare at the bloodstained bark—

But the faces of the Texans bothered her. The men seemed just as hostile as those at the campfires.

Houston smiled and waved as she and Ewing approached. The general was more than six feet tall, with a long, blunt jaw, wavy, gray-streaked chestnut hair and bright blue eyes. His skin was pale. His fine shirt was torn and powder-blackened. So was his claw-hammer coat. A distinctly rumpled and weary-looking Raven—

Houston had been given the name in his youth, when he'd run away from his widowed mother to live with the Indians. He had served in the army, studied law, been elected to Congress as a Jacksonian Democrat, and then won the governorship of Tennessee. In 1829, he'd abruptly resigned in the middle of a campaign for a second term, fleeing the state and an eighteen-year-old bride who had left him after three months of marriage.

Amanda had heard both sides of the story. Houston's partisans insisted the girl had been cold, and Houston had every right to leave her. His enemies claimed the girl feared him; said he was insane—jealous beyond reason; and that his sexual appetites were a disgrace even in the marriage bed.

Whatever the truth, Houston had disappeared for a time along the Arkansas River, where the government had resettled his old friends, the

Cherokees. He used liquor to blot out the past. So much liquor that the Cherokees gave him a second, less flattering name—Big Drunk.

In the early 1830s he had emerged from his alcoholic wanderings and re-established his old ties with the president under whom he'd soldiered in the Creek War. Some in Bexar hinted that Houston had come to Texas for a purpose other than the one publicly announced: to help American traders negotiate treaties of peace with the marauding Indian tribes. The rumormongers said Houston's real mission was to foment a movement for Texas independence, thus paving the way for the territory's eventual union with the United States.

It might have been true. Certainly since the beginning of the Mexican trouble, Houston had been in the forefront of the Texan cause—

"Amanda!" Houston exclaimed in his deep voice as she entered the dappled shade of the oak. "I can hardly believe it's you! When I heard you were a prisoner of the Mexicans, I was almost as surprised as I was when Santa Anna showed up wearing bedroom slippers."

"My compliments on the victory, General," Amanda said. The remark brought snorts and some ugly glances from the men in buckskin and homespun on the other side of the tree.

"You're mighty formal all at once. What's wrong with the names we used in Bexar?"

"A lot's happened since then, General."

"Goddamned if it hasn't. I trust you'll forgive me for not standing up. Orders of Doctor Ewing there. Push those books off that case. Sit down and tell me how you got here."

"She got here because she was yella," one of the men beyond the tree said in a false whisper. Houston glared:

"The next man who utters a remark like that will answer to me." He glanced back to Amanda. "Passions are still running pretty high. I'm not too popular myself since I refused to let the men hang our Mexican friend."

"I can understand their feelings. I was in the mission."

"So I learned from Almeron Dickinson's widow."

"I saw what the Mexicans did—on Santa Anna's direct order."

"I'd like to hear your account of it."

She told him, trying not to let the words conjure sounds and sights and smells. But they did. She was glad when she finished the story.

He reached out to grasp her hand. "Thank you. You've confirmed everything that was reported to me. I suppose I shouldn't have asked. The memory is obviously unpleasant—"

"I try to forget how it sounded—how it looked—and how sickened it made me. I can't."

"No one can forget—even those of us who weren't there. I told His Excellency much the same thing this morning. Before he decided we'd be easy to beat, he should have remembered the Alamo." He squeezed her hand. "Are you up to telling me the rest of your experience?"

She nodded and, in a subdued voice, described how she'd been made a prisoner. She omitted the more personal details of her relationship with the major, characterizing him only as a man who had treated her in a humane way. At the end, she said:

"I hope his body can be sent back to Mexico City. He—he had a wife there."

"That may not be possible. Some of Santa Anna's staff officers are going to do what they can about notifying next of kin. There's no need for you to worry about such things—you're a free woman now."

Some of the men beyond the tree didn't like that either. Houston's lids flickered; he heard the angry whispers. But he didn't turn to acknowledge them. Instead, he went on:

"You can join in the work to be done in Texas. We've got to rebuild. Get the government functioning—"

His hand strayed beneath one of the mussed blankets. He pulled out an ear of corn. Some of the kernels had been nibbled away.

"My afternoon meal," he smiled. His thumb accidentally flicked three kernels from the ear. One of the men on the other side of the tree scrambled forward to snatch them up:

"I could take this corn home an' plant it, General."

Houston glanced at the ear in his hand, then suddenly began shucking kernels from it:

"Here—all of you take some. Plant it in your fields. It's time to cultivate the arts of peace now that you've shown yourselves masters of the art of war."

Pleased by his flattery, the men crowded forward. Amanda was momentarily forgotten as the Texans laughed and jostled one another, straining to get some of the corn Houston dropped from his outstretched hand.

"By God, we ought to call this Houston corn!" one of the men shouted.

The general shook his head. "Honor yourselves, not me. Call it San Jacinto corn."

With his forefinger he worked another kernel loose, then tossed the ear into the crowd. Noisily, the Texans swarmed around the man who caught it. Not a one of them was paying any attention to Amanda now. She wondered whether the byplay with the corn had been a ploy to divert them and blunt their hostility.

Not entirely, she realized, as Houston held out his hand:

"You take this one. It's time for all of us to start thinking about the future."

Amanda tried to speak. She couldn't. With bleak eyes, she stared at the kernel resting in her palm.

"Doctor Ewing," Houston said, "I think you'd better conduct the señora back to the surgical tent. If any man so much as touches her, report it to me and I'll have him whipped till he can't walk."

She leaned on Ewing's arm in the twilight. Along the way, the kernel of corn dropped from her other hand. She was aware of the loss. But she didn't turn back to search. She had no field to plow and plant. Nothing to give the future meaning and value. That she was safe and unhurt seemed of small importance. The fabric of her life had been ripped to ruin—again.

iv

On a gray and showery afternoon in June, Amanda walked through the rubble in the lobby of Gura's Hotel. With her was a small, finely-boned man in cleric's robes, the parish priest, Don Refugio de la Garza.

Don Refugio wrinkled his nose at the smell of human waste left in a corner. Amanda surveyed the smashed counter, then a pile of scrapwood and horsehair—all that remained of the lobby furniture.

Her dress was the only touch of color in the whole dreary scene. It was homespun, dyed yellow with root dyes. A sunbonnet kept her face in shadow as she studied the wreckage. She had been back in Bexar for several weeks, escorted by an amiable soldier in a wagon Houston commandeered for her. The journey had been difficult. She felt weak most of the time, and was troubled frequently by nausea.

Shortly after she'd arrived, she'd been informed that Gura's Hotel was no longer fit to be lived in. Don Refugio had advanced her a small sum to rent a room elsewhere in town. This was the first day she'd been able to summon the courage to visit Soledad Street and see the devastation for herself.

"It's a pity, but there's not much left," Don Refugio said as Amanda gazed at the whitewashed wall. Someone had used charcoal to scrawl a filthy remark about Texans. "There was a good deal of drinking and carousing while Santa Anna's senior officers were quartered here. Also, they were not particularly respectful of property belonging to an Anglo."

Amanda sighed. "Is it the same upstairs?"

"Worse."

"Then there's not much point in going up. I suppose the land and the building will bring me a little money."

The priest's gray eyebrows shot up. "You don't intend to re-open the hotel? I know it would require a great deal of work, but I thought—"

"I'm going to sell, padre. As is. There's bad feeling toward me in this town."

"Yes, I realize. Still—"

"It's even worse than before, when I had girls upstairs."

"You can admit the ill will is understandable, can you not?"

"No. I was the one American woman who survived the battle at the mission *and* stood up to Santa Anna—in return for which, I was made a prisoner. To the Americans around here, that somehow makes me a traitor. Susannah Dickinson, on the other hand, took Santa Anna's clemency—"

"She saw her husband die, Amanda! She was utterly demoralized—"

"I know. I'm not finding fault, just stating a fact. She *did* accept his offer—and spread the message he wanted her to spread. For that, she's a heroine. I don't imagine my name will ever appear on the list of the women who lived through the massacre. I'm confident hers will."

"Ah, but a name on a paper tells nothing! If your name is recorded, you will probably be listed as a Mexican—"

"True. Anyway, that's not the point. I wouldn't accept Santa Anna's so-called generosity—and look where it's gotten me."

"But people wonder why you didn't run away from the Mexicans."

"Because I gave my word to the officer who saved me from execution! Oh, what difference does it make? They hate me, and that's that."

"It will pass, Amanda."

"Will it? I know what people are saying. That I should have refused to go with Cordoba. Broken my word. Fled. And if that wasn't possible, I imagine they believe I should have done away with myself! Well—" Her mouth twisted. "I've always had a strong survival instinct. I gather that's no longer permitted in Texas."

"Nonsense," Don Refugio snorted. "Do you know how many, here and elsewhere, actively supported Santa Anna when it seemed the Texan cause was lost? I assure you the number is not small."

"People might even think differently if I'd lived with a different sort of man," she went on, staring at three holes drilled in the wall by pistol balls. "But Major Cordoba was decent—and I've made no secret of that. Evidently decency on the part of the enemy is also unthinkable."

"That we are all God's creatures, with an equal distribution of devils and saints among all nations, is seldom remembered in wartime."

"General Houston remembered," she said. "He, at least, was kind to me."

The priest nodded. "He has grown to be a man of immense wisdom, I think. They say there'll be an election in the next few months. Burnet will step aside. Houston is almost certain to be named president of the republic. He's your friend, and I'm sure he'd see that you were treated fairly. For that reason, you might want to reconsider your decision. I assure you the hatreds will be forgotten. We are all Texans now. We may eventually become Americans, if the rumors are true."

"The rumors about annexation?"

"Yes. Houston is in favor, is he not?"

"Very much so. He told me before I came back that he may petition Congress—or at least ask the people to vote on whether a petition requesting annexation should be sent. But the newspapers say Jackson's cooled on the idea. He doesn't want a protracted war with Mexico, so he has to maintain neutrality. It's all very muddled—especially since the Mexican legislature repudiated Santa Anna's treaty recognizing the republic's independence. Who knows how it will come out?"

Her words trailed off with an empty sound. The priest pondered, then agreed:

"Yes, in some ways Santa Anna's defeat only compounded the confusion. The matter of chattel slavery will becloud annexation, no doubt—"

Thinking of the dead in the mission, she made a derisive sound. "I trust you heard how Quincy Adams referred to the rebellion? Denounced it in Congress as nothing more than a scheme to restore slavery down here, and bring another slaveholding state into the nation? The fool!"

"There are some who would hope for that," Don Refugio told her. "Here and in the United States."

"Well, I won't be present to see how the whole thing's resolved, padre. I've made up my mind. I have to start over somewhere else. With a new name. Or an old one, rather. The name I had before I was married. I need a fresh start at everything."

The little priest tried to read her face in the shadow cast by the bonnet's brim. He couldn't. But he heard the strain in her voice:

"Whether I've done right or wrong is something someone else will have to decide. Maybe the woman who guards the vine—"

"Who?"

"Never mind."

"Amanda, I beg you to think carefully before—"

"I can't stay in Bexar any longer, padre. There are—too many memories. My husband—my friends murdered in the chapel. The major—"

Her voice broke. She shook her head as if angry with herself. Don Refugio laid his slim fingers on her arm, squeezing gently to comfort her.

"Where will you go?"

"I don't know. Further west, I suppose. I can travel with one of the pack trains. Perhaps to Santa Fe. Even on to California—I hear that's beautiful country."

"Comfortable, certainly. But you would be a subject of Mexico again."

"I'm not trying to escape a government, just the past. Besides, more and more Americans are settling there all the time. Coming up from Sante Fe, or from the east by ship—"

"And across the mountains one day, perhaps."

"The mountains? I doubt that."

"So did I, at first. But a number of the itinerant traders claim the fur companies have sent wagon shipments quite far west to equip their brigades. They believe it's possible to traverse the mountains and reach the Pacific with a wheeled vehicle." He looked amused. "America has a ravening hunger for land. Few obstacles will deter its satisfaction, least of all mountains. I expect your people won't be content until they claim the continent from coast to coast. So I'd have a care about choosing California. You might find yourself embroiled in the same political turmoil you've just endured here."

"There's always the Oregon Territory."

"One more area ripe for dispute and rebellion! Don't the British and the United States occupy it jointly, by treaty—?"

"It doesn't make any difference where I go—so long as it's away from here!"

After a moment, Don Refugio sighed in a resigned way:

"If your mind is made up, I am at your disposal to help with arrangements."

"Thank you." She smiled, but without much feeling. "I won't be going immediately, much as I'd like to. I won't be in any condition to travel for a while. You see, I—"

She experienced a bursting sense of relief at finally admitting it to someone:

"I'm fairly certain I'm going to have a child."

v

"Push," the fat old midwife said with a singular lack of compassion. She rested hard hands on Amanda's huge, heaving belly.

She tried. The pain was intense, and growing worse. The contractions seemed to torment her whole being.

She lay on a table in a room Don Refugio had provided in a wing of the San Fernando church. Her knees were bent, her feet braced against blocks of wood the priest had nailed to one end of the table. Don Refugio, dimly visible at the edge of a circle of lantern light, was in attendance because he'd acquired certain medical skills over the years. But Serafina, the midwife brought in from the country, was in charge.

There was a howling in Amanda's ears. Was it the wind outside the church, carrying sleet and rain from the northwest this gloomy day in January, 1837? Or was it only an imaginary echo of sounds from the past? The melody of the *deguello*? The shrieks of the dying in the mission? The pitiful cries of the routed soldiers at San Jacinto—?

"Push, for the Virgin's sake!" Serafina cried. "I can see the head!"

The insides of Amanda's thighs were wet. She lay naked, only her breasts covered by a scrap of rag. Her hands gripped the ends of a length of pine wood the midwife had given her to bite.

She dug her teeth into the soft, fragrant stick and closed her eyes, writhing.

"Hold her still!" Serafina exclaimed. Don Refugio's hands pinned Amanda's shoulders. The contractions were no longer distinct; they blended into a single, consuming pain. She felt the thick thrust of something being expelled from within her body—

"Push, woman. *Push.*"

She lost her sense of time and of place, catching only fleeting visual and aural impressions as her mind blanked out, then re-awoke—

The thickness between her legs was gone. She saw Don Refugio, white rags draped over one arm of his robe. She heard water splash as Serafina bathed her red-stippled hands and forearms.

She heard a muted gurgling, too; then the midwife's grumbles as she manipulated twine, tying the cord once near the opening from which the child had emerged and a second time close to the belly of the unseen baby. The child must be resting on the mound of rags between her thighs, Amanda realized—

The midwife stepped back.

"Cut the cord, padre."

The sudden glitter of a bowie knife almost made her scream aloud. Then she remembered she wasn't in the mission, nor on the hill of San Jacinto, but in an adobe room with a winter rainstorm raging outside.

Don Refugio's hands dipped out of sight. Immediately after cleaving the cord, he whipped the rags off his arm and began to bundle the infant. Amanda glimpsed a tiny, plum-colored face puckered in a struggle for breath. The baby's skin was wet and shimmering—

"A very good child," Serafina announced. "Now we must wait."

A second later, Don Refugio said, "I don't believe she hears you."

"The Pope send me packing, but it's a mystery to me how you celibates can presume to minister to women. Nothing personal, mind you—" A shrug. "You're a lot better than some I know." A pointing finger loomed before Amanda's eyes. "She hears me. She just doesn't feel like chattering."

"A thousand pardons!" Don Refugio said. "I forget this is your domain, not mine."

Amanda's grimace gentled into a smile. She stopped biting the stick so hard; released her hands from the ends. The priest melted into the darkness as the baby began to squall. In the church tower, the wind struck wild clangs from the bells.

Amanda let her heavy eyelids close. She opened them suddenly at the midwife's cry:

"Ah, Jesus have mercy! She's gotten rid of everything but she's still bleeding—"

Don Refugio's white-haired head bobbed above Amanda. He laid a dry hand on her sticky forehead. Suddenly her loins felt thick again—Serafina had thrust her right hand and forearm into her and was massaging vigorously to stop a warm flow she could feel on her legs.

The midwife grunted anxiously as she worked. At last she withdrew her red hand, disappeared, and once more Amanda heard the sound of flesh being plunged into water.

Presently Serafina returned. She stood immobile, her gaze focused between Amanda's legs.

After what seemed like hours, she nodded:

"The bleeding has stopped." For the first time, she allowed herself a smile. "You can sleep now, señora."

"I—I'd like to see the baby—"

"All right, but only a moment." She swung toward the darkness. "Step lively, padre!"

Amanda heard sandals scraping stone; Don Refugio obeyed the midwife just as any novice would have obeyed a superior.

"You've had babies before," Serafina declared, moving up beside Amanda's torso and re-arranging the cloth that had shifted away from her left nipple.

"None—that lived. I want this child to live."

"Oh, I think he will. He's a hefty one."

"He?" Amanda repeated. "A boy—?"

"From every observable sign," the older woman said with a wry smile. "What will you call him?"

Drowsily, Amanda answered, "Luis, I think. Luis Kent. Only spelled—" She labored for a breath. "American fashion—with an o in the first name."

Louis Kent. How good that sounded! Then she thought of something else:

Now there's someone to carry on the family. I can take him with me if I ever go back to Boston. I can show him where his grandfather and great-grandfather lived—and teach him to be proud he's a Kent.

"Louis, eh?" The midwife sniffed. Amanda barely heard:

Now that I have him, I will go back. We'll go back together—

"Louis—well, I suppose that's all right. Though everyone these days is naming their newborns after the men who fell at the mission. I'd have thought you might pick a hero's name too."

"I—did. The baby's father—was with the Mexican army—"

"Ah yes, I heard they held you captive for a while."

"He—could have killed—a great many. But he didn't—"

"Well, the decision's yours. Why the baby was named will soon be forgotten anyway. Your people and mine, we're no longer much different, it seems. We're all citizens of the republic. Living under the new republican flag with that one star. Judging by the way the voting went in October, I might even be an American presently. It's a remarkable world—"

She whirled to the shadows:

"It's about time, pad—mother of God, keep the feet covered! *Covered!*"

"My profound apologies," the priest murmured, surrendering the child to the midwife. "I'm a mere man—"

"That's quite apparent, I'm sorry to say." Serafina in turn handed the small warm bundle to Amanda. Then the midwife and the priest stood gazing downward, their shoulders touching and their banter forgotten.

Fighting sleepiness, Amanda lifted a corner of a rag aside and stared at the slitted eyes, the wrinkled pink flesh, the mouth that sucked air noisily. Suddenly she clutched the little boy tight against her breast.

"In God's name handle him gently!" Serafina said. "You'll suffocate the poor thing."

But Amanda clutched her newborn fiercely, feeling him squirm, then hearing him squall.

What a strange turn of events, she thought, remembering the tiny kernel Sam Houston had dropped into her hand beneath the oak at San Jacinto. He hadn't known—nor had she—that an entirely different kind of seed would germinate from the war's bloody ground. A seed that would yield this miracle of living flesh within her arms; give her a purpose; a new reason for going on when it seemed that all the rest of her reasons had been destroyed—

The future no longer terrified her because of its emptiness, its uncertainty. Let the wolf run; she wasn't afraid.

Louis Kent howled louder. She had never heard such a sweet, sweet sound—

Serafina slapped her hips:

"Merciful heaven, padre, I give up. Now she's crying too!"

The Journal of Jephtha Kent, 1844:
Bishop Andrew's Sin

April the 30th. Arrived in New York City after a wearying journey by coach, my annual stipend not being large enough to permit riding the rail roads. I have joined my brethren here for General Conference. Am stopping at a modest hotel where the appointments are few but clean, though of course the establishment cannot compare with other local hostelries. Adjoining one of its rooms, The New York Hotel has installed a separate, private facility for the purpose of bathing—or so I was told by my companion, the Reverend Hodding, with whom I took a brief walking tour late this afternoon.

Hodding is a pleasant, if opinionated, fellow. He itinerates in the vicinity of Chester County, Pennsylvania. We compared our situations, which are not essentially different, except in one regard. Freedom for the enslaved Negro is a goal much sought by Hodding, as well as by many of those to whom he ministers.

I in turn attempted to present Hodding with the views of those Christian men and women I have served the past two years from my location at Lexington, in Virginia's valley of the Shenandoah. But I did not press a strong personal view upon him. I have none. Whenever I think on the subject, I end in a quandary.

As evidence of the moral failure of our own Church, Hodding spoke scornfully of the treatment accorded men and women of color at Lovely Lane in Baltimore, where the "Afric" may sit nowhere but the balcony, and receives the sacrament only after it has been served to white persons. He also mentioned St. George's in Philadelphia, where Negroes must hold their own services at an hour different from that at which the whites worship. Clearly my companion is one of those enraged by the failure of the Methodist Episcopal Church to declare a position on the slave issue; twice

during our stroll, he repeated Mr. Wesley's claim that the system of black
bondage in this nation is "the vilest that ever saw the sun."

I continued to refrain from argumentation because, as I noted, I am not
sure of my own heart—and also because I cannot d–n out of hand those
whom I serve in Virginia. To do so, I would have to d–n the very woman
with whom God has favored me, blessing our union with Gideon—

Gideon. A splendid little boy! I must not overlook his coming birthday.
I must take a trinket home.

Before we parted, Hodding insisted the Conference would address the
slavery question. I pray not. Such disputation can only lead to divisiveness
of the sort which has already led the Reverend Orange Scott of Lowell to
withdraw from the Methodist connection.

I fear a confrontation, and wonder why. Is it because there is epic risk
of fostering ill will within the Church? Or is it because I know that, if
forced to search my own conscience, I will find a lack of personal conviction?

Later. Prayed an hour for guidance, but remain as worried and uncertain as before.

*

May the 1st. One hundred and seventy-eight pastors have gathered. As
the proceedings commenced, I was restored and refreshed by the preach-
ing and the singing. How good to hear those stout voices inquiring of each
other's welfare as the opening hymn, *And Are We Yet Alive?*, soared
forth.

Bishop Soule, occupying the chair for the opening session, sounded a
warning to those who would disturb our work among the people of color.
Their souls are for saving but all else is beyond us, the bishop declared in
his address. "To raise them up to equal civil rights and privileges is not
within our power. Let us not labor in vain and spend our strength for
naught."

His remarks produced a few dark looks up and down the benches, but
no open dissent. I trust the Bishop's admonition will be heeded for the
sake of the Church's tranquility and, I shamefully admit, mine.

*

May the 2nd. A quiet day. Another walking tour late in the afternoon.
Even though I twice visited Boston while a student at the Biblical Insti-

tute in Vermont, the splendor and squalor of New York City far surpass anything I have beheld elsewhere.

There are a great many Irish present, and more arriving by ship each month. Simply by listening to street conversation, one is made aware of the animosity directed toward them. A Mr. Harper, a book publisher like my great-grandfather, is to run for mayor here. Harper is what is called a reform candidate, for the city's affairs are in disorder and badly need setting straight. Whether Mr. Harper is dedicated to that task remains questionable, since I was informed that his partisans are preparing banners bearing a campaign appeal that seems to have little to do with reform, and everything to do with stirring hatred of the slum Irish. The slogan is, "No Popery!" Let us hope the campaign will not produce the sort of anti-Catholic rioting which recently struck Philadelphia.

Obtained an edition of Mr. Greeley's *Tribune,* which contains this remarkable information—the rail road trackage within the country now totals close to four thousand miles, with more being laid all the time as new lines open. The United States has several times the trackage of the entire continent of Europe, the paper says. "Thou *art* the God that doest wonders!"

*

May the 3rd. Today, Friday, the cataclysm is upon us. The sectional quarrel which has inflamed tempers in Congress and the press has reached even here. The Conference to which the Reverend Orange Scott formerly belonged put forward a petition opposing slavery, whereupon the meeting erupted into shouting of a most unseemly sort.

The chair has appointed a Committee on Slavery to accept other memorials on the same subject. Hodding told me such petitions are sure to come, then went on to confirm a suspicion I had not uttered or written before, though many of my southern brethren have expressed it to me:

The anti-slavery delegates are operating according to a plan drawn long before we assembled. The ultimate target of the strategy is the worthy and well-regarded Bishop James Andrew of Georgia, whose sin is this: he is the unhappy possessor of a mulatto girl and a Negro boy, neither of which he purchased. Both were bequeathed to him in the estate of his first wife. His second wife is also the inheritor of slaves. Under Georgia law, neither the bishop nor his spouse can manumit the slaves.

When Hodding mentioned Andrew in a most challenging way, then asked my opinion on what should be done, I once again took refuge in ex-

cuses that hide my own equivocation. I said I did not feel qualified to take
part in any general debate, being among the most recently ordained of all
those gathered; I became a pastor not quite two years ago. I said I felt doubly unqualified by reason of age, having just observed my twenty-fourth
birthday.

Did Hodding suspect my evasion? His smirk made me believe so.

Later. I thought much of my beloved wife Fan, and of our son. I asked
myself what the anti-slavery delegates would offer Fan's father, Captain
Tunworth of Lexington, as well as her numerous relatives in South Carolina, in return for the black labor on which they depend. That, it seems to
me, is one of the sticking-places:

Even many in the south accept the fact that the peculiar institution is,
in a great number of respects, inhumane. But abolitionist agitators such as
Mr. Garrison of Boston, whose *Liberator* newspaper insists upon full freedom for Negros, never propose any plan by means of which the southern
agriculturist can replace his Negro labor. And without the labor, there is
no prosperity for those who cultivate the land. The snare is a cruel one,
since human beings north or south are not prone to abandon that which
fosters their survival.

At supper, we fell into a heated discussion of one alternative to slavery
which has been proposed for nearly thirty years by the Colonization
Society—namely, the freeing and re-settlement of the Negro in Liberia.
Hodding bitterly chastised several of the more moderate brethren who
favor this idea. He said the scheme is based on an unspoken belief that
the Negro is inferior to the white—and will somehow contaminate the nation with his continued presence. Hodding then proceeded to put a theo-
logical cast on the subject.

John Wesley, the beloved Asbury, Coke—the pillars of our faith—were
unequivocal about the absolutes of good and evil. Good and evil are the
fixed stars in our struggle as itinerants. Our aim is, first, conversion—
admission of sin—and then redemption; the eradication of human wick-
edness through the grace of Our Lord Jesus Christ. No one could disagree
with those extremities, and the lack of a middle ground. Then Hodding
closed the trap.

If there is no middle ground in our theology, so there can be none regarding the slave question. If slavery is acknowledged an evil, it must be
destroyed, just as confessed sin is overcome by redemptive love for Christ.
Several shouted at Hodding—one subject, they cried, is spiritual, the other

temporal! Hodding sees no difference; he sees, in fact, an irrefutable connection.

I sat silent throughout. Hodding's logic troubled me sorely, but not as much as the intemperate speech of my brethren on both sides of the argument. It seems to me the affair of Bishop Andrew is exacerbating tempers to a dangerous degree.

*

May the 10th. A resolution has been put forward "affectionately" requesting Bishop Andrew to resign his office. And a curious thing has occurred—the use of the word "slavery" has become infrequent in our sessions. Andrew's alleged transgression has somehow been transmuted into a question of Church authority: whose will is paramount? That of the General Conference? Or that of the bishops?

It is a screen, nothing more. The fundamental issue is Andrew's ownership of black men and women.

Screen or no, Bishop Soule today sounded another, even more dire warning. He said that permitting the Conference to remove Andrew without a proper ecclesiastical trial would rend the organization of the Church "beyond repair."

*

May the 14th. The debate continues, heated and unsettling. I absented myself for a time this afternoon, having realized that I will be forced to take a stand unless the committees laboring in private can effect a compromise, which I think unlikely. By leaving the gathering, I hoped to free my mind of the dismaying subject—only to discover it turning to another almost as troublesome.

My thoughts returned to my conversion six years ago by the Reverend Lee of the Willamette Mission in Oregon. Jason Lee was the great man who first revealed to me that my name, Jephthah as it is spelled in the Old Testament, means "God opens." The conversion did not please my father, to whom I have not written in far too long.

Many years ago, my father Jared Kent put the eastern part of the continent behind him forever, accepting both the freedom which the western lands afford, and the struggle they require for even meager success. My father came to love the free spaces, their natural beauties and abundance. He wanted me to remain a westerner as he is. I could never convince him that my given name must have had a pre-ordained significance unknown to him when he bestowed it, for, through the Reverend Lee, God truly did open my soul to His message, and I felt a compelling call to train myself for the ministry. My answering of the call wounded my father not a little.

As I walked along the Broad Way, I was overcome with pity for my father, who saw me onto the ship for the east with the greatest reluctance. His rheumatism, developed from many years spent in icy streams trapping for plews, has made his existence as a wheat farmer trying in the extreme. His sorrow was increased when my beloved mother, Grass Singing, went to her grave three years ago. Thinking of him alone now in Oregon, my guilt was, for a time, nigh unbearable.

Desperate to relieve it, I sought refuge in an act I freely acknowledge as a pandering to human vanity. In answer to my wife's earnest request, I inquired about, and was directed to, a studio where the remarkable Daguerreotype is available.

The sitting required less time than I expected—a minute, no more. But all of the kitchen funds which my dear Fan gave me for this express purpose were required to purchase the little copper plate which now reposes in a silk-lined box on my bureau.

Although the visit to the studio was worldly indulgence, the experience refreshed my spirit in an unexpected way. On the plate I first saw not myself but the Almighty's handiwork—for surely the Frenchman, Daguerre, was blessed by heavenly inspiration when he perfected his method of capturing the human face on a bit of metal.

On returning to my hotel, I continued to marvel at the plate, which is somehow treated with silver salts and then exposed to the light to create an image. I discovered again why my brethren chide me good-naturedly with the name "Indian Preacher." I have the light eyes of the Kents but the dark and unruly hair of the Shoshoni. All in all, mine is a curious and severe countenance. For a few moments, I fancied that, in the eyes of the image, I saw my guilt over the unhappiness I had brought to my father, and I fancied that I also saw my doubt about where I would stand on the question now being debated at the Conference in increasingly heated language.

*

May the 25th. All the city agog with news from Baltimore, where, only yesterday, there was received an actual, audible message transmitted in code from the Supreme Court room in the capital by means of the electric telegraph of Mr. Morse. He is the inventor of the device as well as the code. Four words were sent: "What hath God wrought?"

As the debate grinds on, I ask the same wracking question about the presence of the black man in America. Why was this tribulation visited upon him—and upon us? Why were we so unlucky, or so foolish, as to find this form of labor most suitable to the requirements of an economy founded on tobacco, rice, cane and cotton crops?

Is Garrison correct in his jeremiads? Is our precious Constitution "a covenant with death and an agreement with hell" because it recognizes the right of an owner to apprehend Negroes who have committed the felonious act of fleeing from their servitude? As Garrison claims, does the Constitution at the same time guarantee Negroes every right of citizenship that whites enjoy? Even many in the northern states find that concept too radical—yet the extreme abolitionists have been propounding it for more than a decade.

Decent people disagree on both questions just noted. Mr. Justice Story of Connecticut, for example, expressed a majority opinion of the Supreme Court when the Pennsylvania Act of '26 was struck down two years ago. The opinion was founded on the Court's contention that neither Pennsylvania nor any other individual state has the authority to prevent the owner of an escaped Negro from reclaiming him—even if the Negro has reached non-slave soil. Mr. Story clearly believed that the owning of slaves confers an unquestionable Constitutional right to recapture that slave—that piece of property.

In further opposition to Garrison and his followers, the opinion also implied that our American liberties are solely for the benefit of members of the white race. Story and the Court ignored the Constitutional promise of due process. Conclusion—it simply does not apply to any man or woman with dark skin.

Who is wrong and who is right? I do not know; I do not know!!

*

May the 27th. There is no way in which I can evade the issue before the Conference, so I have given up trying. I am, instead, struggling to reach my own decision.

After digesting the various arguments and praying on the whole matter, I am for the moment tending to side with the faction which would unseat Bishop Andrew, even though the bishop is clearly a man without onus; a Christian man; a Methodist man; a good man. If my present mood prevails, I will in effect turn my back on my own dear wife and her family.

Am I capable? And is it *right?*

Later. Mr. Polk and Mr. Dallas have been nominated as presidential candidates by the Democrats in Baltimore—the news "telegraphed" for the first time in the nation's history. Either Polk or Mr. Clay, the candidate of the Whigs, will be forced to resolve the stormy issue of annexation of Texas. Mr. Clay is in opposition because the Texan Republic has not been recognized by Mexico, and there is talk afloat that annexation will mean war.

Of more pertinence, if Texas should be admitted to the Union, it will come in as a slave state, further promoting sectional strife. It is already known that a treaty of annexation prepared by Secretary of State Calhoun and currently before the Senate will be rebuffed. But opposition to annexation does not end there. The politicians who espouse Garrison's radical philosophy are adamantly against the extension of slavery into any new territory whatsoever—a thorny problem since the country's mood is generally expansionist; among some sectors of the population—the restless and the poor, whose universal answer to unhappiness or failure is westward migration—wildly so.

The northern radicals will never be content merely with blocking the admission of new slave territories, however. They would prefer to completely upset the fragile balance of the "spheres of interest" established by the Missouri Compromise of 1820, by means of which slavery was prohibited in all Louisiana Purchase lands north of approximately the thirty-sixth parallel—Missouri excepted—but made permissible south of that line, while Maine was admitted as a free state to balance Missouri's presence.

They say former president Jefferson, a very old man in those days and but five years from his death, spoke of the Compromise as "a fire bell in the night," warning of a sectional dispute that could rend the nation. I fear he was correct. The abolitionists want the institution of slavery destroyed wherever it exists, and forbidden forevermore.

My wife's people, of course, believe Texas should and will come in slave. So no matter how the issue of admission is decided, the outcome will only provoke more bad feelings—nationally, and in whatever is left of the Methodist Episcopal Church after the Andrew question is resolved. My southern brethren and I now recognize that if the Andrew matter is put to a vote, we will be outnumbered and defeated—

A sorrowful conceit, the inscription of "we"—I am still tormented, uncertain—but tending toward the other side.

*

May the 30th. Perused the book stalls this afternoon. The Conference is recessed while the committees labor, in hopes that some compromise may yet be worked out. Discovered the bins are a-bulge with guidebooks purporting to inform those afflicted with "the Oregon fever" as to the best way to equip themselves for the journey across the mountains.

In the past few years the "fever" has become epidemic. The trains of wagons leaving Missouri in the good weather number in the dozens, so the newspapers say. I would as soon never meet one of those eager pilgrims, for I would be forced to report the truth: that homesteading in the Oregon valleys is fraught with risk.

For one thing, the border dispute with Great Britain remains an irritant and a potential source of conflict. Everyone cries, "Fifty-four forty or fight!" But informed opinion maintains that England will never accept the fifty-fourth degree of latitude as Oregon's northern boundary. For another, homesteading is best left to those thoroughly skilled in agriculture. This I have seen for myself.

My father traveled to Oregon with my mother and me after the summer fur rendezvous of '37. At that time, the price of a plew was already down to the disastrous low of one dollar, due to beaver hats at last passing from fashion. My father and his fellow trappers saw the demise of their trade in that depressed price—but my father, unlike some too old or too disheartened to begin again, was determined to find an alternate livelihood.

Although he has worked diligently at wheat farming in Oregon, my father has not fared well, lacking the proper experience—and the temperament; he was always more suited to the boisterous, unfettered life of the brigades with which he marched and rode for some twenty years.

Yet I can understand why the Oregon territory holds such allure today. The vale of the Willamette is truly beautiful, and this I know my father appreciates, despite the rigors of the labor and his scant success. If he sorrows at what many would call a life of small accomplishment, it is a gentle sorrow, rendered less stinging by what God has shown him of the lovely, though demanding land beyond the Mississippi. "I have looked on wonders," he remarked once, "and while I live I hope I never lose the hunger to behold more."

If my father regrets anything deeply, I suspect it is the stormy temper

which plagued him during his early years. I can never forget his quiet
confession about taking the life of a man named Walpole; a man involved
in a scheme to seize control of the Boston printing firm my great-grandfather Kent founded. My father set fire to the firm to leave the schemers
nothing but ashes, then fled the city of Boston with his young female
cousin.

The confession took place one night when I was thirteen or fourteen,
my father saying I was at last old enough to hear the story. I can still see
him reclining in our tipi that evening while my mother sewed him a new
hide shirt.

I see his sun-lightened yellow hair streaking to gray, and his thick-
knuckled fingers, stiff from the cold beaver streams, turning and turning
his one tangible reminder of his younger days—a fob medallion struck for
him by his father's half-brother, Gilbert Kent, who operated the firm for a
time. The medal bore the family symbol, and a Latin motto—*Cape locum
et fac vestigium.* Take a stand and make a mark.

The former my father felt he had done. He had put the past behind
him forever, and ventured into the far west, both to make a new life and
to search—fruitlessly as it turned out—for his cousin, Gilbert's orphaned
daughter, whom he lost to an abductor in Tennessee in 1814. As to the
latter—making a mark—my father openly doubted his success.

Because my father speaks of the past as closed—an indication, perhaps,
that its memory still holds a power to hurt him—I have felt it kinder never
to write him about my two visits to Boston while I was studying at the Institute. I not only saw the house on fashionable Beacon Street where my
father lived—a house now occupied by an unknown family—but I also
saw, rebuilt, a publishing company called Kent and Son.

What called all this to mind is a volume I discovered among the guidebooks in the stalls—an expensive and obviously new edition of a currently
popular historical romance by the Frenchman, Dumas. The book is entitled *The Three Musketeers.* The spine was damaged, no doubt accounting for the volume's presence in the bin.

I opened the book, smitten by a most ungodly urge to read something
other than Holy Scripture. There on the title page was the family device
which my father carried on the obverse of his medal—the partially filled
bottle of tea. Accompanying the symbol were the words *Kent and Son.* I
located the date of publication. 1844. The firm still survives.

Before I replaced the novel, I briefly entertained the idea of sending it
to my father with my next, long overdue letter. I decided against it for the

same reason I said nothing about my discoveries in Boston. To hide the truth from a man who prized his family heritage and saw it lost, remains, I believe, the most Christian and compassionate course.

Later. Did I do right about the book? I am so unsure of everything, though I try to let no one see. Only these private pages, an outlet for my turmoil now and for my hopes and apprehensions during the past two years, know of my misgivings—only these pages, and Him Who Sees All.

May He have mercy on my weakness and my doubt.

*

June the 1st. All compromise has failed. The will of the Conference majority has proved paramount. A substitute resolution, requesting Bishop Andrew to cease his ecclesiastical function, was adopted one hundred ten to sixty-eight. Having spent a sleepless night in which I prayed almost continuously, and recognizing that I may have committed a grave sin, I abandoned my earlier flirtation with the majority and cast my vote nay.

I did so with the image of my dear Fan's face in my thoughts. When I was assigned the itinerancy in Virginia, I took the people as my own. I discovered my wife among them, and even though God may one day judge them sinners despite their professions of conversion, I cannot condemn them. I chose to stand with them.

In this perhaps I erred. But I am somewhat comforted because I do not believe my beloved mother would see it so.

The Shoshoni are a remarkable people. During the years my mother and I wandered with my father, first with his partner, Weatherby, and then with my father alone after Weatherby perished of the small pox, many of my mother's spiritual beliefs were implanted in my mind, forever coloring my imperfect understanding of Christian tenets.

The Shoshoni do not deny the existence of evil. They only hold a unique view of its source. To my mother and her race, the evil man was not merely sinful, but deranged—a subtle yet important distinction. The man who carried out some heinous act was obviously not in full possession of his God-given reason. Had he been, he would have recognized that his behavior was harmful to himself and, by extension, harmful to the tribal community. Patience and moral instruction, not punishment, were the remedies for such behavior. Perhaps it is from a secret, all but unadmitted faith in my mother's principles that I turned from the shrill posturings of Hodding and the others of the anti-Andrew faction and sided with the slave-holding bishop and, therefore, with those to whom I minister. Perhaps I acted from an unvoiced belief that, if we have sinned collectively, we can one day come to understand our derangement and correct it.

It may be a vain hope. I pray it is not an excuse for cowardice.

Many at the Conference yearned for compromise, but that longing was frustrated by the vote. Lovick Pierce of Georgia has declared the southern Conferences will lodge a "manly, ministerial and proper protest" concerning the Andrew affair. I have this very night heard talk of the form the protest will take:

Separation. The sundering of the Church into two bodies, north and south.

*

June the 2nd. The Conference winds to its grievous end; I will begin my homeward journey tomorrow. Even the name of my lovely little town in Virginia has become as ashes in my mouth—for I have not been able to escape the memory that, near another Lexington, my great-grandfather first stood with those country marksmen who dared to pledge their lives to the promise of liberty which this nation represents.

But liberty for whom? Whispers the worm of conscience now that the vote is done. I could not rest all night, seeing faces of color scorning me for rejecting their cause. My mind is a maelstrom. Is the agitation I suddenly feel on behalf of black men and women a temptation of the Devil, to divert me from my chief task of redeeming souls? What of the souls of my own kind in Lexington—?

In the gloomy hours before dawn, I wrestled afresh with these questions —and Heaven saw fit to deny me an answer. This morning I encountered Hodding. He did not speak. His glance d——d me for lack of courage. Yet even that bothers me less than what his loathing suddenly portended.

After he hurried on, I saw with utter clarity that we must discover a solution to repair this terrible schism. A solution both sides can accept—and one which will deal properly and fairly with the person of color as well. That the black man has a soul the Church does not deny. That he is entitled to be a communicant of American liberty is what tears us asunder. Whether that idea is right, or only an aberration, the side ultimately found to be in error must be persuaded to admit and amend its error.

Who will lead us in a search for truth and accord? Who will speak reason and effect the means of escape from our dilemma? Unless such means are found, I fear passions will rise even as they rose during the dreadful business in St. Louis in '36, when white hysteria inspired by the columns of the Congregationalist Lovejoy's anti-slavery paper, *The Observer*, led to all manner of mistreatment of Negroes, and to the death of a poor black riverman the mob caught, chained to a tree and burned alive. Hodding has self-righteously recalled the incident to me on more than one occasion—as well as the fate of Lovejoy himself, who fled to free soil in Alton, Illinois, only to be killed by five bullets while another hysterical mob wrecked his fourth printing press.

Such damaging passions are present north and south. How often have I heard Captain Tunworth speak fearfully of the deranged Turner? The slave led perhaps as many as one hundred of his fellows on a rampage throughout Virginia's Southampton County in '31, slaughtering fifty-seven white persons, including women and children. Captain Tunworth swears the black man is a beast, to be chained for the protection of society. He says he would die defending that view.

So where is the answer? Passion is rampant on both sides. I have seen that here, in a meeting of men purportedly pledged not to animosity but to its antithesis—compassionate love. Will God show us the path soon, after we have endured His testing and renewed our vow to follow His Son's teachings? Or has He already abandoned us in rage and sorrow because we are so blind; so incapable of governing our passions, and bringing Christian order from them?

Should God turn aside from us, will not the Federal Union find itself in the same wretched state as the Church does today? Irretrievably sundered? Should that transpire, the prospect is holocaust—for we preachers, contentious as we may be, still waged our little war this month with debate and document and resolution. Even with a gulf now opened between northern and southern Conferences, a modicum of Christian love remains for the brethren on the other side—

Will men outside the Church feel that restraining affection?

I fear not.

Later. I have re-read what I wrote earlier. I am humiliated and ashamed and increasingly filled with dread.

How can there be hope of a solution if even men of Christ have come this far, failing to find it? I go back to Virginia not only wondering whether I have done the right thing, but whether these thirty troubled days are but a harbinger of much worse to come.

A man such as my father-in-law, Captain Tunworth, will not yield. The abolitionists still thunder with the ancient Roman jurist, "Let justice be done, though the heavens fall!" Above the whole tumult rings the black man's anguished cry.

Those who seek a middle ground may be cursed and shouldered aside. I feel it—Almighty God, *I feel it terribly*—

Still later—en route. Very hard to write; coach bouncing; and my hand unsteady. So distressed was I during my last hours in the City, I forgot to buy a bright trinket for my little boy Gideon. I fear I am bringing him instead a legacy of much darker hue.

BOOK TWO

Gold

CHAPTER 1

Cry in the Wilderness

ON A BRILLIANT MORNING in the second week of April 1848, the clipper *Manifest Destiny* sailed into the bay, having been en route from the hongs of Canton an intolerable sixty-two days. The clipper dropped anchor opposite the settlement of Yerba Buena, a straggling collection of frame and adobe buildings set near the water against the background of the southern peninsula's grassy hills.

The ship was owned by the Ball Brothers Line, New York. She had slid off the ways only two years before, christened by her builders in a burst of patriotic zeal. In the pages of *The Democratic Review*, Mr. O'Sullivan had referred to the nation's steady expansion toward the Pacific as a "manifest destiny." The words had caught the fancy of Congressmen and China traders alike.

At thirteen hundred and sixty tons, *Manifest Destiny* was a lean and beautiful vessel. But as her canvas came down, and a lighter operated by the local hide merchant put out from the beach, her captain was still cursing her roundly. He had hoped for a straight, swift passage from China, around the Horn and up to New York. Like most captains of clipper ships —so called because their construction helped them clip time from existing speed records—he was always trying to beat some other skipper's performance. His current target was the seventy-eight-day mark of Captain Waterman's extreme clipper *Rainbow*, set in '45. He didn't like Waterman. Few in the China trade did, including Waterman's crewmen, who had nicknamed him Killer.

A typhoon in the South China Sea—a freak storm, blowing months after the fall season—had nearly dismantled *Manifest Destiny's* masts as she started her homeward run. The damage forced her back to Macao for a refitting. With the chance for a record—and the resulting prestige and increased business for Ball Brothers—gone, the clipper's captain had decided to concentrate on profit.

Manifest Destiny had called at the Hawaiian Islands, adding another two tons of Alaskan sealskins to the sixteen thousand tons of tea already in the holds. The clipper then set sail for Yerba Buena, the sunny little port on the California coast. Here the captain would squeeze aboard whatever hides and tallow were available. The captain's primage was calculated at a generous seven and one half per cent of the delivered sale price of the cargo. Since he was already far behind schedule, the more he brought home without making the clipper plow under, the greater his earnings.

Yerba Buena had one other attraction besides the possibility of extra cargo. As the lighter headed for shore, the captain began to think of that, and with considerable pleasure. It took his mind off his anger at the ship, the weather and himself.

The captain sat in the lighter's bow, the oilskin-wrapped parcel from New York tucked under one sleeve of his trim blue sea jacket. He wore a peaked cap and his best black silk neckerchief. He was a tall, slim man with a sharp chin and gray eyes that tended to intimidate those who served under him. Though he was just forty, white hair already showed around his ears. His name was Barton McGill. His home—birthplace, rather—was Charleston, South Carolina.

While the lighter plowed through the chop, he scanned the small crowd gathering on shore. Such a crowd always formed when a ship of size entered the roads. The permanent population of Yerba Buena was right around five hundred, perhaps half of those being Americans. Even at some distance from the beach, Bart McGill could easily spot the Yankees. The darker ones were Coloma Indians, Mexicans, Chileans and Peruvians. There were even a few Hawaiians in the village. He saw white and colored waving with equal enthusiasm; heard halloos across the water—

Then, approximately in the center of the crowd, he spied an extremely tall, yellow-skinned Negro. Bart McGill's eyes were momentarily cool. He and Israel didn't get along too well. But the Negro's height helped the captain spot the person he really wanted to see—

Sure enough, there was Amanda. Standing a little to one side of Israel, and waving. A few steps behind her was her son Louis, recognizable because of his size—he was eleven—and his jet black hair.

Goddamnedest thing in the world, finding someone like her in this penny-ante port, Bart thought, smiling. He'd been married twelve years to a proper Charleston bitch who had borne him three daughters, none of whom had survived infancy. At last the bitch had done the decent thing and left him a widower while he was somewhere in the Indian Ocean in '43. But he'd had to visit California two years ago to discover a woman he really cared for; a woman older than he was; most miraculous of all, a woman who didn't want to knot him up in matrimony.

He didn't call often at Yerba Buena. But everyone knew Amanda was Captain McGill's woman, as well as the proprietor of Kent's, a tavern and eating house on Portsmouth Square—where, he noticed as he squinted into the sunlight, the stars and stripes still appeared to be flying.

Commander Montgomery had sent that banner up the staff for the first time in '46, when the Americans in California heard the news of their country's war with Mexico. That same year, a treaty with Britain had settled the disputed northern boundary of Oregon not at the fifty-fourth parallel but the forty-ninth. With a potential enemy out of the way, the United States had turned its attention to a real one. Provoked by the annexation of Texas, Mexican soldiers had attacked a U.S. dragoon company near Matamoros, and the war was on—

Realizing how out of touch he was, Bart McGill turned to one of the oarsmen:

"Did General Scott capture Mexico City last fall? I sailed right after he took Chapultepec—"

"Yessir, captain, he did. The greasers done signed a treaty, too. I heard Washington got all o' Texas, New Mexico and Upper Californy. Guess it's true—"

"Which was practically American anyway after the Bear Flag revolt and General Kearny's capture of Los Angeles," Bart said in his mellow southerner's voice. "Will California come into the Union, then?"

"Too soon to tell," the oarsman answered. "The treaty ain't more'n a couple of months old. Can't see much reason why the Union'd want us, either," he added. He bent forward and drew back on his oar.

Bart McGill turned his gaze inland, to the green and tan hills receding to the distant bluish haze that might have been only a haze—or the great Sierras. The land was indeed desolate; a wilderness—though he'd heard there was good hunting in the Sierra foothills. He wondered about the territory's status if, at some remote time in the far future, it acquired enough people to entitle it to statehood. The request would touch off another debate about slavery, no doubt. Being a southerner, he had views on the subject of slavery. But he much preferred the sea to the settled east because he got sick of hearing nigra, nigra, nigra. In New York, nobody could talk for half an hour without launching an argument over the south's peculiar institution.

"Bart? Here we are!"

The faint cry borne on the breeze took him away from the tedious and disagreeable subject. A couple of Mexicans with cornets began tootling a welcome. There was some desultory cheering. But the crowd seemed skimpy, even for Yerba Buena.

His eye fixed on Amanda—forty-five years old and looking ten years less. God, what a handsome woman. If only she'd been able to conceive a child. But her time for that had ended relatively early—before he met her.

She strained on tiptoe, her dyed cotton dress a sparkle of red amid the drab rags of most of the other inhabitants. Her son Louis wore a flannel shirt and homespun trousers. Bart didn't even notice what Israel, the tall mulatto, was wearing. He was concentrating on the vibrant, dark-haired woman who kicked off her shoes and dashed to the water's edge, awaiting the lighter.

Bart felt unusually sentimental just then. During all the years of his marriage, his wife had never once generated emotion of the kind that gripped him as he watched Amanda barefoot in the white foam. She was a prize; a genuine prize—

She'd been married once; lived in Texas a while, then in the pueblo of Los Angeles. She'd been in Yerba Buena for the last four years, and on the surface seemed content to earn a meager living selling food and drink. But he knew how deceiving that air of contentment was. He knew because of things she asked of him, and because of the parcel he bore under his arm.

She was waving hard now, her hand flying. On her wrist he saw that peculiar rope bracelet given her by the vanished cousin she spoke of occasionally. She claimed she could have been a Boston heiress if the right cards had fallen. But here she was on the California coast, scraping out an existence in a single-story building she'd put up with the last of her savings after paying sixteen-fifty American for her fifty-vara lot—

And damned if he wasn't glad about the whole business.

Better watch yourself, McGill, he thought, or you'll do some fool thing like deciding you love this woman enough to marry her—and there goes independence and a handsome living with the Messrs. Ball.

The lighter grounded. The cornets blared as Bart prepared to jump down into the surf. Amanda spun toward the crowd:

"Louis? Come here and see Captain Bart—"

"Oh. they's one more thing I forgot to tell you," the oarsman said suddenly.

Bart turned, an inquiring look on his face.

"Folks around here got tired of the old name for the town. Some of 'em are starting to call it after another settlement that used to be near here."

"What settlement?"

"San Francisco."

ii

"*Bart!*" Amanda cried, throwing her arms around his neck. "I nearly fainted when Louis ran in to say they'd sighted your clipper from the hill. I thought you were going straight back to New York this trip—"

"Planned on it. Ran into an out-of-season blow." He bussed her cheek, relishing the clean, soaped smell of her skin. Even in such a public place, the touch of her body produced a decided physical reaction. "Tell you about it later," he added as he hugged her. She felt him, all right:

"I can tell you've been away a while. Lord, how I've missed you—!"

He grinned. "That's why I don't come around too often. I reckon we'd get pretty tired of each other if we slept in the same bed year in and year out—" He planted another kiss on her cheek. "I swear you just keep growing prettier, Amanda."

"No. I'm getting gray, Bart."

She was; strands of white showed in the dark glossiness of her hair.

"It's becoming. You take it from one who's seen all kinds."

"Nice of you to flatter an old lady, Captain McGill—" She caught his arm as they walked from the surf to the damp sand. She picked up her shoes, still teasing him: "You know some of the local women think I'm scandalous, keeping company with a youngster like you—"

"The hell with 'em. Five years' difference is no difference at all." He peeked around her at the sturdy, black-eyed boy with swarthy skin and broad shoulders. He held out his hand.

"How are you, Louis?"

"Very good, Captain Bart, thank you," Louis Kent said with a cheery smile. Bart gave the obligatory nod to the hulking yellow scarecrow lingering a respectful distance away:

"Israel. Things well with you?"

"About the same, cap'n."

In the opaque brown eyes, Bart detected the hostility he'd encountered before. Amanda said Israel bore southern-made scars on his back—Bart had never cared to ask to see them—and so all southerners were anathemas to the mulatto. Israel made no secret of having run away from a Mississippi cotton plantation. How Amanda could treat the ex-slave as an equal, Bart McGill's experience and education did not permit him to fathom.

Amanda had met Israel in Los Angeles, where he'd gone as a member of one of the trading brigades coming up from the southwest. That was early in '44. She'd hired him to accompany her north to Yerba Buena, where she'd hoped to find a more prosperous economy than the one she'd left in the pueblo. In that, she had been disappointed.

Together, Amanda and Israel, who was about thirty now, had built Kent's. It tickled Bart that Amanda approached physical work with an almost masculine directness. He'd watched her split a log for firewood once, and laughed aloud when she raised her palms to her mouth, spit on them, and clamped a grip on the axe—treating him to an arch look because he laughed. He'd assured her he was only laughing because her behavior was such a delightful contrast to the vaporish ways of eastern ladies—including his unlamented wife—who probably would have gone to their graves rather than let anyone see them spit *or* chop wood.

The mulatto had helped supply the knowledge of carpentry required to put up the tavern. He and Amanda had shared the labor equally. He'd remained her devoted—and free—employee ever since. For no rational reason, Bart distrusted him—an inheritance from his own upbringing, he occasionally admitted to himself.

The crowd was dispersing. Amanda and the clipper captain started up the beach toward the crude buildings that comprised the settlement. Israel and Louis followed.

"Feels good to be on shore again," Bart said.

"Feels good to have you here."

"Reckon we should celebrate with a little music after you're finished for the day."

"Not just with music," she laughed, squeezing his arm.

"Miz Kent already hung up the sign saying we're closed," Israel remarked from a pace behind.

Bart was annoyed at the Negro eavesdropping on private conversation. But Amanda's bubbling voice took the edge off his irritation:

"I'm going to cook you the biggest meal you've had in months. And Louis and I want to hear some songs—"

"Got a new one I think you'll like," he said, taking her arm. He noticed her dark eyes straying to the parcel in his other hand. "But you're more interested in these, aren't you?" He bent to whisper. "There's a price on 'em."

Her eyes brimmed with warmth, and she was only partly teasing when she replied:

"You don't have to bargain for that, Bart. You know how much I long for you while you're gone—"

"Still say you couldn't stand me if I was around all the time."

She kept eyeing the parcel. In answer to the unspoken question, he said:

"Yes, Kent editions, every one. Three Coopers. A collection of stories by Hawthorne—*Mosses from an Old Manse*, I think the title is—and a bunch of peculiar—oh, supernatural tales, I guess you'd call them. Written by some fellow named Poe. I didn't care for 'em much. That particular book was second-hand. I was told the public doesn't care for 'em much either."

Amanda's ebullient mood seemed spoiled by the mention of the books. Soon after they had met for the first time, she had spoken candidly about her childhood, who she was and who her father had been. She said she had never imagined her father's firm was still in existence until, by pure chance, she had come across a tattered copy of Headley's *Napoleon and his Marshals* in Los Angeles.

The book was being sold among other odds and ends by a wagon-trader who had passed through the pueblo. It was the twelfth edition of the popular work, published at Boston in 1839 and carrying the words *Kent and Son* and a design representing a bottle of tea on its title page.

After that very first visit, Bart had brought her Kent books on every trip. Whenever possible, he also brought her answers to questions.

Listening to the story of her early years, he had learned in the bargain how she'd traveled this far west. He had been thunderstruck by the account of what she'd endured, and not a little disturbed by her unpleasant expression when she spoke of the man who had won the family firm from her stepfather in a dice game—

Her face had the same grim look now. In New York the past autumn, he had found the answers to some new questions. He wondered whether he should tell her. He disliked seeing the angry streak in her nature assert itself—

She didn't leave the choice to him. She quickened her step so they drew ahead of Israel and the boy. They swung past a smith's and walked on toward the oddly quiet Portsmouth Square. Even Brannan's mercantile emporium looked deserted. Abruptly, Amanda said:

"What about Stovall?"

"What about him?"

"Bart, don't string me along. Did you find out everything I wanted to know?"

He sighed. "Most of it."

"Well, then—is Stovall still running Kent and Son?"

"Yes."

She swore as vehemently and violently as any of his able seamen. He finally interrupted:

"I don't know where you learned all those words, sweet, but I'm suitably impressed. Now you want to let me finish?"

"I'm sorry, go on."

"Stovall's running the company, but through underlings, not personally—"

"The way you say that, you make it sound like I put you to some terrible chore—"

"I'm out of my depth investigating a muckety-muck like Mr. Hamilton Stovall. Steel's a far cry from shipping, and I got plenty of peculiar stares at the saloons where the newspaper writers hang out—"

"You also got answers, didn't you?"

"Eventually. But those reporter fellows sure as hell wonder why a sea captain's buying them rounds and asking about the third biggest steelmaker in the whole United States."

Amanda seemed not to hear:

"Where is he living?"

"A fancy mansion in New York—he and his wife."

"He's *married?*"

"He is. The woman's a good deal younger. They have no children."

"I'm not surprised. From what Jared told me, I can't imagine Stovall being interested in a woman—unless she could confer some kind of respectability on him."

"Perhaps that is why he married. He's certainly not the same man you described to me—at least not in public. He's eminently respectable."

"But treating the book company like a stepchild—"

"Not exactly. A couple of clerks told me Kent's is still a popular and successful imprint."

"Which he keeps going solely because it makes money?"

"Why else would he keep it going?"

"My father and my grandfather believed printing books served a useful purpose."

"So it does. It lines Mr. Stovall's pockets."

"I'm talking about educating people. Having a point of view and not being afraid to express it."

"It's my impression Stovall cares very little about the state of the public mind. The clerks said the Kent and Son list is growing less substantial every year. And the house publishes nothing controversial—though come to think of it, I did see a Kent edition of *Awful Disclosures*."

"I've never heard of it."

"Caused a real stir when it was issued in '36—and discredited soon after. It was written by a girl named Maria Monk. That is, her name's on it—hacks probably prepared the manuscript. Maria claimed to have been a nun. Later it was proved that the closest she got to the Roman faith was a religious home for wayward girls. The whole book's fiction, but it's lip-smacking stuff. Nuns submissive to the carnal will of priests—midnight revels in a Montreal convent—illegitimate babies baptized, then strangled, nine months after the aforesaid revels—"

"That's disgusting."

"But you can't call it controversial. Too many people believe such tales about Catholics."

"Does Stovall?"

"Can't say. But I imagine that if he published the Monk book, he hates the papists—especially all the Irish filling up the eastern cities."

"Did you ask about his politics?"

"Forgot. You know I don't give much of a damn who votes for what. Again, *Awful Disclosures* would lead me to guess he's a Know-Nothing."

"God!" Amanda seethed. "If my grandfather knew a bigot like that was publishing books under his name—" She was too angry to continue.

"I did discover a couple of things about Stovall's main business," Bart went on. "He's opening up a new mill in Pittsburgh. The railroads are using more steel than he can produce. And he's changed the company name from the Chesapeake Iron Finery to the Stovall Works."

"Did you find out who's actually running Kent and Son?"

He shook his head. "But I know who's general manager of the Stovall Works. One of the boys from the *Sun* stood me to a schooner of beer after I bought him three. He got to talking pretty freely. He said—"

Bart's hands grew chilly. How he despised the sight of Amanda's lovely face when it was this white; this intense. She got that way whenever she discussed Stovall—

They had reached the edge of Portsmouth Square. The stars and stripes snapped in the breeze above the rows of turned earth; the square was Yerba Buena's potato patch.

Bart still hadn't finished his last sentence. In front of the Old Adobe, the town hall, Amanda stopped, blocking his path:

"Go on with it, Bart."

"Jesus! You could let me get to your place, at least—"

"*Tell me right now!*"

"All right. The reporter happened to mention the name of the fellow in charge of the steel operation. It's one of the names you remembered. But you didn't have it quite right—" He hesitated again. "It's not Waltham, it's Walpole."

"*Walpole!*"

Louis, who had been dawdling behind with Israel, ran to her:

"Ma, what's the matter?"

"Nothing—nothing."

"You sounded so mad—"

"You and Israel go on to the tavern—*go on!*"

The gangling yellow-skinned man drifted up:

"Do like your mama says, Louis." He took the boy's hand and started off. The sight of black skin pressing white made Bart McGill feel slightly unclean. He'd been brought up to loathe that kind of familiarity between the races.

Amanda showed no sign of moving. One hand shielding her eyes from the sun, she was waiting for the rest. He figured he might as well get it over:

"Walpole," he repeated. "The same name as the fellow your cousin shot."

"He's a relative—one of Walpole's sons?"

"He's the same man."

"That—that can't be!"

"Who asked the questions, you or me?"

"But Jared killed Walpole!"

"I know that's what you said. But I'm the one who spent three gold pieces on more beer and two telegraph messages. The *Sun* reporter contacted a man he knows on a Baltimore paper. The man wired information back the next day. Walpole's old—almost ready to retire. There are employees at the company who've heard him speak of being shot by one of the Kents way back in fourteen or fifteen—whenever it was that Stovall took over your father's firm."

"Then—Stovall let Jared think—"

"Think what? Your cousin never waited to discover what really happened. You said both of you ran away the very same night—" He grimaced. "I'm getting weary of this blasted detective work, Amanda. What I've found out hasn't done any good at all. It only makes you more miserable. When are you going to realize it's downright unhealthy to harbor a grudge for so many years—?"

She paid no attention:

"He let Jared think he'd done *murder*—"

"Jared never gave himself a chance to find out otherwise!"

"Stovall could have tried to locate—"

"Oh, come on, sweet!" Bart broke in, angered that the past had cropped up so soon. It always did eventually. But it seldom produced the degree of rage seething in her right now. Well, he'd guessed this might happen. But he tried to make her see reason:

"Stovall didn't care a damn for your family. Hated them, in fact—you said so yourself."

"And all this time, he let Jared believe that he killed—"

"*All this time!*" he echoed in a sarcastic way. "Your cousin's probably dead."

"That makes no difference. By God, I'm going back there—!"

He sounded tired: "You've told me. Over and over."

"Ten years ago, I had the same idea—but for a different reason. I just wanted to see where the family lived—search for some mementos my father owned. When I came across the Headley book, everything changed. I want Kent and Son out of Stovall's hands!"

"Maybe the first reason was better. This jeremiad against Mr. Stovall eats on you worse every year—"

"Because I'm getting older. I may not have many years left. I swear, if I can ever put together more than twenty dollars at one time, I'm going back and take the company away from him. I'll do more than that to him if I can—"

Inexplicably chilly in the sun, Bart said, "Sometimes, Amanda, you scare the bejesus out of a man. I know this much. You get involved in trying to destroy someone and you'll wind up suffering as much as he does.

Hate works that way. It hurts the one who gets it *and* the one who gives it—"

I have first-hand experience.

"—Christ amighty, that's exactly what's happening back east right now. One section against the other—the tempers hotter, the words more vile and unreasonable with every day that passes—before it's over, people on both sides are liable to be killing each other!"

She didn't want to hear. She snatched the book parcel from his hand, her fingers almost colorless as they clenched the oilskin:

"*If I only had some money—*"

"Dammit, woman, don't you *ever* listen to what I say? I've told you a dozen times you don't need money to pay your way east. Say the word and I'll take you and Louis aboard—"

"I'm not talking about money for passage. I'm talking about a lot of money."

Exhausted and unsettled by the discussion, he was snappish:

"What if Mr. Hamilton Stovall doesn't care to sell Kent and Son the minute you say so? Did you ever think of that?"

Outwardly, she remained the same Amanda Kent: full-figured, with a deliciously wide mouth, lovely dark eyes—and yet the fury in those eyes produced a subtle distortion; the total effect was spoiled.

"I'll make him sell. No matter what I have to do."

"Then you're just as crazy as you claim he is!"

"Thank you."

"Amanda—"

"Thank you very much, Captain McGill!"

Jamming the parcel of books under her arm, she whirled and hurried away.

"Amanda, come back here! I didn't mean to make you fly off—"

She didn't stop or look around. He swore a few blistering words, then followed her slowly across the sunlit square.

iii

She dashed straight in the front door of Kent's and slammed it after her. He noticed the *Closed* sign Israel had mentioned. Puzzlingly, similar signs hung on the door of Sam Brannan's store, and on the door of the small, jerry-built office of the *Star* immediately adjoining. Brannan owned the paper as well as the mercantile establishment.

But Captain Bart McGill had things to worry about besides the curious absence of the town's most industrious citizen. The visit to Yerba Buena had gotten off to a catastrophic start. All he'd wanted to do today was spend a while enjoying Amanda's company—talking with her of inconsequential things; laughing with her; touching her. And then, at an appropriate hour when Louis was bedded down and Israel had retired to his shanty behind the tavern, he would have climbed into her bed and loved her—

Instead, he'd wrecked her customary composure with the one thing capable of doing that—the past; the past she constantly picked over so the wound could never heal.

Goddamn, why had he ever spent so much time and energy on those inquiries? Why hadn't he refused to discuss the contents of the parcel, or what he'd learned last autumn, until later? Until it was dark and calm and they'd taken their sweet fill of one another—?

He knew why. He'd questioned the reporters in New York, and answered her promptly this morning, because she asked—because he liked to please her.

But she *was* getting too old for silly notions about bringing the Kents back to the position of eminence she claimed they'd once enjoyed. Forty was an average lifetime; five years beyond that, she was lucky to be in such astonishingly good health. She should be enjoying what was left of her life, not dedicating it to some fool scheme that soured her disposition and didn't stand a chance of succeeding. Wealthy or not, she'd be no match for a powerful man like Hamilton Stovall—who logically couldn't be expected to hand over Kent and Son to a member of the family he despised.

Yet Amanda was a determined woman; that he knew very well. Maybe she *could* succeed if she tried hard enough, and had a touch of luck. What upset him was the fact that her ambition was so closely tied to an almost fanatic hatred of Stovall. And as he'd tried to tell her, hate was a costly, destructive emotion—

Except when some shipboard crisis sparked him to a fury and drove him to action, Captain Barton McGill was a calm, detached sort of man. He'd been raised in a Charleston home where two aristocratic people of high temper had clashed often. Among his most vivid memories of childhood were the sounds of argument—

Cursing.

Crying.

Crockery smashing—

He'd been fortunate to discover the haven offered by a career at sea. His parents—both dead now—hadn't objected to his leaving home when he was quite young. He felt they had little interest in him, and suspected they were glad to be rid of him. But he'd married unwisely; married a woman who had much the same disposition as his mother and father. Her anger, easily roused, had driven him deeper within himself. He developed a kind of spiritual kinship with the spotted turtle he'd kept as a pet when he was eight or nine—

Kept, that is, until one of the stormiest of the arguments between his parents. His father snatched the turtle from its box on the porch and hurled it at his mother. She dodged and the spotted turtle hit the house, its carapace cracked even though it had frantically withdrawn its legs and head—

The turtle died that same night. Bart never forgot. Over the years he concluded that those who indulged their tempers for any but the most practical and pressing reasons were fools doomed to destroy others, and be destroyed. Even turtles weren't perfectly protected from the wrath of such fools, but at least they had some armor. His was intellectual.

He abhorred, and took no part in, the venomous debate the slave question produced in the north and south. He jeered at the hysterical abolitionists and their bombastic, foully slanted pamphlets and newspapers. But his contempt was nearly as strong for those cotton-kingdom demagogues who puffed out clouds of gas about states' rights and offered sly threats of separation—secession—to *scare* those northern bastards—

No matter what the motive, hate bred hate and, in the end, chaos. He had long ago weaned himself away from such damaging passions. He preferred the steady, soothing beat of the ocean against a clipper's hull; the spirited but essentially civilized bargaining in the Chinese hongs. In the Far East trade, a man could do his task, take pride in it, and make a little money without staking his life on worthless angers and wooly ideas—such as Amanda's notion that Kent and Son was supposed to do more than bring in a profit; that it had some higher responsibility to inform and inspire the people who bought the books bearing its imprint. Ideas like that—turned into crusades—only brought people to grief—

Damnation! He should have lied about the questions she'd put to him on his last visit. Lied outright:

"Kent's isn't owned by Stovall any longer. No one's heard of Walpole in years—"

As he stared glumly at the closed front door where she'd vanished, he realized that if he'd thought things through a little more—or if he cared for her a little less—he *would* have lied.

Now it was too late.

iv

Whittling, Louis Kent looked up as Bart McGill approached the shadowed rear stoop of the sun-bleached frame building. Out back, Israel was pottering in the garden next to his shanty.

Bart wanted to go on inside; into the building's rear room, a large, square chamber partitioned into sleeping space for Louis, and a second, somewhat bigger alcove for Amanda. He could see the room's furnishings —the piano he'd brought on one voyage; the walnut dining table and chairs that had come on another. Amanda and her son entertained visitors at the table, and took meals there. Food came from the tavern's small kitchen, located between the rear living room and the more spacious public room in front. Kent's didn't waste money on fancy fixtures. A plank bar and several cheap tables and chairs satisfied the diners and drinkers of Yerba Buena—

He saw it all, fondly, but he didn't go in because he suspected Amanda was probably still upset. She'd let him know when she was composed enough to see him again.

He sat down beside the boy on the splintery step. "Louis, I've been wondering something."

"What is it, sir?"

"Have I got my days mixed up? I swear last night, my log read Tuesday. But places around here are closed tight, just like it's Sunday."

"You mean Mr. Brannan's store?"

"And his paper," Bart nodded. "Where is the old money-grubber, off palavering with brother Brigham?"

"Oh, no, Captain Bart, Mr. Brannan's given up the Mormon faith."

"He has! Why?"

"He and Young fell out over the place those Latter-day Saints were going to settle after they got run out of Missouri. Mr. Brannan brought some families to Yerba Buena by ship, you know—"

"Yes."

"—and he tried to persuade Young this was the promised land. I guess old Mr. Young saw it differently, back at that salty lake they say lies east of the Sierras. Young threw Brannan out of their church—"

"Good God! I beg your pardon, Louis. Continue."

"—and he said he wanted all the money Brannan had collected in tithes, too. Ma said Mr. Young claimed it was the Lord's money, so Mr. Brannan said he'd return it as soon as Young sent him a receipt in the Lord's handwriting. That Mr. Brannan's pretty good at turning a dollar—"

"Almost as good as your mother," Bart observed with a wry smile. "But you haven't told me where he is."

"I think he must have gone up to Captain Sutter's mill."

Bart blinked. "You mean the fort on the Sacramento? New Helvetia?"

"No, I mean Captain Sutter's sawmill. I guess it's been built since you were here last. About forty or fifty miles beyond the fort, on the American River. Mr. Brannan probably went up to see about the gold—along with Mr. Kemble, the editor of the *Star*."

"What gold are you talking about, Louis?"

The boy shrugged. "Probably isn't real. Probably just pyrites."

"Found in the river?"

"Yes, sir. Mr. Marshall, who was putting up the mill, spied it first." Louis fished in his pocket, produced a crumpled clipping. "This was in the other paper last month. I tore it out—I got pretty excited. But ma calmed me down quick enough. She said a lot of the yellow stuff had showed up around here before—and all of it busted apart the minute someone laid it on an anvil and hammered it. That's one way you tell fool's gold, they say."

Bart scanned the story from Yerba Buena's other occasional newspaper, *The Californian*. The item was dated the fifteenth of March:

GOLD MINE FOUND.—In the newly made raceway of the Saw Mill recently erected by Captain Sutter on the American Fork, gold has been found in considerable quantities. One person brought thirty dollars worth to New Helvetia, gathered there in a short time. California, no doubt, is rich in mineral wealth; great chances here for scientific capitalists.

He didn't read the final sentence, because Louis interrupted: "Nobody believes that now."

"But a few still went to look for themselves—?"

"Yes. Mr. Brannan even fetched along some *aqua fortis*. I don't know what that is, but he said if you poured it on gold, nothing would happen, and that's another way you tell real gold from pyrites."

"Explains why the town's so quiet, anyway. Strikes me that if there were gold up along those rivers, someone would have made certain by now. It's April already—"

"Does seem funny, doesn't it?"

Bart changed the subject: "How are you coming along with your studies?"

"Pretty well. Ma helps me three nights a week. I'm good with sums—I can make change fast in the tavern. My handwriting's only fair. And I don't like all that poetry and those stories she makes me read—"

"Well—" He tousled the boy's dark, curly hair. In the blue shadow of the stoop, Louis might have passed for a Mexican, so coppery were his cheeks. "—you'll have to suffer. Reading's the mark of a cultured man. I brought a new batch of books. Maybe you'll like that Poe fellow's eerie concoctions—"

The door opened behind them. Bart rose. But even before he swung and saw Amanda's smiling face, he was gratified by her calm voice:

"Come in, Bart. And forgive me for carrying on a while ago—?"

Her smile was so warm, he promptly forgot the worry and turmoil caused by her reaction to the Kent books:

"Nothing to forgive, sweet—'less you refuse to pour me a good strong drink."

v

The remainder of the day was merry and satisfying. Amanda cooked up some beef brought in a few days earlier from the fort of the somewhat bizarre European, Captain John Sutter. The fort lay beyond the central valley, where the Sacramento and American Rivers flowed together.

While Amanda worked, Bart told her all the news he could remember from the previous fall—old news, to be sure, but she welcomed it. There were some newer tidbits as well, the most recent concerning the failing health of the famous Mr. Astor.

He was dying at eighty-four, so enfeebled he could take no nourishment except milk from the breast of a woman hired for that purpose. To provide him with exercise, his household servants laid him on a blanket and lifted and lowered him. But sick as he was, the legendary millionaire still kept track of payments made by individual renters of his various real estate properties—and demanded his agents collect a small amount of money owed him by a widow who had fallen on hard times. The gossips said Astor's son had taken the sum from his own pocket, and sent it to his father by special messenger. The dying man was well pleased, Bart said.

He and Amanda exchanged eastern and western perspectives on the war just concluded under the leadership of two Whig generals, the military commander of the southwest, Zachary Taylor, and the commander of all United States forces, Winfield Scott—both avowed political opponents of President Polk.

Though both men were Virginians, a greater personal contrast could hardly have been found. Scott's preoccupation with protocol and proper dress had earned him a national nickname—Old Fuss and Feathers. Taylor, unassuming and unspectacular, seldom wore a uniform, preferring farmer's clothing, with only a cap carrying a general's emblem identifying his rank. While cogitating, scanning dispatches or issuing orders, he usually sat with both legs hanging down one side of the old white nag he rode. His style won him a nickname too—Old Rough and Ready—and Bart said some in the east were already calling him presidential material.

Like previous American wars, the one against Mexico had been unpopular in certain quarters. Many northerners saw it as a means of guaranteeing the presence of a huge slave state, Texas, in the Union. Bart spoke with some derision about a rustic philosopher of Massachusetts, a chap named Thoreau, who had actually refused to pay a poll tax to protest the "immoral" war. He had gone to Concord jail instead.

Amanda had a somewhat more personal, less political interest in the outcome of the war. She'd had first-hand experience with the Mexican president, Santa Anna, back in Texas in the thirties. Bart knew the story; he knew who had sired young Louis, and under what circumstances.

With relish, Amanda described Santa Anna's abdication after the capture of Mexico City in September of '47:

"I only hope they've gotten the treacherous son of a bitch out of office for good this time!"

She said conditions in California were settling down now that Mexico had renounced claim to the land. The territory was currently being governed by a garrison at Monterey under the command of one Colonel

Mason. Exactly as Louis had said, she dismissed the rumor of gold at Sutter's mill as just that.

She served supper in the late afternoon, while the sunlight began to diffuse behind the fog gathering out on the Pacific. At Amanda's request, Louis pronounced the grace. Then the boy asked:

"Isn't Israel going to eat with us, ma?"

"No, he has a touch of the stomach complaint."

She and Bart both knew it was an excuse. Israel didn't enjoy the captain's company. Bart was glad the former slave wasn't around.

He ate and ate, complimenting the cook frequently. After the meal he lit a Cuban cigar and moved to the room's most cherished object, the small, compact piano he had freighted from New York.

Before going to sea as a cabin boy in the Far East trade, he had been forced to study music. Despite his youthful dislike of practice, he was accomplished. Music had become a companion for his adult years; a companion who never argued over damnfool *ideas*, or got het up, except as the composition and the performer dictated—

He ran through the popular song he'd mentioned in the morning, a lively novelty called *Oh, Susannah!* that everyone in the east was whistling. Louis and Amanda quickly learned the words. The trio sang the song four times through, with foot-stomping and hand-clapping to hide the flaws in their voices.

Next Bart played some Chopin for Amanda, finishing with a fiery yet somehow melancholy fantasy—Opus 66 in C sharp minor—whose central passage seemed to speak of unfulfilled hopes and dreams. Amanda rocked in the rocker, her eyes closed, her sun-burnished face golden in the light of the lamp.

Bart finished the piece and looked around. Louis had slipped out, not caring for "fancy" music. He watched Amanda rocking for a moment.

"Amanda."

"Mm."

"What are you thinking about?"

She opened her eyes. "Gold."

"You said there wasn't any."

"I know. If there were, Captain Sutter would certainly have made more of the fact by now."

"Unless he's afraid the gold might bring a lot of people tromping over his ground."

"You know, I never thought of it that way. You're right. He's a farmer at heart—"

"A farmer who pretends he was once a soldier."

She smiled. "Everybody calls him captain out of respect. No one really believes he served in the Swiss Guards in France—any more than they believe in the gold. Still, it's a lovely dream—"

"What is?"

"Owning a piece of ground with a lot of gold in it."

He didn't like the brief, predatory expression in her eyes. He puffed on his cigar, rose and stretched:

"Who does own this country? One of the men on the lighter sounded like nobody's sure."

"That's true. Anyone who wants land around here can claim it, except in town."

"Let's hope they don't want it. Changing the name of this place is too much change already. I prefer Yerba Buena just like it is. Quiet—"

He walked to her side, bent and kissed her forehead.

"With you always here."

She reached up to touch his face, her fingertips warm against his skin. How soft and beautiful she looked in the lamplight. The predatory quality was gone. He stroked her hair:

"You're an amazing woman, Amanda."

"Why do you say that?"

"I want another free meal tomorrow."

They laughed together. Then he went on, "I say it because most females would have tried to lash me up legally long before this."

She shrugged, the movement tightening the fabric over her breasts and reminding him of his long-unsatisfied need.

"You said one marriage was enough. Besides, even though I'm regarded as something of a loose creature around here, I continue to believe it's the loving, not the document, that counts most. If you wish to consider that an invitation, Captain McGill, please d—what on earth's wrong? Why did you pull such a terrible face?"

"Just thinking of the poor devils still on board the clipper. They don't get leave till morning. While I wallow in debauchery—" He grinned.

"No debauchery permitted until children are in bed. Do you want to help me find Louis?"

"With speed, sweet. With the utmost speed."

As she stood up, he leaned forward to kiss her mouth. She caressed his face again.

"Make sure of that," she whispered.

He wheeled and sped out into the clammy fog, shouting her son's name.

vi

She was full of eagerness and heat too long contained. With Louis bedded down in the smaller cubicle, and the curtain carefully pulled across the entrance to hers, they made love with almost desperate haste, Amanda not even allowing Bart to slip out of his trousers before her hands were on him, pulling him to her.

The alcove grew warm. They lay together drowsily afterward, Amanda laughing about how shameless it was for a woman midway through her forties to enjoy a man's body. She teased him about the difference in their ages, calling herself a seducer of innocents—whereupon he rolled over and kissed one of her breasts while his other hand slid down the smoothness of her belly:

"I'll show you how innocent I am. Would you care to learn a certain way Chinese girls make love?"

She laughed and poked him:

"What Chinese girls, you deceitful bastard?"

"Unimportant. Just pay attention—"

"And I thought southerners were honorable men."

"In public. Shut the bedroom tight and we rut just as hard as the next. Harder, maybe. Better, for sure—"

Laughing, hugging, kissing with their lips parted, they went more slowly this time. The play of hands and limbs drove Bart into a frenzy, until he was floundering on her, parting her legs with insistent fingers, opening the way for himself, thrusting forward with a haste that matched her own—

She cried out happily at the impact—only to jerk her head from the mussed pillow an instant later. Her sudden movement jolted him:

"What the hell's wrong?"

"Someone's shouting—"

"Let them shout."

"I hear people in the square—"

He listened. Caught the unintelligible bellow of a bass voice.

"We've had trouble before, Bart. Drifters liquored and starting a scrape. Setting fires—hand me my robe."

"Oh, goddamn it, all right," he said, severely peeved.

She lit a lamp on the walnut table. Louis popped out of his cubicle, asking what was wrong.

"You go back to sleep," Amanda said, reaching past the pile of new books to a board hanging on the wall. Pegs jutted from the board. Two of them supported one of the revolvers manufactured by Colt's of Hartford. The gun was an 1840 holster model, .36 caliber, with a barrel a full foot long. Amanda handled it expertly, flipping out the fold-in trigger and checking the five chambers to be sure they were loaded. Through one curtained window Bart glimpsed a running figure with a torch—the mulatto, Israel, heading for the square—

Amanda rushed through the kitchen and into the public room, Bart a few paces behind. She unlatched the front door, dashed out on the stoop. Struggling to pull on his shirt, Bart saw her stiffen, silhouetted against the weak glow of several torches being carried through the fog toward the source of the shouting. He heard the bass voice again. This time he understood some of the words:

"By God, I tested it myself! Come and look if you don't believe me—"

He ran toward the door as Amanda disappeared in the thick fog. Moments later, shivering, he joined a growing crowd of people who surrounded a spent, bedraggled man. The man held up something that glowed yellow in the blaze of the torches.

Sam Brannan's thick black hair literally bounced on his forehead as he emphasized his words with shakes of his head:

"It's gold, I tell you—" He brandished the half-full quinine bottle. "Right out of the American River!"

Someone on the far side of the crowd went racing away to summon others:

"Brannan's back! He's got gold from the American—"

Within seconds, it seemed that a half dozen voices began to bawl the word through the fog:

"Gold!"

"*Gold!*"

Lights bobbed as people came running with more lanterns and torches. Bart McGill stared at the faces ringing the stocky Mormon displaying the quinine bottle. The faces were sleepy or stunned or stupidly amused—all except one.

Amanda didn't see Bart watching—nor see him shiver a second time. Her dark hair was lit by the fuming torch in Israel's hand. She was staring at the sparkling yellow dust in the bottle. Staring thoughtfully—speculatively—

She had the look of a predator again.

CHAPTER 2

The Fever

THE ARRIVAL OF THE *Manifest Destiny* was a welcome interruption of young Louis Kent's undemanding, if monotonous, routine.

Louis customarily rose before daylight. He laid and lit the fire in the cast iron stove in the kitchen. While his mother cooked for the men who took breakfast at Kent's, he waited tables, collected money and ran dirty dishes back to Israel, who washed them in two large wooden tubs. When the breakfast business slacked off about eight-thirty, everyone began preparing for the noon trade, which actually started closer to ten.

At that hour, Israel moved out front to take charge of the liquor kegs. A phlegmatic Mexican girl named Concepcion took over the serving chores while Louis was demoted to dishwasher for the afternoon and evening. He wasn't especially fond of any of the work, but dishwashing was particularly boring. He knew the work helped his ma keep the place going, though, so he accepted his responsibilities with no complaint.

But the nocturnal shouting in the square, followed by Amanda's departure with her revolver, altered his life more drastically than the return of Captain Bart ever had.

The following morning, he learned the cause of the commotion. Merchant Brannan had rushed back from the American River with a bottle of genuine gold dust.

Almost immediately, Louis noticed a change in his mother. Her mind seemed to be on something other than the operation of the tavern. He hoped she wasn't finally planning the return to Boston that she discussed from time to time. Even though life in Yerba Buena was far from ideal—he had no playmates, for instance—he wasn't sure he wanted to go.

Oh, she painted an elegant picture for him. She said the printing business her family had once owned would be his one day. She promised him fine clothes, and marvelous sights, and an existence that no longer included a broom, scalding water and garbage scraps. He supposed it might be nice to have some friends his own age. And it would be interesting to see the huge cities at the other end of the continent, though truthfully, he couldn't imagine any place as large and crowded as New York. He hardly believed half of Captain Bart's descriptions.

And could faraway Boston give him the fine, free feeling that swept over him when he and Israel roamed the hills of the peninsula, sniping at jackrabbits with the mulatto's antique squirrel gun? He doubted it.

His reservations sprang from something other than simple fear of the unknown, however. When his ma spoke of Boston, a peculiar, almost ugly look came into her eyes. She seemed like a stranger, somehow.

He finally figured out that his mother's absent air was directly connected to the furor over the gold, though Boston might be mixed up in it. He knew a lack of money was all that prevented their return to the east. And now there was a kind of money available right in the inland rivers.

He didn't like the whole business one bit. Practically overnight, his ma stopped smiling—and she always smiled a lot whenever Captain Bart visited. She grew a little curt with him, and with everyone—Israel commented on it. Louis wished Mr. Brannan hadn't raised such a fuss and set the whole village buzzing. He wanted his mother gay and easygoing again—

But things were never to be what they had been before.

Two days after Brannan's return, Captain Bart stormed into the public room about ten A.M. Louis, pushing the straw broom, glanced up and saw the captain wham his peaked cap onto one of the tables.

"Where's your mother?"

"In—in the kitchen, I think," Louis said, next to speechless.

The captain sank into a chair. "Tell her to fetch me a cup of coffee. Then you can uncork that rum keg and pour me—" He jumped up. "No, I'll get the damned rum myself. You get your mother."

Louis put down his broom and raced for the curtain separating the front from the kitchen. He discovered Amanda in the center of a cloud of steam. Perspiring, she was stirring a kettle of beans with a horn spoon.

"Captain Bart wants coffee, ma."

She laid the spoon aside. "I thought I heard someone come in—" She lifted the lid of the battered pot. "The coffee's gone. We had so many customers this morning, we ran through four gallons."

"Where are all those people coming from?"

"Up from the south—out of the hills—from the sky! There must be fifty more men in town than there were this time yesterday."

"Maybe that's why the captain's in a bad temper. I've never seen him so stormy—"

"Louis, for Christ's sake, the rum keg's empty!" McGill shouted.

"Ma, you better hurry—"

Amanda wiped her hands on her apron. "Find Israel. Have him bring another keg from the storage shed. We drained the one out in front last night."

She disappeared beyond the curtain. As the boy headed out the back way, he heard McGill thunder:

"I sent Louis for you *and* some coffee, goddamn it!"

"Don't you talk to me that way, Bart McGill! What in the world's become of that reserve you're so proud of—?"

Her voice faded as the boy darted into the sunlight. He hailed Israel, who was emptying a tub of dishwater behind the privy. A few minutes later, the two re-entered Kent's, the lanky mulatto balancing a small keg on his shoulder.

Israel removed the empty from its cradle behind the plank counter and set the new one in place. Captain Bart was tapping his cap against his knee while Amanda studied a piece of paper. In a moment, she shook her head:

"It's almost ludicrous, Bart."

"A man does ludicrous things when he smells easy money. Jesus, I need *something* to drink—" He jumped up again and stalked toward the counter.

"I'm sorry about the coffee—" Amanda began. McGill paid no attention. Israel reached for a tin cup. The captain snatched it from him:

"I'll pour my own, if you don't mind."

He put the cup back on the shelf and picked up another. He maneuvered the cup under the bung and got the keg open. But his hand was shaking. Rum splashed, soaking the cuff of his blue jacket. He swore under his breath, oblivious to Israel's venomous stare.

The boy realized Israel was mad because the captain refused to let him handle his drinking cup. Louis saw that his ma noticed, too. She tried to blunt Israel's anger with an explanation:

"Two of Captain McGill's crew jumped ship last night."

"My cook and my third mate," McGill said. "Took off up the Sacramento—" He downed a swallow of rum, then gestured with the cup. "The mate left a note for his father. If he thinks I'm going to see it delivered to New Hampshire, he's got shit between his ears."

Amanda glanced at her son. "Bart—"

"Sorry," the captain muttered in a perfunctory way. He drank again.

In a toneless voice, Israel asked, "What's the note say, Miz Kent?"

"Go on, you can read it to him," Bart said to Amanda.

"I can read it for myself," Israel said. "My momma taught me in the pine woods, even though it was against the law. Bark for a tablet. A white oak stick for a pen. An oak ball soaked in water to make ink—and fifty apiece across the back when the driver finally caught momma and me sneaking off together for a lesson. There isn't any nigger more dangerous than an educated nigger, is there, captain?"

"I don't need any goddamn sass from you!" McGill exclaimed.

"Maybe you gonna get some anyway. And something else besides," Israel said, stepping forward.

Bart McGill slammed his cup on the plank counter. Louis saw with alarm that the ex-slave's fingers were fisted. Amanda rushed between the two, a hand on each of them:

"I forbid that kind of behavior around here, and both of you know it! Israel, you go back outside—Bart, you settle down." She tugged his arm. "Come on—" She glanced over her shoulder. "Israel, I'm asking you to leave—"

"Asking or telling?"

"Asking. Please!"

His dark eyes resentful, the lanky man finally shrugged, turned and walked out. McGill was still seething. After the door banged, he exploded:

"That snotty son of a bitch acts like I'm one of those Mississippi cotton barons! The McGills never owned a slave. Not one!"

"But Israel sees all white men alike because a few of them treated him badly. Unfortunately you have the same kind of irrational feelings about colored people—"

Louis heard Amanda with only half an ear, having inched his way toward the table where the paper had fallen. He managed to glimpse a few of the scrawled lines:

—frenzy has seized my soul. Piles of gold rise up before me at every step. Thousands of slaves bow to my beck and call. Myriads of fair

damsels contend for my love. In short it is a violent attack of what I can only term gold fever—

"Now settle down and think about your men," Amanda urged. "Are you going after them?"

McGill started refilling his cup. "By every law on the book, I should. But I decided against it. I plan to load the hold as fast as possible and weigh anchor. I can't afford to lose anyone else—I've already got the first and second mates standing guard. They rounded up the whole crew this morning and sent 'em back to the ship. They have orders to shoot if anybody takes a header over the rail. I hope the cook and the mate dig to hell and find nothing but a ton of those pyrites!" He slumped at the table, staring moodily into the cup.

Amanda's face had acquired that intense look Louis disliked:

"How does a man collect gold, Bart? You've called in Peru and Chile, surely you've heard—"

His head jerked up. "Why the hell are you so interested? You planning to sail off to the American too?"

Louis knew his ma was hiding something when she answered:

"No, I'm just curious. Gold-hunting must take some equipment—"

"Not much more than a pick, a shovel and a pan for placer mining. You wash the dirt out of a pan of water and because the gold's heavier, it stays put. It's hard labor. Even harder if you're working solid rock instead of a river. The South Americans have mechanical contraptions—*arrastras*—for separating gold from quartz."

He finished his drink, jammed the paper in his pocket and his cap on his head:

"I'll see you for supper—provided I get enough hides loaded. I want to get out of this lunatic place—"

When he was gone, Amanda moved quickly to her son:

"Louis, I'd like you to do an errand."

Uneasily, he said, "What is it?"

"I need a new iron pan for the kitchen. Fetch twenty cents and run to the hardware. While you're there, see how many shovels are in stock."

"Ma!" he cried. "You haven't got the gold fever too?"

Amanda laughed in a harsh way. "No, I'm not that addled. But I've been noticing how many people have come to town just in the past twenty-four hours—"

She gave him a pat on the bottom:

"You hurry along and get that pan."

ii

"I need an iron pan, Mrs. Holster," Louis said to the stout woman tending the hardware counter. She pointed to an empty shelf:

"Sold the lot not two hours ago."

"Who bought 'em?"

"Sam Brannan. He bought every pick and shovel, too. Paid twice the going price for everything. He's loading them out in back right this minute."

Disappointed, Louis headed for the front door. Courtesy jogged him into acknowledging the owner's absence: "Is Mr. Holster feeling poorly this morning?"

"You mean because he's not here?" The woman sniffed. "He hired Andy Bellamy to pole him up the river to Sutter's fort. Mr. Kemble the editor went with him. You won't be reading the *Star* around here for a while—or seeing Mr. Holster selling nails! I swear, I don't know what's got into people, traipsing off to nowhere thinking they can wash a fortune out of a stream—"

But Louis knew. He'd read the third mate's note. The fever explained everything from the influx of strangers and his ma's odd behavior to the sudden turnover in hardware.

To verify that last, Louis walked around to the rear of the building. Bare-chested and sweating, Sam Brannan was lashing a canvas over the bed of a small wagon. Louis said hello, then shinnied up one wheel for a look into the bed:

"What are you shipping, Mr. Brannan? A whole lot of pick-axes, huh?"

And pans and shovels, he noted before Brannan shooed him off and covered the cargo completely:

"That's right, Louis. Going to peddle them in the store I lease up at New Helvetia. I figure just one pan will bring me anywhere from half an ounce to one ounce of dust, flake or lump gold."

"How much is that in money?"

"Oh, about eight to sixteen dollars American."

Louis whistled. "How can you ask so much for a twenty-cent pan?"

"Because men need 'em, my boy. And what men need, they'll pay for—

handsomely. Like I told Mrs. Holster—" He grinned. "Spades are trumps now. If there's as much gold in the American as there seems to be, it's going to be that way for a long time."

Louis ran back to the other side of Portsmouth Square and reported to his mother. She thanked him, but her eyes didn't seem to be focusing on the immediate surroundings. She acted much the same as she did whenever she discussed returning to Boston.

"You go help Israel," she said. "I want to look over my account book—"

She left him. He scuffed the toe of his boot against the kitchen floor. Maybe living by herself—without a man—had something to do with these peculiar spells. Maybe it wasn't entirely the fault of the gold—

Amanda always refused to answer Louis' questions about his father. She put him off with a promise that she'd clear up the mystery when she thought the time was appropriate. Did that mean he was still too young? He assumed so.

Every once in a while he keenly missed having a father. Now was one such time. A man might help his ma keep a level head. A man who was around more regularly than Captain Bart might help cure his ma of the fever—to which Louis was convinced Amanda had succumbed, whether she'd admit it or not.

iii

That night Amanda completely forgot her son's lessons. Captain Bart arrived for supper about seven, but the tavern was so busy, she had no chance to serve him until half past nine—which put him in another foul mood. Louis could tell from the sort of music the captain hammered on the piano before and after he ate—wild, noisy music, full of heavy chords in the bass.

Louis couldn't sleep because of the racket. He pushed the curtain aside and asked whether he could go out to the privy. Amanda didn't answer. She was seated at the walnut table, her pencil moving rapidly over a sheet of paper. She was doing sums, he noticed. Puffing on a cigar, Captain Bart stared out a window.

"Ma? Did you hear me?"

Without so much as glancing up, Amanda said, "What? Oh, yes, go ahead."

Frowning, the boy walked toward the back door.

He sat awhile on the rough, splintery board. But the request had been a pretense. Presently he pulled his flannel nightshirt down and stepped out of the reeking little building. The night air was chilly, damp-smelling. Fog drifted. Out in the bay, blurs of light showed the location of Captain Bart's clipper and a small steam packet that made coasting voyages as far north as Oregon.

A lantern was burning in Israel's shanty. Captain Bart started pounding the piano again. Louis didn't especially want to return to the noise. He walked across the damp ground and knocked on the shanty door.

He heard Israel draw in a sharp breath:

"Who's there?"

"Just me, Israel."

"Oh—Louis. Come on in."

The place was cramped but scrupulously neat. A table, a chair, a cot and a box for Israel's few clothes comprised the furnishings. The tall man lay on the cot, one of the new books—Mr. Poe's—propped on his bare stomach.

As Israel sat up, Louis caught a glimpse of the Negro's shoulderblade. Like most of Israel's back, the yellow skin there was a crosswork of hard brown scar tissue. Israel often said—with a certain air of pride—that he'd been whipped more than any other slave on the Mississippi plantation from which he'd run away when he was twenty.

"The captain's music keeping you awake?" the ex-slave asked.

"Yes, that and—" Louis stopped, feeling vaguely foolish.

"And what?" Israel prompted.

"And all the craziness in town."

Israel nodded. "Know what you mean. I heard almost a hundred more folks showed up today."

"I just don't understand the reason, Israel. Why is everybody so excited about gold? What can you do with it?"

The tall man reflected a moment. "The truth is, nothing much—except use it to replace a bad tooth. Gold's not like iron or copper. You can't turn it into needles or kettles or plows."

"Seems to me it's worthless, then."

"No, you can buy things with it. They say it lasts a mighty long time. And it's not found in very many places in the world. Guess that's why it's so valuable—there isn't much of it."

"I still don't see why people would bother to hunt for it."

"That's because you don't think like a grown-up, Louis. Some grown-ups put a lot of stock in being rich."

"Is owning gold like owning people of color? The more you own, the richer you are?"

Israel's gentle smile disappeared. "Yes and no."

"What do you mean? What's the difference?"

"For one thing, a human being can produce something—provided he's scared bad enough. A lump of gold doesn't think, either. Or shed a tear. Or have any feelings to speak of—"

He said it quietly enough. But his eyes were so somber, Louis shuddered.

"I wish they'd never found any gold at Sutter's!" he declared finally.

"Could make California mighty prosperous, Louis. Could be even more important than that—it just might start this part of the country filling up with people like nothing else could."

"But ma's thinking about it too much!"

"How do you know?"

"Well, she's either thinking about gold or Boston. She's hardly spoken to me since supper."

Israel tried to smile. "I expect she's caught a light case of the fever. It'll pass."

Louis shook his head. "I think she has a bad case. She wants money mighty strongly, Israel. You know how she's always talking about going east—"

"Yes, I do, and I have a peculiar feeling that going there wouldn't be good for any of us. I know I couldn't abide the crowds. Guess it's none of my affair, though. You better hurry back inside. You've been out here a while—"

"Bet they'll never notice how long I was gone. Goodnight, Israel."

"Goodnight, Louis."

He left the shanty and crossed the foggy yard. Amanda glanced up from her sums as he entered. She said nothing. McGill sat at the piano, staring into space.

Louis walked to the cubicle, drew the curtain and threw himself in bed, feeling miserable. He could have stayed out half the night—he could have jumped in the bay or run off to the American—and she probably wouldn't have said a word!

iv

The sandy-haired man walked into the public room about nine the following evening. Nine was the normal closing time. But it was already apparent to Louis that, with all the new arrivals, Kent's could have extended
its hours till eleven or twelve and done a brisk business in liquor.

He presumed the tavern would soon be open that long every night. But
right now his ma was occupied with those scraps of paper on which she'd
been ciphering last evening and most of the day. She was at it again, in
the back, leaving Israel and Louis to hang out the *Closed* sign, sweep and
clean the place, blow out the lanterns and lock up. The Mexican girl,
Concepcion, had already gone.

The public room was empty of customers but the front door was still
open when the sandy-haired young man entered. Israel pointed to the sign
lying on the table nearest the entrance:

"We're closed. I was just about to hang that up—"

"I'm powerful hungry," the young man said. "Couldn't I see a bill of
fare?"

"Isn't any," Israel informed him. "For supper we serve salt pork, beans,
biscuits and coffee—and what's left is cold."

The sandy-haired fellow glanced at the open front door. Nervously,
Louis thought. Busy with the broom, he still didn't miss the wood-handled
bowie sheathed over the young man's left hip. The stranger was in his
twenties, with a homely face. His flannel shirt and trousers looked brand
new. Hardly a trace of dust anywhere. The shirt bagged, much too large.

"Couldn't you rustle up a couple of biscuits?" the young man asked. "I
don't care if they're cold—I'm plumb near starved."

Israel shrugged and headed for the kitchen. Presently he returned, and
set a plate in front of the stranger. "You collect his money when he's
finished, Louis," he said as he left again.

The sandy-haired man wolfed two biscuits and was starting on a third
when he noticed the boy watching him:

"What are you staring at?"

"Nothing, sir."

"Tend to your work!"

The abruptness of it—and the flash of color in the young man's cheeks—
alarmed Louis somehow. Ill at ease, he glanced down at the pile of sweep-

ings. A horse clopped along the street. The sound stopped suddenly. The young man whipped his head around, staring through the door into the darkness. Perspiring all at once, he swabbed his forehead with the back of one hand—

He started when another man appeared in the doorway. A lean, severe-looking Army officer in his late twenties. The officer's dark blue fatigue jacket and light blue trousers were powdered with dust. So was his face, which hadn't been touched by a razor in several days. His reddish beard, wrinkled clothing and fatigued eyes were in marked contrast to the mint-bright barrel of the Army revolver in his right hand.

"Evening, Private Pepper," the officer said. His glance shifted to Louis, then back to the young man, who looked as scared as anyone Louis had ever seen.

"How—how'd you track me so fast?" the young man asked.

"Do you imagine it was hard with you on foot and me on horseback? You had a good head start, but I don't suppose I was more than half an hour behind you by the time you got here."

"I—I know I didn't leave any trail—"

"Where else would you be likely to come but the mouth of the Sacramento? I'd have shown up sooner but I had to stop and ask questions. I just came from the store where you bought those new clothes. You should have bought a hat to cover up your hair, too. I knew people would remember your hair if they didn't remember your face—" A humorless smile curled the officer's mouth. "I'm becoming very experienced at chasing deserters, Pepper. You're the third in as many days—though the other two didn't get as far." He gestured with the revolver. "Come on, we'd better start back to Monterey—"

The young man sighed and stood up. The officer turned his head toward Louis:

"Sorry to trouble you, young man—"

Suddenly the deserter leaped to the side and flung an arm around Louis' throat. The next thing Louis knew, the long blade of the bowie was pressed against his throat:

"I don't want to hurt this tadpole, Sherman. But I will if you don't let me go."

"My God, Pepper, what's become of your brains? You pull something like this, Colonel Mason'll order a whole troop after you!"

"Talking won't change my mind," Pepper said. Louis' heart hammered in his chest. He gulped air through his mouth, feeling the deserter tremble. Any sudden move might get him the bowie through the throat—

"Stand clear of the doorway," the deserter ordered. "And put your revolver on the counter."

The officer remained motionless. Louis winced as the point of the knife dug his throat:

"Sherman, you do what I say or I'll cut him!"

A board creaked. Someone was creeping from the kitchen. The officer's eyes jumped past the deserter, startled—

The younger man jerked his knife hand away from Louis' throat and whirled, cursing, just as Israel swung an iron skillet.

Louis felt something warm and wet trickling down his neck. The bowie had pierced the skin. Israel tried to slam Pepper's head with the skillet—and missed as the deserter sidestepped.

A look of panic crossed Pepper's face. Off balance, Israel staggered toward him. Pepper shot his knife hand straight toward the tall man's belly—

Louis jumped, both hands closing on Pepper's forearm. The deserter snarled, lifted a knee and rammed Louis hard between the legs. The boy crashed against the barrels supporting the counter, clutching his groin and fighting back tears. Somewhere in the back of the building, Amanda cried her son's name—

Israel regained his balance and darted forward again, both hands locked on the skillet's handle. Pepper jabbed with the knife. It raked the iron bottom, struck sparks, skittered off. While the officer shouted for everyone to clear away so he could fire, Israel clenched his teeth, dodged another bowie-jab and swung the skillet at Pepper's skull—

Still dazed, Louis heard the frightful crunch—then Pepper's moan. He saw the bowie tumble from the deserter's hand and impale itself, humming, in the floor. Pepper fell beside it, a stain darkening his trousers. Covering his face with his forearms, Pepper rolled his head from side to side, whimpering—

"What in damnation is going on—? *Louis!*" Her Colt's revolver clutched in one hand, Amanda rushed toward her son.

"My deepest apologies, ma'am," the officer said, leaning down to free the bowie and pitch it onto the counter. "Things got just a trifle out of hand. But the young man was very resourceful—"

"He's not hurt badly, Miz Kent," Israel said as Amanda knelt, laid the revolver aside and took Louis' head in her hands. Despite the horrible pain between his thighs, the boy seconded the lie:

"No, ma, not bad."

"Someone better explain why there are knives and pistols and *fighting* in this restaurant—and damn fast!" Amanda said.

The officer looked flustered. "I'm Lieutenant Sherman, ma'am. Lieutenant William T. Sherman, from the Monterey garrison. That fellow's a runaway—"

"A deserter?"

"That's right. We're beginning to lose them at the rate of one or two a day. I imagine it'll get worse. The struggle between right, and six dollars a month, and wrong, and a possible seventy-five or hundred per day, is a pretty severe one—"

Sheathing his revolver, Sherman dragged the cowed young man to his feet.

"You'll wish you'd never touched that boy, Pepper, because the attack will go on the bill of charges." He glanced at Israel. "Do you have any rope to tie him?"

Louis lost track of what happened next, busy fending his mother's hands and answering her anxious questions. Yes, the man had seized him and pricked his skin and kicked him but, no, he wasn't seriously injured; Israel had seen to that.

"Well, you're coming straight back to bed," Amanda declared. "I want you to take those clothes off so I can look at you. Israel, you lock up. Lieutenant—thank you for your courtesy, but I must see to my son—"

Louis limped a little; the pain in his genitals was still pretty fierce. The last he saw, Israel and Lieutenant William T. Sherman were lashing the prisoner's hands behind his back. The youthful offender looked abject, his moment of crazed courage long past. Nothing remained except a doleful contemplation of the trouble into which his yearning for gold had gotten him.

It drives people out of their heads, Louis thought as Amanda helped him through the dark kitchen. *It really does—*

He was stricken anew with fear for his mother.

v

The next evening, Louis lay rigid in his curtained alcove, wakened from sleep by the harsh sounds of an argument:

"If you stay here one day longer, you're a damned fool."

"Bart—"

"Those are the only words for it—damned fool. It doesn't take a biblical prophet to see what's going to happen to this place. More and more drifters—riffraff—piling into town—and you're willing to expose your son to that kind of existence?"

"Believe me, I've thought it over pretty hard—"

"And what have you decided?"

"I've decided to stay."

"*Jesus!* Louis might have been *killed* last night!"

"He wasn't, he came through just fine. He showed a good deal of pluck, Israel said."

"Pluck isn't worth shit if it lands you six feet under!"

"Bart, keep your voice down. Why are you so angry with me?"

"Because I want to see you *safe!* We're sailing in the morning—come with me. I'll take you and Louis—even that uppity nigger if you insist—straight to New York."

"I thought you didn't approve of my going east."

"I don't. But I like the idea of your staying here even less."

"Well, I won't go back without money—and there's money to be made in San Francisco. A lot of money. Now what about the loan from the primage you'll collect at the end of the voyage? You can easily spare a thousand dollars—"

"Am I supposed to do your damn shopping, too?"

"I told you I'd pay you fifteen percent on your money if you would. That's twice as much as you get from the cargo—"

"How the hell can I inform the Ball brothers I'm loading a thousand dollars' worth of pick axes and iron pans for a female acquaintance? It's against company policy. Besides, they'd think I was out of my head."

"They won't think anything because you won't tell them. And you'll figure out a way to hide the extra cargo, I know you will. Why are you so averse to profit all of a sudden? You heard what Sam Brannan's doing.

You know you'll make your fifteen percent half an hour after you bring in the shipment—"

Louis lay utterly still, disheartened by the severity of his mother's tone:

"I've never had a chance like this. Never in almost forty-five years. I'm in the right place at the right time. I can make something of myself! For Louis—"

"Pardon me if I say bullshit to that."

"*Please*, Bart—"

"You're not thinking of Louis, you're thinking of that damn printing company—and how good it'll feel to take it away from Stovall."

"I'm losing patience with—"

"Fuck your patience! It's true, isn't it?"

"May I remind you this is not a New York dock? Your language—"

"Is no worse than what you indulge in when you're mad. Isn't what I said the gospel truth? *Isn't it?*"

Silence. Louis dug his nails into his palms and shut his eyes, wishing they'd stop.

"I'm not going to argue my motives, Bart," Amanda said, very quietly. "I've never made any demands on you before—"

"*No demands?* What about all that damn investigation—?"

"You could have refused. I was very clear on that."

"You're saying I can't refuse this time?"

"Not if what we've been to each other means anything—"

Louis wanted to cover his ears when McGill shouted:

"So the account's finally due, is that it? The whorehouse madam finally presents her bill for services rendered?"

Silence again. Dreadful silence. What did McGill mean, calling his ma a whorehouse madam? Louis knew what a whorehouse was—Yerba Buena had one—but the connection with Amanda was a mystery as impenetrable as the riddle of his unknown father.

Finally, he heard his mother speak in a whisper:

"That's absolutely vile. You promised you'd never bring up what I told—"

"Christ, I know," he interrupted, sounding miserable all at once. "I'm sorry. I truly am. But I can't stand what's happening to you, Amanda! All of a sudden you're acting like the rest of the moon-heads in this town—thinking you can have El Dorado in your pocket before snow flies in the mountains!"

"You're wrong," she said in a hushed voice. "I'm not like the rest of them. I'm not going to the mines. I've talked to Sam Brannan. I know the odds. Men are staking out claims no bigger than twenty feet on a side. Only one in a thousand will strike anything big. There'll be many more losers than winners. I can make a killing off both."

"*A killing*—you see? It's even affected the way you talk!"

"Bart, I am almost forty-five years old! Sometimes I can't sleep at night, thinking of what that means. I'm going to die. I'm really going to die. But I swear, before it happens—"

"Now who's yelling?"

"I don't care! I won't throw this chance away! Will you buy the merchandise for me or won't you?"

Louis was perspiring. He drew a slow, careful breath, fearful of making the slightest sound.

"I shouldn't," McGill said. "I should cart you away from here bodily—"

She laughed then. "Impossible, and you know it."

Through the curtain, Louis heard him sigh:

"Yes, I do. So I guess I'll help you. But Jesus!—you sure do take advantage of a relationship."

"Bart, I'm handing you an opportunity to earn fifteen percent on your money! If you're smart, you'll risk two thousand, not just one."

"I already reached the same conclusion."

He didn't sound overjoyed about it. Amanda was, though:

"Oh, Bart, thank you, thank—*now* what are you angry about?"

"Losing my temper, goddamn it!" But at last his voice had a smile in it. So did hers:

"Not typical of you, Captain."

"Only two things ever get me wrought up. Trouble with the ship, and women."

"Any women?"

"No, sweet, just those I care about."

"How many does that include?"

"One. But she's damn near more than I can handle—"

Louis heard muffled sounds; the sort of sounds which usually accompanied that funny custom of men kissing women—the prelude, he surmised, to what animals indulged in without benefit of hugs or kisses.

In some ways, Louis Kent wasn't overly fond of Captain Bart McGill. The captain treated Israel shabbily. But lying in the dark and listening to the murmurous voices beyond the curtain, this was one time he believed Captain Bart was right.

Because of the gold, Yerba Buena was changing. It was no longer a pleasant place. Maybe not a safe place, either. He'd seen some of the rough characters drifting into town. He'd felt the young deserter's knife against his own throat. He feared there'd be more of the same in the months to come—

Right then, he altered his thinking about the east. It might be better if they left California—

But they weren't going to leave. His ma had won the argument—as usual.

The gold was changing her too, though. Changing her into a new person. Someone even more forbidding than the stranger who spoke of Boston. That he feared most of all.

CHAPTER 3

Christmas Among the Argonauts

"CONFOUND IT, AMANDA! Forty-eight thousand, then."

"Not for sale, Sam," Amanda said, handing cups of Thirty Rod to the miners elbowing Brannan at the plank bar. "Lord knows why you need another piece of property—"

"Not need, my dear. Want."

"Your wants should be well enough satisfied by the dozen plots you've already bought. Not to mention that shipload of carpet tacks which I hear you're selling to carpenters at four times cost."

"Don't act so damn virtuous. Wouldn't you do the same thing?"

"Of course. That's why pouring you a Christmas drink is the limit of my generosity for the evening."

"One side, one side!" Israel yelled, pushing past the crowd at the bar. He held two platters of grizzly meat with side helpings of oysters. Two more were precariously balanced on his forearms. He was jostled and shoved, but he managed to deposit the food on one of the tables. Out in the kitchen, Felix, the recently hired Frenchman, was screeching about the inhuman pace of his work.

Israel's expression made it evident he didn't enjoy the duties of a waiter. But the Mexican girl, Concepcion, had quit to work in a bordello for much higher wages. He scribbled a chit and flung it down. "Pay the boy when you leave." He pointed an elbow at the podium by one of the front windows.

Behind the podium, Louis Kent sat on a stool. On the podium stood a quill and inkstand, a balance and a set of weights. Immediately to Louis' left, six-foot Billy Beadle lounged at the front door, a big slung-shot conspicuously displayed at his belt.

Billy kept watch on the men packing away food and drink in Kent's public room. He was one of the lately arrived Sydney Ducks—Australians transported to San Francisco by a government desperate to rid itself of the criminals in its overcrowded jails. Bruises on Billy's face testified to his fondness for brawling. His size and obvious strength helped keep the customers from sneaking out without paying—or from wrecking the place. Virtually all the customers were miners down from the diggings on a holiday, or would-be miners heading for the camps. Hardly a one of them was sober.

The air in Kent's was heavy with tobacco smoke and the aromas of its eclectic menu. The miners demanded everything from the hottest Mexican chili to duck, plover, trout and antelope. The stink of sweat mingled with the more exotic odors; most of the miners were none too concerned about their grooming.

As he struggled back toward the bar, Israel reflected that white folks had always looked pretty similar to him. That certainly was true of the men who came down from the American and the Yuba and the Feather and all the other obscure forks and branches and intersecting creeks on which strikes were being made. The men the newspapers called the modern Argonauts tended to dress alike after a few weeks in the diggings: flop-brimmed hats which they never bothered to remove indoors; flannel shirts; dark pants; heavy boots. Their individuality was further blurred by an almost universal adoption of chest-length beards. In the whole noisy, smoky, smelly place, Amanda Kent was the only person who looked distinctive and halfway appealing this Christmas Eve in the year 1849. Of course she was also the only woman.

At the bar, Brannan was saying, "You should realize forty-eight thousand dollars is a damn generous offer!"

Israel stopped, leaned over the exasperated man's shoulder and said, "Don't you settle for less than a hundred thousand, Miz Kent."

"A hundred thousand!" Brannan exploded. "Your nigger's a bigger swindler than I am!"

Unexpectedly, that hurt more than Brannan's use of the word nigger. Israel had made his remark without thought. Now he realized he was unconsciously being caught up in the mood of avarice that pervaded Kent's these days.

He showed no anger at Brannan's term for a colored man. With the exception of Amanda and her son, every white person used it. He didn't like it, but shrugging off a word was a lot easier than avoiding outright trouble in San Francisco any more. He thought he'd escaped that sort of trouble when he fled Mississippi—

He walked warily wherever he went. Fear was his companion again, just as it had been on the plantation. There a man toted his cotton basket to the gin house fearing he'd be whipped if he brought in even a few ounces less than his quota. At the same time he feared that if he brought in too much, he'd be expected to deliver the same quantity the next night —and would be whipped if he failed. Israel had been free of that kind of constant fear for quite a few years—and now it was back.

"Sam," Amanda said, "do you want some Christmas whiskey or don't you? You're not going to buy Kent's this evening or anytime. I told you last month and again last week—the property isn't for sale."

She said it with a charming smile. Yet the smile somehow seemed less genuine than the ones Israel recalled from their first days together down south.

Amanda Kent was very alert, brisk and energetic for a woman of her age. In fact she drove her employees—and herself—twice as hard as a man might have. And she always looked handsome in the bargain—

That was true tonight. Her hair was neatly done—though turning grayer, Israel had observed of late. Her dress of yellow taffeta was the sole spot of bright color in the restaurant. She had chosen the dress from the pages of a *Godey's Lady's Book* McGill had brought her. The dress itself had come with the captain's most recent cargo. He was on the lucrative New York-California freight run now; three round trips since that regrettable night over a year ago when Brannan had returned with his quinine bottle full of gold.

At the moment McGill was eastbound around the Horn. Israel was glad. He and the captain would never be friends. And while McGill made an excellent business partner for Israel's employer—and was also her lover, he knew—he wasn't sure the arrangement was doing Amanda any good.

Oh, she'd prospered—mightily. She'd realized four hundred percent from her first investment in a quantity of pick-axes and pans. Then she'd switched to lumber, which couldn't be milled fast enough up in the hills to feed San Francisco's construction boom. Kent's itself had used part of the lumber, adding a second floor—a thirty-man dormitory. For bed and breakfast, Amanda charged twelve-fifty.

Like everything in town, the price was inflated. But the hopeful, pathetically over-equipped arrivals from the packets and clippers paid it without protest, staying a night or two before they bought passage on a river skiff, or set out on foot for the diggings. Right this minute, through the ceiling, Israel could hear one of the goldhunters bellowing an exuberant celebration of his future:

> *"Then blow, ye breezes, blow!*
> *"We're off to Californi-o—"*

Brannan refused the drink Amanda had offered. "All right, Sam," she said. "I don't want to be rude, but you're taking up space for a paying customer." Shaking his head, Israel started on for the kitchen.

> *"There's plenty of gold,*
> *"So I've been told,*
> *"On the banks of the Sacramento!"*

The singer slurred the last notes into a whoop and a couple of stomps that vibrated the flimsy planks overhead. The mulatto's frown deepened. A lunatic with no future except an imaginary one that fumed out of a liquor bottle was of no consequence to him. But Amanda was. And her behavior worried him. She no longer had time for anything but business. No time for the boy, for instance; Israel had taken over Louis' lessons.

"Israel? Hey, chum!"

The yellow-skinned Negro turned in response to the shout from Billy Beadle.

"There's a chap outside who'd like to talk to someone from the establishment."

Israel pointed to Amanda. But she was busy filling cups with Sixty Rod, the godawful whiskey that was twice as strong as its counterpart, Thirty Rod. A whiff of either was supposed to flatten the unwary at the indicated distance; even around corners.

"See what the man wants, Israel," Amanda called as Brannan jammed his silk hat on his head and left.

With a sigh, Israel started for the front. He overheard snatches of conversation. One miner bragged he'd soon see color on his claim now that he'd teamed up with some partners and installed a long tom. Another complained that it was a crime the way greasers could walk the streets as freely as whites. Greaser was a catchall term for the Mexicans, Peruvians and Chileans pouring into the town along with Americans, Frenchmen, Englishmen, Australians and even a few Germans.

The remark put another scowl on Israel's face. Then he reminded him-self that he was a free man. If he didn't like the situation in San Francisco, he could always leave—

Yet he stayed, and would stay, because he was loyal to his employer, as well as fond of her. Amanda Kent was one of the few human beings who had ever treated him as a person. To most of the others he'd known dur-ing his thirty-two years, he'd been either sub-human, or property, or both.

His wife Cissie, whom he'd married at age sixteen in Mississippi, had been property. He'd been forced to stand by and see her whipped when she was pregnant with their baby. She'd brought in too little cotton to the gin house, so the big boss ordered a pit dug in the ground; a pit in which her bulging belly fitted as she lay face down. He was whipped uncon-scious when he tried to interfere. When he woke much later, he learned that Cissie had lost the child. She was sold off within two months. No white person on the plantation had expressed one word of regret to Israel, and he'd never seen his wife again—

Amanda Kent wasn't that sort of white woman. She was kind; thought-ful of others. At least she had been until the damn craziness struck the whole town—

One more example of it was waiting outside. In the spillage of lamp-light through the smoke-grayed plate glass windows, Israel spied a young, yellow-haired miner on muleback. Reeling drunk. Armed with a pistol and a knife, too. A bad combination.

At the door, Billy Beadle said:

"Don't know what the bucko wants, but he's got fat saddle bags."

"So I see." As Israel stepped out to the plank walk, Louis gave him a wan smile. *Isn't exactly the kind of Christmas Eve a boy should have,* Is-rael thought.

He stopped at the edge of the walk Amanda had installed at her own expense. "Something we can do for you, mister?"

The stranger kept himself from falling by hanging onto the mule's neck. He squinted at Israel:

"You a white man?"

Israel gnawed his lower lip. Christmas, he thought sourly.

"That make a difference to you?"

"Well, if you ain't white, you sure as hell ain't the owner of this place."

"The owner sent me out to ask what you want."

"Simple. I want a good swallow of Sixty Rod—"

Puzzled, Israel shook his head. "Then bring in the bags. You've got dust in them, haven't you?"

"Damn right I have. I been up at Sullivan's Creek, pulling out a hundred, two hundred dollars in every pan."

Israel rolled his tongue in his cheek. If the young miner was telling the truth, he was one of the lucky ones; the few lucky ones. There were supposedly fifty thousand men in the diggings; men who had come by ship around Cape Horn, or over the Panama isthmus with a change of vessels, or the whole way across the continent in wagon trains from Westport and Saint Jo back in Missouri. Israel had heard that more than seven thousand wagons had rolled toward California during the good weather this year.

"You want a drink, come on in," Israel said, still not understanding the delay.

The miner leaned forward. He would have tumbled into the mud—it was San Francisco's rainy season now—if Billy Beadle hadn't dashed from the doorway and propped him up.

"For—" The miner belched. "—for a coon, you're a mighty dumb one. I don't want to walk in and drink. I want to *ride* in and drink."

Billy said with a grin, "I don't think your mule would fit through the door with those bags hanging on him."

"I don't want to ride through the door," the young man replied. "I want to ride through *that*."

He jabbed a finger at one of the two glass windows.

Billy looked dumbfounded. Israel started back inside; the windows were recent additions, and costly:

"You better find someplace to sleep, mister. You're already dreaming."

"No goddamn coon's gonna tell me—" the miner began, reaching for his pistol.

"None of that, chum," Billy exclaimed, seizing the miner's wrist just as another voice interrupted:

"What on earth's taking you so long out here?"

Amanda stood in the doorway. The miner saw Billy's other hand lift the slung-shot from his belt, and all at once lost his urge to fight.

Grinning again, Billy took the heat out of the situation: "Why, nothing much, Mrs. Kent. This laddy just asked to ride through the window and have a drink."

"*Ride through—?*"

Amanda stopped, studying the miner. Thunderstruck, Israel watched her smile:

"That's a pretty peculiar request. Why do you want to ride through a window, young man?"

"Ain't ever done it before. Ain't ever seen a window that big, either."

"Don't you have glass windows where you come from?"

"I come from a farm in Illinois and, no, we don't, 'cause my poppa's poor."

"But that doesn't really explain—"

"Listen, are you the owner?"

"That's right."

"Well, we're making progress, anyway. I wasn't gettin' anywhere with the coon." He swept off his filthy hat. "They call me Flaxtop up in the diggings, ma'am—"

"I don't give a damn what they call you—you *get!*" Israel said, reaching for the mule's bit.

"Calm down, Israel!" Amanda snapped. "If you can't keep your temper, go inside."

Astonishment sapped Israel's anger almost instantly. He rubbed his eyes. Lord, he was tired of this upside-down existence, where you never knew what to expect next. He was tired of working seven days a week. He was tired of the noise in town—even on Christmas Eve, shouting and laughter and piano music poured from the plank and canvas and brick hotels and gambling dens and brothels that spread out from Portsmouth Square, lighting the peninsula with hundreds of glowing lanterns. The night was so bright, he could even see the masts of the abandoned ships in the bay—seventy or eighty of them, left to rot at the end of one-way trips from Panama or New York. Their crews had rushed to the diggings right along with their passengers—

It was mass insanity! And Amanda had fallen victim to it. Why, she'd even considered hiring four Chilean whores for the second floor until he talked her out of it, convincing her it wouldn't be suitable with young Louis on the premises.

As further proof of the way her wits had deserted her, Amanda was actually treating the miner's request seriously:

"You really want to ride through one of my windows?"

"I sure do. I struck paydirt and I want to celebrate. I got the dust to pay for the privilege—" He reached back to slap a saddle-bag. "Plenty of it."

Israel headed inside. No doubt she was just being courteous to the young fool—

He pulled up short at the sight of her face. Lord God in heaven. She was *considering* it!

With a cool smile, she said, "Your fun won't come cheap, Flaxtop."

"I guessed not, ma'am. How much?"

She pondered. "Seven hundred and fifty dollars for the window—there's no plate glass manufactured in the United States, you know. It's imported from Europe. Add another two hundred and fifty for general damage. The Sixty Rod will be on the house."

Even Billy Beadle gaped. Israel performed some quick calculations. Allowing for freight charges, Amanda could order a new window from the east coast for maybe five hundred; repair some broken furniture for a hundred or a hundred and fifty. Her terms were outrageous; but she'd presented them with an absolutely straight face. His stomach started to hurt.

"You're sayin' a thousand—?"

"One thousand," she repeated. "If that's too steep for you—why, Merry Christmas."

She pivoted away from the miner. Israel marveled at the way she bluffed. It worked:

"Hang on! I—I guess I can afford it. You got yourself an arrangement, ma'am."

Amanda acted unruffled, as if what was happening was an everyday occurrence:

"Fine. We'll give our guests a little holiday entertainment with their suppers. Billy, you carry those bags inside. Weigh out the equivalent of a thousand dollars. Flaxtop, you wait right here until I move a few tables."

The miner slapped his mule's neck and uttered a long, piercing yell. Louis appeared, drawn by the noise. Amanda spoke to Israel:

"We're out of Thirty Rod. Walk over to Dennison's Exchange and see whether they'll let me have twenty gallons."

"Sure they will," Israel said. "Your credit's good all over town."

Amanda swept back inside. Billy Beadle chuckled, started to unstrap the saddle bags. The mulatto glanced at Louis:

"You walk along with me to the Exchange."

The boy's face fell. "I want to see him bust the window."

"I said you come along! It isn't fit for a youngster to watch grown men act like fools—" Muttering gleefully to himself, the miner paid no attention. "You watch enough of 'em, you'll start behaving the same way. Come on, now—I'll need help rolling the cask through the mud."

He said it harshly, still upset by the way Amanda had taken advantage of the tipsy miner. He yearned for the old days: Yerba Buena quiet and mellow in the sun; a relaxed pace at the tavern; a few slow-moving residents hoeing potatoes in the square—

What the devil had come over her? *What was driving her?* He was afraid he knew the answer.

"Clear away, boys, clear away!" he heard her shouting inside. "Move your legs, mister, we've got a customer coming in by a different route. Billy? Hurry up with those bags!"

"Come *on*," Israel said, with such a savage gesture that Louis shied back. After a moment's hesitation, the boy stepped down from the plank sidewalk. Instantly, the mud hid the soles of his boots.

"You're gonna miss a real fine show, mister coon," the miner said. Israel grabbed Louis' hand and didn't look back.

I mustn't let it twist me up, he thought. *I've listened to every dirty slur ever invented for a black man. I've watched the Hounds beat up Frenchmen and rip down the tents of the Chileanos on Alta Loma, and I haven't let any of it bother me too much because I'm a free man, I can walk away any time I want.*

Maybe I will. She's not the same woman any more.

ii

Israel tugged the boy's hand, pulling him to the left:
"Watch your step!"

Louis had nearly stumbled into the top of a cast iron stove. The rest of the stove had sunk into the mud produced by the December rains.

Neither man nor boy was much surprised by the sight of the stove top. Discovering that charges for shipping heavy freight to the diggings were astronomical, the gold-hunters who came by ship discarded all sorts of personal goods in the public thoroughfares. Speculators who attended the beach auctions and bid on the cargos of the incoming vessels sometimes had to take every item in a shipment when they wanted only part of the shipment. The unwanted merchandise was abandoned in the same places the would-be miners left their heavier belongings. Rotting sacks of flour, expensive commodes, unopened cartons of dress shirts—you could find damn near the whole residue of civilization buried in the winter slime of San Francisco's streets.

One of the stove lids lay in the mud just beyond the sunken obstacle. Angrily, Israel flipped the lid over with his toe:

"I bet when Jason and his Argonauts went hunting the golden fleece, they never left a trail of garbage!"

As the boy and the Negro crossed the square, the noise remained constant. Men and women laughed in the bars. A brass band blared *Deck the Halls* from the lobby of the Parker House. Barkers shouted from the entrances of the gambling tents—"*Come on in, gentlemen, come on in and try to find the little joker! Here's the place to get your money back!*"

They circled around a bearded, wild-eyed fellow in parson's weeds. Clutching a Bible under one arm and exuding a smell of gin, the man bellowed at them:

"Divine services tomorrow morning! Eight sharp in the tabernacle just a few steps up Kearny. Divine services unless there's news of a strike tonight!"

"Thimbleriggers—cheap women—rum-sots—*trash!*" Israel declared, his yellow face changing as he and Louis passed from shadow into the blaze of lanterns. Everywhere, men walked or ran or staggered—going to perdition!

He guided Louis around a signboard on a pole at the edge of a particularly sinister-looking mudhole. The sign bore the words:

THIS WAY IMPASSABLE!

Below, in a rougher hand, someone had written:

not even jackassable

"You surely don't like San Francisco any more, do you, Israel?" the boy said at last.

"No, sir, I don't. They say we have twenty-five thousand people, and that's twenty-four thousand five hundred too many. You no sooner blink an eye than somebody reports one more camp opened up, with fool names that are an insult to the English tongue. Gouge Eye—Whiskeytown—Mad Mule Gulch—Murderers' Bar—people've lost their minds even when it comes to christening towns! Old Polk should have kept his mouth shut."

"What's the president got to do with it?"

"Why, Louis, if President Polk hadn't stood up when Congress opened its session a year ago—"

As he spoke, his eyes were never still. He saw half a dozen rats prowling over a heap of garbage. Heard a passing miner make reference to his color. A Peruvian in rags loitered in the shadows, watching him and stroking the edge of a knife across his thumb. Every time he ventured out these days, it felt like Mississippi again. He needed to arm himself.

"—if he hadn't blabbed about the gold Colonel Mason sent to the Philadelphia Mint in a tea caddy, it might have been a lot longer—years, maybe —before the country got excited about California. Polk should have just gone out of office quietly and let Taylor take over—but no, he had to pop the cat from the bag. They say he always wanted land. The whole continent under one flag. I don't object to that, but I do object to him giving the fever to every rascal, fool and failure on three continents—"

Without a smile, Louis said, "I told you 'most a year ago that ma had a bad case. You didn't believe me."

"I know. Proves how wrong a man can be."

"Know something?"

"What?"

"I don't like it either. I mean, here it is Christmas and we don't even have a holiday pine with some candles on it. And nobody's got time to make presents—we're too busy fixing to serve dinner all day tomorrow—" The boy sighed. "I try not to think about it too much. Most of the time that's easy. I'm so frizzled out from working, there's nothing on my mind but sleep."

"We keep on this way," Israel said, "we're liable to wind up the richest folks in the graveyard."

"Not ma. She's tough."

"Tougher all the time."

"She wants to go to Boston something awful, I guess."

Israel didn't answer. The boy only knew the surface reason Amanda worked so hard. The mulatto, on the other hand, had heard her speak at length about Hamilton Stovall—not only about how he'd gained control of Kent and Son, but how he'd ruined her cousin's life. He believed Amanda had kept that latter part of the family's history from her son.

The man and the boy reached the large canvas tent whose signboard read *Dennison's Exchange.* Like the other establishments around Portsmouth Square, it poured noise into the Christmas Eve darkness—and, from outside, it shone like one immense lantern. Suddenly men yelled in the distance; glass shattered.

Louis spun. "Oh my Lord, she really let him do it!"

Israel refused to look. His face was as bleak as his thoughts:

It's that Stovall driving her. Stovall and those books McGill brings in. She doesn't see what it's doing to her, either—and what it could do to her boy.

To speak to Amanda on that subject would have been overstepping. Israel could argue with her about the advisability of women on the second floor; even though that too concerned Louis, that was business. But he didn't dare intrude in more personal areas. After all, she was his employer—

A white woman.

Once, he'd practically been able to forget about that. But gold had drawn men to California. Men who bore hatreds. The source—the way they'd been taught, or the lack of any teaching at all—didn't matter. Either way, they were dangerous. He'd begun to feel the fear again—

He heard the tipsy young miner, Flaxtop, saying *coon.* The memories tumbled one upon another. The crack of the whip at the gin house. The feel of it flaying his back while he clenched his teeth and struggled to keep from crying out. Cissie's screams as she lay with her belly in the hole, taking her punishment—

Confused and angrier than ever, he jerked Louis through the entrance to the Exchange. His yellow face looked thunderous in the hazy lantern-light.

He knew he was in a bad temper. Told himself so—and that he ought to simmer down. He made an effort—

Then he saw who was on duty behind the bar.

iii

The preceding year, San Francisco had been plagued by ruffianism unusual even for a boisterous frontier town. The source of the trouble was a group of men once called the First New York Volunteers—the last word hardly being appropriate since most of them had been forced to join up or languish in eastern jails.

The Volunteers had been shipped to California to reinforce Kearny during the Mexican trouble. When they arrived, the fighting was over. The unit had disbanded, and some of its members had drifted north a few months after the discovery of gold.

In San Francisco, the men boastfully called themselves the Hounds—because they roamed the streets in packs, harassing women and foreigners with obscene remarks and their favorite weapons: slung-shots and metal knuckles.

The men professed an affiliation with a splinter political party in the east, the American party, which had sprung from an earlier group calling itself the Native American Association. The title capsuled the group's purpose, and that of the party which emerged from it—to keep America the exclusive preserve of those white Protestants who had been born there. Members of the party had secret rituals, passwords and handshakes—never revealed when they were questioned: "I know nothing." An eastern editor —Mr. Greeley, Israel believed it was—had contemptuously christened the party Know-Nothing.

For months, the local counterparts of the Know-Nothings had occupied a tent headquarters at Commercial and Kearny. The tent, its nickname *Tammany Hall* also borrowed from the east, was gone now; torn down as the result of a public outcry when the Hounds invaded Little Chile up on the hill called Alta Loma the preceding July. The Chilean immigrants had been beaten, their women raped, their hovels demolished—and San Francisco had finally risen in outrage. Amanda had contributed fifty dollars to help organize a company of volunteer peace officers who razed Tammany Hall and drove the Hounds out of town.

Officially, they were gone. But some had come back. One, a bald, blue-chinned man named Felker, had found employment as a bartender at the Exchange.

Israel approached Felker warily. He was sure the man would recognize him. Amanda had once used her Colt revolver to back down three Hounds who tried to come into Kent's for a meal; she wouldn't allow the hooligans on the premises. But an offense to one Hound was an offense to all.

Felker was busy telling a story to a trio of miners leaning on the bar:

"—and so the nun says to the priest, let's fuck now, father, and you can hear my confession later."

Scurrilous jokes against Catholics were a staple of the Know-Nothings. Two of the bearded miners laughed. The third, dressed much like the others but standing a little apart, fiddled with his whiskey cup. The man's blue eyes registered his dislike of the story.

Israel stepped between Felker's cronies and the loner. Behind him, Louis watched the conclusion of a three-card monte game. The pale-skinned dealer raked in a two-thousand-dollar bet from his glum victim, whose loss the watchers cheered and applauded.

Felker kept talking with the two miners. The lantern hanging from the canvas directly above him cast an oily light on his bald head. The thin, weathered loner scratched his almost pure white beard and studied Israel, then Felker, who continued to ignore the Negro. Israel in turn scrutinized the miner from the corner of his eye. The man's long hair showed a few streaks of yellow among the gray. He was a decent-looking sort. And Israel guessed he might need help handling Felker.

He was correct. The bald man wouldn't even look at him for the better part of two minutes. Finally, struggling to contain the anger that had been building within him during the evening, Israel slapped a palm on the bar. "Felker."

A slow, almost smug smile tugged up the corners of the bartender's mouth. Behind Felker, Israel saw a knotted rope hanging from a nail in one of the tent poles. When patrons grew too rowdy, men who tended bar used such a rope as a substitute for a ship's cat.

"Merry Christmas," Felker said in a sarcastic way. Israel started to dig in his pocket, then remembered he was supposed to put the order on credit. Felker mis-interpreted the move, reaching across the bar to fasten a hand on the mulatto's forearm:

"I know the rules around town say a nigger is entitled to one drink in any public place. But the rules are suspended when I'm tending the store."

Israel's hand clenched. He jerked free of Felker's grip.

"I came to buy twenty gallons of Thirty Rod for Kent's. We're out."

"So am I."

His stomach starting to hurt again, Israel pointed to a keg on a cradle. "Doesn't appear that way."

"Empty," the balding man shrugged. "You try somewhere else. Niggers give this place a bad odor. 'Course, I have a pretty keen nose. I can smell coon twice as sharp as any hunting dog."

That brought a snicker from one of the two miners on Israel's right. He knew he should leave. Perhaps on a different evening, he would have. But everything that had happened tonight had made him testy.

"All right," he said. "But first I'll have a whiskey."

"No," Felker said. "No, you won't."

"Israel, I think we'd better go along," Louis said.

His brow hot, Israel drew a coin from his pocket. Felker seemed to be bouncing up and down, almost expectantly.

"Pour me one, Felker."

"I said no."

"Pour me one or I'll pour it myself."

Dennison's Exchange grew still. The racket from the street only heightened the silence as the mulatto and the white man stared at one another.

iv

For a moment, Israel didn't believe what he was seeing. Felker shrugged again, as if giving up.

The two miners had stepped back just a little in case of a confrontation. The lone miner, hunched over his drink as he had been ever since Israel and the boy walked in, watched the bartender. Felker wiped his hands on his apron, started to turn and reach for a cup—

Israel's astonishment slowed his reflexes. He wasn't prepared when Felker grabbed the rope from the tent pole, whirled and lashed at Israel's face.

The rope's knotted end nicked Israel's left eye, made him yell in surprise. Blinded and enraged, he shot his hands out to fasten on Felker's neck.

Israel gripped hard, his height helping him lean halfway across the bar. Felker squealed, hit at him with the rope. Israel heard Louis pleading with him to let go, then caught the sound of men rushing forward. But the flick of the rope on his eyeball had shattered his control. He choked Felker harder—

The two miners reached for him. The loner stepped away from the bar. Israel heard the cock of a pistol, then the miner's voice:

"You two stay out. And that goes for everyone else. Let them settle it."

Slobbering curses, Felker tried one more slash with the rope, bringing it up and over his shoulder. The end snapped against the hanging lantern, knocked it off its hook, sailed it behind the kegs where it broke and spilled oil that ignited a second later.

"Jesus Christ, a fire!" one of the monte dealers shouted as flame spurted up the canvas wall.

The canvas caught almost instantaneously, the whole rear wall of the Exchange turning to flame. Israel held Felker's throat, taking satisfaction from the way the man's eyes were starting to water. He applied more pressure, the heat from the canvas popping sweat onto his yellow face—

He wasn't choking Felker alone. He was choking the drivers who had beaten his mother so that she died before her time. He was choking the owner who had sold Cissie. He was even choking old President Polk, who had turned a sleepy little village into a stink-hole—

Felker's eyes bulged. Time held still for Israel, the hate in him almost intoxicating. The fire reached the tent's side walls and ceiling. A pole behind the bar became a column of flame, gave way—

Louis shouted, "Israel—!" as the ceiling started to buckle.

Israel let go, shoved Felker backward against the kegs. The bald man fell, flailing. The lone miner seized Israel by the shoulders, pulling him away:

"The ceiling's coming down—!"

The patrons had started a wild trample for the street. Somewhere a bell began to clang. "Go on, Louis!" he yelled, shoving the boy out of danger as the miner leaped away too. Israel stumbled against a rickety table that collapsed beneath him, tumbling him to the dirt floor—

A third of the canvas ceiling ripped and fell, enveloping Felker. He shrieked and disappeared in roaring flames. Lying on his belly, Israel screamed too when scorching canvas struck the backs of his outstretched legs—

"Burned that white man to death!"

"—own damn fault—"

"Get moving, get moving!"

The distant bell grew louder. Sobbing, Israel dug in his elbows, dragged himself out from under the canvas. His trousers smoldered, caught fire. He rolled over, thrashing the backs of his legs in the dirt. Overhead, another section of canvas tore loose—

"Boy, help me!"

That was the lone miner. Israel felt hands at his collar; vainly tried to focus his eyes. All he saw were leaping tatters of flame and, deep in the center, a charred, crawling thing that bleated like an animal as it died, Felker—

Hands hauled him along. His head banged against the ground. The ceiling glowed red-orange. He wondered whether he was going to hell for murder—

The flames disappeared in total darkness.

V

When Israel regained consciousness, he was lying in the mud of Portsmouth Square. He was dimly aware of people milling against a backdrop of glaring light. He heard loud crashes as the fire swallowed frame and canvas structures near the Exchange.

Bit by bit, his awareness returned—bringing pain that consumed him from his thighs downward. He writhed, groaning.

"Lift his legs, lift his legs! Where's that damn lard they sent for—?"

He thought that voice belonged to the miner who had pulled him out of the blazing tent. He felt hands on his brow, then a cheek pressed to his forehead:

"You'll be all right, Israel. We'll get you fixed up—"

The words grew incoherent as Louis broke down and cried.

"Stand back! Here come the pumpers!"

If he hadn't been in such agony, Israel might have laughed. San Francisco's fire equipment was worthy of nothing but laughter, and no one had taken steps to remedy the situation, even though people were extremely conscious of the hazard posed by the town's shoddy buildings. He thought he saw spokes blurring as men dragged one of the hand-driven pumpers toward the conflagration. Was it the antique from Hawaii, or the old wreck from the east that President Van Buren had once used to water his garden? *Odd,* Israel thought, *odd how your mind works when you're hurt bad—*

"I think we got him out soon enough," the lone miner said, sounding far away. "I hope so. Let's turn him—"

Israel screamed when men rolled him over, tore away the remains of his trousers and began to smear lard on his calves.

"Ma, ma—this way!"

That was Louis. With a great effort, Israel lifted his chin from the dirt. Sure enough, elbowing and pushing, there was Amanda—

Oh God, he thought, *she's getting mud all over that pretty yellow dress.*

Unconcerned, she hiked up her skirt and dropped to her knees beside him. Through his pain, he felt an almost overpowering happiness. She didn't care about her fancy dress. She cared about him. Maybe he'd been too hard on her—

He started to cry, just like Louis. Even the agony of hands patting lard on his legs didn't bother him now—

Somewhere out of his field of vision, the lone miner asked, "Ma'am, does this man belong to you?"

"No—that is—he works for me—dear God, Israel, what happened?" She stroked the side of his face. He felt the roughness of that old, worn bracelet of rope. "Louis—someone—*tell me what happened!*"

A half dozen voices babbled at once. To Israel, the men around him were no more than fire-etched silhouettes. But Amanda's face was visible. He saw her flame-lit eyes widen when the miner grabbed her arm.

"What's the matter with you, are you crazy? Let go of—"

"Where'd you get this piece of rope, woman?"

"Damn you, let go!" She started to punch the miner.

"Where did you get it? What's your name?"

Curious, Israel thought, his pain so intense that it actually numbed and soothed him and sent him drifting back toward sleep. Most curious, the way Amanda was staring into the dark where the miner must have been standing. Her face had the strangest expression—

"My name's Amanda Kent. I don't see why you—"

"Amanda—"

Very strange, how that miner sounded as if he were about to weep too: "I'm Jared. *Jared Kent—*"

Israel heard no more.

CHAPTER 4

To See the Elephant

JARED ADAM KENT couldn't remember when he'd celebrated a more remarkable and joyous Christmas day.

He didn't feel the least bit tired. His occasionally crippling rheumatism —a legacy from the years of trapping with Weatherby in the cold streams of the beaver country—hardly bothered him at all.

He should have been exhausted. He was already weary when he reached San Francisco after the long ride from the mining camp called Hopeful located all the way up on the east branch of the north fork of the Feather River. He hadn't slept a single minute since glancing up outside the burning saloon and seeing a woman whose face stirred a memory; a woman whose wrist, circled by a worn bit of rope, brought a miracle he'd never dreamed he'd witness.

In the first hour after Amanda's mulatto had been dragged from the flames, Jared barely said half a dozen coherent words to his cousin. They'd wept and hugged each other for a couple of minutes, but things were too frantic for much more than that.

Amanda saw to Israel's removal to his shanty behind the restaurant she owned. Then she summoned a doctor. The sleepy physician dressed and bandaged the Negro's burned legs. He dosed the groaning man with brandy, assuring Amanda that although Israel would suffer pain for a few weeks, as well as the unpleasantness of skin sloughing away, in his professional opinion Israel would eventually be good as new.

With that problem attended to, Jared and his cousin spent three quarters of an hour surveying the damage done by the fire. It had leveled several blocks surrounding the Exchange before being brought under control. Booming gambling houses such as the Verandah and McCabe's El Dorado had disappeared into smoldering ashes. Had the wind been blowing in a different direction, Kent's would very likely have burned too.

Amanda introduced Jared to a man named Sam Brannan who apparently owned a good deal of real estate in the town. Brannan predicted San Francisco could expect many more fires in view of the building boom and the flimsy nature of most of the construction. He suggested that volunteer fire companies be organized, and better pumping equipment secured. Amanda pledged financial support of such a program. But Jared somehow had the feeling her heart wasn't in the promise.

Finally, toward midnight, they returned to her place, to begin building a bridge of words across the years since 1814. They talked all through the night.

Now it was Christmas morning. Jared was relaxing in a chair by a back room window, with Amanda's handsome, swarthy young son curled up at his feet.

Jared wiggled his nose. "Smells mighty good, Amanda. My, you've come a far piece in the world. I've never met anybody else who had a French cook."

Because of all the excitement, Amanda hadn't bothered to change her mud-spotted yellow gown. She was seated on the piano bench, hands in her lap, and he had to admit she'd amply fulfilled the promise of beauty she'd shown as a child. She was slender but full-bosomed. Her dark eyes were as lively as ever. And the gray in her hair seemed to enhance her beauty, not detract from it.

Jared's mind could hardly hold all that she'd told him in the breathless bursts of conversation before dawn:

Her life with the Teton Sioux. Her marriage to a Spanish trapper. Her difficult experience in Texas. The Mexican officer, Cordoba—and Louis' birth. Then her migration to California, and now sudden prosperity brought on by the discovery of gold—

Still, all night long, he'd sensed she was holding something back. At those times, her eyes had a hard glint difficult to reconcile with the sight of the happy, self-assured woman seated opposite him, or the memory of the young girl he'd last seen at Stone's River in Tennessee—

"Felix is a jewel," she said. "He came from Paris. He keeps talking about going to the gold fields, but I make it worth his while to stay here. He's cooking something special for dinner. Eggs and oysters. It's quite delicious, the way he spices it. Oh, Jared—" Laughing, she hugged her knees. "This still seems like a dream."

"If it is, I hope we don't wake up before we eat. I'm damn near starved to death."

"We'll sit down the minute Billy finishes nailing boards across the broken window."

From Jared's feet, Louis asked, "Could we sing a Christmas carol first, ma?"

"Why, yes. Though with Bart gone, we've no one to play."

"Who's this Bart fellow?" Jared asked.

Louis glanced questioningly at his mother. From the front of the building, the steady beat of Billy Beadle's hammer thudded. At six in the morning, Amanda had taken what Louis said was a most unusual step. She'd ordered the burly Australian to hang out a sign announcing that Kent's would be closed the entire day.

Still smiling, Amanda told her cousin, "His full name's Barton McGill. He works for a New York ship line. Captains one of their clippers. I guess you could call him my gentleman friend—"

"He's from Charleston," Louis put in. "We don't get to see him often."

"Well—" Jared stretched luxuriously, then leaned back in the chair. The mellow December sun highlighted the few strands of yellow still visible in his white hair. "—I'd be happy to have him here to share this wonderful day. I wish my son were here too."

"A Methodist minister." Amanda shook her head. "I can hardly believe it."

Jared's expression was tinged with sadness for a moment. "I couldn't either when he first broached the idea after his conversations with Reverend Lee. Then I got to thinking. There's a peculiar streak on my side of the family. Rebellious. The Fletcher blood, your mother used to call it. I expect Jephtha inherited it from me. So it was probably natural for him to strike off in some unexpected direction."

"Where is your son, sir?" Louis had missed all of the night's conversation.

"In Lexington, a little place in the Shenandoah valley in Virginia. He and his wife Fan have had four children so far. Three have survived. All boys." He ticked them on his fingers. "Gideon was born in forty-three, Matthew a year later. Annabelle lived only two weeks in forty-five. Jeremiah came along fourteen months after that—"

"Is Jephtha happy in Virginia?" Amanda asked.

Jared frowned. "If I read his letters correctly, no. His last one came on a packet just before I left Oregon. Gloomier than ever. It's the chattel slav-

ery question that upsets him. He's loyal to his wife and her people—
they're southerners. And when the Methodist Episcopal Church split over
slavery five years ago, he stayed with the southern faction. But what he
sees of the system torments his conscience. Of late, unbearably."

"Well, we're a long way from those problems out here," Amanda said.
"Though one of these days, I expect I'll be right in the middle of them."
She gazed at her cousin. "Eventually I'm going back east."

Jared noticed the way young Louis began to fool with the loose sole of
one of his boots. The boy was frowning. Amanda went on:

"I want to see our old home. That's one of the reasons I'm working so
hard to make money."

Jared flexed his fingers; examined his swollen knucklejoints. The hard
glint had returned to her eyes. It bothered him.

"You didn't mention that last night—" he began.

She shrugged, gazing past him to the sunlit window. "It's something I
decided a couple of years ago—" Her stern look softened. "We can discuss
it after dinner."

Louis tried to re-direct the conversation to a more agreeable topic:

"Was your wife really an Indian, cousin Jared?"

"A Shoshoni," he nodded. "A fine woman. She was called Grass
Singing."

"That's a pretty name."

"I wish I'd been able to make a pretty life for her—"

He cut off the thought, much as he'd cut off an earlier frustration by
leaving the failing farm in the Willamette Valley in the late summer of
'48.

"—but all in all—" He spoke for his cousin's benefit now. "—I have very
few regrets. I sired a son to keep the Kent name alive—without ever imag-
ining you'd be doing the same, Amanda. For a long time, I made enough
money to live just the way I wanted. I loved the fur trade until my partner, Elijah Weatherby, died. His passing took some of the joy out of it—
maybe because it made me realize I was getting old. Then business
dropped off. I thought raising wheat in Oregon might be a good thing to
try. I was wrong there. Like my father, I wasn't cut out to be a farmer—"

A sadness touched him. His imagination showed him dim pictures of
the house on Beacon Street from which he'd fled after setting fire to the
printing house and shooting the man who had helped Hamilton Stovall
steal Kent's. He could look back on all of that without anger. Once, he'd
harbored hopes of revenge. But they had been burned out of him by dis-

tance, and time, and his gradual acceptance of the life he'd made for himself in a land he found beautiful—

Aware of Louis and Amanda watching him, he resumed, "I sold the farm when Oregon got the news of the gold. I always did like seeing new sights, and Captain Sutter handed me a perfect opportunity. I tramped down the coast on foot and went straight to his fort. There, I heard about a strike in a new camp called Hopeful, so that's where I headed. I've done pretty well, too. That is, the Ophir Mineralogical Combine's done well—"

Louis said, "Ophir what?"

"Mineralogical Combine." Jared grinned. "Fancy name for a pretty grimy operation. There are three of us in it. We each had adjoining claims along the stream. The first men on the site agreed no claim would be larger than a hundred square feet. By putting three together and building ourselves a cradle to speed up the processing of the dirt, we see more color than we would if we worked alone. Color means the yellow color of the dust or flakes," he added in an aside to Louis.

Amanda inquired about Jared's partners.

"One's an Englishman. He was a draper over in Liverpool. The other man's a little Baptist storekeeper from Georgia. He came across the mountains with a wagon train. He's the one who slapped on the splendiferous name. He said that in the Bible, in King Solomon's time, Ophir was a land famous for apes, ivory, peacocks—and gold. We're getting a fair amount of it, but we could get a lot more if we could hire decent help."

Louis raised his eyebrows. "You mean some of the men in the diggings don't have claims?"

"The ones that are too lazy. They'll pick up a few dollars for day wages, then go on a week-long tear. We've tried hiring a few Pikes. Every one of them's proved to be worthless."

"What's a Pike, sir?"

"Originally it meant a fellow from Pike County, Missouri. Now the name sticks to anybody with small education and a big temper. If a man says he's a Pike, you can be halfway certain he's running from the law, too. There are a lot of men of that sort in the diggings. They even make up tunes about 'em—"

Leaning back, he began to wave his hand to and fro, smiling at Louis as he croaked in an off-key way:

> *"Oh, what was your name in the States?*
> *"Was it Thompson, or Johnson, or Bates?"*

Louis clapped in delight. Amanda looked impatient.

> *"Did you murder your wife,*
> *"And then run for your life?*
> *"Say, what was your name in the States?"*

"I'll have to teach that one to Captain Bart—"

Amanda interrupted: "How much gold are you mining, Jared?"

"Lately it's averaged out to near twenty-four, twenty-five hundred dollars a week—"

He was startled by her look of intense concentration: "You could wind up a millionaire."

"Sure—in about thirty years."

"Thirty! I calculate nine or ten."

"You forgot my partners. It's share and share alike."

"Yes, I did forget that."

"The claim may peter out, too. A great many do."

She looked disappointed. What in the world was going on inside her head?

Louis diverted him with another question: "Do you work every day?"

"Every day except Sunday. It's not a matter of miners being godly—just worn out. Sunday's actually the wildest day of the week in Hopeful. Sometimes we have dances—"

"Are there women in the camps?"

"Once in a while a female of—call it low character—shows up and spends a couple of nights. If you don't believe grown men can go crazy, you should be there when a woman arrives. Women of that sort aren't interested in dancing, though. For dances, the men take turns tying ribbons on their arms and acting the woman's part. But no matter what you do to liven up the routine, camp life still gets boring as the devil. My partners and I drew lots to see who took the first holiday. I was lucky, I picked the short straw. So I got to come down to see the elephant. I've always wanted to see one elephant or another," he sighed. "I guess that's why I never really lived up to this—"

From his pocket he drew a tarnished medal, handing it to Louis for inspection. On the obverse was a design of a tea bottle and an inscription in Latin. The reverse bore the words *Kent and Son* and a date—1810.

"Your grandfather gave me that," Jared explained. "It was part of a fob, but the green ribbon's long gone. The Latin means take a stand and make a mark."

But Louis was more interested in something else the bearded man had said:

"There aren't any elephants in San Francisco, cousin Jared."

"Oh, that's only an expression. From an old story of the farmer who had read about elephants but never set eyes on one. The circus came to a town near his home, so he loaded his wagon with eggs he meant to sell and drove in to watch the circus parade. The elephant frightened his horse, the wagon overturned, and all the eggs broke. But the old farmer shrugged it off—'I don't give a hang, I've seen the elephant.' It means living through a bad experience. Or, the way some miners use it, just satisfying your curiosity."

He retrieved the medal and slipped it back in the pocket of his worn trousers.

"That's practically all I've done since Weatherby and I went up the Missouri in 1814, chase elephants. I suppose a man could do worse, though—"

"But now you're a rich gold miner!" Louis exclaimed.

"Not rich by a long shot, son. Not yet."

Amanda leaned forward. "What are you going to do with your share?"

"Just enjoy it while I can. I've never had much money. I'd like to take a trip back east myself. See Jephtha and my grandsons—"

A stranger looked at him from her eyes:

"And Boston?"

"No, Amanda, that's past history."

"Maybe not." But she didn't amplify the remark.

The back door opened. Billy Beadle ducked as he entered, slapping his hammer against his thigh:

"When's that bloody frog going to serve dinner? I've worked up a proper appetite—"

Amanda rose. "I'll go ask him." As she started out, she noticed the Australian frowning.

"Something wrong, Billy?"

"Nothing much," Billy replied with a too-quick shrug. "Thought you should know that a couple of Felker's chums wandered by while I was nailing—"

"Hounds?"

"Yes, ma'am. I've seen them before, though I'm not familiar with their names. They passed a few remarks about what happened to the little bast—excuse me, Louis. To Felker. Seems they don't think too kindly of any of us. I expect they're all bluff and brag, though."

Jared pointed to the corner where he'd put down his bag and his old Hawken rifle; he'd fetched them from a cheap hotel where he'd taken a room before going to the Exchange.

"I expect that'll handle them if they cause a fuss."

"I doubt they'd do it on Christmas," Billy said. "We can just relax and enjoy the grub."

Jared chuckled, amused at the way California slang had found its way into the Australian's vocabulary. Billy Beadle was a convicted thief, Amanda said. But he seemed a sunny, even-tempered sort.

"I'll stow my hammer," he said.

"And I'll prod Felix—"

Amanda and the Australian left. Jared stretched again, feeling drowsy in the sunlight. His knees had begun to ache a little. But he was supremely content; totally unworried about the dead man's friends.

ii

They began the Christmas celebration with a discordant but boisterous rendition of *Hark! The Herald Angels Sing,* which Billy Beadle directed with considerable flourish. Then Amanda said:

"Louis usually offers the grace, Jared. But if you don't object, I wish you'd do it—being the oldest of the family."

"Don't know whether that's a compliment or not," he smiled, then bowed his head along with the others.

It took a while for him to collect his thoughts. Even when he did, the words were hesitant:

"Lord God, this is Jared Kent speaking to you. I, uh, mention the name because I haven't been one of your most faithful followers. But I—we thank you for the blessings of this holy day, most particularly because—"

He cleared his throat and knuckled his misting eyes.

"—because you saw fit to re-unite the Kents, and for that we are in your everlasting debt. We thank you for the food of which we are about to partake, and for the kinship of loved ones after so many years of—"

He couldn't go on for a moment.

"After so many years," he repeated in a whisper. "Thank you, Amen."

Amanda slipped her hand over his and squeezed, not letting go for a good long time. Jared got himself under control and, smiling again, finally raised his head.

Amanda nodded briskly to the cook who had crossed himself at the completion of the grace:

"Felix, we're ready. Do your utmost."

He bowed low. "Madame Kent—that I have already done. You shall see!"

He bustled out, returning with platter after platter. The meal included his egg and oyster specialty, salmon, wild duck with rice, loaves of bread he'd baked before daylight, and plenty of rum and French champagne to lubricate Jared's tongue and deaden his rheumatic pains.

Amanda left once during the meal, to go out to the shanty and see to Israel. While she was gone, Jared carved himself a second slice of duck. The slightly greasy handle of the knife slipped in his hand. He nicked a finger. Louis ran for a bit of clean rag while Jared sat pale as milk, his stomach churning with the old, inexplicable nausea that had plagued him since childhood.

He had never been able to look at a wound—his or anyone else's—without being overcome by a few seconds of paralyzing sickness. He'd long ago given up trying to fathom why he was so afflicted. By force of will he usually managed to keep his reaction hidden while he waited for the infuriating nausea to pass, as it did now.

By the time Louis returned with the rag scrap and knotted it around Jared's finger, he was his old self again. Amanda came in to report Israel was sleeping comfortably.

Louis insisted on hearing Jared describe his life as a trapper. He obliged, sprinkling the story with anecdotes about the friends he'd made—his partner Weatherby; Old Gabe Bridger; the bandy-legged and pugnacious brigade captain, Kit Carson—and examples of the humor peculiar to the tough, often illiterate mountain men. He repeated their jokes about the Platte River—"The only water in America you have to chew."—and the spaciousness of the country they roamed:

"Since an echo takes eight hours to come back, you just shout 'Time to get up!' when you go to bed. Then of course there's the glass mountain—"

Louis was smiling but dubious.

"I've seen it!" Jared said. "A whole mountain exactly like the lens of a spy-glass. You can look through it and watch elk grazing twenty-five miles away. But it's so clear, there are thousands of dead birds around the base. They try to fly through it and knock their brains out."

"Glass mountain or not," Louis said, "it sounds like you've done some mighty exciting things."

"I've done what I had to do," Jared answered, with considerable truth. He drained the rum in his cup, gazed across the table at Amanda. "I never did find your mother, though. Weatherby and I searched two whole seasons, asking for her among the Teton Sioux—"

"They kept me out of sight whenever white traders arrived. I never got so much as a peek at visitors."

"I do recall a village where there was a brave named Plenty Coups," Jared reflected. "Weatherby and I visited it a year after I threw in with him. No one said a word about a white girl in the tepees. My God—" He shook his head. "If we'd only had sense enough to search a little on the sly—"

"We were probably closer than we knew," Amanda agreed.

"At least we didn't spend all our lives without seeing each other. I was plain lucky to draw the first holiday—"

"And we're delighted your mine's a success, sir," Billy Beadle said, toasting their visitor with a cup of champagne.

"Delighted and envious!" Felix growled from his place beside the Australian. "I should leave the kitchen! Go to the diggings—"

"You'd have a hard time," Jared advised him. "It's sad to say, but the Americans are pretty intolerant of foreigners."

"The same is true here, sir," Billy remarked. "I often wonder if it's a national disease—"

"Sometimes the behavior of Americans does make you think so," Amanda said. "I do get astonished at how easily people forget that everyone in this country is a foreigner—except the Indian."

"I would be happy to take my chances if I could find gold," Felix declared.

"Not many do," Jared said. "I'd guess ninety percent of the men in Hopeful will end up poorer than when they chased out here. I suppose I should count myself fortunate. At the rate the Ophir's producing now, it won't make me wealthy by the time I die. But at least I'll be comfortable."

"Comfortable enough to go east to see Jephtha—" Amanda began.

Unaccountably annoyed, he hedged:

"At this stage, it's no more than a thought—"

"A good thought. Louis and I could go with you. We could visit your son, and then Boston."

Louis' cheerful expression vanished. He snatched a slice of bread, tore it in two and stuffed a half in his mouth. Jared shook his head:

"Talking about Boston is pointless, Amanda. I have no desire to go there."

"I think you'll change your mind."

She didn't say why, though; just gave him an odd, challenging stare. Her face looked chalky in the pale orange light suffusing the room. Jared again had the feeling she wanted to tell him something. He almost urged her to it. But she stood up suddenly, murmuring that the coffee pot was empty.

Felix jumped to his feet. "I will go, madame—"

"No, you sit still." Before she turned away, Jared saw that hard glint in her eyes.

He frowned and plucked a crumb from his beard, wondering sadly whether they could ever be genuinely close again. As he well knew, time and hardship changed a person. It seemed to have changed her.

Yet he felt there was more to it. She was inexplicably tense; expectant—

I'm getting old, he thought. *I'm seeing phantoms where I should be seeing only a capable, grown-up woman who can't help being a stranger in many ways—*

But he wasn't convinced. She was hiding something. What was it?

Gazing at the curtain falling into place across the kitchen door, he asked himself whether he truly wanted to discover the answer.

iii

It was well after dark. A whale oil lamp glowed on the small table next to Jared's chair by the window.

Louis was already tucked into bed in his alcove. Billy Beadle had gone off to sit with Israel. The doctor had called at five, saying Israel would begin to experience a good deal of pain soon, and would need liberal doses of alcohol throughout the night. Felix had departed to circulate among the celebrants in the saloons. Even on Christmas, San Francisco had resumed its revelry.

Jared yawned, sleepy from the huge meal and the rounds of rum and coffee afterward. Amanda entered; she'd gone to settle an argument between two of the paying guests upstairs. He marveled at the expert way she handled the long-muzzled Colt's revolver—

She replaced the revolver on its pegs, then moved to a shelf of books he had noticed earlier. She drew one down and handed it to him.

Puzzled, Jared examined the stamped spine. *"Napoleon and his Marshals,"* he read aloud. "If you're recommending this to put me to sleep, I don't need it."

She ignored his wry smile: "Look at the title page."

He turned the first couple of leaves.

"My God! Kent and Son."

Amanda leaned over him, pointing:

"The date, Jared. Ten years ago."

His hand shook as he closed the cover. Now he understood what had caused her tension. He felt as if he'd walked to the rim of a chasm; a chasm from which he'd retreated years ago. The whale oil lamp made her eyes glare with a fierceness he found frightening.

"Where—where did you get this, Amanda?"

"From a trader down in the pueblo of Los Angeles." She pointed to the shelf. "Captain McGill has brought me others since then." She took hold of his shoulder. *"Stovall rebuilt the company!"*

Jared's head lifted, his eyes revealing his confusion. "I wonder if Jephtha knows. He attended divinity school in New England. He might have seen some books with the Kent imprint—"

"Entirely possible."

"If he did, why didn't he write me?"

"To spare your feelings, perhaps. He might think it was wiser to let the past stay buried. He might assume nothing could be done about it. That's where a minister and I would disagree. I believe something can and should be done."

Fingers still trembling, Jared laid the book aside. He covered his eyes with a palm; whispered:

"I knew there was something you were waiting to tell me. I could feel it all day—"

He dropped the hand to his lap, massaging the enlarged knuckles. The peace of Christmas had left him, replaced by a chaotic churn of emotion. He saw images—

The deck of the frigate *Constitution* on which he'd sailed when he was still a boy.

The hateful, foppishly handsome sixth lieutenant, Hamilton Stovall, who had tried to make him a party to shameful male degeneracy.

He saw Stovall aim a pistol in the smoke that hung over the frigate after its battle with *Guerriere*; saw the defensive slash of his own cutlass sever a cannon's breeching ropes.

He saw the cannon rolling free, and Stovall falling against it; he heard Stovall's shriek as his hands, then his right cheek struck the searing metal of the still-hot gun—

And he saw the morning when Hamilton Stovall, swinging a cane, had strolled into Kent's with his general manager to announce that he'd won the firm by cheating Aunt Harriet's husband at cards and dice—

He didn't want to ask the question that fairly screamed in his mind. But he did:

"Who's operating the printing house now? Stovall?"

"His employees."

"You're sure?"

"Positive."

A long silence. He covered his eyes again.

"I must say, Jared, I expected a stronger reaction."

"What kind of reaction?"

"Interest. Anger."

He shook his head. "Indulging my anger made a shambles of everything. I knew I had to begin a new life or I'd always be a prisoner of the old one." He drew a breath. "Forget Stovall. I have."

"How could you? *He took what belonged to us!*"

"In another life—another world. I'll never see Boston again."

She whispered, "I will."

"Is—is that the real reason you're working so hard out here?"

"Yes. Ever since I found the Headley book, I've worked for nothing else. Jared—"

She turned and walked slowly toward the piano bench. As she sat, her hand brushed the treble keys. A wild, jangling burst of notes filled the lamplit room, then slowly died away.

"—Hamilton Stovall is still alive. Living in New York City—controlling the company from there—I've had Captain McGill make inquiries. He's ruined the firm. It publishes outdated reprints and scurrilous books that run counter to everything our family stood for. I've got to bring Kent and Son back into the hands of its rightful owners!"

"Not for my sake. I don't care any more."

Her mouth thinned. "You don't care that Stovall's let you believe you were a murderer all these years?"

"Let me believe—? What do you mean?"

"Do you remember the man you shot at the printing house?"

"The man I killed? Walpole? Yes—"

"You didn't kill him."

"What?"

She rushed to him, kneeling and gripping his arms:

"He didn't die. He's alive today—just as Stovall is! Stovall probably laughs about it. Jared, believe me. Captain McGill confirmed it—Walpole is *alive.* Isn't that reason enough to fight for the company? *And* hurt Stovall if he gets in the way?"

His emotional defenses broke. Hate seethed through him—fully the match of the hate he saw in his cousin's eyes.

                                        iv

At last, terrified of where the discussion could lead, he fought back his rage:

"No, Amanda—no. I'm done with Stovall. I buried the past—"

"You can't bury the fact that you're a member of the Kent family!"

His mouth wrenched. "Hardly an outstanding one—"

"If that's how you feel, now's your chance to change things!"

"I don't think you and I are talking about the same kind of accomplishment—"

"What the hell does that mean?"

Jared drew the medal from his pocket; held the obverse toward the light:

"I remember your father speaking to me before I went out on the *Constitution* the second time. He talked about the Kents always taking the high road. The road of cause. Contribution. Commitment—I think those were the words he used. If so, I haven't lived up to them. But at least I've lived so I'm not ashamed of myself—"

"By God, I don't see any shame in taking what's ours!"

"But you talk about hurting Stovall at the same time—"

"He deserves it! If he tries to block us, let him suffer!"

Jared shook his head. "I don't want anything like that on my conscience. I'm satisfied with what I finally made of my life. I married a good woman. I earned a living honestly. I fathered a boy who angered and disappointed me when he went his own way—then I finally realized it was a worthy way. In Boston I was—I was headstrong—vindictive—"

The medal disappeared as he clenched his hand.

"I've tried to live differently as a grown man. I don't want to go back to the past! As if we ever could—"

"We can. And it's our duty."

"Not mine. I'm an old man. Fifty-one—"

"An old man? Or a weak one?"

Stunned, he stared at her as she knelt beside him:

"I don't think I know you any more, Amanda."

She pounded a fist on his knee, not realizing the pain it caused:

"I only want what's rightfully ours! We've both lived too long with too little—"

"What is it you're really after? Stovall's money? Stovall's life—?"

"I want *justice,* goddamn it! I want Kent and Son! For myself—and my boy."

"And you don't care what you do to get it?"

A brief silence. Then:

"No, I don't."

In the crucible of memory, Jared saw the face of Hamilton Stovall on the day the printing house burned. He saw the white silk bandana hiding Stovall's scarred flesh, and remembered his own intense rage—

But trying to undo a wrong more than thirty years old was futile. Futile and destructive. He saw the latter very clearly—on Amanda's own face.

His anger left him again. Gently, he touched his cousin's forehead:

"Don't do it. Trying to hurt Stovall, you'll only hurt yourself. And your son. Do you notice how he looks at you when you talk about Boston? He's afraid of you—just as I was afraid of my father before he disappeared—"

He pressed her cheeks with both hands:

"Amanda, I beg you—don't go back."

She jumped up, whirling away:

"God, you've turned spineless!"

Grieved, he shook his head. He stood up; took a step toward her. Darkness seemed to close in from the corners of the room. He thought he heard a foot fall outside; probably Billy Beadle walking in the yard—

"Not spineless. Sensible. The more you hate, the more it poisons y—"

"Oh, yes," she broke in, "I've heard that pious little sentiment before. From Captain McGill, among others. Spare me!"

"Amanda—"

His shoulders lifted. Some of the age seemed to drop from him; his blue eyes grew nearly as fierce as hers.

"—I'm afraid this is going to be a short reunion."

That finally gave her pause:

"Short? Why?"

"Because I don't want any part of rebuilding the Kent family in the way you propose to do it."

"Jared, Jared—!" She came to him, speaking more calmly. "I only want to see the family live again!"

"There's nothing wrong with that—except the price you intend to pay."

"I had hoped you'd pay your share."

His eyes narrowed. "With what I'm taking from the claim?"

"Yes. In a year or two we could rent a decent house in the east. Find that law firm whose name I can nev—"

She stopped, her eyes flicking to the glass beyond the lamp.

"There's someone out th—Jared, move away from the window—"

Her rush to push him came too late. Two pistols exploded in the back yard. He heard glass shatter an instant before he was slammed forward against the piano, struck in the back.

v

Amanda screamed. Louis burst from the alcove—"You stay in there, Louis!"—and Jared dropped to his knees, trying to grip the leg of the piano. He was short of breath. His spine hurt. The skin beneath his flannel shirt was warm and sticky—

"Sneaky, murdering bastards—!"

He heard Amanda's voice from afar; she'd run outside. Her revolver boomed once, then again. In the dormitory upstairs, men shouted questions at one another. Billy Beadle yelled in the yard, but the words made no sense.

He lost his grip on the piano leg, struck the carpet, his beard twisted under one cheek. His eyes filled with tears of pain. Peculiar, disconnected thoughts tumbled in his mind:

Too much cold water gets every trapper one day—

I'm old—

Oh, God, I hurt—

"Cousin Jared?"

That was Louis. He tried to answer. The pain was too consuming. He fainted.

vi

Voices. Faces. Indistinct. Hard to identify.

"—some of Felker's cronies, I don't doubt. Bloody scum! They got clean away in the dark—"

Who was that? He struggled to focus his eyes. He was lying in the shadow of the walnut table. Above him, a blurred figure in the lamplight, he finally recognized Billy Beadle.

Amanda spoke:

"Billy, you run for the doctor. Run like hell!"

The Australian vanished. In his place Jared saw his cousin. But he was only marginally aware of her. His mind distracted him:

So this is how it ends. Unexpectedly—at the wrong time—with too many words unsaid—too many things undone—

He cried his son's name; fought to sit up—

Amanda knelt. Her cool palm pressed him down. He thought he detected tears in her eyes. An inner voice spoke with bitterness:

At least she has enough heart left to weep.

Then he thought of the claim—the Ophir Mineralogical Com—

Com—

The last word eluded him.

What would become of his share?

He knew. The knowledge only sharpened his fear:

I've given her exactly what she shouldn't have—

"Don't," he said in a barely audible voice.

Amanda shook her head; shook it so hard, tears flew from her eyes. He wasn't speaking loud enough.

She rested her cheek against his. How warm her lips felt through the tangle of his beard—

"What did you say to me, Jared?"

"Said—don't take—the Ophir gold—"

"No, that belongs to your son."

"But he's—not worldly, he probably—won't want—"

He had no strength to say more.

"I'd never take it, you know that, Jared," she said, grief jumbling the words together. "But if Jephtha will permit me, I—I'll be the—the steward —of it—"

I know why. DON'T!

Pain shot upward through his neck into his head. A heavy haze obscured his sight of Amanda. He realized she was still on her knees, asking another question. Through the roaring in his ears, he finally deciphered part of it:

"—attorneys."

"What?" The sound emerged as a guttural. His lips moved again, slowly: "What?"

"The name of the family attorneys—Boston—can't remember—"

Merciful God, how terribly he hurt! If only he'd drawn the long lot— never come to San Francisco—he might have seen his grandsons—

But not Amanda. Why were things never clear-cut? Why was there darkness and this unbearable pain? Why hadn't he been given time to persuade her to abandon her scheme for—

"Jared, please—tell me the name!"

Don't, Amanda. That's not the way your father wanted you to live—

"Jared, you're my blood kin. *You've got to tell me!*"

His lips jerked; a whisper:

"Ben—"

"What? Jared, try. *Try!*"

"Ben—" He spoke it as separate words. "Bow."

"Benbow. Benbow—yes, oh God, that's it!"

Was he wrong to tell her? The question savaged him as he arched his back and cried aloud, afraid because the lamplight had grown so dim.

Was he wrong? Was she only planning to do what needed to be done—?

No. It would harm her. He didn't want her harmed. He loved her. He tried to tell her as she leaned her cheek against his again, their tears mingling:

"Jared, oh Jared, don't die, we're all that's left to bring the Kents into the world again—"

Againagainagain wailed the echoes in his mind. The pain was lessening; the dark deepening. One last, clear thought eradicated his fear, now that he realized even fear wouldn't help him:

I have to go, Amanda. All of us have to go to see the elephant.

CHAPTER 5

The Man Who Got in the Way

THE TWO MOUNTED FIGURES were dwarfed by the immensity of the dripping spruces and pines. A gray haze, not so thick as fog and not quite rain, hid the slopes of the Sierras they'd last seen at sunset the preceding evening. The mules struggled over the rocky terrain. Israel, leading the way, frequently had to resort to quirting the animals.

Most of their gear was packed in bags that bulged from the flanks of his mule. His trousers bulged as well. His legs were still wrapped in bandages.

Although the mulatto's burns could have been far worse, they'd nevertheless caused him considerable suffering. He'd never complained once—but the pain had shown on his face from the first day he'd hobbled out of his shanty and taken half a dozen steps before halting in the center of the back yard, sweating and drawing deep breaths.

Amanda had been watching from inside. Israel resumed walking in a moment or so, wincing each time he put weight on his feet but clearly determined to reach his goal. He'd finally come up the steps into the back room. Even though he'd made rapid progress since that first passage across the yard, walking was still difficult for him. Riding muleback was much less of a strain.

"Israel? How much further, do you think?"

"I calculate a mile or so. Unless we took the wrong fork a while back."

"I surely hope not. I'm worn out."

"So'm I. And the Sabbath's supposed to be a day of rest!"

The shod hoofs of the mules rang against rocks on the barely discernible trail. From their right drifted the purling of water, a stream hidden by the murk. Only by copying down the most explicit directions at Sutter's had they been able to wind their way up to this branch of the Feather.

Amanda's statement to Israel was no exaggeration. They'd been on the way from San Francisco six days now, making slow progress because of their unfamiliarity with the country. It was a trip she'd decided they must take, hardship or not.

But she'd be thankful when they reached their destination. Winter dampness seeped up the sleeves of her fleece-lined coat and penetrated the fabric of the jeans trousers tucked into her stout boots. Her thighs hurt from the bouncing and scraping of the saddle. With her hair pinned up beneath a flop-brimmed wool hat, and the holster of her revolver showing beneath the bottom of her coat, Amanda hardly resembled a woman. Nor did she feel much like one.

Since the dark of Christmas night, a kind of daze had enveloped her. Even now, more than three weeks into January of the new year, 1850, she hadn't entirely freed herself of despondency. To find Jared with such abruptness, then lose him just as abruptly, and all within a space of twenty-four hours, had been the profoundest sort of shock.

She had wept over his body for nearly an hour after the breath went out of it. It was Billy Beadle, she learned later, who finally pulled her away. She'd been hysterical. She didn't remember.

She was ashamed she'd behaved that way. She'd always prided herself on her strength. But flesh could only bear so much, and that one Christmas day had strained her physical and mental resources almost to the breaking point.

In the days that followed, she'd alternated between periods of depression whose only antidote was a stiff drink and the security of her bed, and other periods of almost frantic activity. During the latter, she tramped San Francisco with Billy, asking in the saloons and gambling halls for information about the identity of the men who had shot her cousin.

That the murderers were cronies of Felker's she didn't doubt. But the disbanded Hounds proved to be more than close-mouthed. They were elusive. Every known member of the group had vanished suddenly, perhaps fearing civic wrath of the kind that had caused the destruction of the Hounds' headquarters.

Amanda offered five hundred dollars for information, but got nothing more than a few useless scraps: this man had been seen playing cards with Felker; that one had accompanied him on a tour of the brothels. One man mentioned was at last identified as one of the pair who'd spoken to Billy on Christmas morning. He too was gone. The guilty had fled along with the innocent. Amanda soon realized she'd probably never locate the two who fired the fatal shots.

That wasn't the only cause of her troubled state. Jared's burial in San Francisco's crude hillside cemetery had been an ordeal.

The mourners were few. Amanda; Israel; solemn-faced Billy; Felix; and Louis. Only their nearness, and her own vow not to surrender totally to despair had made it possible for her to endure the brief service. She'd hugged Louis to her side, her other hand clutching Jared's fob medallion. As the earth rattled on the plank coffin, she closed her hand tighter and tighter on the medal's edge, using the physical pain to deaden the pain of her heart and her mind—

Afterward, she found herself constantly wishing Jared had been given a few more days at her side. She remembered his eyes during their argument just before the pistol balls shattered the window. He had looked at her with surprise—sorrow—and finally with loathing—

Or did she only imagine that?

Accompanying her depressed feeling was an almost abnormal awareness of the hampering effects of age. She'd been conscious of gradual changes for several years. Her energy seemed to drain away before a day was half done. She was frequently wakeful at night. Routine tasks sometimes looked too formidable until she rested a bit. For a week or two, she dwelled on this deterioration in a morbid way, unable to stop thinking of the ultimate end of the process.

The heightened sense of her own mortality brought on intense self-questioning. However briefly, perhaps Jared *had* seen her more clearly than she saw herself. Perhaps her determination—the determination that had burst inside her like a long-smoldering fire when she first saw the Headley book—had become a ruinous influence.

She'd long believed it was right to plan and work and save in order to go back to Boston. She thought the Kents' past and her son's future demanded it.

Yet recalling Jared's eyes and his dying plea for her to leave the gold alone, she doubted.

Was she letting the fury of wounded family pride warp her?

Or was she on the right course?

She didn't know.

But when it struck her that she should at least look after Jared's interests up in the diggings, she didn't put the idea aside. Instead, she immediately informed Israel that they were going.

Louis had received word of the forthcoming trip in somber silence. To add to the gloom of the departure, she was worried about Bart McGill. The morning she and Israel set out, his ship was seven days overdue. He'd often spoken of hundred-knot winds that created an extreme hazard on the Cape Horn passage—

Now here she was, winding up a muddy track beneath sodden trees. She felt more than a little out of her element. How ridiculous for a woman almost forty-seven years old to go traipsing into the gold country like the very fools she'd once condemned.

Someone had to settle Jared's affairs, though—

To whose benefit? was the immediate response of her questioning conscience.

Confused again, she took comfort in remembering what she'd once told Luis Cordoba about the Mandan's vine to paradise. A human being did what seemed necessary and right, and left it to someone else to judge whether the sum of thousands of such decisions equaled a life lived with honor, or the lack of it. If her plan to recapture Kent's, tainted as it was by her hatred of Stovall, was impure—why, so was life itself. Despite Jared's warnings—and Bart's—she would go ahead. She had in effect made that choice the moment she informed Israel about the journey.

A sudden change in the irregular clopping of the mules' hoofs drew her from introspection. Ahead, between two great shoulders of granite, Israel had brought his mount to a halt.

"Guess we've arrived safe and sound," he called. He pointed. "There's civilization."

Amanda grimaced. Just beyond the mulatto, a hanged man dangled from the branch of a tree.

The corpse twisted as the rope unwound slowly. The tree limb creaked. A young man, Amanda saw as she rode up beside Israel. A young man with a black beard and distended eyeballs and flesh discolored by death. She wondered what his crime had been—and what heaven's verdict on his life would be. The earthly decision was unmistakable.

The two mules clopped by the hanging tree to a place where the trail again descended. Listening, she heard a fiddle scraping *Old Dan Tucker.* The camp itself was still invisible in the mist.

They rode on till they came to a crudely lettered sign on a post driven into the ground:

welcom to Hopeful

Another sign—rather, the sheared-off top section—lay discarded nearby. Amanda leaned forward to read what had been painted on the board:

War! War! ! War! ! !
The celebrated Bull-killing Bear
KIT CARSON
will fight a Bull to the Death on Sunday
the 15th inst. at 3 p.m.

The rest was gone. Somewhere ahead, a gun went off. Men shouted. Her shoulders felt heavy. Foolish old woman, she thought.

Then she recalled the fob medallion in her pocket, and sat up straight. Two more shots exploded. She said:

"We may be sound, but who knows how safe?"

She unbuttoned her heavy coat; laid her right hand on the holstered revolver. Israel fell back to let her take the lead as the mules negotiated the muddy track that led toward lanterns now visible as smears of yellow in the murk.

ii

Even in San Francisco, Amanda had seldom seen such a confusion of humanity as she did that Sunday morning.

Hopeful straggled for more than half a mile along the bank of the Feather's branch, hemmed in on the landward side by nearly perpendicular hills covered with dark firs. The camp consisted exclusively of improvised housing—tents, scrap-lumber hovels and even a number of large packing cases from which the sides had been removed. Inside one of these, a man lay reading. In another, a couple of bearded miners played cards.

Amanda kept her hat brim pulled down as she and Israel rode along the main street. She saw no women anywhere. Men milled aimlessly on either side. Most were white, but here and there she spied a darker face; a Mexican; a Chilean. Two stocky youngsters appeared to be Kanakas from Hawaii. Most of the miners were dressed as Jared had been—heavy coats and trousers. There was an almost universal display of mustaches and chin whiskers.

Being hatless, Israel immediately attracted attention. A group lounging outside a tent identified as Sacramento Tom's started pointing. One man lobbed a stone. Another shouted:

"Ain't no claims for niggers here!"

Israel went rigid. Amanda laid a hand on his arm. He swallowed and gazed straight ahead.

Inside Sacramento Tom's, the fiddle-scraper swung into *The Old Oaken Bucket*. A man approached Amanda's mule, weaving. He doffed a filthy felt hat:

"Welcome, pilgrim! You don right, comin' to Hopeful. We're takin' it out of the ground with jackknives—"

Head down, she didn't respond. The man shrugged, executed a half-turn, unbuttoned his pants and began to urinate in the mud.

On Amanda's left, three bearded fellows were carrying a wounded man out of another gambling tent, to the amusement of a small crowd. Had this been the source of the shots? She heard one of the watchers yell to someone in the tent:

"Frenchie, you be in miner's court at five sharp. The court'll decide whether Dick provoked you. That is—" A glance at the wounded man being borne away. "—if Dick's still alive to state his case."

A somewhat larger tent on the right announced itself as *The Bear Flag Palace*. From all the lanterns burning inside, some positioned above others, Amanda realized an enterprising soul had somehow rigged an upstairs section for the hotel. Immediately beyond the Palace, a general store —another tent—was doing a brisk business. Out in front, a shirt-sleeved clerk waved a pair of boots to half a dozen customers:

"Cowhide, double-soled, triple-pegged and guaranteed waterproof. Fit your road-smashers exactly! Who's going to start with a bid of two and a half ounces? Do I hear two and a half ounces of dust—?"

"You hear three!"

"Three and a half!"

"*Four!*"

Before Amanda passed by, the boots sold for nine ounces of dust. She admired the auctioneer's audacity.

She was so intent on watching the auction's conclusion, she failed to see another man, more tipsy than the first, who came lurching toward her mule from the left. He stumbled against the animal. The mule brayed, bucked—and Amanda went toppling off.

She struck on her right side, sinking three or four inches into the ooze and gasping for air. Her cheeks and forehead were splattered with mud. Israel tried to control his nervous mule as Amanda gained her knees. She grabbed for the top of her head. Her hat had fallen off—!

The tipsy gentleman, pink-faced, middle-aged and bearded, gaped:

"God bless us all, a woman! Madam—" He extended a pudgy hand. "Otto Plankveld, late of Albany, New York. Allow me to assist you—"

"No thanks, I'm all right," Amanda said, jumping up and jamming her hat on her head—too late:

"A woman! The Dutchman's got a woman—!"

"Ah, he's just blind drunk again—"

"No, you are. She's standin' right out there!"

Instantly, men rushed toward Amanda from both sides. The commotion spread, attracting others from up and down the street. The damp air grew so full of alcohol fumes, she might have been inside a distillery.

Poor Otto Plankveld was promptly elbowed to the rear of the crowd. Hands reached out. Teeth shone in sudden grins:

"Hey, dearie, you a workin' girl?"

"How much for a toss in bed?"

"How about in the mud? Is that cheaper?"

"Hell, she ain't no whore, she's too damn old—"

"Yeh, but she's got her nigger bully with her—"

"Gentlemen," Amanda began, not a little alarmed by the ring of jostling, inebriated men, "I'm looking for the Ophir—"

Before she could finish, a particularly foul-smelling fellow with a long white streak down the center of his sandy beard grabbed her left arm:

"The Ophir boys can wait a while to take their turn. There ain't another creature in Hopeful that's got what you got—"

With his other hand, he reached for her crotch.

She jerked out of his grip and took a hasty step backward.

"Hey, Pike, leave her alone, we seen her first!"

The man paid no attention, his smile fixed and ugly. The portly Dutchman had squeezed his way up front again. He stepped between Amanda and the man identified as Pike. Not his name, probably, Amanda thought, recollecting Jared's remarks about the type.

The Pike shoved Plankveld:

"Back off, you fuckin' little sausage-eater."

"No. Can't you see she is a lady?"

"Shit, why would a lady come up here—'less it's to do business?"

"You've swilled too much liquor, Pike. She's a lady. You got to treat a lady decent. Especially on the Sabbath—"

"I'll Sabbath you, you two-legged jackass!" the Pike said in a slurred voice. He shoved Plankveld hard.

The crowd surged back as Plankveld staggered, then righted himself. Amanda intervened:

"Stop it! You've both drunk too much. I'll thank you to get out of my way."

Plankveld almost retreated. The bearded Pike refused, grinning as he faced the German. He wriggled his fingers, an invitation for the other man to attack.

Amanda's mule had wandered to a spot just beyond the two antagonists. The crowd closed in again. Israel, still mounted, was behind her. The only way to reach her mule was to remove the two drunks from her path:

"Did you hear me? Stand aside."

The Pike called her a filthy name.

Muddy and exhausted from the long journey, her temper was short. She saw the quarrelsome Pike as an infuriating obstacle. She started to yell at him. Before she could, he reached for Plankveld's neck.

The German tried to fend him off. The Pike's arms were longer. He locked hands on Plankveld's throat, yanked him forward and drove a knee into his genitals.

Plankveld cried out. The Pike flung him into the mud, laughed. A few watchers applauded. The crowd, completely ringing Amanda, Israel and the mules, grew larger every second. The Pike raised his right boot and brought it down on the German's temple.

This time Plankveld screamed, the right side of his head driven deep into the mud. Amanda shot her hand toward Israel, snatched the quirt from the mulatto's hand. Just as the Pike started to boot the German a second time, she laid the quirt across the back of his neck:

"Now will you stop and get out of the way?"

The Pike stood up to his full height. A hand darted to the back of his neck where the quirt had drawn blood. Amanda's palms started to sweat. Whimpering, Plankveld tried to crawl away.

The Pike faced Amanda. "Well, ain't the little bee got a sting—"

Israel kneed his mule forward to block the Pike's lunge at her. The bearded man pounded both fists into Israel's ribs. With a yell, the mulatto slid off the side of his mule just as Amanda had done, landing on his rump in the mud. Someone flung a handful at him, smearing his face. Almost at the same moment, the Pike stabbed a hand under his tattered coat and pulled a pocket pistol, a cheap copy of the popular large-caliber weapons built by the Philadelphia gunsmith Henry Deringer.

"I got me a sting too, woman—"

Behind Amanda, men yelled and scattered.

Perhaps if she hadn't been so tired and so furious at having been stupidly balked in the middle of the main street, she might have reacted in a different way; tried to reason with the Pike. But he was mad and so was she. His right hand lifted for a shot at close range. She saw the man not just as a witless bully but as a symbol of everything that stood between her and what she wanted—

The Pike pointed the stubby muzzle at her eyes. She darted to one side, freed the revolver from her holster while the Pike tried to correct his aim. Because he'd been drinking, his forearm shook. He closed his other hand over the one clutching the pistol, squinting as the muzzle steadied—

Amanda extended the revolver to the full length of her arm and fired.

The reverberations of the shot died slowly. The pocket pistol slipped from the Pike's hand. He dropped to his knees, astonished at the reddening hole drilled in his flannel shirt between the lapels of his old coat.

He lifted his head and stared at Amanda for one gruesome moment. Then his eyes shut. He fell face down in the mud.

Someone exclaimed, "By Christ, she killed him outright!"

Amanda whirled. "He was going to kill me!"

"He was too drunk to shoot straight. He'd have missed you sure—"

"And I was supposed to take a chance on that? No thank you!"

Men surged around her, shouting. Israel shoved them back:

"Get away! You get away from her—!" He bent to whisper, "Keep the gun handy, Miz Kent. We may need it before we're out of here—"

A violent argument erupted between factions in the crowd. Some claimed Amanda had committed cold-blooded murder, others that she had only defended herself against a man who would have done murder himself. Her right hand was shaking so badly, she could barely hold the Colt's.

Israel slipped an arm around her shoulder. A man demanded she attend miner's court at five. In the midst of the yelling, Plankveld picked himself up and tried to out-shout the others:

"*Nein*, no court! He attacked her! A worthless Pike—everybody knows he had a terrible temper—"

"I'll be in court!" Amanda said.

"Walk with me," Israel whispered, cradling her against him and easing the revolver from her hand. "You bring the animals, will you please, sir?" he said to Plankveld.

The red-cheeked German nodded, grabbing the reins of the two mules. Amanda felt the unsteadiness of Israel's gait; he was favoring his left leg, the one burned worst.

Faces swam around her; glaring eyes; mouths bawling this or that point in connection with the argument. She and the lanky yellow-skinned man took two steps; then two more. They could go no further.

Israel raised the revolver. *Oh God, he's forgotten to revolve the cylinder. What if they notice—?*

Israel spoke politely to the men in front of him:

"We're looking for a claim called the Ophir and we'll be obliged if you permit us to go on our way."

Ugly grumbles. Israel swallowed again, glancing around the ring of miners. He adjusted his grip on the revolver he was holding at waist level. Several men eyed the barrel apprehensively.

"I'm asking you all to stand aside," Israel said.

"Shit," a man grumbled, "the Pike ain't worth gettin' killed over. Let the nigger through, you boys."

"Thank you," Israel said quietly. The men fell back.

Dizzy for a moment, Amanda closed her eyes. "Come on," Israel whispered.

"Hurry—I got the mules," Plankveld said from behind them.

"I can walk," Amanda said. "You ride, Israel. I know your legs are hurting—"

"Be that as it may, just lean on me till we're clear—thank you, gentlemen, thank you—"

He led her past the miners and out into the open. After they'd gone a short distance up the street, he relaxed a little:

"Well, we got out of that. For the moment. Sure wish you hadn't killed that fellow—"

Infuriated, she wrenched away:

"He was aiming that hide-out gun straight at me!"

The mulatto's sad gaze accused her. "Yes, but it holds only one ball. Those men called it right—the Pike was full of whiskey, and wobbly. I think you could have dodged him."

"That's not your place to say!"

Israel glared suddenly:

"Miz Kent, don't you forget—I don't have any *place* except the one I pick."

"All right, all right—I'm sorry."

"Never seen you so riled as when you pulled the trigger—" He sighed. "Guess it's too late to do anything now."

She held back a retort because she knew he was right. She'd lost control; aimed for the Pike's chest when a leg would have served. But her pent-up anger and her desire to reach the claim had pushed her beyond reason. She was terrified to discover that she was capable of such irrational rage when she was opposed.

iii

The Ophir Mineralogical Combine was a plot of ground thirty feet long and ten deep along the excavated bank of the stream. Plankveld led them to the claim's boundary, stopping near a large tent. A piece of mining equipment stood on a sandbar three yards out from the bank. Constructed of wood, it resembled an oversized child's cradle. A long chute jutted from one end.

The bedraggled German handed the reins of the mules to Israel, who kept shifting his weight from foot to foot. Amanda's revolver was back in the holster, but she still felt the after-effects of the shooting—which apparently had already been forgotten by most of the camp. Fiddle music and laughter drifted down to the claim.

"Madam," Plankveld said, "take my advice. Do not go alone anywhere in Hopeful today."

"Why not?"

"Scurrilous as he was, the Pike had one or two friends."

"All right, I'll do as you say. Israel will come to court with me. Where is it?"

"The Bear Flag Palace."

"At five. Thank you for helping us, Mr. Plankveld. I'm sorry you got dragged into a scrape because of me."

"The Pike—Armbruster, I think that was his real name—he was known for his bad ways—" The German picked at a gob of mud in his beard, then aimed a thumb at the lamplit tent. "Those boys won't be too unhappy over what happened. The Pike worked for them four days, got drunk and smashed up their cradle. Cost Mr. Nichols plenty to buy lumber for another—"

"Mr. Nichols is one of the partners?"

"*Ja*, one of the three. Just two left now. Another, Mr. Kent, he went down to San Francisco and never came back. Too bad, you know? The Ophir, she's one of the best. Starting to produce close to a thousand dollars a day—"

Amanda caught her breath. The tent flap lifted:

"I say—someone there?"

She turned to confront a spare, rather handsome man of about thirty. He was bearded and dressed like the other miners. But one touch distinguished him—a bright sash of scarlet silk.

She answered the query in a voice still a bit unsteady:

"Yes, my name is Amanda Kent—"

The man's debonair smile faded. "Kent, did you say?"

She thought of Jared living with guilt all his days. She thought of the man who had caused that guilt. And suddenly, her own guilt over shooting the Pike vanished. She spoke with authority:

"That's right. A third of this claim is mine."

iv

Francis Pelham, the former draper from the British Isles, and Joseph Nichols, the rotund litte Baptist from Georgia, welcomed Amanda into the tent. Nichols brought a basin of water and a few rags. After she'd cleaned her face and hands, they listened to her story. At the end, Nichols shook his head:

"I'm sorry indeed to hear of Jared's demise, Mrs. Kent. You have my most sincere sympathy. Your cousin was a straight sort."

"Can't say the same for that rascal Armbruster," Pelham remarked. "We took him on and later regretted it."

"So Mr. Plankveld told me," Amanda said.

The interior of the tent was crowded with shovels, pick-axes, three cots, crates, a small stove and a table with a crooked leg. A set of balances rested on the table. Amanda saw no evidence of gold. She asked about that.

"We have a sort of community bank in Hopeful," Pelham explained. "Each miner pays a share to cover the wages of the clerk and three guards

who work eight-hour shifts. Three other chaps watch the guards so they're
not tempted. As you discovered, the atmosphere in this camp borders on
the unbalanced—"

"Damnation!" Nichols jumped up from the crate on which he'd been
sitting. He squashed his palm against his left leg just above the knee.
Then he blushed:

"I beg your pardon for the profanity. We're all afflicted with the quicks
and slows."

"Joseph means fleas and lice," Pelham said. "Are you sure I can't warm
a biscuit for you, Mrs. Kent? You look a trifle pale."

"I'm fine," she lied.

"And nervy," Nichols said. "I 'spect you realize by now that you risked
your life coming here."

She shrugged. "I had no choice. I heard from miners in San Francisco
that any man who gets killed or disappears forfeits his claim."

"Entirely correct," Pelham returned with a precise nod. "We had all
but given Jared up for lost. I share Joseph's grief at his unhappy end."

"Well, that's past," Amanda said.

"Would you perchance like some coffee?"

"I'd like some whiskey if you have it."

"We do—for medicinal purposes," Nichols told her.

Pelham grinned. "And the Sabbath."

Nichols poured. No mention was made of refreshments for Israel,
who'd been standing silently ever since the four entered the tent. Nichols
gaped as Amanda downed the half cup of liquor in four swift swallows.

The alcohol was cheap and raw. It hurt her throat and stomach at first,
but quickly began to exert a soothing effect. Feeling a little stronger, she
said:

"Israel might like something—"

She didn't miss Nichols' frown. The mulatto noticed too. Amanda realized he was thinking of her welfare when he refused to turn the remark
into an issue:

"Thank you anyway, Miz Kent, I'm not hungry or thirsty."

Amanda nodded, addressed the partners:

"To business, gentlemen. I came here principally because my cousin
has a son in Virginia. I'll probably be going to visit him soon—"

"You wish for Joseph and me to buy out your cousin's interest?"
Pelham broke in.

"No, I don't. I intend to take over Jared's third."

Pelham frowned. "Absentee ownership is not too practical. Every partner must share in the work—"

She turned her head toward Israel, who was standing near the table. Despite the condition of his legs, his posture was erect. Amanda suspected that was probably for Nichols' benefit. She knew what the effort must be costing the mulatto.

"Israel has agreed to act as my representative," she said.

Joseph Nichols scratched his nose. "Well now, ma'am, I ought to caution you about one thing. Nigras don't receive a very cordial reception in the diggings—"

"Do they anywhere?" Israel asked. Nichols looked flustered.

"Mr. Nichols," Amanda said, "My cousin told me you're from Georgia—"

"That's true."

"Do you object to working with a man of color? As an equal?"

After a moment Nichols replied, "I can't pretend I've ever done it before. On the other hand, the Nichols family doesn't support the idea that slavery is an immutable institution, or even a good thing. Not all southerners do, you know. Too much fuss about cotton at the expense of everything else has caused the south to lag badly in manufacturing—"

"I should clear up one point," Amanda interrupted. "Israel is a free man. He'll return in a few weeks and work as hard as either of you. For that, he'll be paid a percentage of my cousin's share."

"Joseph—" Pelham confronted his partner. "Can you accept a colored man?"

Amanda shook her head. "There's no question of *acceptance*. I'm asking how Israel will be treated by—"

"Please, Miz Kent," the mulatto broke in. "Let him answer. If this is to be a going operation—"

Piqued, Nichols said, "It *is* a going operation."

"All right." Israel replied calmly. "Then if it's to continue as one, we have to be honest about how we feel toward each other. I'll do my portion of the hard labor, that I promise. But I won't sleep outside, or take my meals anywhere but right here."

Nichols reddened again. "I must say you're mighty assertive for a nigra—"

"You'll get used to it."

"Freedom *is* the law in California," Amanda said. "I assume you know the new government down in Monterey adopted an anti-slavery clause in the state constitution—?"

"Yes," Pelham said, "though we were frankly too busy to vote on the constitution. Not that I could, of course—I'm still a citizen of Her Majesty's country. But I do think it's remarkable that California declared itself a state before your federal union did so—"

"The question remains," Amanda said, "will Israel be welcome, or are you going to cause problems for him? If you are, you'll have problems with me."

Unsmiling, Francis Pelham answered, "Based on Armbruster's fate, Mrs. Kent, I would take that for granted. The decision is really Joseph's."

Nichols scratched his armpit. Shook his head, rose and walked to the coffee pot. Painfully conscious of everyone watching, he poured a cup. Then, slowly, he walked back to Israel.

"It'll take some effort, but I guess I can get used to it." Abruptly, he thrust the cup forward. "You sure you're not thirsty?"

With a grave smile, Israel said, "I believe I am now."

"Then here—help yourself."

Israel took the cup. "Thank you, Mr. Nichols."

"You all have any name besides Israel?"

"I don't," the mulatto admitted. "Some slaves adopted the last names of their masters but I refused."

Nichols looked startled: "You a runaway?"

"Many years ago. I was born on a plantation. My papa was a white man. My momma never told me his name. She hated him, I guess. I ran away first chance I got. Is any of that important?"

"No, I 'spose it isn't—"

"Definitely not," Pelham said. "We've no time to dwell on past history, we're too bloody busy. It requires four men to work a claim efficiently, you know. Two must dig, a third must alternately shovel the dirt into the hopper of the cradle you saw outside, and pour in water. The fourth man rocks the cradle to filter the dust and flakes down the chute. The gold is caught behind the chute's transverse riffles, while the water and mud wash on—"

Israel nodded: "I'm familiar with placer mining, Mr. Pelham."

"Ah, but Joseph and I don't want to limit ourselves to placer mining." He began to speak with more animation, waving his cup as he paced back and forth. Amanda decided she liked the cut of Jared's partners. Israel too was interested in what the Britisher had to say:

"We're drawing a fine profit out of the claim now. We can do better if we can ever hire a dependable helper."

"Better than a thousand a day?" Amanda asked.

"In my opinion, yes."

Nichols said, "I heard Chinee boys are showing up in some of the camps, Francis. Hard workers. Maybe we'd have better luck with one of them—"

"And I wouldn't feel so outnumbered," Israel said. Nichols actually chuckled.

"A possibility," Pelham agreed. "My point is this, Mrs. Kent. If there is abundant gold in and along the rivers of California, it follows that it must wash down from somewhere. The Mexicans are undoubtedly correct when they speak about a *veta madre.*"

"A mother vein?"

"The boys around here call it mother lode," Nichols told her.

"Go on, Mr. Pelham."

"Men are already striking off for the slopes of the Sierras. The land's for the taking—no one's quite thrashed out the laws of ownership as yet. Separating gold from the quartz rock will require heavier equipment, however—"

"You've studied the subject, haven't you, Mr. Pelham?"

"I have. I did not leave my relatives—the city where I was born—and the pittance I earned in the drapery in order to enjoy a holiday in America. I came here for a purpose."

"Excellent."

"As soon as Joseph and I—"

"And Israel," she said.

"Quite so. As soon as we can lay up sufficient funds and hire trustworthy chaps to work *this* claim under the supervision of one of us, the other two will go to the mountains. As you undoubtedly know, the size of claims is settled by the common consent of those who arrive first. It's my plan to locate a promising site no one's discovered, and set the limits to suit ourselves." Pelham smiled. "Naturally we'll require your approval of such a venture, Mrs. Kent. But I gather from your remark of a few moments ago, you would not be averse to a speculative expedition—?"

"I wouldn't. If there's more money to be made, I insist you go."

"Capital!"

"The one thing we aren't going to do," Nichols declared, "is squander gold from here *or* the mountains on alcohol, games of chance and traveling prosti—fast women," he amended, beet-colored. "Like Francis, my home's a long way off—and not worth going back to, either. A big combine from Atlanta put up a general store four times the size of the mine and just half a mile away. Drove me out of business. I suffered the miseries of the damned on the Overland Trail. I dosed myself with gunpowder and Dr. Zoril's cure-all medicine and wore one of those blasted asafetida bags to prevent the cholera. Until I got used to the stinking alkali water, I thought a chamber pot would be my life's companion. We never saw an Indian—not one—but I was always scared of being murdered by some fool handling a gun without knowing how. One man in our train thought he heard an Indian whoop, jerked his rifle out of the wagon barrel first and shot himself to death. Why, there were guns popping day and night—!"

"I've heard the overland route is trying," Amanda said.

"Disillusioning would be more like it. I had to throw out most of the heavy goods I freighted from Georgia to Missouri with the last of my savings. I dumped a Franklin stove, a pile of furniture—anyone can find California just by following the trail of abandoned bedroom suites! But I got here, by heaven. I carved my name on Independence Rock, crossed the mountain ranges and even survived the stench of the rotting carcasses of horses and mules that collapsed in the Humboldt Sink. After all I went through, I'm not going to behave like that stupid Armbruster, throwing his dust away as fast as we paid him. I don't mind telling you we had some fierce conbobberations concerning his errant ways—"

"Conbobberations?" Amanda repeated.

Amused, Pelham said, "Arguments. If it's English they speak in this part of America, they're jolly well inventing it more quickly than I can learn it. However, Joseph addresses a valid point. I've observed that those who strike it rich, as the saying goes, need more than a spot of luck. Success requires ample perspiration and a diligent, scientific approach. We can control those two factors. If we also have luck when we move to the higher elevations, we could all be exceedingly wealthy. At very least, this claim alone should keep us comfortable for a long time."

"Comfortable isn't good enough, Mr. Pelham. I prefer rich."

He saluted her with his cup. "We shall do our best to shower you with gold, dear lady."

"My cousin's son is a preacher. I don't think he'll have much use for it. But I do, believe me."

At that, Israel stared down into his cup, visibly unhappy.

v

Amanda stood up. "Do they serve dinners at that so-called hotel on the main street?"

"The Bear Flag?" Nichols said. "You bet—pretty good ones."

"Outrageously over-priced, though," Pelham added.

"I'll pay the bill, so let's not worry about price. Since I have to be there for court at five, we might as well go up to the hotel now. We can eat and discuss more of the details of this—"

She noticed Nichols studying his muddied boots.

"You're not hungry, Mr. Nichols?"

"Ma'am—" A quick glance at Israel. "—please, now, don't anyone be insulted, but the Bear Flag has a policy—that is—"

Scarlet again, he stopped.

"Joseph means they don't serve persons of color," Pelham said quietly.

Weary as she was, Amanda still spoke firmly:

"I think they'll suspend their policy—" She moved her right hand to the butt of her holstered revolver. "—just about as quickly as that jury of miners will clear me when I tell my story."

"God save me," Pelham grinned, "you *are* a determined woman."

"Miz Kent usually gets whatever she goes after," Israel said. A second later he added, "Sometimes that can be downright harmful to a person."

He didn't mean the remark as a joke. Amanda knew she should call him down for it. With Nichols present, she concealed her anger and didn't.

That Israel spoke the truth was a risk she'd already accepted.

CHAPTER 6

The Parting

CAPTAIN BARTON McGILL hauled back his right foot and kicked the rock he'd stumbled over:

"Son of a *bitch!*"

The rock went skittering down the path that led to the top of the semaphore hill. A few steps above him, Amanda waited, her face hidden by her bonnet.

"My," she said as he joined her, "you're in a fierce temper."

"Are you surprised? I go away for three and a half months—" He linked her arm in his. They resumed their climb toward the ramshackle house and the wooden signal tower perched on the hilltop. "—and when I come back, nothing's the same. I waited two hours for the lighter from shore!"

"You just made the mistake of anchoring on the day the mail boat arrived, Bart."

"Ship," he grumped. "Mail ship."

A fragrant cigar clenched between his fingers streamed smoke into the clear air of early evening. For February, the weather was unusually warm and beautiful. He took a puff of the cigar, asked:

"How often are they sending that steam monstrosity out here?"

"Twice a month."

"Never seen such crowds! Kicking, punching each other—must have been a couple of thousand people in those lines at the Post Office."

"You can turn a nice profit if you get a place at the front of a line. You can sell it to someone else for twenty-five, sometimes fifty dollars."

They circled the side of the hill about fifty feet from the summit. On the front porch of the house, the elderly man raised the arms on the semaphore tower to signal when a ship was sighted sat rocking slowly. A paper in his lap snapped in the wind.

Bart's gray eyes searched the soft gold sky, then the shadowed hills across the channel to the north. He didn't want to look behind him. He didn't care to be reminded of what he'd seen when he stepped on shore: masses of people; pack animals and every sort of wheeled conveyance; new buildings of raw pine or red brick—the only word for it was chaos.

What pained him most were all the abandoned ships in the harbor. It was unconscionable that worthy vessels should be left to rot. Their crews had succumbed to the lure of the diggings. Bart's own officers were standing armed guard on the *Manifest Destiny*. He'd threatened to whip and chain any man who attempted to jump ship.

The changes in San Francisco were only part of what troubled him, though. Certain changes in Amanda's situation—and in his own state of mind—were equally responsible. Feeling dour, he was sharp with her:

"That all you can think about these days? Profit?"

She wheeled to face him, her dark eyes catching the western light. He marveled at how lovely she was. She possessed a beauty no girl of sixteen or seventeen could hope to match. She was assured, not gawky; calm-spoken but purposeful. Secretly, he admired her strength, though he wouldn't have admitted it. Her strength was one reason he feared he'd lose her—

He realized he was extremely nervous. He had been worrying about this moment ever since the harrowing passage through the Strait of Magellan. For a time, he'd thought *Manifest Destiny* was going to founder and break apart in the violent winds and towering seas.

They'd run against the gale six days and six nights. Even now he could hear the roar of the waves smashing over the bows; feel the bite of the ropes that held him lashed to the helm.

He'd fought the storm as if it were a human enemy, dogged by a conviction that his luck had played out, and he'd never reach San Francisco. But he refused to give up. Finally, the clipper escaped the worst of the weather.

Although he'd already been awake seventy-two hours straight, he'd sprawled in his bunk for another two or three, thinking. Sorting out what he wanted of life and what he didn't. He reflected that perhaps only the prospect of imminent death could force a man to arrange his affairs. Lying there with the cabin lamps unlit, he'd reached a decision.

The freight-laden clipper arrived in San Francisco harbor nine days behind schedule. He'd been on shore since noon. He'd yet to speak to Amanda concerning the decision. He was fearful she wouldn't care about it. Besides, she had much to tell him about the past weeks—

And now the walk had taken a bad turn. Alone with her, away from the rowdy town, he'd hoped to tell her what was on his mind. Instead, just a moment ago, his nervousness and uncertainty had prodded him to make a remark better left unspoken.

She tugged off her sunbonnet as she faced him. Evening sunlight set her dark hair ablaze.

"Bart, that was unkind."

He studied the cherry-colored tip of his cigar:

"Mentioning profit?"

"No, what you implied about me."

"Maybe so, sweet. But you have a look you didn't have last time I was here."

"I told you—a great deal has happened."

She leaned against him, letting him feel the curve of her body. The contact somehow heightened his uneasiness. He felt exactly like a callow boy, angry with the world because he expected it to reject him—

He tried to smile:

"I found that out the minute I walked into Kent's and Felix informed me Sam Brannan was the new owner. How much did you squeeze out of him?"

"I asked ninety thousand. Firm. He complained but he paid. It's prime real estate."

"That uppity nigra of yours told me he got himself a last name, too."

"Why shouldn't Israel adopt a last name? He's a free man. And he'll have a responsible position, helping to manage the claim—"

"Israel Hope." Bart shook his head. "The whole world's haywire. Niggers naming themselves after mining camps—Billy paid off and gone chasing up the Yuba—your cousin showing up from Oregon one day and getting shot the next—" He fixed her with an uncompromising stare. "And you weren't there when the lighter tied up at the pier."

"I've already apologized for that. I had to sign papers with Brannan."

"Well, it makes no difference."

"You sound as if it does."

"What the devil's my opinion worth? I'm just a common sea captain—" His bitterness grew uncontrollable. "I've never owned a speck of gold. And believe it or not, I've never killed a man."

Amanda stiffened. "How did you learn—?"

"Israel."

"He had no right—"

"Oh, don't score him for it. He was only recounting what happened in the camp. Besides, it'll be all over San Francisco soon. Someone from Hopeful is bound to come down here and talk about it."

"There's no reason why they'd—"

"There certainly is. Most women don't know which end of a gun to pick up, let alone how to shoot one. Have you decided what you're going to say to Louis when he finds out?"

"That I'm not guilty of any crime! The miner's court brought no charges against me. I can explain the shooting to him—"

"For his sake, I hope so."

Bart turned away, glowering down at the sprawling town. Lanterns beginning to wink in the dusk softened its jumbled look. Westward, darkness was thickening above the channel. A fog bank hid the horizon. The air was growing chilly.

He was ashamed of the things he'd said. Yet he'd said them, hadn't he? Hell! He ought to head back for the clipper this instant. The confusions of shore life were too much for him to handle any longer. Ferocious as the tides and winds could be, they were antagonists a man could understand, and master. Here, he understood nothing—not how to deal with the demons that drove Amanda, nor how to control himself so he didn't hurt her.

And he *had* hurt her—to the point where she couldn't even summon anger:

"Would you care to listen to my side of the shooting scrape, Bart?"

"No. The Pike got in your way. And nothing—no one—is allowed to do that, correct?"

She shook her head. "It sounds like you don't think much of me any longer."

Bitterly: "I think more of you than you'll ever realize. That's why I wish I'd never helped you find those books, or asked those damn questions. Now you won't stop until you own Kent's again. I suppose that means you won't be coming back here—?"

She avoided his eyes. "I haven't decided."

"You don't fib very well, sweet."

Her cheeks darkened.

"You going straight to Boston?"

"No, Virginia first—to visit Jared's son. He deserves to know what happened to his father."

"You could write him."

"I considered it. That sort of news isn't easy to deliver in any fashion. But I think I can soften it better in person."

He had no comment. After a moment, he said, "Suppose you get all your humanitarianism out of the way and approach Stovall and he refuses to sell—what will you do then? Aim a gun at his head?"

"You're unreasonable. And very unpleasant, I might add!"

She spun to gaze at the thicket of bare masts in the bay. He all but abandoned his plan to discuss what he'd decided after surviving the storm.

"I plead guilty to unpleasant," he said. "But not to unreasonable. Putting your personal crusade aside, you still don't know what you're getting into by deciding to settle in the east."

"I know very well."

"Permit me to disagree. There's real trouble brewing. Has been ever since that damn Democrat from Pennsylvania tried to tack his anti-slavery proviso onto the Congressional bill for money Polk could use to negotiate with Mexico."

"I've heard some people actually approve of Mr. Wilmot's proviso."

"Nobody down south approves of it! Wilmot tried to violate the 1820 compromise line. Tried to make sure slavery would be banned in any new land acquisitions, north *or* south. The proviso passed in the House, but the Senate voted it down, thank God. Still, ten state legislatures in the north endorsed it. Not that it makes much difference to me personally, but I'll be flogged if I can see how the federal government has any business interfering with the rights of states, new or old. There's no such thing as a state surrendering a little bit of her sovereignty. Just as old John Randolph of Roanoke said thirty years ago, that's like asking a lady to surrender a little bit of her chastity."

"It was my impression you avoided thinking about politics, Captain McGill."

"Who the hell can avoid it when everybody on the east coast talks of nothing else? The hotheads on both sides of the Congress are screaming because of Wilmot. Someone's got to settle the question of slavery in the new territories. And figure out a better system of enforcement for the fugitive slave laws. It better happen soon, too."

"The newspapers on the last mail packet said Mr. Clay proposes to work out a compromise of some sort."

"Yes, he's supposed to introduce a flock of bills to calm the abolitionists *and* the secessionists—"

The last word brought a sharp glance from Amanda.

"That's right, the southerners are raising that threat again. The damn fanatics in the north are driving them to it! You'll be drawn into it if you go back. Nobody can stay neutral—"

Now it was her turn to sink a barb:

"Except at sea?"

"I'm not ashamed to say I've retreated. I don't want any part of such quarreling. It never decides anything, it only hurts people. I hope the situation doesn't get worse, but I'm afraid it may. Zach Taylor was a capable soldier, but as a president, he's a failure. So it's up to the Congress to resolve the differences peaceably."

"Peaceably?" she repeated. "What other way is there?"

"There's war."

"Oh, Bart, the states would never fight over—"

"Slavery? Don't you be too sure. There's a terrible violent streak in this country, Amanda—your own experiences should prove that. In New York, just last spring, the mob nearly tore down the Astor Place Opera House— the one you can't walk into unless you wear kid gloves—"

"I think I read a short item about that. I don't recall any mention of the cause."

"A ridiculous feud between Forrest, the American actor, and Macready from England. The feeling against the high-toned Mr. Macready boiled over when the Opera House booked him in *Macbeth*. The city called out more than three hundred police—the militia—even artillery and cavalry. There were thugs packing the theatre—and thousands milling in the streets. Why, Christ, before it was over, water hydrants were knocked open, the pavement was torn up and chucked through the Opera House windows— more than twenty got killed, and about a hundred and fifty wounded. The police arrested that Judson fellow—the one who writes those pieces against foreigners under the name Ned Buntline—for trying to set fire to the building—while it was still occupied! They dragged him away screaming, 'Working men! Shall Americans or English rule?' If people will behave like maniacs because an English actor spouts his lines on a U.S. stage, just imagine what they might do over the nigra question. I sometimes think we were immortal fools to start this country with a revolution. It's helped put a stamp of respectability on violence ever since."

Amanda had no answer for his assertion. Maybe he'd broken through her unspoken confidence that she could deal with any problem, no matter how large; deal with it and overcome it—without being harmed by it. He pressed his momentary advantage:

"If those Congressional compromises are put to a vote, I've heard Calhoun may go to Washington, sick as he is. He knows the situation's desperate—he and Webster and Clay and the other big thinkers. A big thinker I surely am not. But I'm content with my life because it lets me stay sane—no, you hear me out. You're a good woman, Amanda. A strong woman. But there's another part of you that's dangerous. In some ways you act like the windbag abolitionists—you've somehow got it in your head that you're one of those avenging goddesses of the Greeks or the Romans, I forget which—I read about them at the academy when I was no more than Louis' age. But the difference between you and one of the furies, sweet, is just this. They lived forever. You can't. You can be injured. Back east, you'll have to take sides politically. On either side, you'll be putting yourself in jeopardy. And you've already done it by declaring war on Stovall. So you're doubly vulnerable. I read some Bible when I was a boy, too. I remember St. Matthew. Jesus in the garden of Gethsemane—"

He gazed at her, hoping the meaning wouldn't be lost:

" 'All they that take the sword shall perish with the sword—' "

The wind murmured in the silence. The darkness was lowering rapidly. It muted the ugliness of the town below—but not the determination in her eyes:

"I'll take my chances."

"Yes—unfortunately—" He tried to smile. Failed. "That's the kind of woman you are."

"Why won't you understand, Bart—?" Unconsciously, she touched the rope bracelet. "Jared's death made it impossible for me to turn back. I would never have wished him murdered. But once it happened, I accepted it—and decided to make the most of it. I'll never have the same kind of opportunity."

With considerable cynicism, he said, "You're certainly counting on your cousin once removed wanting no share of what belonged to his father."

"He's a preacher. I don't think he'll be interested. Besides, all I intend to ask of him is the use of the money for a while. He'll be rewarded. Eventually I'll give Jephtha Kent ten times what he'd earn otherwise. I've discovered how to use money to make money—"

She brightened then, her head lifting as she whirled to face the dark eastern sky:

"Try to look at it from my side, Bart. Even apart from wanting to own the company again, it's exciting to think of going home. There's so much

I've never seen. The cities. Fine houses and those huge factories they say are springing up everywhere. I want to ride a horse-car and a railroad—I'll have to educate myself, too. Learn good manners, and how to dress properly. And teach everything to Louis—"

"Staying out of the way of the political trouble all the while? It can't be done. I especially don't think you can do it."

"Why not?"

"Just the way you are."

"Would you mind explaining that remark?"

"For one thing, you have a peculiar liking for nigras—"

Amanda bristled: "And which side were you on during the Astor Place riot, Captain McGill?"

"What?"

"You sound like you might have joined the thugs trying to keep the American stage for Americans only!"

"Nonsense. I never take sides. I was still in the Atlantic, thank God. Besides, I was just using that as an example of the way people in this country knock each other in the head over any trivial—"

"I wouldn't call the slavery question trivial."

"No, I expect you wouldn't. You treat that damn Israel like an equal."

"I treat anyone I respect as an equal! I always have. It didn't matter whether it was a Sioux dog soldier, or a Mexican officer, or a black man—"

"God," he muttered, "you do have an inordinate fondness for inferior sorts."

"Such as my grandfather? You're absolutely right. My grandfather Philip was one of those *inferior sorts*—he was nothing when he came to this country. A penniless bastard boy. But he thought America might offer him something Europe couldn't then. A chance to succeed because of what he could do, not what he was. I'm of the opinion this country stands for that. And if my attitude means I'll get involved in this political furor you're so afraid of, then I guess I will. But first of all, I'm going to bring the printing house back into the family."

Bart shook his head. "You won't listen to reason on any subject, will you? Do you really imagine Stovall's going to sell out to someone named Kent?"

"I thought of that. For a while, I'll use my married name."

Bart's cigar had burned out long ago. With a grimace of disgust, he flung the stub into weeds beside the path. He noticed the old man on the porch of the house watching them, roused from his doze by their loud voices.

A sense of desperation filled him then. He was convinced Amanda was charting a course much more dangerous than she was able to recognize. He had to stop her if he could. There was one possible way. He'd glimpsed death in the seas of the Strait of Magellan, and reached a decision. He *had* to tell her—

"Look, sweet," he began, "I think I've said a lot more than I should have about your personal affairs—some of it in a pretty nasty way. I apologize."

Her expression gentled. "Accepted—if you'll accept mine."

He waved that aside. "We've wandered pretty far from what I wanted to say this evening. I told you about the storm we struck rounding the Horn—"

"Yes—Lord, I was frantic with worry when the clipper didn't arrive on schedule—"

"You aren't the only one whose life has changed. I thought we were all going to die before we outran that blow. When we got through it, I realized it was time to make some changes of my own—"

He reached for her shoulders and pulled her against him, inhaling the fresh-scrubbed scent of her skin. His fingertips moved lightly down her back.

"I thought a good deal about what I wanted. I decided what I wanted more than anything was you. I don't mean just occasionally. I mean all the time—"

He hugged her impulsively, and for a moment, silent in the wind, they savored the closeness. The dark had engulfed the semaphore hill and hidden them from the old man watching.

Finally Bart resumed:

"I'm about to say something I never imagined I'd say to another female after I got rid of the one who played hob with my life for twelve years—"

A hesitation.

"I love you."

She clasped him tightly. "Oh, Bart—you probably won't believe it because of the way I scold you for some of your notions—"

"Scold me!" He managed a chuckle. "Lop my fool head off with a verbal ax, you mean—"

"You hush and let me speak."

"All right."

"I love you too."

Stunning, unexpected joy welled inside him. Emotion made his words halting:

"I—I hardly see how it could be possible. God knows I'm not perfect. Tonight I've demonstrated that amply—"

"A woman doesn't ask for perfection and love in the same package, Bart. To love you, I don't have to agree with every word you utter—"

"Some men expect that of their women."

"Well, you know better than to expect it from me."

He chuckled again. "I surely do. I reckon that's one of the reasons you stick in a fellow's mind—"

Holding her close, his fears of rejection began to seem groundless. He went on with rising enthusiasm:

"If what you say about loving me's the gospel truth, Amanda—"

"It is."

"Then don't go back. Stay here with me. Away from the stump speakers and the wild-eyed philosophers and—all the things that can hurt you. Even though California's filling up, we'll be safer than we would be in Charleston, or New York. I'll make a good life for you. For your boy, too—"

He wiped his eyes. When she spoke again, her words and her tone told him she didn't yet understand all he was attempting to say:

"You work out of New York, Bart—"

"In the desk in my cabin, there's a paper I drew up three days ago. My resignation. I'll hand it to the Ball brothers at the end of this voyage. The next time I sail to California, it'll be for good. I can find a captain's berth on one of the coastal packets, I know I can—"

Again that affectionate merriment in her voice:

"My, it must be love if you're willing to learn to pilot one of those hateful steam ships—"

"To be with you I'd do damn near anything. Marry me, Amanda—"

He held her waist and poured out all the longing that had grown within him after the perilous passage:

"*Marry me.*"

She drew in a breath; she was astonished:

"I had no idea you meant to propose—"

"What's so strange about it? People marry all the time!"

She kissed his cheek. "And I love you all the more for asking me. But—"

He pulled back, cold and fearful all at once:

"The answer's no?"

"I have an obligation, Bart."

"An obligation to what? To some Latin on a cheap piece of metal?"

"Please don't say that. I wouldn't have shown you Jared's medallion if I thought you'd make sport—"

"I'm *not* making sport! I'm trying to save you from what you're going to do to yourself!"

"It's my duty to go to Boston. I came from a family that—"

"A family that's nothing any more. Nothing! Your splendid *family* consists of one Methodist gospel-shouter and one former owner of a Texas whorehouse—"

He could almost feel her wrath like a physical blow:

"You certainly have a very peculiar way of demonstrating your affection, Captain McGill."

"Amanda—"

"Do you enjoy being cruel?"

"I'm trying to show you the truth! I care about what happens to you!"

He spun and stalked off into the high grass, hands clenched at his sides.

He'd suspected from the first that she'd refuse him. That was why he'd been so nervous. And now her refusal had unleashed rage again. He hated her strength almost as much as he hated his own lack of self-control—

He stood with his head down until his trembling worked itself out. Then, over his shoulder but loud enough for her to hear, he said:

"I've botched everything tonight. I'm sorry. I truly am, Amanda—"

He heard her footsteps in the grass. Felt her body against the back of his blue sea jacket. But something in him was dying. Not responding to the clasp of her arms around his waist from behind, nor to the press of her cheek against his shoulder:

"I understand why you're upset. You risk a lot—including pride—when you propose to a woman. I only wish I could say yes—"

His last hope died then; died and disappeared as completely as the house and tower had disappeared, only a short distance above on the hill's black summit. He blinked a couple of times, then pried her hands from his waist. He didn't want to let her know how much he was hurting. He tried to banter:

"All right. If there's anything a man should avoid, I reckon it's a committed woman—"

"If what you say about the east is true, I don't think you can stay un-committed either."

"You just watch! Five thousand miles from New York, I won't be wor-rying about anything except course and cargo."

"No, you're talking differently than you did a couple of years ago. You're much more conversant with both sides of the political argument."

"The hell I am!"

"Then, you thought men who championed states' rights were fools. A while ago, you said the federal government shouldn't tamper with those rights. Maybe you've taken sides yourself. Unconsciously—"

That fueled his wrath all over again:

"Never. *Never!*"

"You *are* a southerner—"

"I'm a seaman—period. The only territory with a claim on me is the deck of a clipper!"

He stepped away from her, unwilling to discuss the subject further. She'd pointed out something of which he was totally unaware, and it had shaken him profoundly. He practically barked the next sentence:

"It's time we went back." Then—with a faint undertone of threat: "I've got a business offer to think over."

"An offer? You didn't say anything about—"

"No point in mentioning it earlier. I thought I'd be berthing out here from now on. Since I won't be, this other proposition has a lot to recom-mend it. Gentleman approached me just before I weighed anchor this trip. The manager of the New York office of the Royal Sceptre Line."

"Sounds like a British firm."

"It is. Headquarters in London. Most of their trade's with Africa and India. Guess I've built a pretty fair reputation with Ball Brothers—Royal Sceptre offered me a mighty handsome command on a brand new clipper, the *Prince Consort*. Might be just what I need to get me away from the mess in this country. 'Specially since there are no personal reasons for stay-ing—"

"Would you be based in London?"

"Yes."

Unhappy, she fell in step beside him, letting him speak again when he was finally moved to it:

"Concerning your own trip, Amanda—I trust you don't have any thought of traveling on *Manifest Destiny*—"

"Why, yes, I do."

"You know there isn't passenger space."

"What about your cabin? You've offered it before."

"Not this time. It—it wouldn't be good for either of us. You find passage on another ship."

A silence, interrupted only by the crunch of their steps on the path.

"Will I see you in the east, Bart?"

"Can't say for sure."

"Does that mean you're going to England?"

He didn't answer.

Negotiating a steep place, she hung onto his arm for support. He almost pushed her hand away.

He smelled the night breeze. It was cold, and carried a salt tang. Already most of the lamps of the town were haloed by fog. But the hateful noise—the music, the braying laughter—grew steadily louder as they descended.

"Bart—"

"What?"

"Will you at least stay with me while you're in San Francisco?"

"Maybe it would be better if I didn't—"

"I want you to stay. I want us to have that much."

"We could have a lot more."

"I know. I'd say yes in a minute if it weren't for—"

"The family," he finished. "I guess I'll never appreciate what that family means to you. But I'll say this and be done. A family feeling as strong as yours is a curse, not a blessing."

"You're wrong," she said. "It's both."

ii

Amanda, Louis and Israel saw him off four days later.

The visit had been strained and anticlimactic, because the parting had really taken place on the semaphore hill. Their two subsequent attempts at lovemaking had been perfunctory. One hadn't even come to completion because something not merely physical shrank his flesh before they were half done.

And yet he stayed, unwilling to surrender his last hours with her even though she was occupied with other matters—packing, purchasing tickets on another vessel, buying Louis a proper traveling outfit. He'd actually seen more of the boy than he had of Amanda.

To fill the time, he taught Louis the fundamentals of playing the musical instrument he'd brought him as a birthday present. Louis was quick, and seemed to welcome the diversion. He obviously didn't relish the idea of leaving San Francisco, though he never said so directly. But he attacked the music lessons with such ferocity that Bart knew the boy was troubled. He suspected Louis was just as conscious of the new hardness in his mother as were any of the adults around her.

In a couple of days, Louis could blow *Oh Susannah!* with only a couple of sour notes, though he absolutely couldn't remember the proper name of the instrument—aeolina—and settled for the easier one, mouth organ.

One afternoon Bart sent out to the clipper for a similar instrument he'd bought for himself. They perfected a pretty fair duet on *Sweet Betsy from Pike.* But the session was strangely cheerless. Neither of them ever laughed aloud.

The morning of Bart's departure was gray and gloomy. He was going home with the holds of *Manifest Destiny* only scantily filled with hides. All the profit these days came from the westbound run. The quicker the clipper returned to New York for another load of freight, the better.

Trim and tall in his best blue jacket, black neckerchief and peaked cap, he said his farewells one by one:

"Israel—"

He forced himself to grasp the other man's hand and shake it. The mulatto looked startled, then pleased.

"—I count on that new last name to bring you good luck in the diggings."

"Thank you, Captain Bart. I'm mighty glad to be getting out of this wicked, overcrowded town. Hopeful isn't a capital of virtue, but at least they christened it sensibly."

Bart glanced past Israel to Amanda. She was wearing the yellow taffeta he liked. At the moment she was fussing with the sleeve of Louis' new coat. The boy was sprouting. He was almost thirteen; slimming down as he grew taller. His dark eyes were a mirror of his mother's but his swarthy skin and jet hair echoed the man who had fathered him in Texas.

So Amanda wouldn't hear, Bart said to Israel:

"I don't think much of her going east, you know."

"Gathered that. I don't either."

"We finally agree on something."

"Indeed we do."

Smiling without feeling it, he moved on. He extended his hand to Louis:

"Take care of your mother."

"I'll try, sir. Are you going to come visit us?"

"Don't see how I can. I don't know where you're planning to settle."

Uneasily, the boy glanced at Amanda. "I'm not sure myself—"

"Besides that," Bart said, "I'll probably be out of the country."

He took the last two steps with great effort. Amanda started to reach for his hand. He noticed the old, worn rope bracelet—little more than a few frayed strings now—and quickly brought his hand up to the brim of his cap in a small salute.

She looked at him, surprised and saddened. But he couldn't touch her. He couldn't or he'd break.

"That was a very decent thing you did for Israel," she said.

He shrugged. "I try to make a conscientious effort not to be a son of a bitch all the time. God keep you safe, sweet."

"Bart—please. Don't cut it off this way. Come find me in the east."

"I'm sure that wouldn't be difficult. Given your money and your ambition, I'm sure that after a couple of years go by, you'll be well known. Eminent, in fact. Unless—"

Unless that man Stovall is more than a match. Fights you—and wins—

"Unless what?"

"Nothing."

It could go either way, he decided. She was smart, sturdy and strongwilled—more of the goddamned Kent family inheritance!

Unexpectedly, he saw tears shining on her cheeks:

"Bart, I beg you—come find me. Just—to say hello—"

He was unintentionally curt:

"Doubt that'll be possible. Right now I feel pretty favorable toward that offer from Royal Sceptre—"

And I don't think I'd want to see how you've been hurt.

Or how you may have hurt others—

"Goodbye, sweet."

"Bart—!"

He spun away as she cried his name, stalking toward the end of the creaking pier where the lighter waited.

As he climbed down the ladder to the bobbing boat, he kept thinking of the ominous passage of scripture that had come to mind on their hilltop

walk. It fit her perfectly. She was too determined; too unwilling to moderate her stand or limit the means she'd use to achieve her goal. In a way,
she was like the zealots—the fanatics—in the north and south who were
surely going to bring destruction down on the whole nation one day—

An oarsman spoke to him. He didn't hear. He was listening to an inner
voice.

*Put up again thy sword into his place: for all they that take the sword
shall perish with the sword.*

iii

Aboard *Manifest Destiny*, Barton McGill immediately turned command
over to his first mate and sailing master, with orders that the clipper depart
as soon as possible. He went below.

In his cabin he opened the drawer of his desk and drew out the resignation he'd labored to phrase properly. He was satisfied with the language.
He intended to submit the letter the moment he docked—but not for the
same reason he'd written it.

With a shake of his head, he returned the resignation to the desk and
opened the locker where he stored his whiskey.

To make room for the bottle on the desk, he cleared away his log and
the one Kent and Son title he'd purchased in New York—some sort of
trashy romantic novel. *A Frenchman's Passion*. The unknown author had
adopted an obvious, and ridiculous, pseudonym—Mrs. A. Penn. Yet a
clerk had informed him, disdainfully, that this latest offering of the once
dignified and prestigious Kent house was attracting thousands of readers,
principally feminine. Bart had somehow balked at taking the book ashore,
and now he flung it on the deck.

He poured a drink, downed it, poured another and shucked off his
jacket. He took his boxed aeolina from one pocket. With his sleeves rolled
up and the bottle for company, he started playing the central melody of
the Chopin fantasy in C sharp minor. Because of the sunless day, the
cabin was dark. He sat with his back to the windows that overlooked the
abandoned ships in the bay, letting the music speak his grief and his fear
for the woman he loved.

The Journal of Jephtha Kent, 1850:
A Higher Law

January the 17th. A most disagreeable dinner-time. Captain Tunworth and my mother-in-law present, but neither ate more than a few morsels, preferring to fulminate against President Taylor. They condemn Taylor as a traitor to his class, and his state, because of his easy compliance with the will of certain northern Congressmen under whose influence he has fallen. Chief among these hated advisors is Seward of New York, who takes an inflexible stand on the slave issue.

Prodded by the northerners, Taylor leans toward admitting California to the Union under the constitution which the state has already adopted, viz., the constitution prohibiting slavery. If this happens, the "South's Sentinel," ailing Calhoun of South Carolina, predicts the cotton states will leave the Union. Captain Tunworth is all in favor—not surprising, since he is the master of twenty-nine ill-treated bucks and wenches.

So deep has the ideological chasm become, I find even my own modest table in Lexington divided. I listened in dismay as my dear Fan hotly seconded her father's views. I think she and Tunworth noticed my silence.

If there is to be peace in our household, I dare not speak what is in my soul. As the preceding pages of this private book will attest, I am coming all too close to complete rejection of Mr. Calhoun's claim that the idea of freedom for the blacks originates in "that blind, fanatical zeal which made one man believe he was responsible for the sins of others; and which, two centuries ago, tied the victim that it could not convert to the stake."

Christ teaches that I *am* the keeper of my brothers and sisters, whatever their color. But am I "blind and fanatical?" I pray not.

The Methodist Episcopal Church, South, will not permit me to voice my convictions, or even my doubts, from the various pulpits to which I itinerate up and down the valley. But even more saddening is my growing fear that should I present even a single counter-argument to the Captain at my own table, my dear wife would look upon me with vexation and, yes, even anger.

*

January the 29th. God has let the merciful light of His compassion shine! A way out of the nation's awful dilemma may exist after all—

In surprisingly temperate conversation with Fan before she retired this evening, I won a concession from her. She agreed that the omnibus legislation which Mr. Clay is bringing to the Congress may offer the last, best chance of averting strife and disunion.

Though she has grown increasingly partisan, Fan yet recognizes the urgency of a program of compromise. If we are to continue to enjoy tranquility throughout the nation, the dispute over fugitive slaves must be resolved. So must the status of the new western lands, which have been thrust into great prominence as a result of the discovery of California gold —an event, I should judge, which has forever altered the course of the country by generating a gigantic migration—thus inevitably filling all the territory between the Mississippi and the Pacific.

Under old Clay's various legislative proposals, California would be admitted to the Union as a free state. The New Mexico and Utah lands would be organized as territories, but without reference to slavery. The boundaries of Texas would be settled, and her debts assumed. Slave auctions in the District of Columbia—an odious sight to diplomats from foreign nations—would be prohibited, though slaves already present would not be tampered with—this as a sop to Maryland, which ceded the land for the District.

Finally, Clay offers one great bone for the south—a fugitive slave law which will at last be supported by vigorous federal enforcement. Any person found guilty of aiding a runaway black would be fined and imprisoned. An escaped slave apprehended in the north would not be granted a jury trial to decide his fate, nor be permitted to testify in his own behalf. A federal official would have power to settle questions of ownership, his fee being five dollars if he decides for the slave, but ten if he decides for the master.

It is the continual escape of slaves—and a lack of effective redress— which most rankles men such as the Captain. Perhaps Clay's bill will pacify them. But I do not believe any law will hamper the activities of certain other persons in our district—of white color—who, in secret and at the risk of their lives, assist blacks in reaching the north. No law will damp the fervor of these "conductors of the under-ground railroad."

But at least Clay's compromise may exert some soothing effect upon those who talk publicly and thoughtlessly of secession.

*

March the 9th. The momentous debate in Congress occupies the minds and fills the conversations of most people throughout the valley and, it is my impression, in the north as well. Two days ago, with the galleries packed and the chamber overheated to nearly one hundred degrees, the eloquent Webster of Massachusetts rose and spoke for three hours in reply to Mr. Calhoun. The substance of Webster's impassioned plea for accord was reprinted today in a newspaper which reached our house from Richmond.

The hour is late, Webster said. Men of good will must reach an accommodation or there will be disunion and war. The senator stated—rightly, I think—that "peaceable secession" by the southern states is a contradiction in terms—

Impossible.

*

March the 15th. How vile and bitter are the attacks upon Webster already! Having boldly stood for the principles of compromise, peace and Union, he is scorned by radical elements of the northern press as "the lion turned spaniel." He is accused of "fawning on the masters whose hands he licks for the sake of the dirty puddings they might choose to toss him."

To a congregation with whom I was visiting, I lauded the senator's courage in risking his reputation and, indeed, his treatment by posterity. I found about half of those gathered agreeing that Webster had taken a noble stand. But there are also those who resist all compromise. They will neither forget nor forgive the bayings of the abolitionists who accuse the south of being "one great brothel where half a million women are flogged to prostitution."

Alas, the president himself, who should be the foremost spokesman of the cause of Union, favors a more limited program than Clay's. He is jealous, they say, of Mr. Clay's renewed notoriety! How mean and petty are the ambitions and angers of some men in high places!

*

March the 31st. A giant has perished. The news was flashed to Richmond and brought on from there—yesterday, Calhoun succumbed to a lung sickness.

Against the advice of friends and physicians alike, he went to Washington earlier this month to address the Senate on Clay's proposals. He was so enfeebled, he could not speak aloud. He sat huddled in a blanket in the chamber's dreadful heat while Senator Mason read his remarks.

Calhoun could not embrace the Clay legislation wholeheartedly. He believed the north has made the south its hapless victim, abusing its people and abridging their rights—and it was in response to this stern view that Senator Webster pleaded for three hours.

When I first read of Calhoun's reaction, I reflected again on the unfathomable purpose of God in creating a race of colored men. Without the existence of such a race, the old "Sentinel" might never have veered from the position he took in Congress nearly forty years ago, when he championed an improved system of national highways and waterways with the cry, "We are under the most imperious obligation to counteract every tendency to disunion!"

But the presence of the black man upon this continent—and Calhoun's conscience, which not even the most rabid northern agitator dared call into question—slowly worked its change. Just before he fell out with Old Hickory over the Nullification issue, he had already replied to Jackson's toast on Jefferson Day—"Our Federal Union! It must and shall be preserved!"—with one that expressed his own conviction—"The Federal Union—next to our liberty most dear." After that, he swung ever closer to his final position—that slavery had somehow been vindicated as "a good—a positive good" and that any other view was "moral and political evil."

To the end, he was a Unionist—but not at any price. Captain Tunworth is fond of quoting Calhoun's remark during the debate on Wilmot's Proviso—"I desire above all things to save the whole; but if that cannot be, to save the portion where Providence has cast my lot." In his last appearance in the hall he loved, a sickly figure listening to another man read the outpouring of his heart, he remained true to his principles.

Shamefully, I cannot claim to have emulated him, except in these pages. I grow more and more circumspect in my remarks to Fan. She will grant that Clay's compromise offers the one chance of averting a separation of the sort which sundered my Church. But like Calhoun, she will not admit there is any wrong in holding men and women in bondage. I fear to dispute with her because Gideon, Matthew and Jeremiah are in her constant care, I am gone a good deal, and she has stated without qualification that she will not permit the boys to hear any of my "softness toward the nigra."

*

April the 10th. Seldom have I heard invective to rival that which Captain Tunworth directs toward Seward of New York. During the March debate in Washington, the Whig senator referred to "a higher law than the Constitution, which regulates our authority over the domain." Nothing worse could have been said to inflame southerners, who insist the Constitution protects the rights of slave owners because of these words:

"No Person held to Service or Labour in one State, under the Laws thereof, escaping into another, shall, in Consequence of any Law or Regulation therein, be discharged from such Service or Labour, but shall be delivered up on Claim of the Party to whom such Service or Labour may be due."

How I weary of hearing the Captain parrot that passage! It is the foundation of his belief that the federal government must assist in returning escaped slaves. True, the word "slave" is not mentioned. But the Captain says the meaning is unmistakable.

The failure of the abolitionist politicians to heed the clause—plus the passage, in some northern states, of those disputed "liberty laws" forbidding recapture of runaways—has led to the controversy which Clay's new fugitive slave proposal would hopefully abate. Clay's bill would in effect enforce the Constitution to the letter—

But while men are struggling for peace, Seward rants of a law "higher" than the Constitution!

Seward, many say, has presidential ambitions. If so, he has destroyed himself with his statement. He has placed himself permanently among those the Captain villifies as "no better than mad dogs."

In truth, Seward was already very nearly classified that way because of his membership in the Whig party. When Calhoun fell out with Jackson, he promptly joined the new Whigs, a faction opposing Old Hickory's autocratic behavior. The faction took its name from the English party which traditionally fought against the unlimited power of the king.

For a time, the Whigs served the interests of an uneasy alliance of southern gentry and northern businessmen. They sought to curb the mounting power of the Jacksonian Democracy, which draws its strength from, and has become increasingly dominated by, persons of lower social standing. The factory class, as Captain Tunworth calls it.

But the Whigs have also come to be dominated and controlled by a certain segment of society—namely the abolitionist element. This drove Calhoun to abandon them and rejoin the Democracy. Thus by his party affiliation, and most assuredly by his statement about "a higher law," Senator Seward has conjured a ghost which will hover close to him for years—and thwart whatever ambitions he might harbor.

*

April the 14th. Returned from the circuit to find—again—no letter from my father.

Two of mine, sent to him in care of the postal office in Sacramento, have gone unanswered. His last to me from California, written in September, stated that he was journeying to a remote area in the hope of locating a profitable claim. I have heard nothing since.

I thought my father's decision to leave Oregon would refresh his spirits and provide him with a new opportunity much needed since his farming efforts came to nothing. Now I think my enthusiasm may have been ill advised. Spent the better part of an hour praying he is safe and well.

*

April the 27th. Damp weather has brought on a fever and confined me to my bed. The household is disturbed again because of the escape of a prime buck, Amos, belonging to a neighbor of Captain Tunworth.

The Captain raged in our parlor for an hour this afternoon, his voice carrying up to the bedroom. He believes the operatives of the "freedom rail road" aided Amos in his flight. The Captain will join the effort to recapture him.

*

April the 29th. Some thirty miles above Lexington, the runaway was caught by a party of armed men which included Captain Tunworth. They came upon Amos wandering south instead of north. The illiterate slave had grown confused because the inclement weather hid the heavens and made it impossible for him to locate the North Star. Being incapable of reading written directions of any sort, he was following the star. When it was lost from view, he blundered straight into the arms of his pursuers.

All this I learned when Captain Tunworth returned tonight. He could not refrain from coming to my room to inform me of the details. He first described the crude pass, with the signature of Amos' owner forged, which the slave had been carrying. Every black out after nightfall must have such documentation of his right to be abroad, or he becomes immediately suspect.

The Captain and his associates interrogated Amos for nearly four hours, using all manner of inhuman persuasion, since it was obvious a literate person had provided the fugitive with the forged paper. My father-in-law said he and his friends suspect Syme, who operates a small granary on the outskirts of Lexington. Syme is a Connecticut Yankee by birth. He inherited the granary from a relative. He has been heard to remark in public that he loathes the "peculiar institution." In an effort to make Amos confess the name of his abettor—Syme or someone else—the slave's owner ultimately resorted to—

It sickens me to attempt to put the actual words on this page. They are an abomination to my sight, and to the eyes of Him who sees all. I will state the despicable truth as decently as I can:

Captain Tunworth's neighbor employed a long knife. It was applied to the private parts of Amos, destroying his manhood and, soon after, his life. He bled to death without revealing the identity of his benefactor. May God have mercy on him, and on his master—

On Captain Tunworth, too. He sees nothing wrong in such base cruelty. He swore that if one of his blacks ever escaped, he would pursue him to the ends of the earth and punish him. Unable to contain my wrath, I ordered him from my room.

Approximately an hour later, when I called to Fan and asked her to bring the boys up to say goodnight, she refused.

*

May the 5th. Itinerating again. I have been unable to banish the death of Amos from my thoughts. It has had a profound effect upon me, beyond all description. Last night, when I rose to offer a meditation at prayer service, I felt as if a mighty hand had seized me, shaking from my lips a condemnation of the cruelty perpetrated against the runaway.

A dozen in my congregation promptly left. Those who remained were obviously stunned and unsettled by the interjection of a secular subject, though afterward, three were bold enough to approach me and whisper their belief that I was right.

I fear repercussions but cannot shrink from them. Some Voice other than mine spoke from within me. I think the Almighty has finally decreed that I shall keep silent no longer.

*

May the 9th. Household atmosphere most unpleasant following my return today. Fan has removed herself to a separate sleeping room. My sons
barely speak at all; I fear she has harangued them in my absence—
Too grieved to write more.

*

May the 11th. While doing an errand this afternoon, I was accosted by
Syme. He is a small, unpleasant-looking man with a pocked face and nervous eyes.

He greeted me cordially enough. But then he began to speak in a
curiously guarded way about my recent remarks at the prayer service,
which are fully known in Lexington. I can tell from the hostile stares of
those I previously called my friends. Twice I have been stoned by small
boys—no harm done, though both incidents deepened my sadness.

A transcript of Syme's words could never be used against him, so carefully and obliquely did he speak. Yet his meaning was unmistakable:

Should my conscience dictate a more active participation on behalf of
the enslaved blacks of the district, he would assist in finding "a means for
expression of my will."

I rebuffed him. My affairs are troubled enough without embroiling myself in conducting runaways to freedom. He tipped his hat and departed,
his manner as contemptuous as that of my father-in-law—though for an
entirely different reason.

It becomes increasingly clear that a man of moderate views can find no
peace in Virginia. Perhaps he cannot anywhere in the nation.

*

June the 3rd. Unable to write a line for three days. Immense and stunning surprise fell on our house, coupled with immense grief.

My father is dead. Foully murdered in California. The news was conveyed by a visitor who has since departed just as she came—swiftly and
forcefully as a summer storm. It was my cousin once removed, a handsome, splendidly-dressed woman of middle years—the very woman for
whom my father searched for so long. Her unexpected arrival, all the way
from California in company with a thirteen-year-old boy of dark complex-
ion and almost Latin appearance, plunged the household into confusion.

She arrived in a carriage secured at Norfolk. She brought much luggage, but there was no hired driver; she handled the reins herself. She goes by the name Mrs. Amanda Kent de la Gura, having been married to a Spanish fur trapper; the father of her son Louis, I presume. She did not specify.

She began her visit in a mood of cordiality and sympathy, relating how she had discovered my father by chance in the city called San Francisco. She described the manner in which he lost his life at the hands of some local toughs. She then stated she was on her way to Boston, but her exact plans were presented in only the sketchiest detail. I gathered she has some desire to buy back the family printing house, of whose existence I told her I knew.

During those first remarkable hours, Fan had the good sense to conceal all hints of the tensions which have divided our family. She treated my cousin once removed and her somewhat willful boy in a friendly and gracious fashion. Regrettably, Captain Tunworth was not so courteous when he called unannounced.

In ten minutes, he and my cousin developed an unconcealed dislike of one another. Mrs. de la Gura chanced to mention that she had employed a runaway slave in California, which caused the Captain to launch a diatribe against those who harbor fugitives. My cousin's retorts were caustic. If not an outright abolitionist, Mrs. de la Gura obviously approaches that persuasion. The Captain departed in foul temper—and Fan's restraint was visibly tried.

She abandoned politeness entirely next morning, when our guest put forth another revelation. Before his death, my father apparently became a partner in a modestly successful gold-mining enterprise. I am heir to his share.

Mrs. de la Gura, who prior to leaving California appointed a representative to act in her stead, urged me to permit her to continue managing my father's interest. I told her I had no experience in business affairs, and so would be willing, provided any monies due my family were scrupulously accounted for. She assured me of it, promising that if she were given leave to administer my father's share of the claim, my sons would benefit to a greater extent than if I were to take an active role.

So strong and lucid a case did she present—remarkable on two counts; she is a female, and no longer young—that I of course consented. This produced an awful argument from Fan. In my cousin's bold and forthright manner, she saw some fancied scheme to deprive our sons of what is rightfully theirs.

At last, after much stormy language, I was forced to demand Fan's silence. I then signed a paper giving Mrs. de la Gura authority to act on my behalf. For the remainder of the visit, she and Fan were decidedly hostile to one another.

Mrs. de la Gura is a person not easily opposed, that much was clear soon after she arrived. She repeated more explicitly her determination to see the printing house restored to the hands of the founding family. In this pursuit, she said she would require the use of the California gold. Fan construed her words as glib fraud. Nothing I said would change her mind.

Before my cousin departed—having assured me she would be in touch when she was permanently located—my wife and I had yet another reason for disagreement. It was caused by an ugly scene which marred the farewell.

My second son, Matthew, six, owns a pet toad of repulsive mien and phlegmatic disposition. The boy Louis wished to examine the creature. Matthew, in one of those contrary moods which seize children from time to time, did not desire to have his treasure handled by anyone else. He refused—politely at first, then more vehemently as Mrs. de la Gura's son continued to insist. Finally the latter snatched the toad from Matthew's hand—whereupon my son burst into tears and the toad hopped into the shrubs, never to be seen again. When my cousin struck her boy's cheek to admonish him, his eyes glowed with fury, and I thought for a moment that he might strike her back.

He did not, fearing her, I suppose. But she was visibly upset by the young man's behavior. I cannot help but observe that he only imitates the behavior of his mother, who descends upon a person like that storm of which I wrote, and sweeps all away before—

When the carriage had departed, Fan berated me. I was so exercised that I could barely keep from speaking un-Christian words in reply.

I wanted to console Matthew over the loss of his pet but he would not admit me to his room. As a result of my cousin's visit, I am more than ever an outcast in my own home.

*

June the 29th. Today I received a communication from my bishop. I have paid dearly for my discourse at the prayer service.

The bishop chastised me for speaking against the cruelty of the death of Amos. My remarks were in violation of the ordinances of the Methodist Episcopal Church, South. The bishop reminded me that the Church is apolitical, concerned only with the saving of souls, not the freeing of physical bodies from bondage.

In his closing paragraph, he removed me from my intinerancy.

*

July the 5th. President Taylor died yesterday, from ingesting too much iced water and a large quantity of cherries. The stomach ailment struck him after he participated in a celebration of our nation's Independence in the capital. Mr. Fillmore has already been sworn in.

On hearing the news of the president's death, I almost wished a similar fate might befall me. I am a pariah in my Church, my own house, and throughout Lexington. Only Christ's ever-present and strengthening hand enables me to endure the tribulation.

*

July the 21st. I can find no employment—no means of supporting my family. Fan and I fell into another terrible argument because of it. I refused her demands that I make a public retraction of my statements concerning Amos, and seek the bishop's forgiveness.

My wife, became as a stranger to me, spoke words about my character whose bitterness I cannot begin to capture on paper. She accused me of robbing my own sons by giving control of the gold claim to Mrs. de la Gura. I confess without shame that I left the house with tears in my eyes.

My son Gideon was scything weeds in the yard. I spoke to him and he turned away. I suspected that Fan had been speaking against me, but this day I saw the proof.

As I stumbled from the yard, I cried silently, "Father, if thou be willing, remove this cup from me!"

When I realized it was not to be, I was shaken by a mighty wrath—and only with the greatest effort did I pray the remainder of Our Lord's appeal—

"Nevertheless not my will, but Thine be done."

I tramped the countryside until dark, pausing once to fall on my knees and clasp my hands. Humiliated by my anger against the Lord, I admitted my sin in prayer.

Despite the day's anguish, my convictions remained firm. I vowed I would neither flee Lexington nor the proximity of my family, in the hope that love and the bonds of Christian marriage would restore me to Fan and the boys. I love her, I thought. I love them. Yea, I love those who scorn me, for that is Christ's way.

A short while later, at dusk, I returned to my home in the hope of effecting a reconciliation. Fan ran out to meet me in the yard. She told me there was no place within her house for a traitor. She then brought out a few of my belongings and, when I requested it, my Bible and this book.

And so I crept away again, to the residence of a man in Lexington who I hoped would display Christian charity—the good Doctor William White, pastor of the First Presbyterian congregation. He has permitted me to sleep in a hut on his property.

By moonlight, seated in the hut's doorway, I scribble out these lines—feeling for all the world exactly like a felon, and praying that the cup indeed may pass; that time may heal the injuries of the dispute with Fan, for whom I still find love within my heart.

But I will not effect reconciliation at the price of recantation. I have pondered long on what I was moved to say at the prayer service. I believe the Lord revealed His truth when he spoke with my tongue. Amos was a child of God just as much as any white man. If that be heresy, let me suffer for it; yea, let me burn!

Later. I feel the Lord's presence. A voice whispers what I would have called unthinkable a year ago—

There is, as Seward said, a higher law. God's law of love and justice for all His creatures; a law which men have perverted.

Believing that helps ease my pain somewhat. I have been tardy in taking my stand. I will follow the heedings of that inner voice even to the gates of Hell.

*

September the 10th. I am reduced to penury—living in a hovel and tending the stables for the smartly dressed young cadets at the Military Institute. I am an outcast among those I sought to serve. Only Dr. White's merciful intercession enabled me to remain in Lexington at all, gaining for me as he did this lowly position. Captain Tunworth has assumed responsibility for the worldly needs of Fan and the boys—and is providing for them more handsomely, I am sure, than ever I could on my slim stipend as an itinerant preacher.

It is an irony that my cousin once removed, would I but make the effort to locate her, could rescue me from this wretched state by virtue of my father's gold. Yet I am not willing to take steps to contact her. To throw myself upon her mercies would be to deny the dictates of my conscience—

So I wear rags. Subsist on the coarsest of fare. Perform menial work while enduring the jibes of some of the cadets. I know I am considered the worst sort of fool—a self-condemned martyr.

I also suspect that many in Lexington wish I would leave. I am conscience made visible. A pricking thorn. That is why I will not go. My resolve has become as a stone. I answer to God and His Son Jesus Christ and Their higher law, and to no others.

*

September the 11th. Only my faith gave me the courage to endure an incident which transpired this afternoon. I saw Fan and the boys on the grounds of the Institute, bound upon some social errand or other.

Little Matthew would have spoken, but Fan pulled him sharply away and struck his hand when he resisted. Gideon showed no expression whatever; I believe he knows it would not please his mother if he recognized me.

Jeremiah, four, is too small to do so—especially as I am an unkempt, threadbare figure—no longer the same man physically or spiritually that I was a mere six months ago.

I watched them until they passed from view. Not even Matthew would look back.

*

September the 12th. A professor at the Institute informed me this morning that California has been admitted as a free state. After much struggle and many portents of failure, Clay's program is at last being maneuvered through the Congress—largely with the help of a senator who belongs to the Democracy, Douglas of Illinois, whose support had not previously been counted on.

Old Webster is now in Fillmore's cabinet, Secretary of State. Clay, exhausted, has gone to Rhode Island to rest. Neither can directly engage in the legislative battle. But Douglas has seen the danger, and responded to it—

If the rest of the compromise bills can be passed, perhaps the Union can be saved. That now appears more likely than it did at the start of this tumultuous season.

Autumn is coming to the valley. The coloring of the countryside, the hue of change, reminds me that men too must undergo change. So I have done, by speaking my beliefs and enduring the consequences.

I do not hate those in Lexington who abuse me openly or in private—the cadets; Captain Tunworth. I pray for reconciliation. I pray the Union may be preserved, though I am frequently pessimistic. I fear the issues are too deep and divisive for Clay's compromise to bring more than a temporary tranquility.

Later. The voice of the higher law spoke to me again. I cannot remain passive in my protest—though I will be circumspect, so that I may be useful to the Lord for many months to come.

Tomorrow, I will seek out Syme and reveal my willingness to help him perform the secret work I am convinced must be done.

BOOK THREE

Perish With the Sword

CHAPTER 1

The Legacy

OUTWARD BOUND FROM Boston harbor, the gigantic six-masted steamship belched smoke from her stack. Louis Kent, watching from the port rail of *Yankee Arrow*, a much smaller coastal steamer, nearly lost his broad-brimmed wide-awake to a sudden gust of wind. He caught the hat as it tumbled off his head, then exclaimed:

"I can't make out her name. But I see the British flag—"

A few steps further along the rail, clutching her parasol with one hand and her spoon bonnet with the other, Amanda turned to her companion, a broad-shouldered, six-foot Negro in his early thirties. He had a prominent nose, deep eye sockets that accentuated the darkness of his eyes, and skin of a lustrous bronze hue. His long hair, neatly trimmed at the line of his collar, tossed in the wind. He was faultlessly dressed in a frock coat and strapped trousers whose elastic bands fitted under the soles of polished-boots.

"Is that one of the Cunard steamers, Mr. Douglass?" Amanda asked. She and Louis had made the gentleman's acquaintance on the voyage up from Norfolk—he had boarded at Philadelphia—and had dined at his table, despite the purser's whispered suggestion that they needn't segregate themselves in that fashion. Amanda had remarked tartly that the other white passengers were the ones segregating themselves—foolishly—since the gentleman was delightful and provocative company.

"No," Douglass answered in a mellow voice. "I believe that's a sister ship of the *Great Britain*. A competitive line. At the end of my lecture tour in '47, I came home on the *Great Britain*. She's screw-driven—just like that one. Those masts are an innovation too. All but one's hinged. They can be lowered to the horizontal for less wind resistance and greater speed. *Great Britain* brought me to America in just under thirteen days."

Amanda marveled: "Thirteen days from Europe. Imagine! It seems machines are changing the whole world—"

Mr. Douglass smiled in a rueful way. "Every part of it except the most important. The human mind. Two years ago, I was the only male delegate at the conference on women's rights in Seneca Falls. Afterward, I said publicly that I agreed with the ladies attending the conference—society does discriminate against women. The good folk in Rochester treated me as if I were twice a leper. Leprous once for being black, leprous again for daring to suggest women are entitled to equal treatment under the law. Those Rochestarians thought I was crazy! There's not much a steam engine can do to change attitudes of that sort, I'm afraid."

"I still don't see why she carries sails," Louis said, absorbed by the sight of the huge ship putting out to sea. He'd hooked his elbows over the rail and was hanging onto his wide-awake with both hands. He looked smart in his trim black jacket, vertically striped railroad trousers, button boots and dark green cravat.

"For the same reason we do," Douglass said, gesturing to the masts of the *Arrow*. He spoke loudly because of the thump of the *Arrow*'s engines and the steady roar of water spilling down from her enclosed paddle-wheels amidships. "To conserve coal—and the engines—when there's a fair wind," he explained to the boy. "To provide motive power if the engines fail."

He settled his white summer top hat on his head. "We'll be at the pier shortly. I'd better go below and sign that book for you, Mrs. de la Gura."

"I thank you for that, Mr. Douglass—and for the pleasure of talking with you during the voyage."

Amanda smiled as she said it. But she was decidedly uncomfortable in the four-foot-wide skirt of crinoline and the flounced, stiffened muslin petticoat beneath. Summer-weight the materials might be. But all the clothing was a burden to someone accustomed to the more casual dress of California.

Still, she was determined to get used to wearing what was proper. She looked quite attractive in the expensive outfit. Her hair was done in the style that had been popular for more than a decade: parted in the center, with the sides drawn down and beneath the ears and pinned up in a bun in back. Mercifully, daytime fashion permitted her to go without the annoying ready-made side ringlets held in place by cumbersome combs. The ringlets were mandatory in the evening.

As Douglass started away, she added, "I do hope I may be able to make a donation to your paper soon."

The black man turned back, pleased. "A shortage of money is the constant plague of *The North Star*. Without the help of friends, my paper would never survive, and my message could never be spread so broadly. As it is, I spend too much time running from city to city presenting lectures and soliciting donations. Your contribution would be very welcome. An address reading Fred Douglass, Rochester, New York will bring it to me—"

"I'll remember."

As Douglass disappeared down a companionway, Amanda turned toward the panorama of Boston, a murky jumble of piers, hills, residences, and commercial buildings that poured smoke from tall chimneys into the already gray air of the late June morning.

"I'm not sure all those factories are as great a boon as everyone claims," she remarked to Louis. "Look at the dirt they spew into the sky."

The boy was more interested in their departed companion:

"Is Mr. Douglass really famous, ma?"

"Louis, I've reminded you before—it's time you began saying mother."

The dark-eyed boy scowled. "What's the difference?"

"One sounds more genteel than the other. And to answer your question —yes, Mr. Douglass is just about the most famous runaway slave in America. People pack his lectures."

"Then why wouldn't anyone else sit with him in the dining room?"

"Because he's a black man."

"But he's very nice." His scowl deepening, Louis surveyed the passengers along the rail. "People should be whipped for treating him that way."

Amanda said nothing. The remark about whipping disturbed her. Louis was beginning to display some less than admirable traits. She recalled the dreadful row with Jephtha's son over a toad during their visit in the Shenandoah Valley.

She tried to recall when she'd first become aware of the boy's aggressive attitude. In California, she decided. Soon after she told him of the shooting in Hopeful. She'd taken pains to explain that the man had threatened her, but it was the fact that she'd killed him that seemed to make the greatest impression on Louis. Quite a few times since, she'd noticed him watching her with a speculative expression.

Now, while his attention was diverted, it was her turn to study him. He was handsomer than Cordoba. Yet he seemed to lack the Mexican officer's softening humanity.

On the long voyage from San Francisco, she'd finally told Louis about his father. The experience had been harder on her than it seemed to be on him. He'd asked a few questions about Cordoba's appearance and character, and accepted Amanda's statement that the officer was an honorable man whom she'd loved.

She deliberately refrained from cautioning the boy about mentioning his illegitimacy to others; he had no friends with whom to discuss it, and she was afraid that undue emphasis would lend it an unhealthy importance it shouldn't have.

Louis hadn't brought up the subject since that one and only discussion. In many ways, the boy was an extremely private person. Not surprising, since she'd been occupied with so many other things these past few years. And would be in the weeks and months to come. She wondered whether their new life in the east would be good for him—

A bit too late to think of that, she reflected. Still, his words about whipping put her on guard. If she were required to perform any unpleasant actions in connection with Hamilton Stovall, the boy must never become aware of them.

The pilot maneuvered *Yankee Arrow* through the crowded harbor. Amanda felt just a bit intimidated by the great city rising before her. She was angered by the reaction. Here she was, about to step ashore to begin a new life just the way her grandfather had done eighty years ago, and her gloved hands were trembling!

Despite her anxiety, she was fascinated by the sprawl of the city, the gush of smoke from the manufactures, the crowded confusion of the docks becoming visible off the bow. Boston, like the other cities she'd glimpsed on the trip, seemed to symbolize the wealth, the power, the human energy and inventiveness of the industrialized east. In all her years, she'd never seen anything that even resembled this part of America.

There were nearly twenty-five million people in the nation now. Population, according to Mr. Douglass, had grown at an unprecedented rate of thirty-six percent in ten years. And there appeared to be no limit to the mechanical genius of the country's citizens.

For two decades, McCormick's reaper had been improving the productivity of the farms. Three rival inventors—Howe, Wilson and Singer—were vying to produce a device for mechanized sewing. She'd overheard a man on the steamer discussing a fellow named Otis, who proposed to build some sort of oversized box to lift and lower passengers within a shaft inside a building. The man had made an extravagant prediction: structures as tall as eight, ten or twelve floors would be commonplace if Otis succeeded.

The marvels were by no means limited to the large and spectacular. In her cabin, Amanda had a half-dozen samples of a remarkable little invention called a "safety" pin, perfected only a year ago. The sharp end was springy, and hid away within a small metal cap when the pin was fastened.

She was both fearful and excited at the idea of creating a place for herself in this restless, fast-changing society. It would be an important place, too. She had the means. In her portmanteau, she carried the document Jephtha had signed, granting her the right to administer the California claim—

For a few moments she pondered the sad enigma of the Reverend Jephtha Kent, a pious, haunted-looking young man who scarcely resembled his father. Something was seriously wrong in Jephtha's family; she'd sensed that all during her visit.

Perhaps it was friction over the slave problem. Jephtha's petite and attractive wife had made it clear she was a partisan of the system. His father-in-law, a detestable rogue named Tunworth, had been even more outspoken; positively vitriolic. But Jephtha himself had given few hints of his own convictions. To Amanda that suggested he didn't feel free to voice them. Having secured what she came for, she'd been glad to leave the tense household.

Thoughts of her cousin once removed reminded her of Bart's warning about the stormy political situation here in the east. She had seen another tangible example aboard the *Yankee Arrow*: the public shunning of a noted man who happened to be black.

Perhaps the socially generated turmoil was one more reason she felt uneasy. She didn't want to be drawn into it. And yet, quite without realizing she *was* being drawn in, she'd taken Louis to sit with Douglass in the dining room. No great damage done by that—snickers and glares could do her no harm. But she'd have to be careful of any deeper involvement. It could divert her from her purpose.

ii

With her autographed copy of the *Narrative of the Life of Frederick Douglass* tucked under one arm, Amanda waited impatiently near the open door of a private office at Benbow and Benbow.

Yankee Arrow had let down its gangplank less than an hour ago. Clerk's pens had stopped scratching the moment she and Louis walked into the dusty-smelling outer room of the law firm.

She was still conscious of eyes turned her way.

Louis raised his head at the sound of faraway thunder. At the open door, a clerk was speaking to the invisible occupant of the private office: "—a Mrs. de la Gura, sir."

A somewhat high-pitched male voice snapped back, "The Benbows have no clients by that name. If she insists on seeing someone, refer her to one of the junior partners—"

Amanda stepped forward. "If you'll excuse me—" The clerk had to move or be bowled aside. "—I insist on speaking to one of the senior partners." She stopped in the doorway. "Is your name Benbow?"

At an ornate desk in front of a wall bookcase jammed with reference volumes, an elderly man with thin white hair and pale skin swung his spectacles back and forth from one hand. He studied his visitor disapprovingly:

"Yes, madam, I'm William Benbow, Junior."

"Well, I'm not precisely a client as yet. But before we finish our interview, I will be. Now if you'll dismiss this young man, I'd like to discuss my business—"

Benbow flung down the spectacles. "See here! I am preparing an important brief. If you insist on seeing me, make an appointment for sometime next week."

Amanda shook her head and walked into the gloomy office:

"You don't understand, Mr. Benbow. I've come all the way from California, and I don't propose to wait. I'm Gilbert Kent's daughter."

William Benbow, Junior, was seized with a fit of coughing. He groped for a crystal water jug and overturned one of the tumblers before he poured and gulped a drink. It was a full minute before Amanda was sure the old man wasn't going to faint away.

Turning to the clerk, she said, "You may go." She took hold of the door and pushed to make certain he would. Louis grinned and darted into the office before the door shut.

iii

"Incredible," William Benbow, Junior, said at the end of Amanda's rapid summary of her history—the portions of it she cared to reveal, that is.

"Absolutely incredible. You do resemble your father. At the time he died, my father—" A gesture toward a dour portrait on one wall. "—was his attorney. I was still clerking in the outer chambers." The lawyer wiped his eyes with a kerchief, replaced his spectacles. "You mentioned business—if it has anything to do with your gold claim, I should advise you that the Benbow firm has no expertise in that area."

Amanda replied, "No, it has nothing to do with the California property. I may need your help with a simple real estate transaction."

Benbow looked a trifle crestfallen: "Real estate?"

"I assure you, Mr. Benbow, if you serve me capably in this small enterprise, I'll probably have a good deal of work for you later on."

"You plan to stay in the east permanently?"

"That depends on a number of factors we needn't go into right now. Are you familiar with the house my father owned on Beacon Street?"

"Quite familiar," Benbow nodded, his manner growing more cordial. "My father took me there to visit on several occasions. A handsome residence—"

Louis was seated in a chair beside his mother's. He scraped the toe of his boot on the carpet. Benbow frowned, as though the noise had interrupted his train of thought. Amanda noticed that Louis stared right back at him, without so much as a blink.

"Who lives in the house now?" she asked.

"Why, let me see—" Benbow thought. "A family named Wheeler. Mr. and Mrs. Charles Wheeler. He's a furniture merchant. He and his wife have owned the home for nearly twenty years, I think."

"I'm asking because my father once kept certain family mementoes in the house. I'm anxious to see whether they might have survived. The items would be of no intrinsic value to another owner—but there's always a slim chance they weren't discarded. Would you imagine the Wheelers would let me inspect the property? Search the attic, and the cellar?"

"Doubtful. Wheeler's an arrogant sort. His wife is quite conscious of her fancied social position."

Amanda smiled without humor. "You're saying they might not permit some strange woman from the west to prowl through their house?"

"Yes, you've put it accurately. I doubt very much that they would."

"Would you guess that items that might have been stored in the house would still be there?"

"I've no way of knowing, Mrs. de la Gura. Wheeler and his wife are antiquaries. I'm told they've packed the place with art objects purchased on tours of Europe. That may indicate a penchant for saving things—but it's still thin evidence on which to base a positive answer to your question."

"Then the only way to answer it is to buy the house."

Benbow's spectacles, swinging in his hand again, fell to the carpet. "You want to live in it?"

"No, I just want to go inside."

"You—you've certainly chosen an extravagant means of entry!"

"I don't think so. The location of the property still makes it valuable, I assume—"

"Very definitely."

"Then it's a good investment. I'll be happy to have the house back in the family. After I inspect it, you can lease it to someone else."

Benbow was speechless. Annoyed, Amanda said:

"I'll be glad to pay whatever fee you require, Mr. Benbow. But I want you to approach the Wheelers and tell them you have a purchaser for the property. How much is it worth?"

"Why—why, I suppose—in that area of town—forty to fifty thousand—"

From her reticule Amanda drew an envelope, and handed it across the desk. "Inside, you'll find a bank draft representing the sale of some real estate in California. The sum of ninety thousand dollars. I'm prepared to pay up to seventy thousand for the Beacon Street house, though if you can get it for less, so much the better. You must stipulate that nothing stored in the house when the Wheelers purchased it is to be removed. Nothing—no matter how worthless the object seems."

Benbow retrieved his spectacles, pulled the draft from the envelope and examined it, shaking his head and blinking. Amanda frowned:

"What's the matter? The draft is perfectly good—"

"Of course, of course. I am only—only—"

"Shocked at my way of doing business?"

"To put it mildly."

"Time is precious to me. I'll call on you tomorrow to learn whether you've been successful."

"*Tomorrow?*" Benbow gasped.

"Certainly." Amanda drew one of his old-fashioned quills from the inkstand; wrote on a slip of paper. "You'll send a representative to the Wheelers this afternoon, I assume—" She tapped the quill feather on the slip. "You can reach me here—the American House—should you get a favorable response at once."

"Very well," the lawyer gulped. He nearly dropped the envelope containing the draft. "But please take this. I'll feel more comfortable if you deposit it with a bank. I suggest the Rothman Bank on State Street— where your faher had his accounts. Ask for the president, Mr. Joshua Rothman. He's the grandson of the founder. I—I think you'll find he has some important information for you—"

Thunder rumbled again, louder this time. "What sort of information?"

"I would prefer you learn that from him," the lawyer said, still acting stunned.

iv

Mr. Joshua Rothman was a slim, dark-haired young man with graceful hands and thoughtful dark eyes. Behind his high-backed chair, rain spattered the windows of his private office.

The office was conservative, as befitted an important Boston bank, yet opulent. Thick carpeting deadened sound. The marble top of Rothman's desk showed not a speck of dust. Wood paneling reflected the bluish light of the gas jets hissing within wall-mounted glass bowls. Until today, Amanda had never been in any building with gas illumination, though her hotel, the American House, boasted that it had installed gas fixtures in its rooms and upper halls in 1835.

From beyond a heavily carved door came a sudden, rapid clicking. Curious, Amanda swung toward noise.

"My apologies for the racket, Mrs. Ken—Mrs. de la Gura," Rothman corrected. "That's a private telegraph wire. The bank maintains constant contact with Wall Street. Where large sums are involved, fast and confidential communication is important."

The young banker rose, walked to the door and opened it. He said to Louis, "You're welcome to go in and watch the operator."

Louis shook his head, clearly unhappy at being trundled from office to office. Joshua Rothman shrugged, closed the door and strolled back to the desk where Amanda was seated.

"I only wish my grandfather Royal were here to greet you in person. He often spoke of the Kents—and with great fondness. The publishing house your grandfather founded has added luster to Boston for a long time."

"I have the impression absentee management has dimmed that luster quite a bit."

"Hamilton Stovall, you mean? Yes, his orientation is—how shall I say it? More blatantly commercial than that of the Kents. You know, I've always been curious about the loss of the firm to Mr. Stovall. There's still a fanciful tale that the transfer came as a result of a wager—"

"The story's correct," Amanda said. "My mother's second husband was cheated by Mr. Stovall. In a gambling game."

"Is that a fact. I never believed it. I do know the printing house burned. I heard the fire was started by—ah, but forgive me for bringing up an unpleasant subject."

"It may be unpleasant, but it's the truth. My cousin set the fire. He died in California. That part of the past is closed."

The banker nodded without replying.

"I'd like your opinion on something, Mr. Rothman. Suppose that in a few years, I were to accumulate a substantial amount of money from the mining claim I described. What are the chances of my purchasing Kent and Son?"

"I would say excellent."

Relief swept over Amanda as the young man went on:

"The firm earns a decent return, I'm told. But Mr. Stovall has a reputation for being more interested in the current balance sheet than in long-term stability and growth."

"He milks the company, in other words."

"Exactly. He does the same with his steel factories. He's in his mid-fifties, but he's still quite preoccupied with—ah—call them worldly pursuits. He's not a favorite of the lending community because he gives too little attention to sound management. He prospers only because the domestic market for steel is voracious. Since he devotes even less time to the publishing operation, I should imagine he'd be happy to dispose of it if he could realize a profit."

With never a flicker of change in her expression, Amanda stored away the bits of information about Hamilton Stovall—including the hint of licentiousness in Joshua Rothman's choice of the words *worldly pursuits*. She stored the information away just as she'd already taken note of the use of a private telegraph line.

"Very good," she said. "The draft I handed you for deposit should convince you I'm serious about purchasing my family's former home—well, I'm every bit as serious about buying Kent and Son."

"I don't doubt you for a moment, Mrs. de la Gura. But you needn't delay making an offer to Mr. Stovall."

For the first time since entering the busy bank, Amanda was genuinely surprised:

"What do you mean?"

"Rothman's has enjoyed a peculiar relationship with the Kents over the years. The bank has been the steward of certain assets of your late father of which you are probably unaware."

"What assets?"

"Have you ever heard of a cotton spinning firm in Pawtucket, Rhode Island, called the Blackstone Company?"

"Never."

"My grandfather Royal, your father, Gilbert Kent, and a number of other local men founded the Blackstone Company in 1803. It's still operating. Very successfully, I might add. For certain reasons of his own, your father preferred that your mother not be aware of his investment of one hundred thousand dollars in the firm—forgive me if this is offensive in any way—"

"No, go on," Amanda said softly, a strange expectancy gripping her.

"Your father, in short, took steps to protect a portion of his estate by placing his Blackstone voting stock in the bank's keeping. Your mother drew income from, and controlled, only the printing house."

Immediately Amanda understood why. The way in which Harriet Kent's poorly chosen second husband had gambled away Kent's made her father's decision wholly comprehensible.

"Rothman's has long since assumed there were no Kent heirs," the young man went on. "Nevertheless, we have administered the Blackstone shares as if there were. Contrary to much popular opinion, bankers are not thieves. You are the recipient of your father's legacy—which has grown to be worth a great deal of money."

"How much money, Mr. Rothman?"

"At current market value—conservatively—six million dollars."

v

"Oh my Lord, ma! Six *million?*" Louis burst out. She was so overcome, she quite forgot to correct his use of the word ma.

The initial shock passed in a few moments. But not her awareness of the stunning possibilities opened by the young banker's announcement.

While the rain ticked at the windows and a glare of lightning paled the gaslight, she collected her thoughts. She said finally:

"For the time being, Mr. Rothman, I want the bank to continue administering the shares."

"Certainly. The dividend income will be credited to your new account."

"I'll also want to inspect the Blackstone Company."

At that, he looked dubious:

"If you wish, I can arrange it. But not even the male stockholders go there very often. It's a noisy, unwholesome place—a typical factory, I'm afraid."

"But I own part of it—"

"Yes, a substantial part."

"You said it's voting stock—?"

"It is."

"How can I cast intelligent votes if I've never seen the business? What it does, or how?"

"Why—" He smiled in an admiring way. "You can't, obviously. I'll be happy to schedule a visit at your convenience."

"Excellent. I'd appreciate your doing two other things for me. First, approach the owner of Kent and Son regarding a purchase. Operate through Benbow if you wish, but above all be discreet. I don't want it known that I'm a member of the family. Mr. Stovall might not be willing to sell to a Kent. He harbored quite a grudge against my cousin. That's why he took the firm away in the first place."

"So I remember hearing," Rothman murmured. "We can make the proposition this way—you are a woman of means who seeks to diversify her business holdings. At all times, we'll refer to you by your married name."

Amanda smiled. "You're very quick, Mr. Rothman. We'll get along splendidly, I think."

"I think so too. But I wish you'd call me Joshua."

"Very well—Joshua."

"You mentioned a second request—"

"Mr. Frederick Douglass is in Boston to present a lecture at the Park Street church—"

"My wife and I plan to attend." His glance said he was testing her political sentiments.

"I met him on shipboard, and I promised him a donation. Send him a draft for one hundred dollars, drawn in my name so he knows I kept my promise."

"With pleasure." He started to make a note, then noticed her upraised hand. "Yes?"

"A week from now, send a second draft to him in Rochester. Don't identify the donor."

"Is the sum also a hundred dollars?"

"Five thousand."

"Your generosity's commendable. But why give so much anonymously?"

Amanda's face looked oddly pale in the gaslight. She framed her reply with care:

"Two reasons. One, I don't think the purpose of charity is to earn public approval for the donor."

"Nor do I—though many people wouldn't give a penny to any cause unless they were honored for doing so. Still, Mr. Douglass is hardly in the same category as churches and orphan's homes. Boston *is* the center of abolitionism, but there are also quite a few local citizens who detest Garrison, Douglass and everything they stand for—"

"That's my second reason. I prefer not to be too closely identified with the movement. A small sum attracts small notice. A large one attracts a great deal. I'm sure you understand."

He did, but he said nothing. Amanda knew she'd diminished herself in his eyes. But she was determined not to become actively involved in the slavery dispute. Whether Joshua Rothman thought she was cowardly or not, she had no time for extraneous struggles. Kent and Son came first.

"I have one final question," she said. "Negotiations with Stovall will take some time, will they not?"

"Yes, though we'll make our initial approach immediately."

"I'd like to see the firm."

Rothman tented his fingers. "I'd refrain until we have at least sounded out the owner on his amenability to a sale. Actually, it would be better if you didn't visit Kent's at all—"

"That's out of the question."

"Very well—" He was obviously not happy. "I'll inform you when I think it's all right. I'd only caution you that when you do inspect the property, do so in a businesslike way. Keep your remarks very general—you'd be astonished at how a seemingly trivial word or action can sometimes upset a negotiation."

"I'll follow the advice, thank you."

The banker smiled.

"You're amused?"

"Forgive me—I am. I have an odd feeling you'll accept advice from Rothman's when it agrees with your wishes—and disregard it when it doesn't."

"You're an astute young man, Joshua," Amanda said, smiling back. "Good afternoon. Come, Louis."

vi

July rain streamed down the marble headstones in the little burying ground in Watertown. Amanda's parasol was soaked through.

The thunderstorm had blackened the sky. Behind her, at the edge of the narrow drive, the carriage horse whinnied. She didn't look around. Her eyes were moving across the rain-blurred inscriptions on the monuments.

Philip Kent

Anne Ware Kent

That was her grandfather's first wife. She was the daughter of a Boston patriot, a member of the small band of men who had led Massachusetts into open rebellion against George III. Amanda knew Anne Kent had been lost at sea during the Revolution; no mortal remains lay beneath the headstone, which stood to the right of Philip's. An equal distance to the left rose the marker belonging to her grandmother.

Peggy Ashford McLean Kent

To its left—she walked that way in the driving rain—the final monument.

Gilbert Kent

A bird had left a spatter of white on the top of the stone. It made her angry. Heedless of dirtying her glove, she smeared the white until the rain dissolved it and washed it away. Then she put the parasol on the ground and laid both hands on the wet marble and let the tears pour down her cheeks.

Presently the sadness passed. She had discharged a small debt by coming to the graveyard. Now she must discharge a larger one—and give new life to the name a stonecutter had chiseled four times. Lightning glared on it—

Kent

She was home. Home and ready to return that name to its rightful eminence.

The parasol offered no protection as she groped her way back toward the closed carriage, her eyes still damp and her emotions as turbulent as the thundery skies.

"All ready," she called to the soaked driver huddled on the seat.

In the carriage's small oval window, a lightning-burst showed her the handsome face of Louis Kent. The lightning flickered out. The face vanished.

She had asked, but not ordered him to leave the carriage and walk to the graves with her. He wasn't interested.

What sort of emotional legacy was she passing on to him? she wondered. Was there *anything* he cared about?

vii

Below, the cavernous rooms of the house on Beacon Street steamed in the heat of the late September evening. With a whale oil lamp in one hand, Amanda slowly climbed the front staircase toward the second floor landing. The lamp's flame cast shifting patterns on the wall beside her.

She was vaguely aware of Louis making noise as he wandered back in the kitchen. She heard occasional shouts and catcalls from the Common. A torchlight procession had ended there at seven. Bald, bespectacled Garrison was addressing a crowd about the injustice of the recapture of a slave named James Hamlet.

The escaped black had been seized in New York City, only a few days after the Congress had passed the new fugitive slave law. Clay's compromises had finally won through, even though important legislators on both sides—including Senator Seward of New York and Senator Jefferson Davis of Mississippi—had withheld their support.

The Kentucky statesman had endured the worst sort of personal abuse during the debates on the bills. At one point, an opponent had gone so far afield as to jeer at Clay's thwarted presidential ambitions. Clay had replied that the work of averting national catastrophe was far more important than personal considerations. He would rather be right, he'd declared, than be president.

Once the various bills had finally been passed, the ringing of bells and an orgy of public drunkenness throughout the north celebrated the Union's salvation. But the members of the noisy throng listening to Garrison undoubtedly hadn't taken part in the revelry. The Massachusetts Anti-Slavery Society had been denouncing the compromise as a betrayal of American liberty.

Slowly, Amanda started toward the third floor. The darkness depressed her. She thought of Bart McGill; longed for him—for the simple physical presence of someone she cared about. A son could never satisfy that need in quite the same way—

Her knees ached as she climbed the stairs. Age. Time was running out for her. Thinking of that, she almost regretted refusing Bart's proposal—

Why was she troubled by regrets so keenly now? The matters she had set in motion early in the summer were moving toward completion. Through the Benbow law firm, Joshua Rothman had made his first tentative offer on Kent's. The sum had been rejected by Stovall's New York attorneys, but the door was left open for further negotiations at a higher price.

And the Wheelers had succumbed when Benbow increased his offer on the house to sixty-seven thousand dollars. The Wheelers had removed the last of their belongings only this morning, transferring them to a new residence in Cambridge.

In California too the future looked promising. Amanda had received a letter from Israel Hope the last of August. The letter said the Ophir Mineralogical Combine was generating ten thousand dollars in gold per week, and on the basis of this, Francis Pelham was purchasing equipment for a prospecting trip into the Sierras.

Despite all the favorable developments, she was still depressed. Louis' behavior was one reason. He was surly with the tutor she'd engaged to instruct the boy in their hotel suite. Louis did his lessons in a perfunctory way, or not at all—it depended on how he felt that particular day. He bowed to Amanda's discipline, but with the greatest reluctance. She hoped the waywardness was merely the effect of adolescence, and that it would pass. Soon.

But you can't blame the boy for the way you're feeling, she thought as she climbed on toward the narrow landing outside the attic door. *The blame's yours. You rejected Bart. You decreed that you had to go your own way. Alone—*

Sometimes she questioned the worth of the effort. And even wished she didn't feel such a strong family obligation.

With a sigh, she approached the attic door. She pulled back the latch, then walked into the musty, cluttered interior. True to their bargain, the Wheelers had left any number of old crates scattered about the attic.

Amanda set the whale oil lamp on the floor. She tried loosening the slats on the side of one crate. The wood was thin, and so old she could break it bare-handed.

She opened the crate, coughing as dust clouded from feminine garments that smelled of mold. Old clothing of her mother's? Or the possessions of the people who had owned the house before the Wheelers? Impossible to tell.

She walked around the lamp and started to insert her fingers between two slats of another crate. Something standing against the back of the crate caught her attention. She swept off the tattered muslin cover—

A framed painting. A large oil. She pulled it into the light—

A dark-haired, almost truculent man gazed at her from the canvas. In her mind's eye, she saw the stern face in its proper setting—the wall of the library downstairs.

Philip Kent's painted eyes stared at the cobwebbed attic and the woman who wept with happiness as she attacked the slats of the second crate.

viii

"Louis? Louis, come see—!"

At the open front door, the boy turned. Amanda came rushing down the darkened stairs, grime on her cheeks and fingers, her gray hair festooned with cobwebs. On the Common, the mob yelled and waved torches.

As Amanda hurried to her son's side, she noticed a figure above the crowd on the far side. A man storming back and forth across an improvised platform, waving a piece of paper—

"Louis, I found them!" She gripped her son's shoulder. "Your great-grandfather Kent's portrait—the sword, the rifle, the bottle of tea—all packed away in the attic. Come see them!"

The boy shook his head, pointed at the scene on the Common:

"I want to watch this. A man who went by told me the fellow speaking is Mr. Garrison. He's going to set fire to a copy of the Constitution."

Disappointed, Amanda said, "I really feel you should show an interest—"

"I want to watch!" Louis declared, turning and dashing out on the stoop.

Someone passed a torch to the platform.

"Look, mother—he's going to do it!"

Just as the boy uttered the last word, the mob howled and the paper in the hand of the distant figure burst alight. The roar died gradually as the man with the burning paper gestured for silence. Amanda heard him shout:

"—so perish all compromises with tyranny! Let all the people say amen!"

The mob roared, *"Amen!"* Garrison flung down the charring document and stamped on it.

"We must go to hear him speak sometime," Louis said. "It takes a lot of nerve to burn the country's constitution—"

The boy turned, a smile on his handsome face.

"Mr. Garrison's a lot like you. He does exactly as he pleases and no one dares to stop him."

One bright eye caught the torch-glare as Louis waited for her to respond to what he fancied was a compliment. Cold clear through, Amanda started to speak.

She couldn't. She turned and walked slowly back into the darkness, leaving her son staring after her, first with confusion, then outright anger.

CHAPTER 2

Of Books and Bloomers

THE STREET TO WHICH the carriage brought Amanda several weeks later testified to the parsimony of the firm's owner. Kent and Son had been relocated in a dingy district of warehouses and chandler's shops near the North End piers. Despite the October sunlight and the brisk, salty smell of the air, Amanda was in a cheerless mood when she alighted from the carriage, paid the driver and told him to return in an hour.

As the hired rig clattered off, a scrofulous man in a blue jacket limped from a nearby doorway. A grubby blue bandana was wrapped around the man's forehead, hiding his eyes. Amanda noticed him sidestep a rotting fish carcass.

The man extended a dirty hand. "Penny for a Mexican veteran, ma'am?"

Furious over the appearance of the frame building that housed Kent's, she whipped up her closed parasol and whacked the beggar in the side of the head.

"Jesus Christ! Have you no charity, woman?"

"I'm as charitable as you are blind, my friend. Go cheat someone else. But first I suggest you pull that bandana down more snugly. I can see your eyes move."

Muttering, the man hobbled away. The limp vanished after he'd taken a few steps. And he did adjust the bandana before he slipped down an alley, cursing her.

Well, his anger wasn't any stronger than hers. The building was a disgrace. Its warped, split clapboards were layered with grime. So was the signboard swaying from an iron fixture over the door. The board's gilt lettering was blurred by accumulated dirt. The lower half of the e in Kent had flaked away, and the o in Son was totally gone. The tea-bottle design was barely discernible. She swung up the parasol and gave the sign a smack to set it swinging. Then she headed for the door.

While Joshua Rothman continued to negotiate with Stovall's attorneys, she had deliberately avoided driving by the firm. Now she decided that had been a mistake. She should have prepared herself gradually for the sorry state of the company.

Finally Rothman had given grudging consent to the visit. She had set out from the American House this morning with great enthusiasm. That enthusiasm was already destroyed.

At the door, she stopped, recalling the banker's caution about behaving with restraint. Rothman believed the seller's lawyers might well approve the current offer. She didn't want any actions of hers to upset that—nor did he.

She got her anger under control. But it took her almost two full minutes to do it.

ii

Sunlight from the open door spilled over the stained floor. The light seemed to stir the resentment of the five decrepit men bent at desks covered with untidy piles of paper. They blinked like animals roused in a cave.

The front office area was badly lighted. Only two oil lamps hung from ceiling fixtures. The management evidently relied on daylight through a pair of plate glass windows flanking the door. The smallness of the windows—each was less than a yard on a side—was another indication of Stovall's niggardly ways. On a gloomy day, Amanda imagined the office would be stygian. It wasn't much better now.

The five men watched her from their desks. Not a one of them looked younger than fifty. All had a dispirited air. Three went back to work as she slammed the door, cutting off the sunlight.

The floor vibrated. The presses—located in the basement, she guessed—had a slow, ponderous sound, as of someone laboring for breath.

"Who is in charge here?" she asked, advancing toward a rail that separated the desks from the small waiting area. Her voice made one of the employees start. The gutta-percha cane leaning against the back of his chair toppled over and clanged on a spittoon. The floor around the spittoon showed that the spitter missed frequently.

One of the human wrecks shuffled to the rail.

"Mr. Payne is chief editor and general manager, madam. He's busy."

"Where's his office?"

"There—" A veined hand fluttered toward two partitions walling off the back part of the room on either side of a corridor. "But I tell you he's occupied. Conferring with one of our authors."

"Who are you?"

"Mr. Drew. Office manager. May I ask your business? Are you a bookseller interested in the Kent line?"

"If I were, one look at this place would convince me the Kent line is probably as outdated as—never mind."

Watch your tongue, she thought as she pushed through the gate in the railing. But she was still angry.

"See here!" Drew snorted as she headed down the aisle toward the partitioned offices. "You have no right to thrust yourself—"

She wheeled around. "I certainly do, sir. I'm trying to buy this company. I've come to look it over."

He gaped. "You're the one—?"

"Yes, and if I'm successful, I guarantee there'll be some immediate changes!"

Sullen, Drew watched as she continued on, her cheeks scarlet.

iii

The narrow corridor dividing the walled office space ran straight to the back of the building. At the extreme rear, Amanda glimpsed a dark stair leading to the upper floors. The first door on her left bore a small, tarnished metal plate reading *T. Payne.* The door was ajar.

She reached out to knock, only to be stopped by the weary sound of a man's voice:

"Of course I don't like the manuscript. But I don't have to like your vaporish fantasies to publish them. I have instructions from Mr. Stovall! Drew will write your check before you leave the city."

"Theo—"

Amanda blinked. The voice, deep and almost masculine, belonged to a woman.

"—I frankly get goddamned sick of your Harvard snobbery. You know how many copies *A Frenchman's Passion* sold. *Bartered Virtue* did twice as well. This manuscript will outstrip both of them put together."

"The title makes me ill."

"What's wrong with *Convicted by Love?*"

"If you don't understand, I can't possibly explain. Will you stop puffing that disgusting weed in my face?"

Amanda's mouth rounded. She'd assumed the unseen man was the source of the cigar fumes. In response to the complaint, the woman laughed—a rich, cynical laugh that somehow tickled Amanda.

"Indulge me, Theo. You have your habit, I have mine. And I can't plunk myself down at Commodore Vanderbilt's dinner table and smoke a cigar. I have a position to maintain in New York! That's why I like coming to Boston to bring you a manuscript—and discuss the words dropped from *Bartered Virtue*. Here's the list. Sixty-two adjectives, eighty-nine adverbs—"

"Good writing doesn't need those crutches, Rose."

"Who said my writing's good, dear boy?"

"Not I, certainly."

"Theo, were you drunk when you edited the manuscript?"

"That's insulting."

"Well, goddamn it, I corrected the proofs till my eyes watered! I put back every word you took out. And you ignored them!"

"Rose, please," the man pleaded, sounding tired. "You know Mr. Stovall has given orders—expenses are to be kept to an absolute minimum. We can't bear the burden of re-setting once I've edited the copy."

"You'd better *start* re-setting, or I'll take my next manuscript to Mr. Harper in New York. He'll appreciate the value of my work! If it weren't for the sales of my novels, you couldn't afford to publish that dull literary drivel everyone praises and no one buys. I understand the book trade better than you do!"

"Then why don't you take over my job? I happen to be thoroughly sick of it. God, I wish I'd never quit the newspaper!"

At that point, Amanda finally knocked and thrust the door open:

"Excuse me—"

The man behind the cluttered desk was about thirty-five. He was small-boned, with pale skin, bloodshot hazel eyes and a thick pink nose. His neck-cloth and silk shirt had seen better days. He smelled of whiskey.

"This is a private conference, madam! Deal with one of the gentlemen up front."

She was amused rather than annoyed. The little man in the large chair resembled a small boy physically; his face, by contrast, suggested a hundred years of debauchery crammed into a third of that time.

The woman with him, exceptionally robust, was about Amanda's age. She had a blunt chin, forthright blue eyes and white hair. Her crinoline skirt was wider than Amanda's—and far more expensive. In one gloved hand she held a green-wrapped cigar, half smoked.

"I prefer to deal with you," Amanda said, turning sideways and tilting the bell of her skirt to maneuver it through the door. "My name is Mrs. de la Gura. I hope to purchase Kent and Son."

His reaction was similar to Drew's: *"You—?"* He jumped up. The top of his head barely reached her shoulder. "—I had no idea—that is, Mr. Stovall's attorneys wrote that someone was interested, but no names were mentioned—"

"I've come to look over the premises."

"You mean Stovall's going to sell?"

"It's a distinct possibility."

"Jubilee!" the editor cried, doing a little jig. "I think I'll go out and get a drink to celebrate."

"Not right now, please," Amanda said. "What's your first name?"

"Theophilus."

"I prefer Theo. I heard your guest using it—"

She acknowledged the stout woman gazing at her through a curl of smoke from the cigar now clenched in her teeth. Realizing he'd neglected introductions, Payne blurted:

"Oh, excuse me—Mrs.—de la Gura, you said? This is Kent's romantic novelist, Mrs. Rose—that is—"

His cheeks turned as pink as his nose. His eyes appealed to the elegantly groomed woman. She rescued him:

"It's all right if she's going to own the place, Theo." She extended her hand. "Rose Ludwig. Mrs. Adolph Ludwig of New York City."

"I'm pleased to make your acquaintance, Mrs. Ludwig."

"Down in New York, nobody knows I'm Mrs. A. Penn," the woman confided. "Being an authoress isn't an occupation my late husband—or his friends—would consider proper."

"I'll keep your secrets," Amanda told her.

Rose Ludwig drew the smoldering cigar from her mouth. "Including my vice?"

Laughing, Amanda nodded. "Now, Theo, although the sale hasn't been consummated, it's far enough along so that you and I should get to know one another. I'm buying Kent and Son to diversify my holdings—" The lie came glibly. "—and if Mr. Stovall comes to terms, I'll probably want you to continue acting as editor and manager. Provided you and I find we can deal with one another."

Payne took the candid remark as a threat. He started perspiring. Amanda decided that Hamilton Stovall had reduced the man to a state of fear.

Rose Ludwig settled herself in a chair beside Payne's cluttered desk. "Where are you from, Mrs. de la Gura?"

"California."

"One of those new gold millionaires?"

"Not quite yet."

The woman intimidated Amanda a little. She'd caught the reference to Commodore Vanderbilt, the steamship magnate. Mrs. Ludwig obviously had important social connections.

But she didn't act as if she did. She disarmed Amanda by tossing her cigar butt in Payne's spittoon and nodding emphatically:

"Well, by God, I'm glad you're here. I like your cut. How about you, Theo? Isn't she a big improvement over Mr. Stovall?"

"Careful!" Payne warned, a finger at his lips. He mouthed a name silently. *Drew.*

Amanda realized the doddering office manager must be a spy for the owner. She kept her voice low as she asked:

"Do you know Stovall personally, Mrs. Ludwig?"

"Unfortunately I do. My late husband forced me to entertain him several times. Adolph once owned a fairly substantial block of shares in the Stovall Works. The last time Mr. Stovall graced our house, he drank too much—nothing personal, Theo—ignored his wife—she's dead now and I'm not surprised—and fawned over another guest. A gentleman," she added pointedly. "And he pretends to be so respectable! He's really a dreadful man—a grotesque. He wears a white silk scarf that covers half his face, and never takes his gloves off indoors because his hands are scarred, they say."

Theo Payne shut the office door and added to Rose Ludwig's comments in a whisper:

"He's also a political primitive. He boasts about membership in the Order of the Star Spangled Banner."

"I'm not familiar with that," Amanda told him.

"The inner circle of the Know-Nothing party."

Amanda merely nodded. It was evident Payne detested Stovall's politics, and perhaps hoped to draw her out about hers. She changed the subject:

"It's obvious you're not happy here, Theo. Why haven't you resigned?"

Scratching his pink nose, he walked back to the desk. "I have four youngsters in my family, Mrs. de la Gura—and positions aren't easy to locate these days."

Amanda wondered whether he meant he personally had a hard time finding jobs because of a fondness for alcohol. She tried to reassure him:

"Well, I hope you'll stick with it a while longer. If the sale can be completed, perhaps you'll be happier with your situation."

"As you said, that depends on whether we can work together. Also on what changes of policy you might institute—"

Again Amanda stayed on safe ground:

"I can assure you I'd do anything to keep Mrs. A. Penn content." She turned to Rose. "I saw two women at the American House carrying copies of your last novel."

"Did you, now. I know Theo's right—the books are trash. But I have to do something to keep from suffocating in that mausoleum Adolph left me!"

Amanda turned back to Payne, who had slumped into his chair:

"I do think new management could find the money to re-set corrected copy for Mrs. Ludwig—provided you and she settle your differences on style, of course."

"Jesus Christ, that's an improvement already!" Rose declared. "Just for that, Mrs. de la Gura, I'll treat you to dinner this evening. If you're free—"

"I am," Amanda said, delighted. "Could we take a short tour now, Theo?"

"Yes, of course."

"Mrs. Ludwig, would you excuse us for a while?"

"No, I'm going to tag along. I hope you realize Theo and I don't really hate each other," she continued as they left the office. "Those goddamned Harvard literature courses softened his mind a little, but he's still a smart boy. And he works under very trying restrictions. Instead of Mrs. A. Penn —with or without adjectives—he'd rather publish tracts on abolitionism—"

"Not so loud!" Payne said, glancing down the corridor. Amanda turned and saw the emaciated Mr. Drew dart back out of sight.

iv

Amanda found herself growing angry again as they walked through the cramped, disorderly warehouse area on the top floor. She saw bins full of cheap reprints of popular works—novels by Scott and Cooper—issued first by other publishers. When they passed a bin containing Maria Monk's *Awful Disclosures*, she exploded:

"You're still selling this?"

Payne grimaced. "Mr. Stovall's orders."

"You can be sure the moment the company changes hands, we'll destroy all copies."

"I'd be happy to see it gone from Kent's list."

Another appalling sight waited for Amanda in the basement. It was noisy, damp and badly lighted. It smelled of ink and the sweat of eight slovenly men in leather aprons who operated the antiquated flatbed presses. Amanda raised her voice to be heard above the rhythmic thumping:

"Doesn't the ink take a long time to dry in this dampness, Theo?"

"Of course it does," he shouted back. "And I can't tell you how many sheets we smear and ruin. But Mr. Stovall's accountants reckon that loss to be smaller than the cost of installing proper ventilation."

"I don't know much about the printing business, but it's obvious this equipment doesn't belong in a cellar."

"No, it belongs on the second or third floor."

"Why isn't it located there?"

"Too expensive to brace the flooring properly."

"How old are these presses?"

"Oh, thirty or forty years."

"Isn't there anything newer on the market?"

"Certainly. Mr. Hoe of New York has perfected steam-driven rotaries that print much faster. Some of the newspapers have installed them—"

"We really will have quite a few changes to make," Amanda said as they left the basement.

Payne burst out suddenly, "I hope you'll permit changes in our list as well—I mean beyond dropping the Monk book. We've been severely limited by Mr. Stovall's tightness with money on one hand, and his political bias on the other. For instance, two years ago, I wanted to buy the American rights to *Jane Eyre*. Too costly, I was told. One of the country's foremost poets, Professor Longfellow, lives just over in Cambridge and we can't afford him either—"

"With all this emphasis on culture, we can kiss Mrs. Penn's future goodbye," Rose sighed.

"Definitely not," Amanda laughed. "I told you before—I wouldn't lose Kent's most popular writer."

"But I *am* controversial to certain clergymen, Mrs. de la Gura—"

"Call me Amanda, please."

"My pleasure. You *do* know some churchmen find my books offensive?"

"Does the public?"

"Not generally. I practice moderation. When Mr. van Dugdale, the horse-car tycoon, raped Mercy Twickington in *Bartered Virtue,* I closed the bedroom door well before the actual moment—and only alluded to the deed afterward. Still, I know why women read my books. The subjects of sex and money are irresistible—sometimes an author doesn't even need money! Look how handsomely Mr. Hawthorne's doing with *A Scarlet Letter*. Theo's right, though. Kent's could stand the addition of some substantial authors writing on important subjects."

"I had a chance to bid on the right to reprint Fred Douglass' autobiography," Payne said. "I didn't even raise the question internally because I knew the owner would veto the idea."

Amanda shook her head, outraged:

"And that book's done well!"

"Exceedingly well. As a category, narratives of the lives of escaped slaves are highly popular. They also serve a worthwhile purpose," he added as they reached the entrance to his office and went in.

Amanda realized she was approaching controversial ground again. But she asked one more question:

"I assume most of the authors of such books have professional help in preparing their texts—?"

"Generally, yes. Douglass did his own—he's a rarity."

"It's premature to say this, Theo, but I know a man in California who might be persuaded to assemble notes on his experiences as a slave in Mississippi. The man's a mulatto. He manages my share of a mining claim—"

The mention of California caught Rose Ludwig's attention:

"You really do come from the far west?"

"Yes, I spent some years in Texas, and then California."

"Then you're just the person I'm looking for! You can help me with background for my next book. Theo, I haven't mentioned this to you, but I'm fed up with sighing heroines. That's one of my quirks, Amanda—I'm easily bored. After Adolph was buried, I started writing because I was bored, and after three novels with a New York setting, I'm bored again. The growing, important part of this country is the far west. I want to do a tale about a genuine western hero."

Payne looked dubious. "I doubt the public would accept that kind of novel from Mrs. Penn."

"Of course they will if it's interesting and the detail's authentic. And here's my source!"

"If you'll settle for an imperfect recollection of my husband's career—he was a fur trapper—I'll provide you with whatever detail I can," Amanda said.

"I knew you were a proper sort the second you walked in!" the other woman declared. "Theo, I believe we're all going to be much happier as a result of this meeting."

"So do I," Payne agreed. "I hope the sale goes through promptly."

Amanda asked, "You will keep everything we've discussed in absolute confidence?"

"Naturally, naturally!"

"When the lawyers finish haggling and we have Mr. Stovall's signature, I'll be in touch with you by telegraph."

"Telegraph?" Payne repeated. "You don't plan to remain in Boston?"

"I intend to buy or build a home in New York City. That's the financial center of the country, and that's where I must be if I'm to make my business ventures a success. I may install a private telegraph wire between my home and my local bank, though."

"My God, Mrs. de la Gura, do you have any notion of how expensive that will be?"

"I don't," Amanda replied. "If I have to worry about the cost, I'd have no business doing it."

Rose Ludwig laughed. "Theo, I think you've met your equal. Maybe your better—even though she didn't go to Harvard."

v

That evening, under the gaslights of the dining room at the American House, Amanda and her son shared a table with the authoress. Amanda had already confirmed her first reaction to the deep-voiced woman. Rose Ludwig was outgoing, opinionated, occasionally profane—and the two of them got along famously.

On the carriage ride from Kent and Son, Rose was candid about her beginnings. Her father had been a lock-tender on the Erie Canal near Buffalo. Her first meeting with her deceased husband, the owner of a fleet of brightly painted canal passenger boats, had been accidental. Ludwig had been touring the Erie system—which was still in operation, but gradually declining in importance because of the spread of the railroads.

Rose frankly admitted she was drawn to Ludwig's wealth and his status as a widower more than she was to his physical assets:

"He was four inches shorter than I am. A wispy little fellow. His head had this unfortunate point—which his baldness didn't help. On the other hand, he was no fool. And he was kind to me the first time my father introduced us. So when he came back on another inspection trip a year later, I was ready for him. My God, I was thirty already—a spinster!— because I refused to marry the first canal-boat captain who came along! I'd learned my lesson from my older sister Lily. She rushes to the altar the moment some man makes her pulses flutter—and she never worries about the wisdom of the choice until afterward. She's had seven—no, eight husbands—the poor creature's been wed so many times, her cheeks are pitted from the rice. The last one who carried her off pretended to be a Bavarian duke. I think Lily's in Europe with him right now—no doubt having discovered he's only a pastry cook with an accent. That's not my style. I wanted to be sure I had a good catch. The second summer that Adolph happened by, I'd looked through enough old newspapers to be certain he was the one. I hooked him in record time. Six days, two hours and twenty-three minutes. I think that's why I took to you, Amanda—you're as direct as I am. That is—as direct as I am when I'm hobmobbing with Theo. In New York, it's a different story."

"I'd like to hear about your life in New York when we have dinner," Amanda said.

"I'm afraid most of my comments will be negative. I despise so-called society. Unfortunately, by virtue of marriage, I'm considered part of it. By and large, the people are pretentious mummies—except for one or two, like Vanderbilt, who can cuss the paint off a wall, and does. God, I hate these hoop skirts—!"

She writhed on the carriage seat, cursing so floridly that the driver opened the sliding partition behind his feet to see what was wrong.

At her own hotel, Rose Ludwig brought Amanda up to her suite while she rid herself of the hated muslin petticoat with its four steel hoops sewn into the fabric. Amanda, who had thus far relied on stiff petticoat material to give her skirt the fashionable bell shape, inspected the hoops with interest. The style was coming into fashion.

End to end, the hoop at the top of the skirt measured about a yard and a quarter, she guessed. It was a complete circle of steel. The three lower hoops, increasingly longer, didn't meet in front; there was an opening of about ten inches in each.

"No matter how carefully you walk," Rose called from the bedroom, "they jab the hell out of your thighs. I'd be in a fix if I was young enough so a man would want to look at my thighs—"

She appeared in the doorway in a costume that brought a gasp to Amanda's lips: a jacket and knee-length skirt in cerulean blue and, underneath, men's trousers of the same material, gathered at the ankle.

"But I'm not supposed to say a word like thighs, am I? Women don't have *thighs, breasts, stomachs*—or some other anatomical features I'd be ostracized for mentioning—Amanda my dear, why are you staring?"

"I'm sorry, I've never seen real bloomers before. Those *are* bloomers?"

"Copied after the very ones worn by Amelia Bloomer herself. I don't dare put them on in New York as yet, though I predict they'll be popular in less than a year, no matter how the churches howl about immodesty. I hope I won't be barred from the dining room at the American House—"

She almost was. The head waiter frantically clenched his teeth and darted his eyes from the bloomers to the turned heads of scandalized guests. Amanda tipped the man heavily to overcome his moral scruples and, with Louis in tow, she and Rose sailed toward their table. They did grant the head waiter a little amnesty by permitting him to seat them in a corner. The position of the table hid the lower part of Rose's costume from most of the room.

Rose Ludwig's presence had one additional benefit. Louis was overwhelmed by his mother's new friend. He was more polite and biddable than he'd been for several weeks.

As the three sat finishing their dessert ices, Amanda concluded her considerably censored account of the circumstances that had brought her to Boston. She had told Rose of her family connection with the printing firm, and won her promise of secrecy. But she implied the firm had first changed hands in a normal manner. Rose looked surprised:

"Theo's always said there was some scandalous story about it being lost in a gambling game."

"I don't know how fictions like that get started," Amanda replied, concentrating on her ice. She felt the other woman studying her. Did Rose believe her? If not, she didn't make an issue:

"We certainly have a lot in common, Amanda. We both had rough beginnings. Fortunately, once I snared Adolph, my way was smoothed. Though it wasn't all pie and roses! I immediately had entree to the best homes. You'll be spared that tribulation."

"What do you mean?"

"You won't have to mingle with all those dreadfully self-important people. You *don't* have any notions about cracking society, do you?"

"No. You heard what I told Theo Payne—I'm moving to New York because it's the business center."

"Good. Then you won't be disappointed. Really, you'd be amazed at the number of Ohio widows who remove themselves to New York with a little capital, thinking they'll soon be dining with the Rensselaers and the Belmonts and the Vanderbilts. Society has closed up like a clam in the last twenty or thirty years. Today you're either born into it, you marry into it— or you wait a generation before you get your first invitation to tea with Mrs. Belmont. Some poor creatures foolishly try to shorten the wait—"

And she launched into an anecdote about one such parvenu, a young woman who learned that New York gentry frequently rode on a certain bridle path above Forty-second Street early in the morning. Though terrified of horses, the young woman contrived a system of straps to keep herself lashed to her saddle. She made herself visible on the bridle path, where she attempted to strike up conversations with affluent bachelors:

"Now God as my witness—this is true, Amanda. One morning a thundershower struck. The horse reared and the young lady was dumped on her ass—excuse me, Louis; derriere—with all her hidden straps, and her pretensions, exposed. She left the city a week later."

Amanda laughed. "I don't want to meet any bachelors, Rose. Or any society people, for that matter."

Except one.

"Good for you." She leaned her elbows on the snowy tablecloth and pointed a finger at Amanda's nose. "You did promise to tell me what you know about frontiersmen. I'm sure Theo loathes the idea, but I'm convinced the public's ready for a rousing western tale."

"I'll tell you everything I can."

"Wonderful! Why don't we travel to New York together?"

"I'd love that. As soon as we arrive, I want you to show me where to buy a pair of bloomers."

"Delighted. You'll forgive an old lady for being sentimental, but I think we're going to be the best of friends. Friendship's a rare commodity—I have hundreds of acquaintances, but I'll bet I've had no more than two real friends all my life No, three—I considered Adolph a friend. It's much more comfortable being married to a friend than to a lover, you know. I like you, Amanda—"

She reached across and touched Louis' dark hair.

"And I like your son. My God, with those eyes, he'll be breaking hearts in a few years. If I weren't such a tottering wreck—oh, well." A sigh. "Are you two finished? I'm about to perish for want of a cigar. Bad vice I picked up from Adolph. He smoked them even in the bath. Have you ever looked at a tub full of floating ash? Ugh!"

As they left the dining room, still drawing shocked stares and comments, Amanda was immensely pleased. At long last, it seemed that events were moving in response to her will, instead of at the random whim of chance. Before the year was out, she'd be well established in New York—

With Kent and Son in her possession.

vi

Two mornings later, a grim Joshua Rothman called at Amanda's suite in the American House. She was in the midst of packing, with trunks open everywhere.

"Mrs. de la Gura, what did you say when you visited the publishing company?"

She looked chagrined. "A little more than I should have, perhaps—"

"That became evident first thing this morning."

Amanda set aside the skirt she'd been about to fold into one of the trunks. "What do you mean?"

Upset, Rothman stamped to the windows:

"A banker can be of no use to you if you refuse to follow his suggestions!" He spun around. "You made some remarks about getting rid of a certain anti-Catholic title on the Kent list? Some other comments about wanting to publish an autobiography by a runaway slave—?"

"What if I did? I got angry at what I saw at Kent's—the decay—the indifference—besides, I only spoke to the general manager, Mr. Payne. In private. He promised not to repeat a word."

Rothman leaned across the top of a trunk:

"Theo Payne is a notorious drunk! An excellent brain—but a loose tongue when he imbibes. And he imbibes constantly."

A little knot of dread tightened in Amanda's stomach. "I—I did catch some hint of that," she admitted.

"Did you also meet a gentleman named Drew?"

"Briefly."

"Mr. Stovall's informant within the firm. After you left, Payne was so delighted, he spent all afternoon in an alehouse, celebrating. As I get the story, he returned late in the day, barely able to walk, and boasted to the entire staff about all the changes you intended to make. The *entire* staff—including Mr. Drew. You should have stayed away—I warned you. More important, you should have avoided political subjects at all costs—that, I didn't warn you of specifically. So we're both paying for it."

"Get to the point, Joshua."

"This morning, Stovall's attorneys wired from New York. The negotiations have been broken off. Permanently."

"Oh my God."

"It's my error for not telling you Stovall's an active member of the Know-Nothings—"

"No, don't blame yourself. I was aware of it."

"Then how could you imagine he'd sell out to someone who plans to turn Kent and Son a hundred and eighty degrees politically?" Rothman sighed. "I'm sorry—it's not my position to speak so frankly—it's just that I know how much you want the company—"

"I didn't stop to think about the danger in Payne's drinking. The blame's mine, Joshua. I accept it."

"That won't make Stovall relent, I'm afraid."

"If we can't buy the firm straightforwardly, we'll have to get control some other way."

Thunderstruck, he stared at her.

"Are you serious?"

"I am. This is a setback, nothing more—"

But she felt it much more deeply than the words suggested. She hadn't been all that outspoken at the firm—yet she *had* realized she shouldn't be speaking. Her anger had overcome caution.

Stovall's immediate reaction to her comments spoke volumes about the sort of man he was; the sort her grandfather would have detested—

In a calm voice, she resumed:

"I'm sorry you've labored so hard, only to have my carelessness undo your efforts." She touched his arm. "I'll see you're well compensated when we finally get control."

"Mrs. de la Gura, I really think you'd be wiser to abandon any hope of—"

"No," she said, "I won't."

"I can see no open, legal means of—"

"Then we'll do it secretly if we have to! Illegally! One way or another, Joshua, *I am going to own Kent's.*"

CHAPTER 3

The Man Who Thundered

SOME SIXTEEN MONTHS LATER—a Friday evening in February, 1852—Amanda and Rose Ludwig were seated in a box at The Bowery Theatre, a structure already twenty-five years old but distinguished among New York's playhouses because it had been the first to install gas.

The jets throughout most of the auditorium had been turned off for the meeting, which was being held in lieu of a performance of the Bowery's current attraction. Together with the footlight candles, the gas fixtures flanking the proscenium opening illuminated the half dozen speakers seated behind the podium. The six were paying dutiful attention to the preacher addressing the three thousand people who had packed the main floor, the boxes and the galleries.

A few feet upstage from the half-dozen chairs, a drop painted to represent a European drawing-room added an incongruous note; the theatre management had declined to remove all the scenery for the comedy now playing six nights a week. But since the comedy was not particularly successful, the management had been happy to rent the theatre for an abolitionist rally.

The preacher, a Congregationalist, had been talking for twenty minutes. His function was the same as that of four of the men behind him—to lengthen the program and build anticipation for the featured address by Frederick Douglass. The guest of honor sat directly behind the podium, motionless and attentive.

Mr. Bryant, who was to introduce him, began consulting his notes, conscious from the flow of adjectives that the cleric was reaching his conclusion. And so he did, with much arm-waving and a shrill burst of oratory devoid of logic but long on heat. He called down divine damnation on the entire south—but drew only perfunctory applause from the restless crowd. They'd heard essentially the same message four times already.

An audible sigh ran through the dark threatre as the preacher sat down, mopping his forehead. William Cullen Bryant, the Massachusetts lawyer turned poet and journalist, straightened his two pages of notes and stood up. A hush settled on the hall. Amanda heard Rose murmur:

"Finally! Old Horace has fallen asleep over there. So has my rear end."

Gazing across the main floor to the front box on the far side, Amanda saw the publisher Greeley straighten up in his chair, roused by the applause that greeted Bryant's arrival at the podium. She glanced to the box directly behind Greeley's; it was still a puzzle. No one seemed to be occupying it, though every ticket for the meeting had been sold for weeks. If there were people in the box, they'd seated themselves quite far back, to avoid being seen.

"Ladies and gentlemen," Bryant began, "I shall be brief in my introduction—"

A raucous cry of approval rang down from the gallery. The audience laughed. Bryant smiled. He was in his late fifties, held the editor's chair at the *New York Post,* and appeared tonight as one of the city's most outspoken foes of slavery. In the national election of '48, Bryant had been a member of the Barnburner faction that had split off from the Democratic party, enraged because the party adopted a platform containing only one plank of substance: a vague endorsement of the conduct of the Mexican war. Out of the Barnburners—who had offered former president Van Buren to the electorate in '48—had come the even more militant Free Soil party, ardent reformers unalterably opposed to the extension of slavery into any new United States territories.

But Bryant refrained from comments on the meeting's theme, confining his remarks to a quick summary of the career of the man everyone had come to hear.

He touched on Douglass' birth as a slave in Maryland; mentioned his early years in Baltimore, when, through the kindness of an enlightened master, Hugh Auld, he had been able to learn to read and write while serving as a houseboy and a laborer in Auld's shipyard.

It was Auld's death, Bryant reminded the audience, that had brought Douglass to St. Michaels, below Baltimore, and confrontation with another Auld, Thomas, who proved less liberal.

Douglass had already begun to feel resentment of his bondage. He was quarrelsome. Auld took steps to correct that. He hired out the young black to a noted slave-breaker named Edward Covey.

Covey attempted to apply the whip once too often. Douglass turned on him, and fought. After the struggle, Covey, all but defeated, never again touched the Negro whose spirit he had been paid to destroy—

"And thus," Bryant said, "in our distinguished guest's own words, a slave was made a man!"

Applause. Amanda and Rose joined in. Then, as the clapping died away, they heard a startling sound from the darkened box behind Greeley's.

The rest of the audience heard too. Heads turned. There were scowls. Greeley rose all the way out of his chair and tried to see who had hissed.

It wasn't uncommon for foes of the abolitionists to attend their programs. Sometimes the unwelcome guests tried to disrupt a meeting. That was evidently the case tonight. Amanda's vantage point still prevented her from seeing the occupants of the box in question.

Bryant was plainly angered. He lost his place in his notes and took a few moments to resume. Douglass looked unperturbed.

Rapidly, Bryant went through the rest of his introduction, describing the speaker's first, aborted effort to escape to the north, and his second, successful one in 1838. With seventeen dollars and an identification paper borrowed from a free Negro seaman, Douglass had boarded a train in Baltimore and waited nervously for the conductor to collect his fare and examine the paper. The conductor gave the paper only a casual glance. After a boat trip from Washington to Philadelphia, then a train ride, Douglass arrived in New York, a free man.

Bryant paid tribute to Douglass' family; to his long and earnest dedication to freedom for America's enslaved blacks; to his career as editor and publisher of *The North Star* at Rochester. Then, folding away his notes, he said:

"It is my great pleasure and high honor to present Mr. Frederick Douglass."

The audience surged to its feet, applauding wildly. Douglass smiled for the first time, tilted his head to one side to acknowledge the ovation and approached the podium.

ii

The speaker began quietly, using no notes:

"Mr. Bryant—ladies and gentlemen—I too shall be brief. My message to you is essentially a simple one. But just let me state that I never stand before an audience like that which I see before me without feeling my incompetence to do justice to the cause which I am here to advocate—"

He allowed himself another faint smile.

"Or to the expectation which is generally created for me by the friends who precede me. Certainly, if the eulogiums bestowed on me this evening were correct, I should be able to entertain this audience for hours by my eloquence. But I claim none of this. While I feel grateful for your generosity, I can certainly claim very little right to your applause—for I was once a slave. I never had a day's schooling in my life. All that I know, I have stolen—"

The oblique reference to his escape produced a scattering of cheers, which he acknowledged with another of those carefully controlled smiles. As the cheering faded, there was another loud hiss.

This time, a man in the orchestra leaped up and shook his fist:

"Shame, shame!"

Others took up the cry. Douglass didn't dignify the dark box with so much as a glance. He held up his hand, settling the crowd into silence.

"I wish at once to relieve you from all expectation of a great speech. That I am deeply and earnestly engaged in advocating the cause of my brethren is most true, and so, this evening, I hail your kind expressions toward me with the profoundest gratitude. I will make use of those expressions. I will take them home in my memory. They shall be written on my heart, and they will give me courage as I travel throughout this land of boasted liberty and light—"

His voice had grown stronger.

"—yet this land of abject slavery, for the purpose of overthrowing that system and restoring the Negro to his long-lost rights!"

Applause louder than before greeted this first emotional peak in the speech. Amanda watched the dark box. Sure enough, just as the outpouring of sound began to diminish, the hiss was heard again, prolonged and ugly.

More yells of anger burst from the audience. One burly fellow started out of his seat, intending to go up the aisle and on to the box. His two companions restrained him.

Douglass moved quickly to the subject of his address—Section Two of Article IV of the Constitution. He first quoted the Section's third paragraph verbatim. Then he reminded his audience that the authors of the Constitution had included the paragraph in order to acknowledge the right of slave owners to reclaim runaways in non-slave territory, even though the paragraph carefully avoided the use of the word *slave* in favor of the more general *person*.

"Upon the face of this," Douglass said, "there is nothing of injustice, nothing of inhumanity—it is perfectly in accordance with justice, perfectly humane. But what does it *really* mean in the United States?

"It means that if any slave shall in the darkness of midnight, thinking himself a man and entitled to the rights of a man, steal away from his hovel or quarter—

"Shall snap the chain that binds his leg—

"Shall break the fetter that links him to slavery—

"It means that if he shall do these things, then by night and by day, on his way from a state where slavery is practiced to one where it is not, he shall also be liable to be hunted down like a felon and dragged back to the bondage from which he has escaped!"

Amanda leaned forward, stirred by the man's eloquence. Douglass' forehead showed a light sheen of perspiration. He still had no scrap of text before him. But he obviously needed none. Much more than thought had gone into what he was saying; his life's fears and angers and hopes had gone into it.

He let go of the podium, his hands clenched.

"This clause of the Constitution," he thundered, "is one of the greatest safeguards to that slave system which we have met here this evening to express our detestation of!

"This clause of the Constitution—upheld and endorsed by an abominable fugitive slave bill promulgated by misguided men in the Congress—gives to the slave-holder the right at any moment to set his blood-hound upon the track of the fugitive, hunt him down and drag him back to the jaws of slavery!

"*This clause of the Constitution consecrates every rood of earth in this land over which the star-spangled banner waves as SLAVE-HUNTING GROUND!*"

The booming voice was drowned under a roar of, *"Shame! Shame!"* If the unseen antagonist in the box bothered to hiss, no one heard.

Douglass then launched into a ringing demand that all men of conscience disobey the Fugitive Slave Act. While Amanda had applauded during the earlier portions of the speech, here she held back. She wasn't certain the speaker was right. Congress had passed the law in the hope of mitigating sectional strife and preserving the Union. Douglass rejected such compromise. He said the law was immoral—and perhaps it was. He said it should be overturned—that might be true as well. But when he said that until the law was repealed, it should be ignored, Amanda found herself disagreeing.

"This being the state of things in America—" Douglass' quieter tone immediately hushed the hall again. "—you cannot expect me to stand before you with eloquent outbursts of praise for my country. No, my friends, I must be honest with America—

"Unmask her pretensions to republicanism!

"Unmask her hypocritical pretensions to Christianity!

"Denounce her pretensions to civilization!

"Proclaim in her ear the wrongs of those who cry day and night to heaven—'HOW LONG, HOW LONG, OH LORD GOD!'"

The Bowery Theatre literally shook from the hand-clapping and footstomping. Douglass bowed his head, breathing hard and clinging to the podium for support.

The ovation continued for one minute; two; three. Rose was clapping furiously. Even Amanda cast aside her reservations and joined in, caught up in the spell of the man's oratory.

Finally, when the tumult died, Douglass resumed:

"Let me say this to you in conclusion. Despite the dark picture I have presented—despite the iniquity of the present law which can only be an abomination in the eyes of all men who consider themselves believers in the principles upon which this nation was founded—no, despite all this, I do not despair of America.

"There are forces in operation which must inevitably work the downfall of the unjust law and the entire system of slavery. 'The arm of the Lord is not shortened.' The doom of slavery is *certain!*"

Once more, little by little, he had begun to build volume. Amanda's spine tingled. The stately figure held every eye in the theatre.

"While drawing encouragement from the Declaration of Independence —from the great principles it contains—and from the genius of American institutions, my spirit is also cheered by the obvious tendencies of the age in which we live.

"No nation can now shut itself up from the surrounding world and trot around in the same old path of its fathers. A change has come over the affairs of mankind!

"Walled cities and empires have become unfashionable. The arm of commerce has borne away the gates of the strong city. Intelligence is penetrating the darkest corners of the globe. It makes its pathway over and under the sea, as well as on the earth. Wind, steam, and lightning are its chartered agents. The fiat of the Almighty—'Let there be light!'—has not yet spent its force. No abuse, no outrage can now hide itself from the all-pervading and cleansing light of decency, democracy, and honor.

"Unjust laws shall perish. Unjust men shall die unmourned and dishonored. There will be universal freedom if we dedicate our hearts, our minds and our mortal souls to its accomplishment—if we resist the tyranny of the law where it must be resisted—and if our prayer of fervent aspiration forever remains that of William Lloyd Garrison—"

Douglass flung his hands high over his head, roaring:

" 'God speed the year of jubilee—the wide world o'er!' "

iii

It took Amanda and Rose nearly twenty minutes to work their way through the long line of people filing onto the stage to congratulate Douglass. He was particularly gracious with Amanda, recalling their meeting on the steamer to Boston, and thanking her warmly for the donation she'd sent. She promised to send another, then said:

"But I must tell you honestly, Mr. Douglass, I can't agree with you on one point in your address."

"Which point is that, Mrs. de la Gura?"

"That the Fugitive Slave Act must be disobeyed. Overturned—perhaps. But as long as it *is* the law—"

"I can understand your attitude—even though I consider it wrong. The working of that particular law remains an abstraction for you. Something you read about, and consider intellectually. I think you'd change your mind if you were face to face with one of the law's victims. Or were a victim yourself."

"I'm not certain of that, Mr. Douglass."

He smiled. "But I am."

The press of the line behind them forced Amanda to break off the conversation. As she followed Rose up one of the aisles, she glanced at the box from which the hissing had come. If the box was still occupied, it was impossible to see by whom.

Presently the two women reached the packed lobby. Through the open outer doors, Amanda saw that snow had started falling in the February darkness. Forward movement was almost impossible.

The crowd filled the lobby and spilled outside. Lines of hacks and carriages waited three deep. As each vehicle maneuvered for a place at the curb and loaded its passengers, she and Rose were able to take another step or two. But progress was infernally slow.

As she slipped her hands deeper into her muff, Amanda felt Rose tap her shoulder. She turned and saw Mr. Greeley of the *Tribune*.

Amanda had met the Whig publisher at a Christmas fete at Rose's mansion in Gramercy Park. She'd been struck by his aura of age. Though Greeley couldn't have been much more than forty, his mutton-chop whiskers were already whitening. His piercing eyes seemed those of an old man who viewed the world with simmering discontent.

Greeley had been intrigued when Rose mentioned that her friend had survived the Alamo massacre. He had also been openly skeptical, reminding the women that there were no American survivors save a lady named Dickinson.

Amanda pointed out that the list of Mexican survivors was much less precise. She expected she'd be shown on the record not under her maiden name but under her husband's, which was Spanish, if the record carried any mention of her at all.

A few details of the massacre soon convinced Greeley that Amanda was telling the truth. He suggested an interview with one of his reporters. She declined, saying that the idea of personal publicity struck her as ostentatious, and she didn't care to be painted as any sort of heroine; she'd merely survived as best she could. Actually, her real reason for turning him down was a wish to avoid any chance of the Kent name appearing in print. Mr. Greeley had been testy with her the rest of the evening.

Now, though, the incident was forgotten. He tipped his hat in a cordial way:

"Mrs. de la Gura—Rose—good evening."

"Happy to see you awake again, Horace," Rose said.

Greeley ignored the jibe. "Douglass gave a splendid talk, didn't he?"

"Splendid," Amanda agreed.

"Marred only by those disgusting interruptions from the box behind me."

"Did you see who was doing it?" Amanda asked.

"Of course. A certain gentleman who enjoys making his obnoxious opinions known in public. A member of the exalted Order of the Star Spangled Banner. I prefer not to discuss the subject any further. His performance made me sick."

"But Horace, who was it?"

Greeley paid no attention to Rose's query. He was staring at two men in the crowd. With a sour expression, he said:

"And I'm experiencing the same feeling right now."

Amanda recognized handsome, blue-eyed Fernando Wood, a wealthy politician with ambitions for the mayor's office. With him was his brother Ben. Both were Democrats, and hence Greeley's foes.

Fernando Wood and his brother were arm in arm with a pair of gaudily dressed young ladies who might have come straight from a Paradise Square brothel—but then, the Woods made no secret of having the poor, and even most of the city's criminal element, in their political camp.

The Woods had grown rich in real estate, and also by operating as licensed gamblers, under a dubious "charter" granted them in Louisiana. They were close friends of the Tammany politician Isaiah Rynders, who bossed the Sixth Ward, owned several slum saloons—and could always rally a street gang to harry an opposition candidate. Rynders was notorious for his hatred of blacks and foreigners—his Irish constituents excepted. He had been in the crowd that had started the Astor Place riot. The ringleader, some said.

But none of this seemed to rub off on the Wood brothers tonight. They waved and chatted with friends as they worked their way out of the lobby. They saw Greeley; Fernando Wood said something that was obviously contemptuous. His brother and the young girls laughed. Greeley's jaw showed a tinge of scarlet as he turned back to the women.

"By the way—have either of you read Mrs. Stowe's novel?"

"It's not due out until next month, is it?" Rose asked.

"No. But Jewett's of Boston is distributing advance copies."

The conversation touched off Amanda's anger. If only the secret campaign she and Joshua Rothman were waging had proceeded a little further —if only she'd been in control of Kent and Son—the firm might have had a chance to publish what everyone predicted would be the literary sensation of the year. Perhaps of the decade. She forced herself to speak calmly:

"I'm afraid Rose and I aren't important enough to be on Jewett's list. How did you like the novel, Mr. Greeley?"

"Oh, not very well. I read several episodes when it was serialized in the *National Era*. The complete version's more of the same—too sentimental for my taste. The book's purpose is worthwhile, though."

"Rose introduced me to Mrs. Stowe's brother last week," Amanda told him. "We drove over to Plymouth Church in Brooklyn to hear Reverend Beecher preach."

Greeley whipped a small pad from his coat and jotted on it with a pencil:

"Must remind Dana to send a reporter over there to see whether Henry's still planning that mock slave auction. Last time I saw him, he was trying to find a good-looking young Negress who wouldn't object to being paraded before a crowd, and sold from his pulpit—"

As Greeley put the pad away, Amanda said, "The Reverend told us they're working up a dramatization of *Uncle Tom's Cabin* for Purdy's Theatre in the fall."

"Meanwhile," Rose said, "I'll have Kent's send you another review copy of *The White Indian*. It's obvious you misplaced the first one."

"I doubt that," Greeley retorted.

"Really, Horace! You should pay attention to the book. We've gone to a fourth printing already."

"Rose," Greeley said, "I'm very fond of your hospitality. But not of your characters."

"Not so loud!" she cautioned. "You're one of the few people in New York who knows Mrs. Penn's identity."

"Well, I wish Mrs. Penn would change her style. Characters who make four-page declarations about virtue of courage put me in a torpor."

"I can certainly say the same for those incomprehensible foreign features you're publishing!"

"Mr. Marx and Mr. Engels are astute observers of the European social and political scene."

"I fall asleep after the second paragraph. Many more essays of that sort and I'll start reading Gordon Bennett's paper. Or the *Times*."

"The *Times!*" Greeley sputtered. "Upstart rag! I'm astonished it's survived this long. It certainly won't last till the end of the year. As to your fable of the fur business—"

"The story may be fictional, but Amanda here provided me with the background. It's absolutely authentic."

Greeley still looked put upon. "All right, send another copy to my editor, Mr. Dana. At your own risk!"

The stout woman pulled a face. "Horace, you can be positively vicious."

"The function of the free press is to provoke, not pacify, dear lady."

"But I thought you fancied the west."

"The real west," he nodded, with a clear implication that he still believed Rose had written about something else. "It's astonishing how the public prefers fancy to fact. I'm already enthroned for having urged some anonymous young man to go west, when it was Mr. Soule, who edits the *Express* out in Terre Haute, Indiana, who actually turned the phrase last year. I merely repeated it in a letter to a friend—which he promptly made public."

Rose teased him: "The price of fame, Horace."

With another sarcastic expression, Greeley tipped his hat. "There's my carriage." He began to elbow his way outside.

Rose stood on tiptoe, trying to find her own driver in the confusion of vehicles and stamping horses in front of the theatre. A few gusts of snow began to blow into the lobby. Suddenly the heavy woman exclaimed:

"I've had enough of being pushed and shoved—let's do a little of our own. Follow me, Amanda—"

She turned sideways.

"I wonder if you'd excuse us—we're trying to get through—*damn it, get off my skirt!*"

The man turned abruptly. Inside her muff, Amanda dug her fingers into the palms of her hands.

She'd been in New York City for over a year. And although she'd driven by the immense house just off Washington Square a number of times, she'd never set eyes on its owner—though she'd kept track of his activities through items in the press.

And now, unexpectedly, he was directly in front of her, slender and erect despite his age—fifty-eight or thereabouts. If Rose's outburst had angered him, he didn't show it. His shoulder cape displayed its crimson lining as he raised a glove to the brim of his black top hat. In his other hand he held a gold-headed cane.

A white silk scarf was tied around his head. It cut obliquely from the left side of his forehead, across the bridge of his nose to the right side of his chin. The scarf fluttered in the wind. Amanda glimpsed a bit of ugly, discolored scar tissue. The man's left eye, brown and amused, seemed to glow like a dark gem.

Amanda held herself rigid, somehow afraid to speak or even be noticed. "My sincere apologies, Mrs. Ludwig," Hamilton Stovall said.

CHAPTER 4

Suspicion

"MR. STOVALL! I DIDN'T see you in the audience—"

"I don't sit with the *audience*," he said. "I always take a private box."

Rose's eyebrows shot up. "Behind Mr. Greeley?"

"Quite right."

"So it was you interrupting Douglass!"

Stovall chuckled. "Really, the man's incredible. If he didn't have such a grip on so many minds, baiting him would be amusing. Under the circumstances, I view it more as a public duty—"

Thus far he'd hardly taken notice of Amanda. She was trying to breathe evenly; maintain a polite but none-too-interested expression.

"I wonder if there's a city ordinance prohibiting a baboon from dressing in a man's clothing," Stovall went on. "If not, there should be—and it ought to be enforced against Mr. Douglass. However, I do apologize for making my presence known to you so clumsily, Mrs. Ludwig."

Stovall's words carried a faint sarcasm that robbed them of any sincerity. He turned to a man twenty years his junior hovering at his elbow.

"May I present my secretary, Mr. Jonas? Jonas, this is Mrs. Rose Ludwig—"

"Ah yes, one of the bloomer ladies," Jonas replied, his eyelids drooping briefly. He had an effeminate face, and pink, pouting lips.

Stovall turned to Amanda. "I'm afraid I'm not acquainted with your companion, Mrs. Ludwig."

Amanda felt her cheeks must be red. To be so close to the man who had made Jared suffer was almost unbearable. She wanted to strike at his face—

She fought the irrational impulse. She tried to appraise Hamilton Stovall without emotion, as she would a business adversary. It was obvious he had once been exceedingly handsome. But his exposed cheek had a purplish, blotchy look. What little she could see of his hair was pure white. His teeth were so perfect—and so yellow—she was certain they were false. Their artificial uniformity gave him a sort of a skull's grin. His glittering brown eye seemed to spike into her mind, drawing out all her secrets—

Foolish! Get yourself under control! He doesn't know who you are—

Rose remedied that in an instant:

"Amanda, let me introduce Mr. Hamilton Stovall. This is Mrs. Amanda de la Gura."

Stovall's good eye blinked. But it was young Jonas, standing unusually close to his employer, who spoke first:

"Indeed! So you're the free-thinking lady who tried to buy Kent and Son!"

Amanda's stomach hurt. "Yes, I tried to buy it. The rest is your judgment, Mr. Jonas."

Stovall's eye held hers. "I'm fascinated to make your acquaintance at last. Of course I regret it was impossible for me to accept your offer—I could have put the money to excellent use. But I simply couldn't turn the firm over to someone whose views are so far removed from mine. Misguided, if you don't mind my saying so—" He obviously didn't care if she did. "I might even go so far as to call them dangerously radical."

Hoping she sounded sufficiently calm, she replied, "Making you aware of those views was my error, Mr. Stovall."

"You're quite correct." The yellow-tinged teeth glared in a fixed smile. But his eye held no humor.

"Of course I wasn't aware you had informants at the firm."

Stovall dismissed it: "Oh, one must—to protect one's own interests."

Abruptly, Jonas asked, "You're from California, are you not?" Amanda's stomach quivered again. Stovall had checked into her background.

"I am." She gave them no more to work on. But Stovall refused to quit:

"Why in the world would someone with substantial mining and textile holdings—"

He knows that too.

"—abruptly decide to venture into book publishing?"

"I was searching for a way to diversify. A publishing house seemed a sound investment."

"Yes, I do recall hearing some such explanation from the gentlemen who acted on your behalf. I find one thing odd, though."

"What's that?"

"I'm not aware that you've attempted to buy another book firm. Was Kent's the only one in which you were interested?"

Amenda hedged:

"At the time we negotiated—yes."

"The fact is, you've bought no other properties at all—at least under your own name. Forgive me, but it's almost as if you had some reason other than a business one for wanting Kent's."

"That's purely your speculation, Mr. Stovall."

"I admit it. There could be no personal basis for your interest, could there?"

"None."

"We've never met before—"

"Never."

"Well—" He shrugged. "I must be wrong."

"A rare occurrence with Mr. Stovall," Jonas informed them with a smug smile.

The outrageous flattery pleased the older man, though. He touched Jonas' gloved hand in an almost affectionate way. Then he said to Amanda:

"Financially speaking, I really wish we had been able to reach an agreement. Publishing is a risky enterprise—another circumstance which makes me wonder why you chose it for diversification. I have very little interest in the firm, actually—only in what it earns. I never wanted the company except as the means to an end. But perhaps you don't know the story. I assumed ownership many years ago as a result of a sporting wager—"

Amanda heard Rose's sudden intake of breath. Stovall's brown eye watched her for a reaction—

Or did she just imagine that?

"—and a desire to see the founders, a clan of wild-eyed Boston mobocrats, put out of business." He licked a snowflake from his lower lip. "The heirs of a Mr. Gilbert Kent. Despicable people."

Amanda's lips pressed together. She was trembling. Hands clenched tight inside the muff, she was conscious of both Stovall and Rose watching her closely. She hoped she hadn't given herself away—

"I know nothing about them other than the name, Mr. Stovall. I've spent most of my years out west."

"Of course," he murmured. "Well, there's no need for civilized folk to quarrel over an aborted transaction—" He patted the secretary's arm. "Jonas, be a dear chap and see what you can do to hurry the carriage."

The secretary started for the curb. He whistled and motioned. Again Stovall touched his top hat.

"Mrs. de la Gura—Mrs. Ludwig—my distinct pleasure."

His good eye raked Amanda as he turned away. Did he know more about her than he was revealing?

No, that was impossible. Outside of her immediate household, only Rose, William Benbow and Joshua Rothman knew she was Gilbert Kent's daughter—

A man blocked Stovall's route to the carriage door which Jonas was holding open. Stovall lifted his cane and prodded the man with the ferrule:

"One side!"

The man, much less elegantly dressed, whirled around:

"Who the hell are you poking with—?"

"You, my shabby friend. It's quite obvious you couldn't afford a private carriage—while mine's waiting just there." Stovall pulled the gold-headed cane close to his chest, as if ready to lash outward with it. His voice had a savage note in it: "If you want to be impudent, I'll give you impudence that'll lay you up for a week!"

The man glared, then shifted his glance to the cane head. Amanda couldn't see Stovall's face, but the other man obviously had a good view of it—and it intimidated him. Stovall's voice was equally intimidating with its unmistakable suggestion of violent temper held in check.

The man stepped back.

Hamilton Stovall climbed into the carriage. Jonas touched him, apparently to assist him on the step. Then the carriage door slammed. The driver whipped up the matched grays and the vehicle lurched off.

Amanda watched it until it was completely hidden by the wind-driven snow. *I blundered,* she thought. *After the Kent negotiations fell through, I blundered by not covering myself with another purchase—immediately.*

And had she reacted too visibly to Stovall's remarks about the family? That worried her most of all; she might well have given herself away—or at least aroused his suspicion to the point where he'd think about making further inquiries. Perhaps even in California—

That's too far-fetched, she decided.

But was it?

Abruptly, she realized Rose had spoken to her. The stout woman repeated what she'd said:

"The carriage is at the curb. Do you want to go home? Or just stand here all night?"

She glanced around. The lobby had finally emptied.

"I'm sorry—certainly, let's go."

She was conscious of Rose scrutinizing her as they hurried outside.

ii

The city of New York looked almost beautiful this February night, covered as it was by fresh snow.

New York's population had climbed to almost three-quarters of a million people. A construction boom was steadily pushing the northern boundary toward the Croton Reservoir at Forty-second Street. Tonight, the ugliness of an expanding city of rich and poor—its unfinished buildings, its piles of uncollected refuse, its free-roaming herds of pigs and cows —was hidden by the wind-blown whiteness.

The streets were empty for a change. It always seemed to Amanda that half the city's inhabitants must be Irish—and indigent. They were forever loitering on the main thoroughfares. In some areas ruled by the immigrants, a lone woman—or a lone man who wasn't Irish, for that matter— dared not walk after dark. Michael Boyle, who would be waiting for her at home with the late afternoon's business matters yet to discuss, was a product of one such festering district, the Five Points.

The inside of Rose's carriage was ice cold. Or was the coldness within her? She couldn't escape an uneasy feeling about her reaction to Stovall's mention of the Kents.

Lamps and gaslights in passing buildings lit the carriage interior from time to time. The wheels jolted into a rut in the unpaved street. The driver whipped the team. The carriage lurched. Rose swore, singeing her glove on the locofoco she'd been trying to apply to the end of a cigar.

When the cigar was lit, she slid a window down and tossed the charred match into the storm.

Amanda felt questions were imminent; perhaps some of her own would forestall them:

"Rose, you spoke about Stovall's wife once. When did she die?"

"Oh, let's see. Early in fifty, I believe. She came of a good family. Baltimore—precious Hamilton's own city."

"When did he marry her?"

"Years ago—and only so he could use her family's capital to shore up his steel business. Or so I've been told."

"He has no heirs, isn't that right?"

"None."

"And I assume his wife died of natural causes—"

"That was the story—publicly."

"What do you mean?"

"I heard a whisper or two that it was suicide."

Amanda smiled without humor. "Perhaps she found out Stovall's not quite so respectable as he pretends to be."

Thoughtfully, Rose puffed out smoke. The thick blue cloud made breathing difficult.

"Well, he does admit to a few vices. He drinks a good deal. He's been known to gamble heavily. But if you removed everybody who does either one, New York would have a population of approximately forty-six. I had a peculiar feeling about that Mr. Jonas, though. I wonder if he's something more than a secretary—"

"He might be Stovall's lover."

"That was exactly my suspicion."

"There's evidence to support it."

"What evidence?"

"Michael goes back to the Five Points now and again," Amanda explained. "To visit some of the friends he knew when he worked on the docks. There's a story circulating about Stovall to the effect that he occasionally takes a little holiday with some people on Mulberry Street. Under another name."

"Who does he visit?"

"A young whore—and her brother. I gather they're all part of a—call it a triangular relationship."

Rose shivered. "My God. I fancy I'm liberal about a lot of things, but I don't care to know any more details of a sordid situation like that!"

"Maybe Stovall's wife caught a hint of it—"

"Perhaps," Rose nodded. "Stovall's tony friends didn't, I'm sure. I've heard nothing like that about him. If he prefers male companions instead of female—"

"I've been told there are some who like both."

"Well, you can be sure he'll be careful no one can prove it. Any more than people can prove your relationship with Michael Boyle's something other than business."

Aghast, Amanda said, "Do they accuse me of having Michael for a lover?"

"Naturally! I've told you—the ruining of reputations is a popular sport of some of our finer citizens."

"I didn't realize I was sufficiently well known to merit that kind of attention."

"In a little over a year, my dear, you've made the city very much aware of your presence. You'll still never crack that so-called social barrier we've discussed before—but a rich, good-looking woman who owns gold in California and part of one of the most successful textile companies in the northeast is grist for the conversational mills of society."

"I had no idea there'd been filthy talk about Michael—"

"Well, my God, he *is* good-looking. He *is* your private clerk—and you *did* give him a room as well as a position."

"He's a bright young man. Why shouldn't he have a better place to live than the slums? I'm disgusted about the stories—"

"Oh, stop," Rose chuckled. "At least Michael's the right sex—which can't be said for Mr. Stovall's employee. Stovall will have to give that up if he's serious about marrying again."

"*Marrying*—! That, I hadn't heard."

"It's true."

"Who's the woman?"

"Miss Coralie Van Bibb. Her father's a pushy clod, but he's done handsomely building carriages—this is one of his vehicles, I think. The irony's delicious. The best people ride in the products of Van Bibb's Westchester factory, and he can't get past their front doors."

"What's his daughter like?"

"Unattractive. She's thirty-four and never had a husband—doesn't that tell you? Pious as a Plymouth puritan, too—if what you say is correct, dear Hamilton will have to mend his ways. Or make a mighty pretense of it. No more Mulberry Street excursions. No more Mr. Jonas—unless he sticks strictly to business. Any sensible girl wouldn't let Stovall court her, you know. But he does have a certain dubious social standing—which old Van Bibb's desperate to share. For his part, Stovall won't be acquiring a wife so much as another source of financing. Papa Van Bibb's money—"

Amanda's eyes narrowed. "Yes, that would jibe with something Joshua

Rothman told me. Stovall's trying to float a big loan for modernization of his Pittsburgh plant. He's having a difficult time of it—the eastern banks don't consider him the best of risks."

"No wonder! He refuses to devote the time needed to run the company properly—and his board is hand picked so he encounters no opposition."

Quietly, Amanda said, "That's right. He has two cousins on the board— his only relatives. And he owns by far the largest single block of stock. Forty percent. No other shareholder owns anything close to that."

Rose took another puff of the cigar. "You seem damn conversant with Mr. Stovall's affairs."

"No more than you. I've found out some things about him since he refused to sell Kent's, that's all. The information from Michael came quite by accident."

"You don't have any hope of trying to buy the printing company again, do you?"

"No," Amanda said, truthfully. *I'm going to get hold of it another way.*

"Do you think he suspects who you really are?"

"I hardly see how he could, Rose—unless I gave myself away completely tonight."

"Not completely, though your reaction *was* noticeable. Amanda—" She hesitated. "We're friends, aren't we?"

"The closest of friends, Rose—you know that."

"Then I wish you'd be honest with me."

"About what?"

Rose leaned toward her, the cigar in her hand casting just enough light to put pinpoints of orange in her eyes.

"Stovall alluded to having won the firm in a wager. When we first met in Boston, you gave me the impression he'd bought it. Which is it?"

Amanda sighed. "Stovall was telling the truth. I misled you. At the time, I thought it was prudent."

"That's why you kept your family connection out of the negotiations— the Kents have a grudge against him?"

"And vice versa. He cheated my family years ago—"

"Is that the real reason you're in New York, not Boston? Because he's here, and you can make inquiries about him?"

"Partly."

"Two can play the game, you know."

"That I realize."

"Do you honestly mean to say you've given up doing anything further about taking over the company? That's not in character, my dear."

"Rose, I think we should drop the subject—"

"Sorry, but I can't. I don't want anything to happen to you. And Mr. Hamilton Stovall isn't the sort one crosses swords with in a casual fashion. You saw what he almost did to that poor chap in front of the theatre—a man he didn't even know. He's vicious. And based on what Michael told you, maybe even a little deranged. Leave him alone, Amanda. Whatever reasons you have for hating him, leave him alone—he could hurt you."

The warning echoed ones she'd heard before. But too much past history remained to be set aright for her to be frightened off by one failure—or an unfounded fear that she might have given her feelings away when Stovall insulted the Kents.

"I've faced worse than Mr. Stovall, Rose. I'll be careful."

"Then you haven't abandoned the idea of taking the firm away from him—"

"No," she admitted. "But there's no point in dragging you into it."

"He refused to sell! What other legal options do you have?"

Amanda didn't answer. Rose glowered at her cigar.

The carriage was slowing. Amanda glanced out the window. They'd arrived in Madison Square, one of the more fashionable residential areas developed in the last decade. Light from large homes dappled the snow with patches of yellow. The carriage swung up the east side of the square and under the portico of a three-story brownstone house Amanda had purchased, gutted and rebuilt after consultation with an architect Rose had recommended.

The driver climbed down and opened the door. A snow-dusted figure, he stood shivering in the night wind. The lights of Amanda's home lit Rose Ludwig's dismayed face.

"Rose, don't be angry with me—"

"I am not in the least bit angry! I'm worried. I'd as soon go strolling in Five Points naked and carrying gold ingots as keep up a feud with Stovall. You'll be the loser. He already suspects you wanted his company and no other. And after tonight, he knows the name Kent produces a reaction. He may figure out a good deal from that—"

"Yes, I'm afraid it's possible."

"Then for God's sake leave him alone, Amanda. Please!"

"Good night, Rose. I enjoyed the dinner and the lecture. Let's have lunch early next week—"

"Amanda—"

She shut the carriage door.

She stood in the blowing snow at the foot of the balustraded marble stairs. The carriage careened out of the drive, its lanterns rapidly diminishing to blurs. A sleigh crowded with young ladies and gentlemen went skimming by on the opposite side of the square. Laughter and the sound of bells lingered long after it had passed from sight.

She was tired; drained by the confrontation with Stovall, and by jousting with Rose. But she couldn't call it a day just yet. She had to deal with the problem of Stovall's suspicion.

Perhaps nothing would come of it. But if he did look further into her background, she couldn't afford to wait and discover it after the fact. She had to accomplish what she wanted to accomplish *now*, before he found out any more—

She hurried up the steps into the house.

CHAPTER 5

The Girl Who Refused

LOUIS KENT CAME DOWN the staircase, walking past the entrance to the dining room on his right and the music room—containing the piano no one played—on his left. The clock in the library chimed nine.

Despite the chill permeating the house, his cheeks felt hot. *Not much more than an hour left—*

All evening he'd thought about her; wild, confused thoughts that set his heartbeat racing. All evening he'd struggled to convince himself that what he wanted to do was perfectly proper for a wealthy boy going on fifteen. Some of his classmates at Professor Pemberton's Day School—the sons of merchants and professional men—boasted of their affairs with household girls. One boy repeatedly bragged that he'd begun when he was twelve!

That, Louis could hardly believe. But the boasting left him feeling inferior all the same. Finally, when his mother had hired the new Irish girl a few weeks ago, he'd decided to go ahead.

The other two maids and the cook were older; unattractive. Kathleen was neither. She was seventeen; on the plump side, but pretty. Clean-smelling, too—though he recalled she hadn't been the first day she presented herself for an interview. She came from a tenement somewhere in the Five Points.

His mother had left at three to have dinner and attend an abolitionist lecture with Mrs. Ludwig. The opportunity was perfect. But he was afraid. Inexperience heightened his certainty that he'd blunder; that Kathleen would refuse him. Or laugh. So instead of waiting for her upstairs—she began her rounds of the three occupied bedrooms shortly after nine every night—he'd fled down here to the first floor. Now he was telling himself his scheme was entirely too dangerous.

He walked softly across the Oriental carpeting of the long front hall.

On his left, forward of the music room, the doors to the drawing room were shut. The library, on the right between the dining room and the front sitting room, showed light, its two doors ajar. In the hall, a single gas jet flung Louis' shadow on the huge front doors. He opened one and let out a gasp of surprise. Snow was falling in Madison Square.

He remained at the open door for a few moments, unable to keep his mind off Kathleen. *You don't ask them, Lou,* the boys at Pemberton's said, *you tell them. You threaten 'em with discharge if they hesitate. Anyway, most are eager for it. They'll say no a few times. But then they'll relent.*

Why had he listened? Why had he rashly promised that he'd bring it off before classes resumed next week? He'd actually gotten in another fist-fight when two of the boys scoffed—

Of course he could lie on Monday. But they'd question him. Demand intimate details. He feared that if he tried to pretend, they'd trip him up.

And it *would* be a relief to end the nightly wakefulness in which he imagined bare breasts, and legs, and lips caressing his face—more and more these past months, he thought of such things frequently. Dreamed of them, too, in dreams that caused an embarrassing aftermath.

He pressed his belly against the edge of the open door. No matter how he tried, he couldn't prevent his flesh from betraying his feelings at the most unexpected moments—

I must do it, he said silently. *Tonight, while it's quiet and ma's away.* He still thought of her as ma, though Amanda had long since trained him to use the word mother when he spoke.

Sweating a little, he watched the falling snow. He knew he'd never be heard upstairs. Except for Kathleen, the servants didn't venture beyond the first floor. Right now, before going home for the night, they'd all be taking supper down in the mansion's raised basement—

The insistent pressure between his legs refused to go away.

But it's too risky!

An inner voice mocked him:

It isn't too risky. You're frightened, that's all.

What would his ma do in a comparable situation? He thought he knew. She did whatever she wanted; went where she pleased, and brooked no interference. That had been apparent to him ever since the time in California when he heard she'd shot a man who interfered with her up in the mining camp—

His swarthy face troubled and his dark eyes focused at some remote point beyond the snow-whitened square, Louis slowly backed up and shut the door. He was afraid of his mother. Her toughness and her preoccupation with business affairs made her forbidding, somehow. Yet he admired her—

He decided he was being foolish to worry about repercussions. *She* never seemed to—

All right. What he wanted, he'd take. That was the privilege of wealthy people, wasn't it?

Turning, he stepped on the tail of the white tomcat before he realized it. The cat, whose name was Mr. Mayor, had evidently crept out of the library and approached him silently.

Mr. Mayor miaowed loudly and went bounding back toward the library doors—which opened all the way a moment later.

From the doorway, Michael Boyle looked at Louis. The boy was sure Michael could see guilt on his face.

Mr. Mayor sought protection behind Michael's legs, peering at Louis with green eyes that caught the gaslight and shone. Suddenly Louis realized what he needed in order to proceed with his plan. He should be able to get it, too. In the darkened dining room—

If only Michael didn't suspect, and try to stop him.

"What are you doing skulking out here, Louis?" the young man asked, cheerily enough. "I thought I'd caught myself a burglar."

"I was only looking at the snow."

Louis walked back toward the entrance of the library. He wanted to glance down, to see whether there was a telltale bulge to give him away. He didn't dare.

ii

Michael Boyle was a head taller than Louis. Almost six feet. He was twenty-two, with a handsome, fair face, rust-colored hair and golden-brown eyes. He had wide shoulders, a narrow waist, and looked elegant in whatever he wore—tonight a loose-fitting white silk shirt, snug gray trousers and expensive Wellington boots. Only a long white scar across his forehead marred his appearance.

The scar was the result of trouble on the piers. Michael Boyle had worked as a longshoreman since he was eleven years old. At twenty, he had joined a worker's movement to increase wages five cents per hour during the twelve-hour day.

The bosses who controlled the dock crews worked more on behalf of the ship owners than on behalf of their own men. Someone had informed on the leaders of the wage movement. One by one, those longshoremen had suffered mysterious accidents. On his way home one evening, Michael Boyle had been waylaid by unknown assailants and beaten until he could barely crawl. During the beating, a man had slashed at his throat with a knife. Michael had dodged. The blade cut his forehead open.

After that, he'd never been able to get employment as a longshoreman. All the dock bosses knew him as an agitator. He had worked at odd jobs until a year ago, when Amanda had hired him over eleven other applicants who had presented themselves in response to a newspaper advertisement for a confidential clerk. The advertisement was one of the few in the paper that didn't carry the line *No Irish need apply*.

From all Louis could tell, Amanda was well pleased with her choice. Michael was self-educated; a voracious reader—something uncommon in the Five Points. His parents had come from a village in County Antrim, where his father had belonged to the Hearts of Steel—one of the gangs that harassed the English landlords. "A brawling boy," Michael had once said of his father, without implying praise or admiration. "The village matched his temperament exactly. My father often repeated a joke—true or not, I can't say—about one of the local ladies who walked out of her cottage one morning and said with a smile, 'A lovely day—ten o'clock and not a blow struck yet.'"

When the first of the famines devastated Ireland in '22, the Boyles had removed to America—going no further than New York because they had no funds, and because they were soured on the idea of working land; the land in Ireland had already rejected them. Five years after Michael was born, his father had died in a bloody confrontation between two of the Five Points gangs. His mother had lasted only two years more. Michael had survived by determination and his wits.

Louis admired the young Irishman's obvious strength. He liked his quiet cheerfulness. At the same time, he occasionally resented Michael's growing closeness to his mother.

Now Michael leaned down and scooped up his white cat. Mr. Mayor was a huge, rather sinister-looking tom. He regarded Louis from the crook of his master's elbow. The young man said:

"You're looking odd, Louis. Got a bellyache?"

"No," Louis replied, too quickly. "I'm fine."

Michael grinned. "Whatever you say. I've a plate of mutton in the library. Care for some?"

"No thanks."

"Come in and keep me company for a bit, at least."

Louis hesitated. To lull Michael's suspicions, he'd better do it: "All right."

He followed Michael through the double doors into the overheated room.

About half of the library's wall space was filled with ceiling-high bookcases. Near the outer windows stood a desk littered with papers and ledgers. Along the wall on Louis' right, another table held the telegraphic equipment that connected the house with the Rothman Bank in Boston.

Michael's booted feet scraped on the carpet, a sound slightly louder than the hissing of the two gas jets over the mantel. Four logs burned in the grate. Beside Michael's chair, a small taboret bore a platter heaped with slices of meat.

Mr. Mayor jumped from Michael's arms. The cat had come with the young man from Five Points, his only possession. Michael had christened him Mr. Mayor "because he's ten times as intelligent as most incumbents, and could do a better job even without the power of speech—which in the case of a politician is usually a hindrance, since it permits his idiotic ideas to be heard."

The cat put his forepaws on the edge of the taboret, shot out his head as if to sample a bit of the mutton. Michael batted him away.

Then, stepping carefully between two piles of manuscript paper at the foot of the chair, Michael sat down. He helped himself to a slice of mutton which he tore into smaller pieces, stuffing them into his mouth one at a time.

"I've never seen one person eat so much, so often," Louis said. "And how can you stand this heat?"

"Because I spent the winters in the streets when I was growing up. Never felt the warmth of a fire—nor tasted decent food, either. I expect in forty years, I might get my fill of both."

Louis wandered to the mantel, gazing at the French infantry sword hung horizontally above the Kentucky rifle. The small green glass bottle half filled with powdery tea shimmered in the gaslight.

He heard Michael riffling some of the manuscript sheets; then caught the distant creak of a floorboard overhead.

Kathleen.

Turning down the beds—

He couldn't stay here long. Not if he meant to do what he'd promised his classmates.

"How is Professor Pemberton treating you?" Michael wanted to know.

Louis turned, wondering why Michael had raised that subject. He avoided the young man's eyes, gazing instead at the oil painting of his great-grandfather hanging on the outer wall. On a smaller table underneath the painting and behind the desk, a glass display case with wooden ends held cousin Jared's medallion. The medallion stood vertically, wedged into a slot in a small velvet pedestal. Lying on the velvet in front of the pedestal was a frayed circlet of tarred rope.

Louis answered the question carefully:

"The school's boring."

"Ah, but you must suffer through if you're to go on to Harvard as your mother intends."

"I wonder if she'll let me use my right name in college. I feel funny being called Louis de la Gura. Everyone thinks I'm a foreigner."

Bitterness crept in when Michael replied, "And *foreigners* aren't the most popular souls in New York, are they?"

"Michael, do you know why I'm not allowed to call myself Louis Kent?"

"Why, how should I know that? I'm only hired help. What does your mother say when you ask her?"

"Nothing that makes much sense. She just says it's necessary to keep the Kent name hidden a while longer—"

He shook his head, gesturing at the sword and rifle:

"If she's so proud of our family, you'd think she'd tell everyone who we are."

"I can't give you an explanation. It's not in my province," Michael answered, his voice so flat, Louis suspected the clerk knew more than he was saying. He'd brought up the subject with Michael once before, receiving the same sort of evasive answer.

"I wish you'd stop your fidgeting, Louis. You're making me nervous."

Louis forced his hands to his sides. "Was I fidgeting?"

"You were. Are you sure nothing's bothering you?"

"No," Louis lied. His eyes slid to the wall clock above the telegraph equipment. The hands had reached ten past the hour.

I must go upstairs. She'll be finished soon—

"What is Professor Pemberton having you read these days?"

"Plutarch."

"In Latin or English?"

The boy grimaced. "Latin. I just can't get the hang of it—the other boys have studied it for much longer—"

"Don't feel discouraged. I've listened to Latin mass for years, and I can't get the hang of it either."

Mr. Mayor jumped up on Michael, purring audibly. After digging his claws in Michael's trousers a couple of times—earning a gentle knock between the ears—the cat settled down in the young man's lap. Michael slid the polished toe of a boot toward the stacks of manuscript:

"If you need something to read, perhaps you'd find this a little more interesting. It came late this afternoon, delivered from one of the California Steamers."

Louis craned around to study the closely written sheets. "What is it?"

"The autobiography of your mother's nigger manager."

"I don't understand why she had him write it—Kent's will never publish it, will they?"

"Not under present management," Michael agreed. "Your mother had the nigger go ahead because she's confident she'll own the company soon."

"How?"

Michael's eyes moved away. "Oh, she's working on it in various ways—" Another evasion.

"Is the manuscript any good?"

"Not half bad, actually."

"Mr. Hope's a bright man."

"Also an enterprising one. The parcel contained a letter saying the Ophir Combine's about to begin work at the claim in the mountains. They've completed the flume that brings in water, and Hope and Mr. Pelham look for handsome profits." He grinned. "You're going to be richer than ever."

Louis didn't answer.

"I am a bit surprised a colored fellow could do so well in business," Michael added. "And turn out an acceptable manuscript."

"You don't care for the colored, do you, Michael?"

Michael Boyle's bright hair glittered as he raised his head.

"I don't hate them, if that's what you're asking. Neither do I think all this effort on their behalf is warranted. You see, Louis, the famines in the old country have grown worse and worse. You know how many boatloads of Irish dock in New York every year—"

"Dozens."

Michael nodded. "I've read we may have two hundred thousand arrivals this year alone. Hoping for a fresh beginning—which includes work. To every such family, a black face means competition for the job that can spell the difference between survival and starvation. It's not surprising abolitionism is hated in the slums. If the abolitionists had their way, there'd be just that many more free nigger laborers pouring into the northern cities. Poor white people are starving to death not twenty blocks from here, Louis! Yet some of the great thinkers can talk of nothing but the unfortunate colored man. They should look closer to home! To the babies who die out in the heat of Mulberry Street in the summer, put there because some girl can't afford to feed her own mouth, let alone her infant's when it grows. I've seen other babies who were gnawed to death by rats that got into their cradles. The babies were left alone while their mothers strolled Paradise Square to earn twenty-five cents with a man. Walsh knows the way it is, right enough—"

He was referring to a colorful, audacious city politician. With the aid of a group of raucous roughnecks Walsh called his Spartan Band, he had finally forced recognition of New York's Irish constituency by the Tammany Democrats, and gone on to represent the constituency in the State Assembly and, in 1850, the Congress.

"—Walsh told those dogooders in Washington that the only difference between the nigger slave in the south and the white wage slave up here is that one has a master without asking for him, while the other has to beg for the privilege—!"

He was interrupted by the rhythmic clanging of a gong attached to the wall above the telegraph equipment and just to one side of the clock. He jumped up—ruffling Mr. Mayor, who stalked off to a corner.

Michael crossed to the table as the Morse sounder clicked off a rapid series of dots and dashes. He scowled at the sounder until it was silent.

"That's the third time the bank's telegraphed since five o'clock. I keep telling them she hasn't returned—"

Louis knew Rothman's kept a telegraph operator on duty in Boston until midnight five days a week, and until noon on Saturday. His mother paid the operator's wages.

Michael pulled a chair up to the table, noted the time of the query on a pad between the sounder and the transmitting key. He wiped his fingertips on his trousers, then began to operate the key, a horizontal knife switch that opened and closed the circuit to form the dots and dashes.

Louis walked quickly to the door—the interruption provided a good excuse —but Michael had trained himself so thoroughly in Mr. Morse's code, he was able to keep sending his message and swing around to look at Louis at the same time—

But Louis was already out the door. As he shut it, Michael's golden-brown eyes fixed on his, puzzled—

He suspects something, Louis thought, flushed again.

All at once he resented Michael's curiosity. The young Irishman *was* just an employee, not a member of the family. It wasn't his business if Louis had decided to—

To—

He couldn't even complete the thought.

Did he have enough nerve to go ahead? If only he hadn't made those rash promises to his classmates—!

But he had. So there wasn't much choice, was there?

All right, he'd take the first step and see what happened.

He stole into the darkened dining room. At the sideboard, he pulled out a decanter of whiskey. He'd tried whiskey before, surreptitiously, and detested it. But he'd heard whiskey made a person bolder. He unstop-pered the decanter, tilted it and let a little of the liquor trickle down his throat.

He winced, wiped his eyes, shivered in the darkness as the telegraph key went silent on the other side of the dining room wall. He listened. Heard Michael's footsteps. Then silence. He'd evidently returned to his chair. Somewhere below, rattling crockery told Louis the servants had con-cluded their meal—

Except for Kathleen. She would be finishing the bedrooms. Lighting the gas; plumping the pillows; arranging the coverlets—

One more swallow of whiskey set his head to aching faintly. He drew a deep breath, returned the decanter to the sideboard and, after a soft belch that burned his throat, started for the rear hall.

As he climbed the steps, the brief headache passed. He felt warmer. Al-most bold. What did he care if Michael Boyle wondered about his behav-ior? What did he care what anyone thought? His mother was a wealthy woman whose money permitted her to do anything she wished. He was no different—

He felt the stiffness again, without shame. He'd have a juicy tale to re-port on Monday.

iii

Louis stole along the second floor corridor toward the spill of light at the open door of his room. As he approached, he could hear small sounds. The rustle of bedding; Kathleen humming—

He squared his shoulders and pressed his palm to his mouth to hold back another belch. The whiskey had produced a feeling of confidence that enabled him to smile as he turned in at the bedroom door.

He was on the point of speaking when he noticed the curve of Kathleen's hip. She was leaning over the large bed, adjusting the covers. Her shiny black skirt shimmered in the glare of the gas. Snow ticked against the far windows.

The sight of Kathleen bent that way, the curve of her buttocks accentuated by her posture, brought him to full and painful rigidity. He knocked on the open door.

Kathleen screeched and spun around. One hand flew to the bosom of her dress. She had coppery hair all but concealed by her cap, a blunt chin and heavily freckled cheeks. Her mouth was full, her eyes pale blue. Her black dress and over-the-shoulder apron fit her ample breasts snugly.

"Good evening, Kathleen," he said, taking a step inside but blocking the door.

"Good evening, master Louis," she said, still red in the cheeks. "You came in so softly—startled me half to death."

"Thinking of something else, were you? A gentleman friend—?"

The girl was obviously stunned by his directness:

"No, sir, I—I don't have any—"

She swallowed.

"I'll be finished in a moment."

"Good," he said, pivoting away. Kathleen's eyes had a peculiar, almost alarmed look. She hadn't missed the telltale bulge of his trousers.

Louis strolled to the window. His palms itched as he stared out at the snow-dusted roof of the mansion next door. But he didn't really see it. He saw only Kathleen's body—

"All done, sir. I'll be going now—"

He turned around. "Close the door."

For a moment she appeared not to understand. She took a hesitant step backward.

"Master Louis, did you say—?"

"You heard very clearly what I said. Walk to the door and close it."

Fright shone in her eyes. She shook her head:

"Sir, that isn't proper—"

"I don't care what's proper, I want you to close the door!"

He moved toward her. His hand shook as he raised it to her left breast. She closed her eyes and shuddered.

With his other hand fisted and quivering at his side, he touched her breast with the back of his hand, then pressed upward. Kathleen appeared on the point of tears:

"Please, master Louis, may I leave?"

"You may not. I've been taken by your looks ever since my mother hired you, Kathleen. I've wanted to talk to you—get acquainted—"

Her eyes opened, tearful and angry:

"And what else, sir?"

"Oh, don't act so innocent. Don't tell me you've never had a man before—"

"Jesus and Mary be my witnesses, I have not! I'm a decent person—"

He guffawed, his dark eyes like black stones. "Come on! No Irish wench from the Five Points stays decent for long."

"That's a nasty thing to say! I've taken no man, and I won't till I'm properly wed by a priest."

"I think you're going to change your mind very shortly, Kathleen."

"You've been at the whiskey!" she exclaimed, pulling away from the press of his hand. "I can smell it. The whiskey's the reason you're saying all this—"

"I'm saying it because I like you."

She lunged for the door:

"I won't stay here another—ah!"

She cried out when he caught her forearm and dragged her back, stretching out his leg to catch the door with his toe and set it moving. Softly, the door clicked shut.

He maneuvered against her, his hands slipping around her waist. He drew her close. She shook her head and muttered incoherent syllables. She tried to pull away from the stiffness thrusting against her skirt but he held her fast, working his fingers in the fabric of her skirt—

"I ask you for the sake of decency, master Louis, stop this—"

"I won't—"

He put his mouth near her left ear, aroused all the more by the tickling touch of her hair and the lace of her cap.

"—because I know you're like all Irish girls. I know what you really want—"

"You don't! It's filthy of you to accuse me of—"

Angry at her protests, he slid his mouth across her cheek and found her lips.

At first they were cold and unyielding. She continued to struggle. But after a moment he felt a little heat.

He laughed, a soft, harsh sound. He held her tight as he pushed his tongue between her teeth.

Her tongue touched his for a fraction of a second. Then, as if realizing her own feelings were getting out of control, she wrenched her head away:

"You mustn't do this! If your mother should find out—"

"She won't. We'll be done before she's home."

"I swear to you, I'm virgin—"

"We'll remedy that."

He slid his hand down the front of her apron and pressed, feeling the curve of her belly. He moved his hand lower, his head all at once throbbing from the whiskey. The gaslit room seemed isolated; cut off from the real world. And the pressure between his legs had grown unbearable—

When he tried to thrust her back onto the bed, she broke away again, slipping around him toward the door. She'd nearly reached it when he called out:

"Kathleen!"

Slowly, she looked back. Her blue eyes widened at the harshness of his face.

"What—what is it?"

"Do you want to be arrested for thievery?"

Her mouth shaped into a horrified O. She could barely repeat the word:

"Thievery?"

He gestured to a bureau where he kept loose change. "I'll say I found you rummaging through my belongings—searching for money—unless you do exactly as I say."

"Oh, God, master Louis, you wouldn't—"

"I would unless you undress and lie down on the bed, Kathleen."

Her eyes grew hateful then; so hateful that he was terrified; tempted to let her go and be done with it.

But she hid the hatred, begging:

"I need this position. I'm the only one of the McCreerys old enough to work—"

"Very well. If you value your six dollars a week, do what I say."

"You—you imagine you have a right to demand—"

"I *do* have the right." He wiped his perspiring upper lip. "What's it to be, Kathleen? The six dollars—or a charge of thievery? It'll follow you wherever else you try to work—"

She started crying, the tears dampening her freckled cheeks as she glanced helplessly from one side of the room to the other. Seeing how she weakened so easily, he laughed aloud.

"You—" Her voice was ragged. "—you're only a child. Not even fifteen—"

Flushing, he said, "I have a man's cock, if that's your worry."

"But not a man's heart. Not a speck of Christian kindness—"

"I want to love you, Kathleen."

"—anything you want, you think you can take!"

"I can."

He took a step toward her.

"*Don't touch me!*"

Then, less stridently:

"Not—not till I'm ready."

He stepped to the door and slid the bolt.

"Just pull your skirt up and bare yourself, that'll be satisfactory—"

He heard the bed creak as she lowered herself onto it. He heard garments rustling; then her voice again:

"Will—will you be good enough to turn the gas down?"

"I don't think so. I want to see you—"

Unfastening his trousers, he faced her, his heart hammering in his chest as he moved his gaze slowly, slowly upward along her freckled white legs.

iv

She lay still beneath him, her eyes open and fixed on the ceiling. Louis slid between her thighs and probed, hurt at first by the roughness of her flesh.

Finally, her body changed in reaction to his presence. He jerked back and forth. Within a few seconds, his loins quivered and exploded. He felt a deep sense of disappointment—

Kathleen maneuvered her hips so their bodies were no longer joined. He rolled onto his side, stretching a hand toward her wrist as she stood up and started to lower her skirt.

The moment his fingers closed, she glared at him, miserable and angry at the same time:

"I've given you what you wanted, haven't I?"

"Once," he nodded, feeling distinctly sober and angry himself. The experience had been much less fulfilling than he'd imagined; a quick abrasion of flesh on flesh, then an abrupt end—nothing worth boasting about—

"Lie down again."

Disbelieving, she shook her head:

"You can't again so soon—"

"But in a little while—Kathleen, damn you, *lie down!*"

"I must go—"

"No, we—" He yawned. "—we've plenty of time." It seemed that way; it seemed as if only a minute or so had elapsed since he'd entered the room. "Besides, no one ever disturbs me after I've shut my door for the night."

She bowed her head, knelt on the bed and stretched out, weeping softly again. He was caught in a storm of conflicting feelings:

Satisfaction because he'd had his way.

Fear that he shouldn't have done it; he tried not to dwell on the hate he'd glimpsed in her eyes.

And a peculiar sadness that came over him because the act so long anticipated had been so curiously coarse and unrewarding.

The second time would be different. He'd enjoy it and so would she—

She lay with her back toward him. He pulled her over and forced her fingers to curl around him. She didn't want to touch him that way—her palm was cold; she cried harder—but he held his hand over hers and forced her, staring at the ceiling as she had done earlier, awaiting the first tingle of a response from his own flesh.

CHAPTER 6

Of Stocks and Sin

AMANDA LET HERSELF INTO the dim front hall. She drew off her hat and cast the snow-dampened muff aside, then paused to study her face in a peer glass.

She'd be forty-nine before the year was out. She felt every one of those years this evening. The glass showed wrinkles around her eyes, and more gray in her hair. How much of that gray had been put there by her preoccupation with Stovall—?

Feeling incredibly weary, she drew a deep breath and walked to the library doors. She opened them and gasped at the heat.

Busy cleaning himself on the telegraph table, Mr. Mayor paused with a paw athwart his nose. He recognized her and went back to bathing. Michael rose from the chair beside the hearth.

"Hallo, Mrs. A," he said with his mouth full.

She was always amused by Michael's passion for food and warmth. He never seemed to sweat, or put on an ounce of fat. She understood the reason for both cravings and seldom said anything about either—although withstanding Michael's temperature preferences required a good deal of forbearance.

"Bad weather out there," he went on as she came toward him. "I was growing a mite concerned. How was the lecture?"

"Douglass is an eloquent speaker. It's hard not to be moved by what he says. His chief target was the fugitive slave law."

Michael's pleasant expression vanished. Amanda knew his feelings about those who championed the cause of slaves. The young Irishman would have preferred to see the same amount of time and energy spent improving the lot of his own people, who had come to the United States to escape the privation and the legal tyranny they'd endured for generations. Instead, the Irish had found tyranny of a different sort—the kind produced by hatred of foreigners. As a result, they'd found privation too.

"I told Douglass I'd send him another draft soon. Will you take care of it? A hundred in my name, and two thousand anonymously."

At the desk, Michael jotted a note without saying anything.

"Stovall was at the theatre."

He spun around. "What the devil was he doing at an abolitionist meeting?"

"He wanted to disrupt Douglass' speech. He didn't succeed."

"Did he have a crowd of cronies with him?"

"No, just one companion."

"My Lord, Mrs. A, that takes brass."

"Stovall's been accused of a good many things, but I don't believe cowardice is one of them."

"Did you speak to him?"

She sank down in the chair opposite Michael's. Her eyes moved to the piles of manuscript. But her mind was elsewhere:

"It was unavoidable. Rose introduced us afterward. My tactics have gotten me in trouble, I'm afraid. Stovall knows my story about diversifying was a sham. He knows I've bought no other properties—"

Rapidly, she described the encounter at the Bowery Theatre. Some six months earlier, when she'd decided she could trust Michael Boyle, she'd revealed her plans concerning her adversary—and her reasons for them. He had to know if he was to function as her confidential assistant. She suspected he didn't wholly approve of her effort to regain control of Kent and Son. But he kept his personal views to himself, and always executed her orders without question.

She concluded, "It's possible Stovall will look more closely into my background—"

"Why should he?"

"Apparently I reacted very visibly when he made a derogatory remark about the Kents. I didn't mean to—it simply happened."

"Um."

"I think I'd better instruct Rothman's to move faster."

Michael gestured to the telegraph equipment:

"You can take care of that yet tonight. Mr. Rothman's operator has queried you three times since five P.M. I told him to try again at ten-thirty."

"Is there a problem?"

"I gather so. Something to do with an emergency meeting of the Blackstone board. If you were in Boston, communication would be less of a problem. Of course I realize Stovall is *here—*"

She looked up at the broad-shouldered young man. "You think I should drop the campaign to take back the firm, don't you? You—and Rose."

"It uses up a hell of a lot of your time. And your strength, I should imagine. Still, it's not for me to say whether you should or shouldn't. I am after all just your employee."

"Nonsense, Michael. You know you're closer to me in some ways than my own son. Where is he, by the way?"

"Popped off to sleep, I think."

"Rather early."

"He seemed—oh, nervous. Quite nervous, as a matter of fact."

"Did he say there was anything wrong?"

"No, *he* didn't say—"

Thinking about Louis, she didn't catch the significance of the emphasized word. She mused aloud:

"I'll have to talk with him in the morning—"

She smiled then, reminded of something her friend had said:

"Would you like to hear a bit of gossip Rose passed along? It seems some of the finer folk of New York have come to the conclusion you and I are lovers."

Michael burst out laughing. Amanda loved the sight of his smile. That such a handsome young man should be marred for life by the ugly scar on his forehead was a kind of blasphemy.

Still shaking with mirth, he turned to warm his hands at the hearth:

"Didn't mean to bray like that. It just tickles me that the filthy sods would come up with such notions. They've missed the truth entirely—" He faced her. "I am fond of you. But not for the reasons they imagine. No one's ever treated me more decently than you. I'd never dare say this to anyone else for fear of being hooted at—but you're as kind as I imagine my own mother would have been, had she lived."

His words heartened her; helped soothe away some of the tension she'd felt ever since the encounter with Stovall.

"That's sweet of you, Michael." She teased him: "I hope it's not pure blarney."

"An Irishman only dissembles with those he despises, not those he loves—" He pivoted back to the fire. "Faith, I'm carrying on like some convent girl—"

"I don't mind one bit."

They looked at one another for a moment.

"What's that manuscript on the floor?"

"Ah!" He scooped up a few of the pages. "Your nigger—beg pardon, I forgot you don't like me saying that—Mr. Hope's narrative. Delivered from the docks late this afternoon. There's also a letter describing the promising nature of the new mining claim in the Sierras. Plus one from your cousin in Virginia, and two others—"

Amanda scanned the few sheets Michael handed to her. Mr. Mayor put his forepaws on her skirt, studied her to see whether she'd resist. When she didn't, he hopped into her lap and curled up, his green eyes closing.

She went on reading while Michael took a clay pipe from the mantel, filled it with tobacco and lit it with a splinter of wood ignited in the fire-place. The odor of the Virginia leaf sweetened the stale, overheated air. But Amanda was hardly conscious of the warmth any longer, absorbed by the flow of Israel's prose:

"He writes extremely well."

"Yes, he does. As much as the subject of—ah—nigras leaves me cold, I confess the first few chapters caught my interest. I think his title's a bit dull, though. *The Life of Israel Hope* would mean nothing to the general public—he's not famous. I suggest something slightly more dramatic if Kent and Son ever publishes the book—"

"Kent and Son *will* publish it."

Her determination brought another smile to his face. "Then why not call it something like *West to Freedom?* It avoids the cliche of a reference to the north—it suggests the escape theme—and people are intrigued about the west."

"Yes, that's very good. I'll be anxious to read all of it—"

She laid the manuscript aside, causing Mr. Mayor to open his eyes and regard her with annoyance. She was almost embarrassed to bring up the next subject:

"Did you drive down to the Royal Sceptre office?"

"I did," he nodded. "The situation's just as it was last month when your letter was returned from London. The owners of the line still don't know anything more about Captain McGill."

Saddened, Amanda ran her hand aimlessly over the tomcat's neck. He arched and purred.

What in heaven's name had become of Bart? He'd sailed back from India the preceding November and abruptly resigned his command, that much she'd learned. But he hadn't told anyone in London where he was going—he'd just walked out and disappeared.

"I suppose it's time to give up on him," she said presently.

"We've no other options that I see."

"God, I hope he's all right—"

"You loved him a great deal, didn't you?"

"More than I realized when I said no to him. However—" She shrugged to hide the hurt. "—we should be worrying about other things. How much Stovall stock do we own at the moment?"

"I can't be positive without consulting the records. Mr. Rothman and Mr. Benbow have so many friends and clients buying small amounts on your behalf, then re-selling them to the dummy company, the total changes daily."

"Where's the ledger?"

"In my room. I was trying to bring it up to date before dinner, but I confess I fell asleep. I believe Boston Holdings owns somewhere above twelve thousand shares now."

Amanda nodded. For months, she'd been engaged in a cover campaign to accumulate stock of the Stovall Works. Her strategy was simple. When she'd acquired a controlling interest, she intended to present Stovall's attorneys with a demand that Kent and Son be sold to her—in exchange for the number of shares that would return Stovall to the position of majority stockholder.

She'd planned to take as long as necessary to acquire the shares; Rothman and Benbow moved with great circumspection, approaching one investor at a time, through intermediaries. So far, she didn't believe Stovall realized the true reason for the activity in shares in his company— nor did she think he knew of the existence of Boston Holdings.

"Find the book and get me the exact figure, would you?" she asked. "Meantime, I'll read Jephtha's letter."

Michael brought it to her from the littered table, then left the room.

Amanda stared at the soiled envelope that had come from Lexington for three cents' postage. But she didn't really see her name and address written in an irregular hand. She was thinking of Bart McGill.

Yes, she had loved him. Not in the same way she'd loved Jaimie de la Gura, and then Cordoba. More deeply—that was the hurtful truth she admitted to herself.

He hadn't sent her a single letter from London, or, so far as she knew, tried to ascertain her whereabouts. And now he'd left England, and no one knew where he was. Jaimie and Luis Cordoba had been taken from her by events over which she had no control. But Bart's departure had been her own doing, and she faced that bitter truth often—especially in the dark hours of early morning when she couldn't sleep; when age made her bones ache, and the shadows around her bed seemed to whisper of her life running out all too rapidly—

She rubbed her eyes to clear them of tears, then turned her attention to the letter.

It proved almost as disheartening as her memories.

ii

The letter, scrawled with a blunted pencil, was dated three and a half weeks earlier. Either it hadn't been mailed promptly, or had been delayed in transit.

The lines slanted across the page. Jephtha's hand was uneven; far less readable than it had been two months ago, when he'd reported his continuing alienation from his family and refused her offer of the income due him from the Ophir claim. The handwriting said the Reverend Jephtha Kent—a Reverend no longer—was a tormented man. The opening paragraphs told her he was still living and working on the grounds of the Virginia Military Institute:

> *My only friend is Thos. Jackson, the professor of whom I believe I have spoken before. He is a strange, deeply religious person—a Presbyterian—who has risked unpopularity by taking an active role in support of the local Negro Sunday School. My father-in-law, by contrast, would deny the colored people even the solace of God.*
>
> *Jackson—whom many of the cadets deride with the name 'Tom Fool' despite his outstanding record in the late Mexican conflict—is opposed to all the secessionist talk. He is humane. He once taught one of his own slaves to read in exchange for the slave's help—holding a torch—while he studied. It is Jackson who renews my hope that all in the south are not prey to the philosophy of a vile human being such as Captain Tunworth.*
>
> *Jackson is married. He and his wife are the only persons in Lexington willing to welcome me into their home occasionally. It is true that his habits are peculiar. To prevent distraction when he is pon-*

*dering problems in military tactics, he will turn his chair to the wall
and sit motionless for long periods of time. But I am comfortable
with him, and can share my thoughts freely—my sadness over Fan's
continuing refusal to allow any contact between myself and the boys
—and my growing certainty that the south's system of servitude will
bring its own dire harvest.*

*Compromise will never avail—it is too late. We have sinned as a na-
tion—I firmly share this belief with the noted abolitionist and Free-
Soil advocate, John Brown of Ohio. Sin is always punished. So the
nation will be punished. And not lightly. In the words of Paul the
Apostle to the Hebrews—'And almost all things are by the law
purged with blood. And without shedding of blood is no remission.'*

The gloomy prediction disturbed Amanda, because there were already
signs that Clay's compromise bills had bought nothing but a temporary
peace.

The Fugitive Slave Act, designed to mollify the south, had generated an
even greater militancy on the part of the northern abolitionists. And
influential Congressmen were toying with a doctrine which could renew
sectional antagonism.

The doctrine's chief ideologue was Stephen Douglas of Illinois, a senator whose combative temperament and slight stature had earned him the
title Little Giant. Sometimes the doctrine was called popular sovereignty,
sometimes squatter sovereignty. Basically it stated that people in a newly
organized territory had the unqualified right to determine what form their
government would take; specifically, whether the government would allow
or forbid slavery.

To Douglas, this was nothing more than the working of the principle of
democracy. To the abolitionists, it was betrayal. If the doctrine were followed to its logical conclusion, a territory could adopt or reject slavery
whether the territory lay above or below the Missouri Compromise line.
Not only did the doctrine run counter to the 1820 compromise, but by its
very nature it denied Congressional right to limit the spread of slavery.

Whig opponents abused Douglas as the south's toady, claiming he was
advancing the scurrilous philosophy to enhance his own chances as a future presidential candidate on the Democratic ticket. Others, less partisan,
said Douglas acted only out of a solid belief in the rights of the majority.
But whatever the Little Giant's motives, the papers had been filled with
the debate over his doctrine.

There was bound to be a test of it in the Congress in the next year or so. Legislators were already talking of the need to organize one or two large territories between Missouri and California. There had even been discussion of a transcontinental railroad, and for this to become a reality, the western lands had to be under some form of government.

If the intellectual debate led to a practical attempt to put the doctrine into effect in the organization of new territories, the Missouri Compromise would be severely threatened—and all of the efforts of Clay and Webster to secure peace might come to nothing. Some pundits predicted that if popular sovereignty ever passed into law, abolitionist groups would launch open warfare—

Open warfare. *Remission of sin through the shedding of blood*—

Sometimes it seemed to Amanda that the nation was heading inevitably toward it—and toward the even more grave Constitutional crisis that might be precipitated. The crisis was implicit in the south's traditional response to harrying by its enemies: secession.

Did one section have the right to separate itself from the rest to protect and preserve what it believed? Though she was no great expert on government, she thought not. If it did, the words *United* States would become a mockery.

Yet how to stop the quarrel before it brought disunion? Jephtha's church had broken apart over the slave issue. Even his own household was divided. How could the nation hope to fare any better?

Clearly, Jephtha didn't think it could.

The issues underlying the letter in her hand—and the letter itself—had upset her. She concentrated with great difficulty on the closing paragraphs:

> *Unhappiness is my lot. But I consider it God's will that I remain in that state; and I do what He has commanded. I continue to be engaged in certain activities at which I have hinted before, though the fugitive slave bill has made the labor increasingly difficult. Previously used points of refuge in the north are now under the closest scrutiny by southern sympathizers. We grow desperate for safe destinations for certain freight, and may be forced to call upon some we would otherwise not burden or endanger.*

Amanda gazed over the lines she'd just read, noting that the word *freight* had been heavily underscored. In previous letters, Jephtha had indeed alluded to mysterious activities, leading her to believe he'd involved himself in the work of what was popularly called the Underground Railroad.

The letter concluded with a few phrases containing her cousin's wish for her continued health and prosperity. Her eye was drawn back to the quotation from St. Paul.

And without shedding of blood is no remission.

She believed the slave system had to be done away with eventually. But was bloodshed the only course left open to accomplish it? She couldn't imagine that people of good will in any part of the country would want that kind of a solution—

Yet every paper she read told her the positions were hardening dangerously. The furies were loose on both sides. What if the compromise of 1850 ultimately proved unworkable? What if the threat of popular sovereignty proved real, and its advocates widened the chasm again, until it could never be bridged—?

She shuddered. The white cat yowled when she jumped up, startled by the loud, interruptive ring of the telegraph gong.

iii

Amanda had taught herself Morse's code so that she could send and receive messages when Michael wasn't present. She seated herself at the table, a steel-nibbed pen poised over a pad on which the young man had noted the times of the evening's previous transmissions. A moment after she acknowledged the query from Boston with a tapped-out A. K. D. G. READY, the operator at the Rothman Bank began to send:

APOLOGIZE LATE HOUR. SERIES OF MILL ACCIDENTS REQUIRED SPECIAL MEETING. BLACKSTONE BOARD DIRECTORS DEADLOCKED THREE FOR THREE AGAINST EMPLOYMENT TWO PHYSICIANS TO TREAT INJURED WORKERS ONE A CHILD. OPPONENTS ARGUE STEP UNNECESSARY AND EXPENSIVE. SAFETY AND WELFARE OF WORKERS NOT MANAGEMENT'S CONCERN. MR. ROTHMAN VOTES AYE HOWEVER. URGENTLY SOLICITS YOUR VOTE ON MATTER. END.

Amanda's pen flew across the pad, copying down the final words of the message. She chewed the end of the pen for perhaps ten seconds, then began to work the key:

EXPENSE NOT FACTOR. BELIEVE WE HAVE CLEAR RESPONSIBILITY. MR. ROTHMAN AUTHORIZED TO CAST AYE VOTE FOR A. K. D. G.

The library doors opened. Michael came in carrying several papers and a ledger. While the sounder chattered out ACKNOWLEDGED WITH THANKS, he took Amanda's pen from her fingers and scribbled on her pad:

12,875 shares as of last Wednesday afternoon—representing 38% of outstanding shares.

She nodded, aware of Michael lingering just behind her as she rapped out the signal for a further transmission, then began to send the dots and dashes:

SPEED UP ACQUISITION STOVALL WORKS STOCK BY BOSTON HOLDINGS. URGENT REPEAT URGENT WE REACH FIFTY ONE PER CENT OWNERSHIP SOON AS POSSIBLE. END.

In a moment, the sounder replied with words Amanda didn't bother to copy:

ACKNOWLEDGED ROTHMAN'S BANK.

Satisfied, she stood up.

"You think Stovall will attempt to block your purchase of shares?" Michael wanted to know.

"Of course he will—if he finds out who I am before we have a controlling interest. I'm sure he's aware of movement in the issue. He may not realize the individual blocks have been re-sold to Boston Holdings, but he could certainly track down that fact if his suspicions were sufficiently aroused."

"You're quite right. The bank that acts as the registrar of the stock has the information. There's no legal way to prevent them having it. You're gambling they'll neglect to inform Stovall—"

"I'm gambling they haven't yet. Joshua Rothman and I have already agreed to the final step. When Joshua's intermediaries have acquired the shares representing the last thirteen percent, those shares won't be transferred to Boston Holdings in small batches, as we've done in the past. They'll all be held and transferred in a single day. It'll be too late for Stovall to do anything about the takeover then. Still, you're right—the risk has always been high—" She paused only a moment. "I think it's time we developed an alternate plan. Just in case the stock scheme's uncovered."

Michael looked wary: "What sort of plan, Mrs. A?"

"You told me some nasty gossip about Stovall—that he's spent time with a brother and sister on Mulberry Street—both of whom are prostitutes?"

Glumly, Michael nodded. "Yes."

"What are their names?"

"I fail to see how their names could be of any—"

"Tell me anyway."

His face had lost its cheerful look. "The Phelan twins. Joseph and Aggie."

"Are they still—what's the term for that sort of thing? Practicing?"

In a clipped voice: "I don't know."

"I think you do."

"I really don't inquire too deeply into such matters—"

"Well, I want you to inquire. I want you to see whether you can get a deposition from them. Concerning what goes on during any one of Stovall's visits. In detail, Michael. Such complete detail that there can be no doubt of the—the customer's identity. Or his intention."

She tried not to see his stunned look.

"Christ!" he whispered. "You don't mean that—"

"I do."

"Manipulating stock is one thing. But mucking around in slime is quite another—"

"Are you telling me you won't do it?"

A long silence. Amanda said:

"If you won't go to the Five Points, I will."

He studied her face for a sign that she was bluffing him; saw none. With a shake of his head, he said softly:

"All right. I suppose I'm obligated to do whatever you ask as long as I'm in your employ."

"And you *are* still in my employ—"

"For the moment."

The dull-voiced threat didn't even make her blink:

"Can these Phelans be persuaded to give you the information I want?"

"Mrs. A, listen! You mustn't soil yourself in this sort of—"

"Answer me, Michael!"

He sighed. "Yes, I think the information could be gotten—if the Phelans were given enough money, and frightened a little in the bargain."

"Would they speak to you in front of a notary?"

"I tell you it's all a matter of how much you pay them—and how much they imagine they're threatened. I could take not only a notary, but a couple of pretty tough lads I knew on the docks. If I were to go," he added.

"You'll go. Because I'm willing to pay the Phelans five thousand dollars —and whatever it takes above that to relocate them in another city. Someplace quite distant—out of Stovall's reach. New Orleans, St. Louis—"

Dourly, he said, "For five thousand, I imagine the Phelans would climb in your bed and put on a performance that would stop your heart with shock—and if you were still alive afterward, they'd hand you their souls in a white hanky."

"Go see them. Get me the statement. Prepare two identical copies."

"What are you going to do with the copies?"

"For the moment, nothing."

"But if you were to use them, how—?"

"Why, I expect one copy would go to Mr. Stovall—with a suggestion that the other might soon be delivered to his prospective bride. I just heard about her this evening. A very proper young woman, I'm told. He's in desperate need of her father's money."

He stared at her, disbelieving.

"I find your reactions damned annoying, Michael!"

"Be as annoyed as you please! I can't reconcile that—" He pointed to the display case holding the medal. "—with what you're proposing. You told me once the Kents always took the high road—"

"There are times," she said angrily, "when the *high road* won't get you where you must go. *I want Kent's!* The statements are only insurance. I really think we'll be successful with the stock, so let's not quarrel—" She fanned herself. "My God, I can't stand this heat a moment longer. Is there anything else we need to discuss?"

"Well—"

"Speak up before I suffocate."

"It—it concerns Louis. I think I know why he's behaving oddly. I tried to suggest as much a while ago, but you were all caught up in Mrs. Ludwig's gossip."

"Go on."

"Professor Pemberton wishes an appointment. He sent round a note. Your son isn't performing satisfactorily in school."

"You mean he's failing?"

"It's not that he lacks interest or aptitude—he simply doesn't wish to do the work. So he doesn't. He's also indulged in a bit of scrapping—"

"A bit or a lot?"

"Well—the latter. You can read the professor's note. He says that when Louis doesn't get his way in some trivial dispute with his classmates, he swings a punch. Rather a mean one, too, I gather. You can be thankful you're not raising a coward, anyway—"

He tried to smile. The effort failed. The dispute about the Phelans had soured his mood.

She wondered sadly whether her own pattern of living was responsible for the way Louis was developing. The change in him dated from the time she'd tried to explain why she'd shot the man in the mining camp. Ever since, she'd had the uncanny feeling that her son was imitating her behavior; doing exactly as he pleased—just as she appeared to do. He didn't realize that every action she took had one motive: to see Kent and Son restored to its rightful owners. She'd have to try again to make him understand she was working toward a goal—a goal that mattered almost as much as life itself—

She glanced up, aware of Michael studying her. He said nothing. But she felt accused. In concocting the scheme with the Phelan twins, wasn't she acting just as irresponsibly as her son? Taking what she wanted, regardless of the means—and regardless of who might be injured?

No! There *is* a difference! she thought.

But she was uneasy with the conclusion.

She didn't want Michael to see that. She spoke briskly:

"Does Louis know about Pemberton's note?"

"No. When the boy dropped in here a while ago, I asked him one or two questions about school, that's all."

"How did he answer?"

"He said he was bored."

"Let me have the note."

He rummaged on the desk. "Oh—here's one more that arrived with the late mail. A solicitation of funds from Mr. Thurlow Weed in Albany. He's the newspaper publisher, isn't he?"

"And the power behind the Whig party in the state—he and Seward. Should I read that?"

"It depends on whether you want to contribute funds to support the party's convention in Baltimore in June."

"I suppose I'm closer to a Whig than to anything else," she said. "I can't quite bring myself to be as rabid against slavery as the Free-Soilers. But I'll be damned if I'll give a penny to a party when I can't vote for it. Put that in a letter to Mr. Weed. Tell him the moment the Whigs support votes for women, he'll have my contribution."

"Do you really mean that?"

"Of course I do!" She looked rueful. "I also know it's impractical as the devil."

"You are a somewhat contradictory creature, Mrs. A."

"Did you ever know a person who wasn't?"

He inclined his head again, almost smiling as he agreed. Then:

"Shall I or shall I not write Mr. Weed?"

"Yes, write him a polite note," she sighed. "Enclose a draft for a hundred dollars."

"Very well."

"And don't forget your trip to the Five Points."

"That would be impossible," he said. "May I plead with you once more not to—?"

"No."

"You can be a hard woman, Mrs. A."

"When it's necessary."

"You've never been hard with me before. Demanding, but not hard." He rubbed his knuckles across his upper lip. "You know how much I hated the tenements—and the crookedness on the docks. You know very well I'd sooner die than be forced back to either. You're taking advantage of that. Still, that isn't what bothers me the most. So far, everything you've done to get the firm is legal. Surreptitious, but legal. The Phelans, though—that's something else."

His steady gaze frightened her; blunted her anger. Her mind echoed with Bart's biblical warning; and Jephtha's—

For remission of sin, the price was blood.

"That's my worry, not yours."

She started for the door, then swung back:

"Oh, yes—I'd better take Pemberton's letter. I want to read it before I talk to Louis in the morning."

"Here. Mrs. A—?"

"Yes, Michael?"

"I really am glad you got home safely. That storm's growing nasty outside—"

With a dispirited smile, she held up the note from the headmaster: "It appears we've one of our own brewing inside, too."

iv

Amanda climbed the stairs slowly. She stopped on the landing to catch her breath beside the stained glass window. The window contained a small portrait of Lord Byron set above a pattern of figures representing the muses.

Under the gas fixture, she read what Pemberton had written. It was every bit as grim as Michael had hinted. Louis was willfully refusing to settle down to his studies—

Damned if she'd wait till morning to have it out with him!

Instead of proceeding to her room, she turned the opposite way on the second floor, toward his. She frowned when she tried to open the door.

Locked.

She thought she heard a voice—not her son's—whispering inside. Curious and a little alarmed, she knocked:

"Louis?"

No answer.

"Louis, this is your mother. Why do you have the door bolted? Please open it at once."

CHAPTER 7

The Box

AN IRRATIONAL DREAD settled over Amanda while she waited for a reply. The wind whined across the roof. A door closed below; Michael leaving the library. In her son's room, she heard furtive footsteps and, if her ears weren't tricking her, that unfamiliar voice.

"Louis, unless you answer me—" she began, only to be interrupted:

"I'm here, mother." The sound of a yawn—too exaggerated to be genuine. "What do you want?"

"I want you to open the door immediately."

"You woke me up."

He's lying, she thought, the knowledge a sickening shock. She'd never known her son to lie before. The other voice whispered again. This time she identified it as a woman's; the shock was instantly compounded.

Amanda had long ago realized Louis would probably have his first experience with a girl without her knowledge. She'd decided she would have little control over the time and place, and that about all she could do was exert her influence to see he didn't become involved with some diseased tart from the slums. But she hadn't expected the encounter to happen so soon. Nor in her own house—

Who was with him?

Of all the females who worked for her, she suspected Kathleen McCreery. Kathleen was young; not unattractive. Who had taken the initiative, the boy or the maid? Kathleen didn't strike her as a scheming sort. But obviously the girl knew she was working in a wealthy household—

Her mind a chaos of questions, Amanda finally realized the door was still closed.

"Louis, I'm not going to continue to speak to you this way. Let me in!"

The door opened. But not far.

That Louis had been lying to her was immediately apparent. He was still dressed. But he was barefoot. The tail of his shirt hung over his left hip. Far from sleepy, he was sweating.

"Mother, you woke me out of a sound—"

"The devil I did!" She shoved the door and rushed past him before he could stop her.

Beside the bed, looking utterly terrified, was the McCreery girl. She was clumsily trying to smooth her black skirt. And sure enough, there was the evidence: the rumpled bed with covers tossed back; a damp stain tinged pink at one edge—

Louis started to speak. Kathleen was quicker:

"Ma'am—please—believe me—he forced me—"

"What do you mean, *forced?*"

"Just—just that. I was fixing the room for the night. He came in—he said—*ohhh*—"

"For God's sake, Kathleen, don't start crying! I can hardly make sense of what you're saying as it is—"

Louis stormed between them:

"Who cares what she's saying? Every bit of it's a lie! She practically begged me—"

Kathleen's face convulsed with shame and rage:

"You filthy boy. You filthy, *filthy* boy—"

To Amanda:

"I've never been with a man before—God as my witness! He locked the door—"

"*Shut your mouth!*" Louis cried, running at her with his hand raised.

Amanda lunged, caught her son's wrist, flung his fist down to his side. He glared at her; tried to strike her—

Amanda slapped him across his left cheek, then across his right.

The boy stumbled back, upsetting a chair. He almost blundered against one of the windows before he righted himself, staring at his mother with astonishment and fear. His normally swarthy face had drained of color. The sight of him sickened her.

She pointed to the overturned chair.

"You sit down while I listen to Kathleen's side of this. Then I'll give you a chance—"

He hesitated. But he finally obeyed, righting the chair in front of the window and sinking down. Outside, the rooftops of the square showed thickening crusts of white—so clean in contrast to the ugliness she'd discovered—

The boy watched his mother apprehensively as she shut the door. Walking back to Kathleen McCreery, Amanda felt her belly aching again, worse than ever—

She put her arm around Kathleen. With their backs to the boy, she gave the girl's trembling shoulders a gentle squeeze:

"Don't be afraid to speak. If Louis abused you, he'll be punished—"

"Oh yes?" the girl retorted. "He's never punished for anything."

"He will be this time. Now tell me precisely what happened."

Kathleen tried, her speech breathy and punctuated by loud sniffles that might have made Amanda laugh in other circumstances:

"He said that—he said he wanted me—in his bed and—if I wouldn't, he'd—he'd say he caught me—trying to steal something—"

Amanda studied the maid's red, puffy eyes. Unless the girl was a superb actress, she wasn't pretending.

"So you consented?"

"I consented because I'd have been accused if I didn't! He demanded that I undress—"

"Demanded?"

"Just the way he demands everything. Don't you know how your own son behaves with the people who wait on him?"

"No, I—I guess I don't. Evidently I've been too busy to give Louis the right sort of attention—"

But I've given him the pattern to follow, haven't I? She remembered California; the boy's odd, almost admiring smile when she talked about the man she'd shot—

Struggling against rage that was directed more toward herself than her son, she faced him. Walked to him. Stood before him, her stare fixed on his guilty, evasive eyes—

"Louis, do you deny what Kathleen says?"

"Yes—yes, I do," he answered, though without firmness. "She flaunted herself—"

"May the saints summon me this minute, *I didn't!*" the girl burst out. "I'd never do such a thing, Mrs. de la Gura. I'd never risk losing this job— I spent months searching for a house where they'd take Irish. Do you think I'd throw that away even—even if I wanted the likes of him?"

"No," Amanda said wearily. "No, that wouldn't be at all likely."

"Ma, I tell you she's making it all up—!" Louis began.

"Louis—" Her voice was pitched low, her eyes stark. "I am not going to tolerate a single lie from you. Did you or did you not demand that Kathleen obey you?"

He still evaded her gaze. She dug her nails into his shoulder:

"Louis, *answer me.*"

"I—"

He wiped his mouth with the back of his hand. Then, as if realizing he was trapped, he turned defiant:

"What if I did? Why shouldn't I have her if I want? This is my house, not hers—and she's nothing but slum trash."

Kathleen began to weep again. As Amanda let go of his shoulder, her lips were almost colorless:

"*Of all the insufferable arrogance—*"

"Are you taking *her* part?"

"Yes! I am! What gave you the right to think you could order her about any way you wished? No one—nothing gives you that right!"

"No?" A kind of cowering nastiness wrenched his face. "*You* seem to do exactly what you please. Anywhere—and any time."

She struck him with her fist, savagely. He toppled off the chair, fell on one knee, still glaring. She shook with fury—realizing belatedly that she'd really been striking out not at him, but at his accusation—

Because she knew it was true.

ii

She ordered Louis to remain in his room. With as much control as she could muster, she put her arm around Kathleen again, shepherded her out to the hall and led her toward her own quarters.

Amanda pitied the young girl. But she also knew what had to be done. Louis must be dealt with firmly, decisively—and at once. Kathleen's presence would only compound the difficulty of taking him in hand.

She turned up the gas in her private sitting room and eased the girl gently into a chair. Then she sat down opposite her, trying to speak calmly:

"Kathleen, I can't tell you how ashamed I am of what Louis did—"

The girl made a faltering effort to straighten her disarrayed hair. "If only—if only he hadn't used me like—like some piece of goods—"

"I'm afraid I must bear the blame for that. I've inadvertently let Louis believe he can do whatever he wishes. I intend to correct that—"

Provided it isn't already too late.

"However—" Here was the thorny place. "—I think you can realize it would only make things more difficult if you were to remain in the house."

Kathleen's head lifted. Her coppery hair glinted in the flickering glow of the gas—and so did her reddened eyes:

"You're going to turn me out?"

"I don't want to, but you wouldn't be happy here in the light of what's happened. Nor would it be good for Louis to—"

"It *is* his part you're taking. It *is!*"

"Kathleen, I assure you it isn't. I'm thinking of your welfare too."

"Then for God's sake think of how much I need this position!"

"I've considered that."

"You're not going to punish him, that's it," she declared.

"I assure you I'm going to punish him. Severely."

"No, you're getting rid of me so you can smooth it over. Pretend it never happened—"

"You're being unreasonable, Kathleen. Don't you appreciate the problems it would cause for you to see Louis every day, feeling as you do about him? I'm asking you to leave for your own sake. In fact I want you to go tonight."

"Tonight—!"

"Yes, go downstairs and speak with Michael. Tell him to write you a draft for eight weeks' wages. Give him your address, and I'll do my utmost to locate another position for you—"

"So I'm to be thrown out as though I'm the criminal?"

"You don't seem to understand I'm doing it for your peace of mind as well as—"

"I *want* him to look at me! I want him to remember how cruel he was!"

Amanda shook her head. "That won't serve any useful purpose. In a few days you'll see the wisdom of—"

"I won't be treated this way, Mrs. de la Gura. I did nothing wrong. The wrong's all on the boy's side."

"And mine," Amanda said wearily. "I've admitted that." Her voice hardened just a little. "But I still insist you go."

All at once Kathleen's eyes brimmed with resentment. Her face showed a wrath Amanda had never seen her display before:

"You'd better not do this to me—"

Amanda bristled. "Young lady, I'm trying to act in your own best interests. I won't be threatened."

"If you force me to leave, I have friends who'll take my part."

Somehow the plain words made Amanda's spine crawl.

"Friends?"

"My uncle's a pal of Mr. Rynders. You know who Mr. Rynders is, don't you?"

"Isaiah Rynders? Of course."

"I'll make sure he learns what you've done."

"Have you heard nothing I've said? I know you're the one who's been wronged. I'm trying to make what amends I can—"

To salve my conscience?

"I need this position," the girl repeated, more firmly. "It's the best I've ever had, and no one else in my family is old enough to bring home steady wages. If you put me out, Mr. Rynders will hear about it."

"And do what, may I ask? Send some of his hooligans to throw stones at the house?"

"I—I don't know what he'll do, but he'll do something. And it won't be just stones, either."

Her reddened eyes seethed with anger—the same kind of anger Amanda had occasionally seen on Michael's face when he spoke of blacks, or the crowded, filth-ridden stews of his childhood. But understanding the girl's rage didn't mean she could condone it:

"I'm afraid I'm losing patience with you, Kathleen—"

"You'll lose a lot more before this is over!"

"Don't you dare utter one more threat, young lady! You go see Michael this instant!"

The girl started to retort, recognized how deeply she'd stirred Amanda's wrath, and kept silent. With a last, hateful glance at her former employer, she rushed from the room, slamming the door behind her.

Amanda sat motionless for the better part of five minutes. Then, overwhelmed by misery and exhaustion, she buried her face in her hands and cried.

iii

When the crippling despair passed, she went to her bedroom. She found the whiskey she kept at hand for those nights when sleep refused to come easily. She poured a generous measure and drank it in swift swallows.

The effect of the whiskey was almost instantaneous. A semblance of control restored, she walked down the hall to Louis' room and knocked.

He replied with a sullen monosyllable.

"I'll be back to speak with you as soon as I've talked with Michael," she said.

Silence.

Amanda shook her head, wheeled and strode toward the staircase.

She found Michael at the desk in the library, his demeanor as melancholy as it had been following their discussion of the Phelans. She closed the doors and leaned against them.

"Has Kathleen been here?"

"Yes, Mrs. A, she just left. I wrote the draft as you instructed. She's downstairs, packing her belongings. Considering the snow and the late hour, I doubt we can whistle up a hack. I'll have to hitch the carriage and drive her home myself."

"How much did Kathleen tell you?"

"Enough to make it clear master Louis all but raped her." He hesitated. "What do you plan to do about the boy?"

"We'll discuss that in a moment. Do you agree Kathleen should go?"

Michael rose and walked toward his chair. He'd refilled his plate with mutton. He picked up a slice and bit into it without much relish. Eventually he answered:

"Under the circumstances, I do."

"The girl made some wild threats about setting Isaiah Rynders on us."

Michael's brow hooked up. "The ward boss?"

"Yes. She claims he's a friend of her uncle. Could she make good on a threat like that?"

"I expect so. There isn't a major gang with which Isaiah Rynders doesn't have connections—the Patsy Conroys, the Daybreak Boys, the Shirt Tails, the Plug Uglies. If Rynders could do her uncle a favor—rather, have some of his thugs do it—he would. Such little acts of kindness insure loyalty to the Society of Saint Tammany come election time."

"Do you have any idea what they'd do?"

"None whatever. It could be a friendly little street assault when you least suspect it. Or Louis might be the target. Some of the roughest gangs specialize in such charming touches as stomping a victim with shoes in which they've embedded a couple of knife-blades—"

"Dear God!"

"They're also fond of quick raids to wreck and loot a house. Or arson—that's relatively safe. The possibilities are almost without limit—" He shrugged. "On the other hand, Kathleen's threat may be more heat than substance."

"You're not entirely convinced of it."

Michael's eyes slid away. "Not entirely."

"Well, I suppose it's time for me to resurrect my old revolver and keep it handy."

"Not a bad notion," he agreed.

"As for Louis—I know what I'm going to do. First I intend to punish him personally. Then I'm going to withdraw him from Professor Pemberton's Day School for a while. Put him to work around the house. Any sort of project that needs doing—or can be invented. I want you to take charge of that phase. Work him to exhaustion."

"What are you trying to do, Mrs. A, break him like a horse?"

That irritated her: "Do you have a better suggestion?"

"I think so—though it'll make you even more angry."

"I'm listening."

Michael drew in a deep breath. "Set him a different kind of example."

She turned red. "Just exactly what do you mean?"

"Simply this. You're a determined woman. You go after what you want, no interference allowed—and you make no secret of it. I suspect Louis is only showing his admiration of that."

"In a very warped way!" She said it sharply. But she knew Michael had touched the essential truth of the problem.

"Agreed," he said. "Still, you might find things changing favorably if you displayed—shall we say—a less aggressive attitude?"

"I can't be what I'm not."

"Certainly. But you *can* be less outspoken about your intention to own Kent and Son at any cost. Louis may not understand the reason for it, or know how you're going about it. But he can't help being aware of your hostility. You're quite a different woman when Mr. Stovall occupies your thoughts than you are, for example, when you're entertaining Mrs. Ludwig or arguing the pros and cons of abolitionism. You may not even realize the disparity—"

"I'm sorry, I don't."

"Then perhaps I've made you angry in a good cause."

Amanda gazed restlessly around the library.

At the painting of her grandfather highlighted by the flicker of flames from the hearth—

At the polished scabbord of the French sword and the lustrous wood of the Kentucky rifle—

At the shimmering green glass of the tea bottle—

She sounded almost despondent when she spoke:

"Everyone wants to convince me I'm a fool for trying to get control of the firm."

"Everyone? There have been others before me?"

"Quite a few," she said, sourly. "Rose Ludwig just this evening. My cousin Jared before he died. Captain McGill—but that's immaterial. I consider it my duty to deal with Stovall."

"I'd say your sense of duty has become a fixation."

"Call it anything you like. I won't stop now. He blocked me once, because I was careless, but he won't a second time. You must understand how I see it, Michael—Louis behaved inexcusably. But every step I've taken against Stovall, I've taken for a good and sufficient reason—"

"You could lecture Louis for days, Mrs. A, and I don't believe you'd get through to him. He's not old enough to comprehend the subtle difference between an appetite for a woman and an appetite for revenge. If there *is* a difference—"

"There is!"

His shrug said the question was debatable.

"Michael, what Louis did to Kathleen was pointless and—"

"Forgive me again," he interrupted. "I may be expressing a narrow male attitude, but a boy with a physical craving hardly considers the craving pointless. It's the most important thing in the world to him. It took me months to work up nerve the first time I—well, never mind the details."

"I am talking about the despicable way Louis went about it!" she insisted.

Michael's gaze rested on Mr. Mayor sleeping in a ball on the marble in front of the fire. "You wouldn't call my planned expedition to the Five Points despicable?"

"I was very explicit on that subject. The material from the Phelans would only be used in an extreme situation, so let's not permit that to confuse the discussion."

He flushed. "I think it's very pertinent to the discussion. You *did* ask for my suggestions—"

"Well, I don't agree with them. Hamilton Stovall and my son's behavior have nothing to do with one another."

"Who are you trying to convince? Me? Or yourself?"

"Michael, you're overstepping—!"

"The hell I am! You've enrolled me as your son's disciplinarian!"

"I told you I intend to punish—"

"For God's sake, Mrs. A, why won't you recognize that it's your obsession with Kent and Son that's damaging the boy? Until you reach that conclusion, no punishment will make a whit of difference in Louis' character. If you change, he may. Otherwise—"

"Enough, Michael."

"No, goddamn it, I want to have my say about—"

"The subject is *closed*."

There was a heavy silence.

"And you'll take charge of Louis as I instructed."

"Ordered!" he growled, turning toward the fireplace. He saw the white cat lying in front of him. He kicked it.

Mr. Mayor woke with a start, nearly as astonished at the young man's cruelty as Amanda herself. Michael slammed a fist down on the mantel, then bent to stroke the cat, murmuring apologies almost as if he'd struck a human being.

She *couldn't* admit Michael was right. Or Jared. Or Bart McGill. She couldn't admit she was being destroyed by her own dedication to owning the printing house. She was strong. She'd survived challenges before. Survived and overcome them. She would survive this one; bring Louis into line *and* gain her objective—

Michael's back was still turned as she said, "Be sure Louis is wakened at six. I'll inform him before I go to bed that you'll be—"

A commotion at the rear of the house whirled them both toward the doors.

Michael started into the hall, only to step back as the butler, Mr. Hampton, rushed into sight, still struggling to slip his arms into his black coat. He smelled of gin; he'd evidently been relaxing downstairs before trudging home—

"Mrs. de la Gura, there is an Adams Express wagon in the alley."

"At this hour?"

"I hardly believed it myself when I saw the accumulation of snow. Nevertheless, two deliverymen are bringing in a large crate."

"We've ordered nothing big enough to be delivered in a crate—" Michael began.

"I can't help that, Mr. Boyle," Hampton said with a dogged shake of his head. "The crate has come from the railroad station, addressed to this house."

"Oh my God," Amanda exclaimed, an incredible suspicion forming in her mind. "Jephtha's letter—"

"What's that to do with a crate from Adams Express?" Michael wanted to know.

But Amanda had already dashed past him toward the butler's pantry. With astonished looks, he and Hampton hurried after her.

iv

The crate, dripping melted snow and exuding a faint acrid smell, had been brought down the rear service stairs into the room at the rear of the raised basement. The room was a cheerless place without gas fixtures, used principally for storage.

The servants clustered around the crate. One of them, Brigid, the downstairs maid, held a flickering oil lamp that cast slow-moving shadows. Two sodden and distinctly unhappy draymen stood eyeing the box as Amanda entered, Michael and the butler right behind.

The outer door blew open, whirling snow and freezing air into the room. The flame of the lamp jumped in the sudden gust. Grotesque shadows leaped across the walls and ceiling. One drayman kicked the door shut while Amanda surveyed the crate. It had been crudely addressed in black paint:

> *Mrs. A. de la Gura*
> *Madison Square*
> *New York City*

It also bore a return address—*J. Jared, Clifton Forge, Virginia*—and, across the ends, an additional legend:

> *Books & household merchandise*

The contrived name of the sender—meaningful to Amanda but to no one else—strengthened her growing conviction about the crate's contents.

With a sinking feeling, she recalled a passage in Jephtha's letter about regular destinations for *freight* being unsafe—

"Come off the train from Baltimore," one of the draymen informed her. "We ain't to blame for the stink. One of the handlers down at the terminal must have pissed on—"

His companion nudged him, then held out a scrap of paper and pencil to Amanda:

"You'll have to sign."

"Why did you deliver it on such a bad night?" she asked, scribbling her name.

" 'Cos the goddamn sender paid extra," the first man grumbled. "Special delivery within an hour after it arrived—"

The draymen left. Outside, wheels crunched snow. Hoofs clopped softly. The sounds faded.

Amanda circled the box, spotting three small holes neatly drilled through the wood. She didn't know whether to laugh or weep over the additional burden thrust so unexpectedly on the already disturbed household.

Michael voiced the confusion of the whispering servants:

"Who in God's name would be shipping you books and such, Mrs. A?"

"That *J. Jared* is the Reverend Kent in Virginia. Jared was his father's name. I'm sure he painted that on the box so we'd identify the sender."

"Well, we can leave it sitting till morning, anyway—"

Amanda shook her head. "We have to open it. Fetch a crowbar."

"Why?"

She pointed. "Do you notice those holes?"

"What of them?"

"Do you remember reading in the paper last year about a black man in Virginia who had himself shipped to the Philadelphia Anti-Slavery Society? The underground railroad's used the trick several times before."

"Oh my Lord!" the cook exclaimed. "Is your cousin mixed up in that, ma'am?"

"I've had hints of it in his letters—Michael, bring the crowbar!"

In half a minute, the young man returned and fell to prying one side off the case. Amanda was outraged that the Reverend Jephtha Kent would make her a party to his illegal work without so much as a word of warning—

But there *had* been warning, she realized belatedly. In Jephtha's delayed letter, hadn't he made a reference to *calling on some we wouldn't otherwise burden or endanger?* If those weren't the exact words, the sense was the same. He'd been telling her in a cryptic way that he might need her help. Perhaps he'd avoided saying it straight out in case mail from suspected underground railroad operators was tampered with. At the time she'd read the lines, she'd simply been too dull-witted to grasp his meaning.

A nail squealed as Michael worked the crowbar. He was starting to pry loose another when the bar slipped from his fingers and clanged on the floor.

"Can't hold onto the blasted thing. There's a bit of grease on it—"

"Spit on your hands," Amanda said.

Bent over and reaching for the length of iron, Michael stared. The reaction was more pronounced from the servants. The butler uttered an audible gasp.

Amanda snapped at him:

"Haven't you ever used a little spit so you could get a better hold on something, Mr. Hampton?"

"No, madam, I have not," the butler said, plainly horrified by the idea.

"Well, you're not taking advantage of the saliva God gave you. For heaven's sake, Michael, get that damn thing open!"

"Right away, Mrs. A—I was about to do the very thing you suggested."

He moistened his palms while Mr. Hampton raised his eyes to the ceiling.

Presently the last nail came free. Michael scrambled back as the side of the box crashed to the floor. One of the maids shrieked softly. Amanda almost felt like crying again:

Not this on top of everything else—!

Huddled inside the crate in a tangle of cheap blankets was a light-skinned colored girl. Her frayed cotton dress barely covered her emaciated thighs. Amanda judged her to be sixteen or seventeen. She looked undernourished and nearly frozen. With the crate open, the smell of urine was much stronger.

The black girl started to crawl out, tears in her eyes:

"I thought I die in there. I thought I die from the cold and the shakin' on the train—"

Amanda forced herself to stay calm. She knelt and slipped an arm around the trembling girl:

"You're safe, child. Safe. What's your name?"

"Mary, ma'am."

"Mary what?"

"Mary's the only name I got."

"I'm Mrs. de la Gura—"

"Praise God! The Reveren' Kent, he took me over to Clifton Forge hid in Mr. Syme's wagon. He stopped in some woods outside of town, an' before he nailed me in the box, he say you help me get to Canada—"

"Christ, that's all we need—black contraband!" Michael groaned.

"Hush, Michael."

"But you can be arrested for concealing a runaway sl—"

"I said hush! Mary—how long have you been shut up in that box?"

"Mos' part of two nights an' all day, I guess—what day's this?"

"Friday night—Saturday morning by now."

"The Reverend, he drove me to the Virginia Central depot Wednesday —trip's almos' thirty miles—"

"Why couldn't they simply have shipped the creature to Canada?" Mr. Hampton asked, disdainful.

"Watch your tongue, Mr. Hampton," Amanda warned. "She's not a creature—she's a human being. And a hungry one at that, I imagine. Have you had anything to eat, child?"

"Biscuits. No drinkin' water. Breathin' was the hardest. Breathin' and bracin' my hands an' feet so I wouldn't roll around and make noise when men lifted the box—"

"Does that answer you, Mr. Hampton?" Amanda asked in a waspish voice. "If they shipped her all the way to Canada, she'd probably suffocate before she got there—or make such a stink in the box someone would surely open it."

The girl grew agitated. "I couldn't help wettin' myself. I tried and tried not to—I tried hard, but I couldn't—"

"That's all right, that's all right," Amanda whispered, patting her. "You did just fine, Mary. Who do you belong to?"

The girl blinked. "To me. I get to Canada, I won't belong to nobody ever again."

"But who did you belong to in Virginia?"

"Cap'n Tunworth."

"The Reverend's father-in-law?"

"Yes'm. He's a proper gentleman with other white folks, but he can be mean as hell to his niggers when the spell's on him."

Amanda nodded, her anger at Jephtha all but erased by the courage and fragility of the young girl who had entrusted her life to two white men, and ridden rattling trains in a lightless wooden cage with mortal fear for her companion.

"I've met the captain," she said. "You've confirmed my impression of him—"

"I knew Mr. Syme could get me started to Canada. Mos' every nigger 'round Lexington knows that. I never wanted to go till the cap'n sold my mamma and papa to a man in Carolina. But the cap'n wouldn't sell me. I figure I never see my folks again, so I might as well take a chance on bein' a free person—"

"But why did the Reverend send you here?" Michael asked. "Why not to an organization like the local anti-slavery society?"

"Jephtha's letter indicated that was getting too dangerous," Amanda said.

Mary nodded. "He an' Mr. Syme say they got slave-catchers watching those places now. Watching for colored—even for boxes like the one I come in—"

Suddenly she hugged Amanda, burying her head on the older woman's shoulder.

"I hate that old box! It was all dark an' I made it smell bad—I couldn't help it—I'm so glad I'm here—I'm so glad—"

"Someone bring a couple of clean blankets," Amanda said while the girl sobbed. "We'll put her in the third floor bedroom next to Michael's until I decide what we can do with—"

She froze. At the storeroom door beyond the cluster of servants, she saw Kathleen McCreery.

Kathleen was bundled in a shabby coat. Her pale eyes rounded at the sight of the crate and the black girl in the circle of lamplight.

"*Michael—!*"

Amanda's warning spun him toward the door.

"*Get her out of here!* When you take her home, warn her that she'd better not say a word."

"I'm afraid we're not in much of a position to issue warnings," Michael whispered. He stalked to the door and thrust the dumbfounded Kathleen out of sight.

The black girl began to cry in earnest, long wailing sobs. Whether of pleasure or pain, Amanda couldn't tell. She was still fighting the impulse to cry again herself.

That Jephtha Kent had relied on her willingness to harbor a runaway—

a clear violation of the Fugitive Slave Act—was upsetting enough. That the McCreery girl had seen the runaway was an absolute disaster.

v

Michael returned to the house about half past one in the morning, reporting to Amanda in the library:

"I did the best I could but she's still in a rage. I promised her an additional two weeks' wages one month from now—*if* she keeps silent about what she saw."

"Do you think she will?"

Amanda wasn't encouraged when he answered, "It depends on how angry she's feeling in a day or two. There's one commodity that's not for sale in the Five Points, Mrs. A—an end to an Irishman's wrath once he's down on you."

"Well, let's hope for the best."

"What are we going to do with the nig—the girl?"

"Put her on the first steamer heading to Canada. You inquire at the piers in the morning."

"What about the disciplining of your son?"

"That can wait a few hours. I still must go up and speak to him—"

"You haven't yet?"

"No, I haven't yet!" she lashed out. "I've been attending to the girl! We tried to feed her and she threw up everything. I finally got some brandy down her. That put her to sleep."

"You'd better sleep a little yourself. You look exhausted."

"I'll see Louis first."

But even that went wrong.

When she climbed the staircase and reached the door of her son's room, she found it unlocked. She opened it quietly. The night sky had cleared. The winter moon shone. Its reflection on snowy rooftops cast a luminous whiteness into the room.

Louis lay on his side in the soiled bed, fully dressed. His head was all but hidden in the pillows, as if he'd tried to burrow deep into them to escape the world.

Her face drawn, Amanda stared at him for a long time, thinking.

vi

She found Michael still in the library. His legs were stretched out toward the dying fire. The white cat was dozing on his knees. He looked startled when she slipped inside.

Her glance went briefly to the display case. Jared's medallion reflected the last red gleams from the hearth.

"Michael—"

"Yes, Mrs. A?"

"I want you to forget about going to the Five Points."

He blinked. "You don't want me to contact the Phelans?"

"No."

She expected him to smile. Instead, quite soberly, he nodded:

"That's good. Because I had decided I'd resign rather than do that particular chore. I'm thankful you changed your mind. May I ask why—?"

"I looked at Louis upstairs. And I thought of what you said about the high road. I—I don't want the ruining of my son to be the price I pay for Kent's."

"Why don't you wipe the slate all the way clean? Forget the stock too. Dissolve Boston Holdings. You've more than enough money to start a new firm."

"It wouldn't be the same. The stock acquisition is legal. I'll go ahead with that and hope it succeeds." She was very much aware of how much she was staking on a single strategy.

Michael smiled then. "At least what you've decided should make you feel a mite better."

"In a way it does. At the same time, I think I've walked away from a fight. I've never done that in my life."

"I'd say your decision took more courage than any fighting ever could."

"I wish I believed you," she said softly. As she turned to go, the admiration in his eyes was of little comfort.

CHAPTER 8

The Slave-Hunter

SATURDAY MORNING BROUGHT brilliant sunshine and the drip of melting snow from the eaves. Amanda slept until nine—three hours past her usual time for rising. When she saw the clock on the mantel of her bedroom fireplace, she got up in a rush, drew on a fur-trimmed robe and went straight to the third floor.

She found Mary just finishing an immense breakfast brought up from the kitchen. The girl seemed in good spirits:

"I never had so much food at one time in all my life! Never slept in a bed so soft, either."

"Are you feeling well?"

"Reckon I am. I couldn't eat that food fast enough."

"Good. Today we're going to look into the schedules of steamers to Canada."

"It scares me some to think about goin'," Mary admitted. "I don't know anybody there. An' the Reverend, he didn't have no names to give me—"

"I've been told there are anti-slave societies in almost every large Canadian city. I'm sure you'll have no trouble locating one. They'll help you get settled."

The girl clutched Amanda's arm:

"You don't think they send anybody after me from Virginia, do you, ma'am?"

"I think it's very unlikely," Amanda reassured her, hoping she was right. She left Mary sitting on the bed, bouncing up and down and enjoying the resilience. Mary's expression was almost rapturous.

Amanda went to her son's room next. It was empty. In Kathleen's absence, no one had yet made up the bed. She returned to her own room, dressed and hurried down the staircase.

As she descended the steps, she heard the bell of a horse-car clang on the far side of the square, then the prolonged rasp of a large chunk of snow sliding off the roof. In the front hall, the sun shone through the narrow windows on either side of the door, casting rectangles of light on the carpet. Somehow that glow restored her spirits a little. She felt more competent to deal with the problems that had arisen during the night.

Hamilton Stovall was far from her mind as she entered the dining room and saw Louis, still in his velvet-collared robe, dawdling over a cup of coffee.

He glanced at her, then back to the cup, his manner subdued. A moment later, the maid Brigid appeared. She was a plain, buxom girl in her late twenties.

"Only tea, I think, Brigid," Amanda said. "But no cream. I'm putting on too much weight."

Brigid smiled, murmured, "Yes, ma'am," and left.

Amanda unfolded the stiff linen napkin set at her place at the head of the long mahogany table. Louis was seated on the side, to her left, near a weighty breakfront displaying some two dozen pieces of fine silver. Amanda laid the napkin in her lap; she could feel the tension her presence created. Rather than confront Louis immediately, she began with another subject:

"Where is Michael?"

The boy's quick exhalation signaled his relief. "Off in the carriage already. To the steamer offices, he said. He told me about the crate Adams Express delivered last night."

"You're to say nothing about it outside this house. The girl will be gone within a few days."

Louis nodded. "I don't know who I'd tell, anyway—"

"I was thinking of your associates at the Day School," Amanda said in a quiet voice. "The ones with whom you've been quarreling."

The boy's head jerked up, his dark eyes wary.

"We had a note from Professor Pemberton yesterday. About your fighting. And your refusal to study. I've decided to withdraw you from school for a few weeks."

He almost smiled. He'd hardly consider that a severe penalty, she knew.

"As to what happened with Kathleen, I'm going to punish you for that when we finish breakfast."

"Punish me? How?"

"You'll discover in due time. First I'd like to ask you a question. Have I somehow given you the idea that you can take anything you want in this world with no thought of how you might be hurting other people?"

The boy frowned. "I don't know, ma—mother. Sometimes, I—I do have the feeling you do whatever you please—"

"Then I am to blame—even though there are good reasons why I behave as I do. You had no good reason for what you did to Kathleen. And nothing like that will ever happen again, Louis. Nothing," she repeated. "I'm afraid I've spoiled you. That too is going to change. While you're out of school, I expect you to work around the house. Under Michael's supervision."

He accepted the announcement in stoic silence.

"Now I'd like to know something else. After mistreating Kathleen last night, did you feel nothing? No shame? No sorrow—?"

He pressed his lips together, toying with the handle of his cup. When he looked at her again, she felt almost dizzy with relief. There *was* a spark of contrition in those blazing black eyes:

"Yes, I—I felt wretched." He lowered his head. "But not until it was over."

He stood up suddenly, hurrying around the corner of the table to stand beside her. "I went to sleep thinking of how I tried to lie to you—and how much you despised me. I can't stand to have you hate me, ma—"

She closed her eyes a moment, immensely relieved. Perhaps he wasn't beyond hope after all.

"I don't hate you, Louis. I love you. But I can't forgive or excuse what you did. You hurt Kathleen. You shamed her, you abused her as if she were an animal. You caused her to lose her job because I couldn't keep her in this house after what happened. No matter how rich a person may be—or how self-important money makes you feel—and it does, sometimes—that still gives you no right whatsoever to hurt another human being who's done nothing to hurt you. I'm going to impress that on you in a way I trust you'll never forget. At the same time, I acknowledge my part in your guilt—I expect I've set you a bad example because you don't understand why I do certain things."

"Would those things have anything to do with that man who still owns Kent's?"

"What do you know about him, Louis?" she countered softly.

"Why—I know he won't sell the company back to you, and that makes you mad. You bring up his name with Michael a lot, and you're mad then too. I've read in the papers that Stovall runs a huge steel factory. And I remember once in California, you and Captain Bart had a terrible argument while I was trying to sleep. I heard his name even way back then—"

Amanda sighed. "Well, you're correct. A good deal of my activity since we've come east is connected with Stovall. I expect I owe you a full explanation. You'll have it—in a week or two—when you've shown me you mean to change your ways."

She couldn't keep affection out of her voice as she clasped both of his hands in hers:

"I can't permit you to go the wrong way now, Louis. There's too much at stake—principally your future. You'll be in charge of Kent and Son one day. I want you to work with Theo Payne if he'll stay on. Learn from him—"

"But we don't even own the company!"

"We will," she assured him. "And you'll re-build it into the kind of firm your great-grandfather would be proud of. There's no limit to the possibilities open to you, Louis. A useful life—a good marriage—*entree* to the best homes—by the time you're grown," she added with a wry smile, "the sour old society ladies who consider me new rich will be in their graves. Their children will welcome you as an equal. That's what I want for you —because you're a Kent. And because I love you."

He pulled his hands loose and flung his arms around her neck, hugging her:

"I know I did wrong last night, ma. I'll make it up to you—I want you to be proud of me—"

She wrapped her arms around his waist and pressed her cheek against his chest, the relief almost unbearable—

She heard Brigid enter with her tea and broke away. The tea smelled delicious. She drank it eagerly. An image of the portrait of Philip Kent drifted into her mind. She thought, *It isn't too late. I'll turn him into a Kent worthy of the name*—

The sound of boots stamping in the front hall caught her attention. She heard Michael speaking to Hampton, set her teacup down and hurried from the room.

Michael stood in an oblong of sunlight, unwrapping a long scarf of red wool from around his collar. His hair shone almost as brightly as his smile:

"We're in luck, Mrs. A. We've only to wait until Tuesday night. There's a White Star steamer sailing from North River at ten o'clock.

Straight up the coast, overnight at Boston, then along the St. Lawrence to Montreal—"

He pulled a manila envelope from his coat.

"I bought the girl's ticket."

"Wonderful!"

Michael flung the scarf onto a bench and raked droplets of melted snow from his hair. "Have you spoken with Louis?"

"Just now. He seems contrite."

"Is he ready to work?"

"He will be in an hour."

"Why the delay?"

"I've one thing yet to take care of—" Her eyes were hard.

"Very well. While I'm waiting, I'll chop up that crate and burn the pieces. As soon as Louis is free, I'll set him to clearing the slush out of the front drive. My, won't that raise eyebrows next door! Mrs. de la Gura's son doing servant's work—"

Amused, he walked toward the dining room. Amanda followed.

"Come with me, Louis," she said.

"Where?"

Michael gaped when she answered:

"The carriage house."

ii

The dapple-gray mare whickered as Amanda and her son entered the frame building at the rear of the property. The light was poor and the interior smelled of straw and manure. The mare's breath streamed from her nostrils in the cold air. She bumped the side of her stall.

Water dripped from the wheels and springs of the carriage Michael had only recently returned to its place. Amanda reached up and drew the stiff-handled whip from its socket.

"Louis, take off your robe."

"My robe? What are you going to—?"

"You heard what I said. Take the robe off and stand against that post, facing it. Put your hands on the post, over your head."

The boy swallowed. The ferocity she'd seen on his face last night might never have existed. He looked terrified; young and vulnerable—

She ached at the thought of what she was about to do. Yet it had to be done.

Louis dropped the robe; lifted his hands to grasp the post. She watched his back prickle into gooseflesh as he waited, his head turned slightly, one eye visible.

"Now," she said, "you remember this moment, because I'll never do such a thing to you again—just as you'll never treat another person the way you treated Kathleen. I remind you once more—she did nothing to deserve the hurt you gave her. Not just the physical hurt—she'll carry the memory all her life. I want you to carry the memory of this. How it feels to be hurt by wanton cruelty. You remember, Louis—and let it keep you from hurting any other blameless person—ever again."

"Ma—" he began. The whip flicked up past her shoulder, and forward. The tip struck between his shoulderblades with a sharp, smacking sound.

Louis' hands tightened on the post. He clenched his teeth.

She whipped him again. This time he cried aloud.

The cry disturbed the mare. She kicked the side of the stall. Louis' whole body was trembling. Sweat covered his cheeks. The second blow had left a thin scarlet stripe on his skin.

Amanda struck a third time. He cried louder, digging his fingers into the post. The mare whinnied, kicked again. One of the stall boards cracked.

She forced herself to fall into a rhythm: the long, flexible tip of the whip came back, then flew forward to mark him. The whip butt grew slippery in her hand—

Six strokes.

Seven—

Blood began to run down the boy's back. The mare was wild with terror, bucking and slamming her hoofs into the stall's side, smashing the boards—

Eight.

Nine—

Louis groaned, started to slide down the post. White-faced, Amanda whispered:

"Stand up. Stand up and *feel it.*"

The savagery of her voice made him pull himself erect. He braced for the next blow; listened for the whisper of the whip cutting the air; closed his eyes—

Screamed when the whip flayed him.

The mare kicked, the sound thunderous. Two more boards in the side of the stall splintered apart.

"All right," Amanda said, ashen.

Louis turned. His hands jerked at his sides. He stared at her, tears in the corners of his eyes. There was no hate in that glance; only dull suffering—

She walked to the carriage, picked up a handful of straw, wiped the blood from the whip and replaced it in the socket. Then she faced her son.

"Come here."

He walked to her, stumbling the last couple of steps. She caught him in both arms, cushioning him against her, arms around his waist.

"Cry if you want. Cry—no one will hear you—"

He did, letting the long sobs free him of some of his pain. Amanda cried too, in silence, holding him close until the worst of his shuddering passed—

Finally he got control of himself. She stepped back, barely aware that the sleeves of her dress were stained red.

"If you're ever tempted to hurt someone again, remember today."

"I will, ma."

"Swear it, Louis."

"I swear. Before God, I swear it."

A knot seemed to break within her. She could barely speak:

"Now—" She wiped her cheeks with the back of one hand. "Put your robe on—"

He did, groaning when the fabric came in contact with the lash-marks.

"We'll go upstairs. I'll dress and bandage the cuts. You can rest for an hour. Then you're going to work. You'll hurt quite a few days, I expect. It's proper you should."

The dapple gray blubbered her lips, still stirring restlessly in the broken stall as the two of them walked into the winter sunlight, the boy leaning on his mother for support.

iii

At twilight on Sunday evening, Amanda was at work at the desk in the library, comfortably dressed in one of the three bloomer outfits she owned —a matching top and trousers in lavender. She was going over the list of investments she'd made using Jephtha Kent's earnings from the Ophir Mineralogical Combine. If the Sierra claim looked as promising as Israel Hope's letter suggested, those earnings should soon increase sharply.

She figured the different percentages of growth for each of the issues in which she'd invested the mining profits. None of that money had gone to purchase Stovall Works shares, as she'd originally intended. Boston Holdings operated solely on income from the Blackstone mill.

She worked slowly. Her eyes itched from scanning the columns of figures. After jotting a final note on two stocks whose poor performance merited immediate sale, she turned to the weekly edition of Mr. Greeley's *Tribune.*

She read an account of a lecture given in New York the preceding week by the philosopher, Emerson, then a review of a concert by the Swedish opera star, Jenny Lind, who was touring America under personal contract to the showman Phineas Barnum. She found both articles informative but dull. In the livelier side was a scathing feature about the poor performance of New York's police.

The writer accused the chief of taking criminal bribes—including one from the city's foremost female abortionist—and argued that city police protection would never be satisfactory until the force was given some semblance of professionalism, the first step being uniforms. But those, the police had steadfastly refused to wear ever since Mayor Harper had suggested the idea in the mid-40s. The police contended they were "free Americans," and thus should not be required to appear in public in "livery befitting servants."

A dispatch from Illinois caught her attention next. It dealt with the Whigs in that western state, and quoted a lawyer named Lincoln who had served one term in Congress during the Mexican war and was apparently becoming a power in the party.

The lawyer's first name was Abraham. Amanda wondered whether he could be the same person she'd seen briefly when she and Jared had been traveling to Tennessee years ago. Because Jared had contracted an illness, they'd stopped for a couple of weeks at a cabin in Kentucky. She remembered farmer Lincoln's boy Abraham quite clearly. Though he had only been five years old, he'd displayed an unusual curiosity about letters and words.

Expressing himself on the strength of the Whigs in Illinois, Lincoln was then quoted on his personal views about the Know-Nothings. The nature of his opinions made it instantly clear why Horace Greeley had given them space:

"How can anyone who abhors the oppression of negroes, be in favor of degrading classes of white people? Our progress in degeneracy appears to me to be pretty rapid. As a nation, we began by declaring that *all men are created equal.* Now we practically read it 'all men are created equal, *except negroes.*' When the Know-Nothings get control, it will read 'all men are created equal, except negroes, *foreigners and Catholics.*'

"When it comes to this I should prefer emigration to some country where they make no pretense of loving liberty—to Russia, for example, where despotism can be taken pure, without the base alloy of hypocrisy."

The statement summed up Amanda's own beliefs about as well as she'd ever been able to do herself. She decided to show the piece to Michael. It might help abate his deep-seated antagonism toward colored people, pointing out as it did that there was little difference between those who would deny the black man liberty, and those who wanted to keep the immigrant Irish in much the same kind of inferior position.

She had just started to tear the article from the page when the door opened and Mr. Mayor miaowed. She glanced up, rubbing her eyes—the older she grew, the longer they took to re-focus from close work to something more distant.

Hampton presented a silver tray bearing a rectangle of white pasteboard.

"A gentleman in the sitting room, Mrs. de la Gura. He's most insistent about seeing you."

"I wasn't expecting any callers—"

"The gentleman isn't from New York. From his speech, I would judge he comes from one of the southern states."

The peace that had begun to settle over her since Saturday morning shattered as she snatched the engraved card and read the name.

Virgil Tunworth, Capt., U.S.A. (ret.)

iv

The card fell to the floor. Hampton peered at her:

"Is everything all right, madam?"

"Yes—yes—" She retrieved the card, her pulse racing. "Where's Michael?"

"In the carriage house, I believe. He and master Louis are repairing the broken stall."

"Give him the card, bring him in here and tell him to wait—"

She started out, whirled back:

"No, go upstairs first. Lock Mary in her room. Tell her to keep absolutely quiet, no matter what happens." When Hampton seemed slow to comprehend, she exclaimed, "The man is her owner!"

Hampton frowned. "The name did seem slightly familiar—"

"Mary mentioned him the other night. How in God's name he got here, I don't know."

In the sitting room, Captain Virgil Tunworth paced back and forth before the windows overlooking the bare trees of Madison Square. The captain was a small, spare man in his early fifties. Wisps of gray hair lay across a bald skull. He spun around when Amanda entered.

Feigning cordiality, she smiled:

"Captain Tunworth—!"

She noted the sooty shoulders of his cream-colored tailcoat; a black smudge on his stand-up collar. The gaslight emphasized the white stubble on his chin; he apparently hadn't shaved for a day or more.

The captain had served in the army for several years before taking up a more profitable career—the supervision of his family's lands near Lexington. He still carried himself in an erect, military fashion, and affected a severe manner.

"Good evening, Mrs. de la Gura." His glance said he hadn't forgotten their unpleasant meeting in Virginia—and his expression quickly registered disapproval of her lavender trousers.

Still smiling, she said, "This is indeed a surprise—"

"You needn't pretend it's a pleasant one. You know why I've come."

"I'm afraid I haven't the faintest idea," she said, drying her palm on the handkerchief she kept tucked in her sleeve. She approached the bell pull. "May I ring for a drink for you?"

"Thank you, no." Politeness was clearly an effort. "I'm filthy and worn out from the train, so let's conclude our business promptly."

Amanda walked past him to the window. Saw a hack waiting under the portico, its side-lamps aglow in the lowering dark.

"What business, sir?"

In a clipped tone, he replied, "You're harboring a nigger girl who belongs to me."

"Captain Tunworth, that—that is the most astonishing—and preposterous—accusation I've ever heard!"

"Astonishing, I grant you. I'm sure you weren't expecting me. But preposterous? Hardly. You see, Mrs. de la Gura—"

He stalked toward her, openly belligerent.

"Some whose niggers run away are content to let them go. I am not. My wench Mary was conducted to Clifton Forge last Wednesday and shipped in a packing case to this house—"

He raised a hand on which a diamond ring glittered.

"Before you trap yourself with denials, allow me to finish. I know how Mary got away because I whipped one of my bucks half to death—until he told me he'd seen her conferring with Mr. Syme when my wife sent Mary and the buck to town on an errand. You certainly know who Mr. Syme is —your cousin's fellow-conspirator? After the buck confessed, we caught him."

Suddenly Amanda felt terror:

"Who caught him?"

"Why, some gentlemen who feel exactly as I do about fugitives and those who assist them. Congress has passed a law denying niggers sanctuary in the northern states—and so we're entitled to their return. I regret to say that after Mr. Syme admitted his perfidy—following a little moral suasion with a board applied to his bare feet—he tried to escape. He couldn't walk, let alone run. Took a pistol ball in the back. He's dead. I'm of the opinion Syme's wife warned your cousin, the Reverend. He's disappeared—"

"Jephtha's gone?" Amanda gasped. "Where?"

"To hell, I sincerely hope," the captain replied with a tart smile. "He was interfering with the law of these United States. He conspired to rob me of my property. As I say, Mary was spirited away on Wednesday. By sundown Friday Mr. Syme had departed this earth—but not before he told us your cousin had driven Mary all the way to the Clifton Forge depot of the Virginia Central line. Some cash and some threats loosened the tongue of the express agent there. That's how I learned the destination of the box the Reverend shipped. This morning, an hour after I got off that infernal train, I fetched the local manager of Adams Express straight out of church. I only had to remind him that abetting the escape of a slave now carries serious penalties—"

Captain Tunworth's hand dipped into his coat and came up with a paper.

"He gave me this copy of the delivery order, and that's all there is to it. I don't suppose the crate is still in this house. But I imagine Mary is. Return her and there's no need for us to quarrel—or to make the incident public."

Amanda sank down on a sofa in front of the Virginian. Jephtha a fugitive! That upset her as much as the arrival of Mary's master. She fought to keep tension from her voice as she said:

"I imagine you're congratulating yourself on being rid of your son-in-law—"

"Woman, don't change the subject on me. I demand—"

"The hell with your demands!" Amanda said in a scathing voice. "I want to know what's become of my cousin!"

Tunworth shrugged. "I expect he's hiding out somewhere in the Blue Ridge. The truth is, no one in Lexington will be grieved at his going. For almost a year he's been suspected of being a conductor on the nigger railroad. His wife and boys want no part of him. Except for that crazy Professor Jackson at the Institute, he hasn't a single friend in the county. And now that we've split up his nefarious little partnership with Mr. Syme, we'll be happy to be quits with him. Let's get back to the matter of my property—"

"You're quite glib about referring to a human being as property!"

"And you're misguided to term niggers human beings."

"Then what are they, captain?"

"Well—human, I suppose I'd have to grant you that. But not to the same full degree as white persons. The nigra is basically inferior in all respects."

Amanda felt desolate. He spoke so calmly—with such an air of conviction—that she knew he'd expressed the bedrock of his belief.

"And nothing will change your mind about that?"

"Nothing. If the abolitionists have their way, the next step after freedom for the niggers will be equality with whites. I can't accept that, I never will accept it—I'd take up arms before I would obey any law that tried to coerce me into accepting it—but you're trying to sidetrack me again, Mrs. de la Gura."

"Because discussing your so-called property is a waste of time, sir—mine and yours."

"You're getting me exercised, woman—" He wiped his forehead with his sleeve. "You can't deny she's here."

"I refuse to discuss it."

He shook the express receipt at her. "Goddamn it, I have the evidence!"

Amanda tore the paper from his hand, ripped it in half. "That's what I think of your trumped-up evidence! I'd be obliged if you'd leave, Captain Tunworth."

"Not without Mary. Not without my propert—"

A peremptory knock broke the tension and whirled them both toward the door. Michael stuck his head in:

"A word with you, Mrs. A?"

She scowled. "This is not the time—"

"Very urgent. Please!"

To Tunworth she said: "You wait here, sir."

The moment the door clicked behind her, she whispered, "What in the hell is so important that—?"

"Hampton gave me the card. How did Tunworth wind up here so quickly?"

In terse sentences, Amanda repeated the essence of what Jephtha's father-in-law had told her—including the dismal news that her cousin had fled Lexington, evidently in fear of his life. Michael shook his head:

"Then you'd better give her up without a fuss."

Amanda looked stunned. "Let him take the girl?"

"Yes. Unless you surrender his wench without a row, you may be in for serious trouble. Do you know whether he has an order from the court—?"

"He didn't mention one. He only arrived in New York this morning."

"Then he'll probably have to wait for court to sit tomorrow. That's even worse."

"Why?"

"You know fugitive slaves are juicy newspaper copy. If Tunworth stays in the city very long, one of the anti-abolitionist sheets like the *Journal of Commerce* may get wind of the whole affair. If it's true your cousin's role in the escape is known—"

"It is. But what's the point?"

"The name Kent could very well be smeared all over the press, along with yours. If Mr. Stovall saw it, I suspect he'd be astute enough to make a connection—"

Amanda's face was bleak as she stared at the young Irishman. He was right. Damnably right—especially in the light of Stovall's already-aroused suspicion.

"Furthermore, Mrs. A, I should remind you that obstructing the recap-

ture of a fugitive slave is illegal. It's one thing to send donations to radical
lecturers, quite another to violate a federal law."

She paced to the front door, then all the way back, her knuckles pressed
against her teeth. Quite apart from the threat to her personal plans, the
question of legality was inescapable. This was the very thing Bart McGill
had warned her about. The moment when she would be confronted with
a line, and only two choices: step back—or cross.

Wearily, she realized Bart had been right when he said it would be impossible for her not to be drawn into the slave controversy. But she'd never
imagined it would happen so precipitously—or pose such disastrous consequences—

She thought of Douglass at the Bowery Theatre. In the abstract, he'd
said, the Fugitive Slave Act was tolerable to some people. But the frightened face of the girl Mary made it intolerable—exactly as Douglass had
predicted.

She faced Michael.

"I'll have to take the risk. With Stovall *and* the law."

"Captain Tunworth is entirely in the right."

"I know he's in the right—according to what's written in the statutes.
But I can't be a party to sending that child back to bondage. If Tunworth
was a decent master—if he treated his slaves in a half way humane fashion
—it might be different. But when I was in Virginia, Jephtha made it abun-
dantly clear the captain's a cruel man. Mary said the same thing. I won't
turn her over to the likes of him."

Michael's smile was tinged with a curious sadness:

"I had a feeling that might be your decision. Do you want me to come
in with you?"

She shook her head. "I want to convey my answer to the captain myself."

v

When she did, and asked him to leave, Virgil Tunworth exploded:
"Damned if I will! You bring me Mary this instant!"

She smiled. "I told you she isn't here, Captain."

"And I say you're a villainous liar!" He snatched up his broad-brimmed
wool hat and stormed for the door. "I'll root her out myself—"

Amanda caught his arm and jerked him around. Tunworth's eyes popped; he hadn't realized how strong she was.

"You're not going to set foot in another room in this house without an order from the appropriate authorities."

"Then by Christ I'll see the Fugitive Slave Bill Commissioner in the morning! I'll be back and I *will* look in every room!"

"Captain Tunworth," she said in a low voice, "I do pray to God that when you die, someone forbids your burial in Virginia. That a state that gave freedom—and great leaders—to America should spew up the likes of you—"

"Sermonize all you wish, Mrs. de la Gura. The fact remains, the Constitution and the law of the land give me the right to reclaim my property. I will. I know the wench is on these premises—or if not, that you know her whereabouts. Mr. Syme revealed everything, you see. *Everything*—"

He jammed his wool hat on his balding head. His smile matched Amanda's for coldness:

"A man doesn't lie when his bare feet are bleeding from fifty blows of a pine board. I'll call on you again. In company with a federal marshal."

He jerked the door open and stalked past Michael who was lounging under the gas fixture. The front door crashed behind him. In half a minute, Amanda was surrounded by Louis and the servants, all clamoring to know what had happened.

As the hack clattered away, Amanda raised her hands to stop the questions. Quickly and calmly, she explained the visitor's identity, and the reason for his call. Hampton, clearly alarmed, said:

"We should get the girl out of here at once!"

"The steamer doesn't sail till Tuesday evening," Michael said.

"Remove her to another location, then. Mrs. de la Gura, the newspapers have been most explicit. The law in effect since 1850 puts all the right on that gentleman's side—"

"The law be damned! I'm thinking about Mary. But perhaps moving her isn't a bad idea. Michael—?"

"Won't work, Mrs. A."

"Why not?"

He crooked a finger and led her to one of the narrow windows flanking the front door.

"Take a look at what I spied when you were inside with the captain the second time."

She peered out; saw a man huddled against a tree in the small park in the center of the square.

"Hell of a chilly evening to be taking the air, don't you think?" Michael asked. "There's another chap similarly occupied opposite the entrance to the alley. I saw both climb out of Tunworth's hackney. That captain may be a countryman, but he's no fool. I'll wager he was prepared for a refusal and hired those lads from some saloon or other."

"To keep watch."

"Aye. You know the law says bystanders may be summoned to help recapture a slave. Or a *posse comitatus* can be formed—"

"So if we remove her, they'll follow us."

"Undoubtedly."

"Then we'll have to keep her here for the moment. But I won't let them take her, I don't give a damn how many orders they produce. That bald bastard helped drive Jephtha out of his own home—and now he's turned him into a fugitive too—Michael, you examine all the locks and latches downstairs. Make sure they're fastened. Hampton, I want someone awake and watching the front and back entrances at all times. I'll take my turn—you will too, Louis. I've also got to speak with Mary. It isn't fair to conceal what's happened—especially since we may have unexpected visitors crashing in on us in the next day or two—"

She started for the library.

"But first I think I'd better do what I forgot to do Friday night. Locate my old revolver."

The library door closed with the sharpness of a gun firing.

Louis and the servants stared, still too stunned to react. Only Michael Boyle showed animation—lifting a hand to his mouth and rocking back on his heels as he laughed, half in admiration, half in dismay.

CHAPTER 9

Besieged

IN THE EARLY HOURS of Monday morning, the temperature climbed a few degrees above the freezing mark. Rain began to turn the last of the snow to slush. Amanda woke around five, having tossed restlessly most of the night. Her knees and elbows ached; she felt ancient.

She put on a robe and lit the gas. While the rain pelted the windows, she sat worrying about Jephtha, and pondering the dilemma created by Captain Tunworth's arrival. When it grew light, she walked to the bedroom window that overlooked Madison Square.

Among the dripping, leafless trees of the little park stood a small kiosk with latticework sides. Inside the kiosk she glimpsed a man pacing to and fro beneath the conical roof. Whether it was the same watcher Michael had spied the preceding evening, she couldn't say. But *someone* was there—

By the time she went downstairs, the servants had already lit the gas to dispel the gloom. She quickly became aware of the strained atmosphere in the house. The two remaining maids, the cook and Mr. Hampton all knew the mansion was under surveillance. They went about their work with drawn looks and few words.

She had no appetite for breakfast. She went directly to the kitchen, poured herself a cup of tea and carried it into the dining room, where Michael sat in front of an untasted platter of ham and fried potatoes. As she sank into her chair and unfolded her napkin, she asked:

"Did you sleep badly, Michael?"

"I didn't sleep at all, Mrs. A. I looked in on our guest, though. She was snoring. You *did* tell her about Tunworth—?"

"Yes."

"Well, she evidently feels reasonably secure in this house." He grimaced as Mr. Mayor prowled from under the table and leaped into his lap. "I think she's the only one," he added, stroking the cat in an absent way.

"Is Louis up?"

Michael nodded. "Polishing the woodwork on the third floor."

"I wonder how soon the captain will be back."

"Not before the end of the day, I should imagine. The court procedure will take time."

"We've got to get Mary out of here."

"I agree. But the two men are still on watch."

"Then we'll take her out right in front of them."

He blinked. "How?"

"I've been thinking about a way. I want you to take the horse-car to Rose's house. Ask her to come here in her carriage. And to wear something bright—with a shawl and a parasol or an umbrella. Also gloves—gloves are particularly important."

He smiled. "I think I see what you're driving at. It's risky—but audacious enough that it just might work."

"When you leave, use the front door. So you'll be clearly seen."

He nodded. "Do I have your permission for a slight detour on the way to Mrs. Ludwig's? I think it might be prudent if I spent a short time browsing around Paradise Square. Just to see whether there's any sign of Kathleen stirring up trouble."

"If you don't take too long at it," Amanda agreed. "Try to be back by noon."

Michael Boyle said, "I will," dumped the white cat off his lap and strode out.

ii

The young Irishman returned about eleven thirty, rain-soaked, with a paper tucked under his arm. He found Amanda in the library.

The old Colt revolver lay on the mantel next to the tea bottle. He flung his cap and scarf on the chair by the hearth and walked to the desk, where Amanda had been vainly trying to examine some figures on the preceding year's profits of the Blackstone Company. Somehow the figures blurred and refused to make sense—

She set the ledger aside with great relief. "Is Rose on the way?"

"She promised to be here inside of an hour—" He managed a grin. "She made a hell of a fuss when I showed up. I forgot she never rises until twelve."

"Oh heavens, so did I. Well, I expect she'll forgive me when I explain the urgency of the situation. What did you learn in the Five Points?"

"Nothing. All quiet. A little too early in the day, I think. I may pop back later this afternoon. Provided I'm not needed here—"

He unfolded the paper in front of her.

"Stop-press edition. Out two hours early. Most of the news is a re-hash of last week's. But there's one fresh item—"

He pointed out a feature story on the front page of the *Journal of Commerce,* a paper founded in 1825 by the Tappan brothers, who had followed a stern abolitionist policy. But the Tappans had later sold the *Journal;* its current management was pro-southern.

"Didn't imagine we could keep the affair quiet for long," Michael murmured. Pale, Amanda scanned the story:

FUGITIVE SLAVE IN MADISON SQUARE?
Virginian lodges accusation
against textile heiress;
seeks warrant.

A warrant permitting search of the residence of Mrs. Amanda de la Gura, wealthy resident of No. 12 Madison Square, will be sought by Captain Virgil Tunworth of Lexington, Virginia, it was learned at eight this morning by the *Journal* reporter assigned to the court of Judge Develbess, Fugitive Slave Bill Commissioner for the city.

Captain Tunworth, who arrived in New York yesterday, alleges that operatives of the so-called underground railroad did cause to be stolen from him and delivered to the Madison Square address late last week one female slave who goes by the name Mary. The Captain, who is stopping at the Astor House, informed this reporter that he anticipates Judge Develbess will issue a search warrant, together with another for the arrest of said escaped slave, late today or early tomorrow.

Tunworth charges that the fugitive was aided in her escape by a former Methodist pastor, one Jephtha Kent of Lexington. Kent is a relative of the lady who occupies the Madison Square manse, and has since fled the district from which Captain Tunworth traveled—

Despondent, Amanda laid the paper aside with the rest of the piece unread. Michael said softly:

"We can't say it was unexpected."

"I know. I only wish they hadn't dragged in Jephtha's name—"

She sat staring at the column of type, wondering whether it was being read in a certain residence in Washington Square.

iii

"Take off my *clothes?*" Rose Ludwig exclaimed when Amanda met her in the front sitting room shortly after one. "I've received some odd propositions in my life, but that has to be the most—"

"Rose, don't say anything—not till you've read this." She held out the copy of the *Journal of Commerce.*

With a puzzled expression, Rose took the paper, the unlit Cuban cheroot in her hand momentarily forgotten.

While Rose studied the front page, Amanda went to the window. She could see both the man in the kiosk and her friend's carriage under the portico. The carriage driver looked miserable in the wind-blown rain.

Once more Amanda judged the angles and the distance. From the kiosk the watcher not only had a clear view of the carriage, but of the front door as well. Yet he was far enough away so that facial features would be indistinct. Provided Mary kept the parasol down; kept her dark skin hidden—

A rustle of the paper turned her attention back to Rose. The other woman laid the *Journal* aside, her eyes grim:

"Is it true, Amanda?"

"Yes. The girl's up on the third floor." Quickly, she described most of what had taken place since Mary's arrival.

"Then you're in serious trouble with the law," her friend said when she concluded.

"I know. But that's of less concern to me than getting Mary out of the house. When Tunworth produces his warrant, there's no way I can prevent him from seizing her. And I want her on that steamer for Canada tomorrow night! Rose—"

She walked to her friend; laid a hand on her arm.

"—if you'll stay here until then, you can help Mary escape."

"How, for God's sake?"

"You were seen coming in—"

"By whom?"

Amanda led her to the window, pointed out the dim figure pacing in the kiosk. Rose peered through the rain-streaked glass:

"Who is that?"

"Some fellow Tunworth hired to stand watch. There's another keeping an eye on the alley and the carriage house. The captain was shrewd enough to realize he couldn't get the warrant issued immediately—and that we might try to spirit Mary away. I'm sure you were observed when you arrived. If that man in the park sees the same dress and umbrella going out again, I don't think he'll realize he's been tricked—"

Rose's eyebrow hooked up. "Is that why Michael insisted I wear something like this—?" She touched the sleeve of her yellow velvet dress. "Which I must say is entirely inappropriate for the season and the time of day!"

"That's exactly it. I want Mary to stay at your house until about nine tomorrow evening. Then your driver can deliver her to the White Star pier on North River. Please, Rose!" Amanda pleaded. "I wouldn't ask if I could think of another way—"

"What am I supposed to do, loll in my pantalets until Wednesday morning? I was planning to do some shopping at the Lord and Taylor store this afternoon. And I have engagements tomorrow—" She sighed. "But of course I'll do it."

"Bless you! I should tell you one more thing. We might be in for some difficulty from another quarter. Louis—well, let's just say he got into a bit of trouble with one of the maids. I discharged her. Before she left, she threatened reprisals. I wouldn't take them seriously, except that she has an uncle who's cozy with Mr. Rynders, the Sixth Ward politician. It's possible he could send some of his gang friends to vandalize the house—"

Rose sighed a second time, louder:

"When you stir up a stew, you do a thorough job of it."

"I'm not positive there'll be any trouble from Rynders. I only thought it was fair to warn you."

"Well," Rose said with an emphatic nod, "that's fair enough. Take me up to the girl and let's get her on her way."

Amanda hugged her friend, then hurried her out of the sitting room to the third floor.

iv

"I never wore a skirt like this," Mary said. "I liable to fall—"

"You won't fall," Amanda assured her, slipping a folded paper into the reticule the girl carried. Rose stood just behind Amanda, wearing an embroidered robe several sizes too small.

The gas in the front hall had been turned down so the interior would be dim when the door was opened. The yellow velvet dress with its immense hoops fitted Mary poorly, but with the shawl drawn around Mary's head, gloves on her hands, and the umbrella for additional concealment, Amanda thought the ruse could work.

"Just watch your step going out to the carriage," she said. "And give that paper to Mrs. Ludwig's butler. He'll see you're driven to the White Star pier tomorrow night."

Mary's eyes misted with tears. "Oh, Miz de la Gura, you been so good—"

She patted the girl's arm. "I want you to be safe in Canada, Mary. Safe and free—"

Peering through one of the narrow panes beside the door, Michael pointed:

"That chap in the park's paying close attention. He hasn't moved since the carriage pulled up." To Rose: "I'm worried about your driver. He's sure to notice the difference, and react—"

Rose moved up beside him. "Let me handle Carney."

Amanda knew the next few seconds would be critical. She tried not to show her anxiety as she opened the door wide. After embracing Mary briefly, she took the girl's elbow and guided her outside.

The carriage driver gaped. "What the hell's going on? Who is—?"

"Carney, don't say a goddamned word!" Rose hissed from the shadows just inside the door. "I'm staying here. The girl's going to my house—in my place. Help her into the carriage! *Look at her, not me—!*"

The dumbfounded driver climbed down. Mary's hoop skirt swayed in a gust of rain that swept under the portico. Biting her lip, she put her foot on the first step below the top one.

Amanda watched the man in the park. He had come to the near side of the kiosk, so he could observe the activity at the front of the house. There was no doubt he had a clear view of the yellow-clad figure moving unsteadily down the steps—

Mary had one hand clutched to her bosom, holding the ends of the shawl covering her head. But her other hand was rising too high; unconsciously lifting the umbrella so that it didn't conceal her face—

"*The umbrella!*" Amanda whispered from the doorway. "*Lower it—!*"

She did. Just as Amanda let out a relieved breath, Mary's foot slipped on one of the steps. She uttered a low cry, staggering—

"Oh, Christ, that's the game," Michael groaned. Amanda gripped the edge of the door, her hand white. The watcher in the park ran out of the kiosk—

"*Help her, Carney!*" Rose Ludwig whispered.

The driver darted up three steps and caught Mary's forearm just as she started to fall.

He steadied her, his eyes wide with astonishment as he got a close look at the black face beneath the umbrella.

But he held onto Mary's arm; assisted her down the final steps and into the carriage. When the door slammed, Amanda gulped and closed her eyes a moment.

She waved and called goodbye. The driver clambered up the wheel, still mightily confused. He popped his whip and guided the team out from under the portico—

Chilled by the wind-driven rain, Amanda turned her back on the square, walked inside, shut the door and leaned against it. The faces of the watching servants were white blurs in the gloom.

Rose re-tied the sash of the robe Amanda had loaned her, then clucked her tongue:

"I imagine that added a few years to my face. I thought for certain she'd fall—"

"Do you feel like a whiskey, Rose?"

"I may drink a quart."

"I don't want that much—but I'll join you."

Michael swung from the window, grinning:

"I think we pulled it off. At least the lad across the way hasn't moved since the carriage turned the corner."

He followed the two women back to the library. Rose immediately noticed the old Colt revolver resting on the mantel. She pointed to it:

"Is that for moral encouragement—or is it loaded?"

"Look in the cylinder," Amanda said.

Rose squinted. "My God! Ready to fire."

"So long as it's handy, I suppose there's no need to keep it on display." Amanda took the revolver down and carried it to the desk, shutting it away in a drawer.

Rose shook her head. "It's unbelievable, the things I permit myself to get into for the sake of friendship—"

"And I can't possibly repay you for what you've done," Amanda said.

The stout woman accepted the brimming whiskey glass Michael handed her. "I'll think of a way, my dear. For instance—when you finally get hold of Kent's, you can increase my royalty rate—"

Amanda smiled, but without feeling.

"Better still, I'll settle for peace and quiet until tomorrow night." She toasted the thought with an upraised glass, then consumed the liquor in several rapid gulps.

Looping his scarf around his coat collar, Michael said to Rose, "Peace and quiet are now in the hands of a certain Miss Kathleen McCreery. I'll be back in a couple of hours, Mrs. A—I'm going to make a second trip to see whether all's calm in the Five Points."

The white cat padded after him out the door.

v

The afternoon dragged on. The February sky darkened. By three o'clock, every gas jet downstairs was turned up full.

Repeatedly, Hampton answered knocks at the front door. He turned away reporters from other papers who had seen the story in the *Journal*. Twice he got into a shouting match before he managed to slam the door in a newsman's face.

Despite the inclement weather, occasional curiosity-seekers came by, on foot or in closed carriages. One group of small boys flung stones at the house before Hampton shouted at them and chased them away. Sequestered in the library with her friend, Amanda was still aware of the attention the house was receiving; it made her nervous; it seemed a harbinger of worse to come—

Rose had pressed for some of the details of what Amanda had referred to as the incident with the maid. Amanda finally obliged, though she concealed the fact that Louis had actually taken the girl sexually, hinting instead that it had been an attempted seduction.

"But I've permitted him to be far too headstrong. In fact I think I've encouraged him without realizing it. That will change."

Rose nodded, then yawned loudly. "Excuse me—it's that damned business of being hauled awake before noon—"

"Why don't you go upstairs and nap for a while?"

"Excellent idea. I'll be down for dinner—unless a riot wakes me sooner."

In the silence of the library, Amanda found herself again unable to concentrate on any of the business details to which she should be attending. She kept staring at the portrait of her grandfather, wondering whether he'd have approved of her aiding Tunworth's runaway. She hoped he would have—

Even now, she didn't know precisely why she'd done it; she wasn't sure whether she'd acted out of a sense of moral conviction, or from a guilty conscience—belatedly trying to live up to the Latin inscription on Jared's medallion in the display case.

A little of both motivations had played a part, she suspected.

She began to focus on other concerns. On Jephtha, for one. She knew there was little she could do to help him until he got in touch with her—if he ever did. She prayed he was safe.

She was bound to have another encounter with Captain Tunworth. She looked forward to it. When the clock showed four-thirty, she was actually a little disappointed the Virginian hadn't returned with his warrants.

Well, he'd surely arrive tomorrow. And she'd have the satisfaction of telling him that—

The telegraph gong shattered her reverie. She jumped up and hurried to the table. She tapped out an acknowledgement of the query signal, then readied her pen to copy the message:

CONFIDENTIAL WALL STREET SOURCE ADVISED FOUR P M TODAY STOVALL WORKS BOARD HAS AUTHORIZED NEW STOCK ISSUE. WILL DOUBLE NUMBER OF SHARES OUTSTANDING. ISSUE ENTIRELY REPEAT ENTIRELY SUBSCRIBED PRIOR TO ANNOUNCEMENT.

A knot formed in the pit of her stomach.

SUSPECT SINGLE BUYER OR CONSORTIUM BUT HAVE NO INFORMATION. WILL ADVISE IF SITUATION CLARIFIES. AWAIT YOUR INSTRUCTIONS. ROTHMAN'S BANK

Amanda flung down the pen; pressed her palms against her eyes. The sounder began to click again:

AWAIT YOUR INSTRUCTIONS.

Wearily, Amanda clicked out NO INSTRUCTIONS, then added her initials. In a moment, the sounder replied:

ACKNOWLEDGED. END.

The stillness of the library was broken only by the steady beat of the rain on the windows and the sound of Mr. Mayor scampering through the main hall in pursuit of some phantom adversary. Amanda stared at the message the bank had transmitted.

"God*damn* it!" she cried, slamming her fist down on the pad while tears welled in her eyes. The last few words smeared from the impact of her hand—

She knew who had moved so swiftly to convene the Stovall board and make it impossible for her to acquire the needed fifty-one percent. It was no consolation that she'd increased the risk of discovery by her decision about Mary—and that she'd made the decision of her own free will.

When Michael returned at ten past five, looking dour, she showed him the information from the Boston bank:

"Stovall doubled the number of shares—and then bought them. He or someone acting on his behalf."

"I expect so, Mrs. A."

"Because of the *Journal* story."

"Yes," Michael said. "We've always suspected he'd be aware of steady movement in the shares over the past year or so. The story undoubtedly prompted him to look into it—very closely."

She covered her eyes again. "Then I've thrown away my last chance to own Kent's—"

Michael strode to the hearth, knelt and began laying logs on top of kindling. "I'm afraid we have more immediate concerns than that."

She wiped her eyes and looked at him. He said:

"Something's brewing in the Five Points."

"What?"

"I saw copies of the *Journal* being passed around in three saloons. Heard your name mentioned—"

He applied a locofoco to the kindling. As it began to snap and blaze, he stood up.

"—plus a lot of nasty talk about a runaway nigger. I managed to draw one of the lads into conversation. Ever since the paper came out, Mr. Rynders has been buying a powerful number of whiskeys for certain selected acquaintances—"

"You think the money I paid Kathleen—and the extra you promised—wasn't enough to pacify her?"

"That's exactly what I think. Also, Mr. Isaiah Rynders has made no secret of the fact that before the day's out, he's going to look up someone at the Astor House."

"The Astor—! That's where Tunworth's staying—"

"I'm sure Mr. Rynders read it in the paper. He's a clever bastard—Tunworth will fit into his plans beautifully. Here's how it works. Kathleen appeals to Rynders for succor. He spots the *Journal* piece. It's a fine pretext for his friends to do devilment on Kathleen's behalf. They can screen their real motive behind false moral outrage—you've concealed a fugitive slave! You've broken the law! Hell, I wouldn't be surprised if some of those gang boys showed up as part of Tunworth's search party—"

"In other words," Amanda said quietly, "you definitely believe we'll be visited."

"Tonight," Michael nodded. "Or tomorrow."

"But there's nothing they can do! The girl's gone!"

"Why, that gives Rynders' chums an excuse to act even angrier. I suggest we follow a sensible course of action. Leave. Now."

"Be frightened out of my own house? I'll be damned if I will!"

"You're also involving other people, Mrs. A. It's not fair to the servants—"

"Can't we contact the police?"

"Not until something happens—unless you're willing to admit the entire story—Mary included. That might lend credence to—"

"No! Mary won't be out of New York until tomorrow evening."

"Well, the police won't act on suspicion alone. Especially not when Mr. Rynders is a pal of quite a few of them—"

Amanda drew a long breath.

"All right. Gather the servants in the kitchen. Wake Rose. And bring Louis downstairs."

vi

What Amanda had to discuss with the assembled group seemed incongruous in the cheery atmosphere of the large kitchen. Smells of baking bread drifted from the huge iron stove. Three capons browned on the hearth spit, giving off a savory aroma.

Rose puffed one of her vile-smelling cigars—causing Hampton to cough in an exaggerated way—as Amanda spoke:

"I've asked you here because I'm afraid the dismissal of Kathleen McCreery may have put this household in a dangerous position. Michael went to the Five Points twice today. It seems clear Kathleen won't be satisfied until she takes revenge for the injustice she feels was done to her—"

Louis stared at his feet, scarlet.

"You're aware we've been under observation by men hired by Captain Tunworth. The girl's gone. But you can be sure the captain will be back. Further, Michael said Isaiah Rynders was going to the Astor House late today. It's possible he went to see Tunworth—to offer the help of some of his thugs. Hunting for a fugitive slave would be a perfect pretext for an invasion of this house—and perhaps worse—"

She left the thought there. But she saw from the faces of the servants that their own imaginations were painting vivid pictures.

"It's my responsibility to defend my own property. But it's not yours. You normally leave late in the evening to go to your homes. I'd suggest you start leaving now, one by one. Go through the alley. I don't think you'll be stopped by the man on watch—especially when he sees you're white," she added with a touch of cynicism. "We might have trouble tonight, it might come tomorrow—or it might not come at all." She tried not to let them know she didn't believe that last.

"I don't want any of you endangered," she said. "So decide who's to go first, and leave. Rose, that includes you."

"Hell," the heavy woman shrugged behind a cloud of smoke, "I don't have any clothes to wear."

"I'll loan you something."

"Won't fit. I'm staying."

"I'll stay too, madam," Brigid said. "My old man once got his head broken by some of Rynders' bullies, 'cos he wouldn't vote the way Rynders ordered."

"Very well, it's your choice. Louis—I want you out of the house along with everyone else—"

"Leave you here with just Michael and Brigid and Mrs. Ludwig?" He shook his head.

"Louis, I really insist—"

"No, ma. I'm not scared of a fight."

As she stared at the boy, she fancied she saw Cordoba's face glimmering in a kind of lapped image. She smiled in a tired way.

"All right. But the rest of you hurry."

vii

By eleven that night, the house lay silent. Rose had gone to bed after three stiff whiskeys. Louis was keeping watch at the back entrance. The rain slashed the sitting room windows. Michael glanced out, then resumed his nervous pacing:

"Still just one chap in the park. Perhaps the rain's spared us tonight."

"The rain and Captain Tunworth failing to get his warrants," Amanda replied. "I almost wish they'd come and get it over with—the waiting's worse than the battle. It's always worse—"

A moment later, noticing her odd, bemused smile, the young Irishman said:

"Doesn't seem to me our predicament's a subject for humor, Mrs. A—"

"No." She brushed a tired hand across her forehead; her smile faded. "I was only thinking of how the past comes around and around again—like a wheel. I was remembering Texas. When I was in the Alamo mission. By my own choice. When I got out alive, I thought I'd surely never go through anything similar. But here I am, besieged again—and again with no one but myself to blame."

"Blame, Mrs. A? Why do you talk of blame? In your position, most women—men, for that matter—would have gone scurrying out of town hours ago. But you never run. That's rare—and certainly not worthy of blame."

"I ran from Stovall."

"Bosh! You canceled your plans concerning the Phelans because your family's always stood for honor. Decency—"

"Neither of which will buy Kent's now that I've lost my lever for forcing the sale."

"We're not positive Stovall's behind the big stock acquisition—"

"Don't try to be consoling, Michael. Of course he is. He saw the paper."

"Well, at least you can balance the other side of the ledger with several favorable entries. You didn't mire yourself in blackmail. You just may have saved your son from ruin. You certainly saved Mary from recapture—"

"And I lost the one thing I wanted most!"

She exhaled loudly; slumped in her chair. "I must be crazy to stay here like this—"

"Why no," Michael said, "you're a Kent. You've always said they were a brave lot—"

Amanda studied the painting of Philip. How she longed, this moment, for a fraction of the courage those eyes conveyed—

She shivered as wind spattered rain against the windowpanes.

"A member of the Kent family's no different than anyone else in one respect, Michael. Being a Kent doesn't make me any less frightened of what's going to happen."

CHAPTER 10

Destruction

DURING THE NIGHT THE rain stopped. The clouds cleared. By morning, Madison Square glowed in winter sunlight.

Amanda hadn't slept well again. But she was up and dressed when Michael ran into the library a few minutes after nine:

"There's a hack at the door, Mrs. A. And some witnesses over in the park—"

"Witnesses?" She jumped up, following him to the hall.

"Eight or ten chaps who don't have the look of belonging in this neighborhood. They've been gathering for the last half hour. Expecting the hack's arrival, I imagine—"

From the window beside the front door, Amanda saw the men loitering near the kiosk. They were shabbily dressed, in patched trousers and jackets too thin for the weather. They huddled close together, their breath making white plumes in the morning air.

Under the portico, the door of the hackney opened. Captain Virgil Tunworth stepped down, followed by a portly, mustached man in a black alpaca suit and broad-brimmed hat. A bulge on the man's hip hinted at a holstered side-arm.

Brigid came up behind Amanda; started to open the door—

"No," Amanda said, patting her hair to make sure it was arranged. "I'll answer."

Puzzled by Amanda's cheerful expression, Brigid bobbed her head and stood back. Michael took up a position against the wall, his coppery hair catching the sunlight. A smile of rascally delight curved his mouth.

Before Captain Tunworth could lift the knocker, Amanda pulled the door open.

"Captain! Good morning."

The greeting confused the Virginian. He glanced at his companion, who was reaching into his jacket. The portly man produced two folded legal documents.

Recovering from Amanda's unexpected cordiality, Tunworth snapped: "This gentleman is Mr. Bowden—"

"United States Marshal, ma'am," the other man said, rather apologetically. "I have to serve you with this warrant. It permits me—"

"To search my house for the runaway girl the captain fancies I'm hiding?"

"Yes, ma'am."

"Put the warrant back in your pocket, Mr. Bowden. It's totally unnecessary."

"What's that?"

"I informed Captain Tunworth Sunday evening that I wasn't harboring a runaway slave. He wouldn't believe me. You come in and see for yourself."

The marshal stared at Tunworth. "I thought you said she'd refuse—"

"This is some kind of damned flummery!" the captain exploded. "She's gotten rid of the nigger—"

"Why, Captain, how ungentlemanly of you," Amanda said, relishing his discomfort. "You continue to accuse me of breaking the law. Even if I had been hiding this imagined runaway, how could she have escaped?" She pointed past the stamping hack horse to the men near the kiosk. "You've had me watched day and night."

Captain Tunworth flushed; clamped his lips together. Amanda retreated a step:

"Marshal, the house is yours. I have a guest staying on the second floor. My friend Mrs. Ludwig. She came to visit yesterday and became indisposed. Brigid will show you her room—if you must search it—"

"I'm afraid we must search the entire premises, ma'am," Bowden advised her.

"Then would you be kind enough to knock before you disturb Mrs. Ludwig?"

She said it so sweetly, Bowden couldn't help smiling. "Of course."

Tunworth glared as he followed the marshal inside. Michael could barely stifle a guffaw. As the law officer stumped into the sitting room, Tunworth wheeled back to Amanda:

"You had a guest yesterday, right enough. But I know she left an hour after she arrived."

"Really, Captain! You should hire reliable men, not the dregs of the saloons. Her carriage left, that's all."

"Goddamn it, I was told explicitly! Your visitor got into—"

"Please don't swear at me, sir," Amanda broke in, that charming smile still in place. "I don't care what you were told. I'd suggest you inquire whether the man who passed on that doubtful information drank a little something to warm himself while he kept watch. Something that dulled his powers of observation—"

Her dark eyes mocked him. He in turn understood exactly what she was telling him without words: the black girl had departed and he had no way of proving it; the Federal marshal's search was pointless.

But the heavy-set official caught none of that. He came bustling out of the sitting room. "All clear in there. Shall we proceed, Captain?"

Virgil Tunworth slapped his hat against his leg and followed the marshal toward the library.

ii

Bowden took forty-five minutes to comb the house from garret to basement. Now and then he ostentatiously rapped a wall, as if searching for one of those secret rooms so popular in ladies' novels but seldom found in private homes. Amanda and Michael retired to the dining room for coffee, saying little but smiling at one another at the occasional loud sound of Tunworth's hectoring voice.

When he and the marshal reappeared in the downstairs hall, Amanda went out to them:

"Are you finished?"

Bowden nodded. "We are."

"And satisfied?"

"Yes, ma'am. I'm sorry we had to trouble you. It seems the captain was in error when he requested the warrant—"

"*The nigger was in this house over the weekend!*" Tunworth said. He waved his hat at Amanda. "She got the girl out. Wearing the clothes of that harpy upstairs!"

The marshal reddened. "Afraid we did disturb your guest, Mrs. de la Gura. Can't say I've ever heard a female use such a collection of cusswords before—"

"Marshal, you come across to the park with me!" Tunworth demanded.

"You talk to the man who kept watch yesterday. This woman smuggled my slave away in disguise!"

"Unless someone can swear positively to having seen a nigra person leave the house—not just a person, Captain; a *nigra* person—you've no grounds for pressing your complaint." The marshal displayed his search warrant. "Mrs. de la Gura's allowed a complete examination of her home. I can't use the other warrant to arrest someone I can't find."

"Take her into custody! Question her! *Force* her to tell you where—"

"That exceeds my authority, Captain," the marshal interrupted, sounding annoyed for the first time. He settled his hat on his head and executed a stiff bow. "Ma'am, we thank you for your cooperation."

"I'm sorry I couldn't be of more help," Amanda smiled, ushering him to the door.

Bowden went out. Captain Tunworth stormed down the steps after him. Amanda closed the door and moved to the window to watch, Michael at her shoulder.

Louis came running from the kitchen with half a sweet bun in one hand and sugar showing at the corners of his mouth.

"Oh, ma, you sure fooled 'em! I never saw anyone as mad as that captain when he paraded through the kitchen—"

"He's still fuming," Michael said, pointing outside.

The marshal and Tunworth stood by the hack's open door. Amanda couldn't make out the words, but it was obvious Tunworth was insisting on further action, and the marshal was refusing. Finally, red-faced, the marshal thrust both warrants into Tunworth's hand, climbed into the hack and jerked the door shut.

The hack clattered off. Tunworth glared at the house, then stalked across the street. He went straight to the crowd of rough-clad watchers near the kiosk and disappeared in their midst. Amanda drew a tense breath when a couple of the men spun away and started walking toward the house.

Tunworth immediately caught them and pulled them back. Presently, the men began to drift away. Captain Tunworth headed for the opposite side of the square, alone, and was eventually lost from sight in dray and carriage traffic.

"Well," Michael said, "that's it—for the moment."

"I should think we've seen the last of the captain," Amanda said. "There's nothing more he can do."

"There's nothing more he can do *legally*. But I'll bet a gold piece those boyos who came to watch the girl's capture are friends of Rynders—"

After a moment he added, "And they operate best after dark. We've not gotten out of the woods yet."

iii

Despite Michael's pessimism, Amanda couldn't help being elated about frustrating Tunworth. She went up to see Rose, and described the search in detail. Rose complained profanely about having two men poking around her room while she was still in her bed-clothes—

Amused, Amanda asked, "Did they see something they shouldn't?"

"Hell no. They wouldn't even give me a second glance!"

"*That's* why you're angry—!"

"Not funny," Rose barked, lighting a cigar.

Presently she dressed and joined Amanda downstairs. The two ate lunch. At the end, Amanda suggested her friend go home, to insure that the black girl was taken to the White Star pier on time:

"There's really no more danger here, Rose." She sounded more confident than she felt.

Rose finally agreed. Michael walked her across the square to catch the horse-car, returning to report the park free of Captain Tunworth's spies. Amanda was more convinced than ever that Jephtha's father-in-law wouldn't bother them again. She told Michael that in the morning, he was to take the carriage and collect the servants. Meantime, he and Louis could resume their work repairing the broken stall in the carriage house.

In the library, she laid a fire, lit it and settled down in a chair to read through Israel Hope's manuscript. She couldn't concentrate on it. The morning's elation was quite gone.

She thought about using the telegraph to query the Rothman Bank concerning the stock situation. But she decided against it, sadly certain she'd hear nothing to cheer her up. The item in the *Journal of Commerce* had totally wrecked her scheme to force Stovall to sell Kent's. The more she thought of that, the more depressed she became.

One simple choice—one moment of commitment to the welfare of a girl she'd undoubtedly never see again—had undercut the effort of the past two years—and the hopes, the hard work, the struggle of many more years than that.

Amanda had never been one to dwell much on past mistakes. But with the problem of Captain Tunworth resolved, she couldn't escape a deepening despondency. If she used the telegraph, the bank would only confirm that Boston Holdings had failed in its mission—

Was the freedom of one uneducated and frightened black girl worth the sacrifice of what she wanted most in the world?

Foolish question. She knew she couldn't have refused to help the runaway. In that kind of situation, a Kent could never refuse—

But the price of Mary's safety was so high; so unbearably high—

Again she tried to read what Israel had written. It seemed pointless; by its very existence, the manuscript mocked her. It would never be published with the Kent imprint—

The words blurred. The sentences lost all meaning. The strain and exhaustion of the past few days finally caught up with her. Sometime after three, she dozed off—

She awoke with a start to find Brigid hovering beside her. Except for the glow from the hearth, the library was dark.

"Visitor, ma'am. In the hall—"

Her palms turned cold. Not Tunworth again—

"Who is it, Brigid?"

"He didn't present a card, ma'am. But he says his name's Stovall."

"*Stovall—!*"

Amanda seized the arm of the chair. The pages of manuscript spilled off her lap.

"Where's Michael?"

"In the kitchen, ma'am. He and Louis are eating a bite of supper I fixed. 'T'isn't as good as cook's fare, but I did my best. I looked in at seven to see if you'd want some, but you were asleep—"

"Seven? What time is it—?"

The clock showed half after eight.

Tense, Amanda picked up the manuscript pages and piled them at the foot of the chair. Brigid noticed her extreme nervousness.

"Would you like me to tell the gentleman you're indisposed?"

"No, Brigid, I—" Fear crawled in her like some venomous invader. "—I'll receive him."

"In the sitting room?"

Amanda dabbed at her perspiring upper lip; glanced from the objects on the mantel to the painting of her grandfather. Her voice grew a little firmer:

"In here. Light the gas, please. Did you bolt the front door again?"

"Of course, ma'am."

"All right. I'll see to the visitor—"

Still plagued by an ominous feeling, she left the library and walked toward the front door where Stovall waited, his gold-knobbed cane under one arm and his silk hat held in his gloved hand.

Outside, Amanda heard a carriage horse stamp. The immaculate white scarf bisecting Stovall's face had a silken sheen in the gaslight. His visible eye sparkled bright as a bird's.

Staring at him, her sense of dread worsened. Her gaze went past his shoulder to one of the narrow windows flanking the door. Except for the flare of the lantern on his carriage and the dimmer lights on the far side of the square, she saw nothing but darkness. Somehow that terrified her too—

"Kind of you to receive me, Mrs. de la Gura," Hamilton Stovall said with a slight bow. "Or would it be more proper if I addressed you by your correct name? Kent?"

iv

From a shadowed place in the hall, Mr. Mayor miaowed. The sound of Brigid's footsteps faded at the rear of the house. She kept her voice as steady as she could:

"Whatever you prefer, Mr. Stovall. Please come this way—"

"Thank you."

Amanda's arm trembled as she held the library door open. Inside, the gaslight glowed.

Stovall went in. She wanted to strike him. But she held back, struggling for control; for mastery of the inexplicable mixture of loathing and terror his presence generated.

Yet he behaved politely enough, taking the chair she'd vacated beside the hearth. She walked around the desk and sat beneath the painting of Philip, almost as if she needed some sort of physical barrier to prevent her from attacking him.

Stovall acted quite relaxed. Smiled—though there was no cordiality in his eye. His artificial teeth glimmered like old bone as he laid his cane across his knees and set his silk hat on the floor.

"It seems my suspicions weren't entirely unfounded," he said.

She didn't answer.

"You *do* recall our little encounter at the Douglass lecture—?"

"Quite—quite well."

Never had ordinary speech required such effort; never had she churned with such overpowering hate. At the same time, her fear of him grew; she was terrified of his assured manner; that skull's grin—

Almost as if he were chiding an infant, he continued:

"You lied to me. Your motive for wanting to buy Kent and Son was not entirely a matter of business—"

"That conclusion hardly seems a sufficient reason for you to call in person, Mr. Stovall."

He wouldn't be prodded:

"You can imagine my stupefaction after I browsed through Monday's *Journal* and saw the mention of your relative—"

"Get to the point!"

Her outburst amused him; he clearly enjoyed unsettling her. Breathing loudly, she brushed a stray lock of white hair from her forehead.

"Certainly," he murmured. "I drove here to satisfy my curiosity—and to pass on two items of information. Shall we take those in order—?"

He leaned forward slightly:

"Who are you?"

"The cousin of a young man named Jared Kent."

He sat bolt upright; a point scored.

"That's right," she said. "The boy who served with you aboard *Constitution*."

He touched the white silk with a gloved finger. "The boy who attacked me—"

"Oh, that's very funny—you speaking of an attack. Wasn't it the other way around? Once in your cabin? And once on the deck?"

Now, finally, she'd cracked his defenses; he spoke with soft, seething fury:

"Jared Kent forced me to live my life as a grotesque—" *Flick* went the gloved finger against the silk. "He gave me this." He held out his gloves, palms up. "And these. Hands so scarred, I can't display them in public—"

"I think you extracted payment ten times over. You stole the printing firm from my stepfather—"

"That foolish Piggott? My dear woman, I won a wager from him!"

"Not honestly, I suspect."

Stovall's lips pressed together in prim pleasure. "Impossible to prove, of course."

"Of course. When my cousin shot your companion—"

"Poor old Walpole. Retired now. Hopelessly senile."

"—you never took steps to correct Jared's belief that he'd done murder."

"Great God, woman, what do you expect from a man who's been the target of a pistol? Charity? Compassion? Besides, your cousin fled Boston—"

"Thinking he was a murderer. He carried the guilt all his life."

"May I ask where he is now?"

"He died in California over two years ago."

"While you amassed your wealth partly in—"

A supple gesture of his right glove.

"California! Now I begin to perceive the pattern. A reunion. A pledge of retribution—in the form of regaining the family business. Really rather cheap theatrics, don't you think? Well, you have at least satisfied my curiosity. And as regards your effort to buy—or in the case of the stock manipulation, I might say steal—Kent and Son, you have failed."

He leaned forward again.

"How utterly you've failed is one of the points I wish to impress on you this evening."

She watched the play of firelight on his flesh and the concealing silk. She felt unclean. He was more than a physical grotesque; the shine of his eye said his very soul—if he had one—was malignant.

"Happily," he continued, "I checked your little stock scheme in time, thanks to the fortuitous appearance of the Kent name in Monday's press. I am not entirely the thoughtless and unqualified steward of my own affairs that I sometimes appear to be, Mrs. de la—forgive me. I simply can't use that name any longer. Mrs. Kent. For some months, I've been aware of a good deal of movement in Stovall Works shares. Much more than the firm's reputation merits, I might add. But if investors had confidence in my company, excellent! That I failed to scrutinize the movement more closely is a tactical error I readily admit. My head's been busy with other things. Attempting to float a loan. Courting a young woman—at any rate, I was not aware the acquisitions of Stovall shares were in any way organized until the *Journal* item prompted me to make certain inquiries—and very rapidly, I don't mind telling you. Naturally the information was there—in the hands of the bankers who act as registrars of the stock. Those fools had neglected to see any significance in the pattern and hence had never called it to my personal attention. All the individual purchasers, it seems, re-sold their shares to a company known as Boston Holdings.

Whose principals, I learned, are the very same Jew financier and the very same attorney who attempted to arrange your purchase of Kent's—"

He kept smiling that hateful, insincere smile; his teeth glared red in the firelight.

"What was your ultimate goal? A majority position in the stock?"

She could barely nod:

"Yes."

"Which you would then exchange for control of the company you wanted?"

"Yes."

He clicked his tongue against his teeth. "I don't accept that lightly, my dear woman. Not lightly at all. You maneuvered against me—"

"Get out," she breathed. "Get out of here before—"

"Before what, Mrs. Kent? You've no trump cards to play—they're all mine. As you'll soon see—"

She shivered. His voice had dropped low. He lightened it, almost teasing her:

"Naturally when I unearthed your little manipulation on Monday, I acted. At one thirty in the afternoon, I convened the available members of the board—which now includes my prospective father-in-law, by the way. By two, we had agreed to issue the new stock. Thankfully, Mr. Van Bibb had already agreed in principle to invest in the Stovall Works. Instead of making a loan to the company, he and two associates subscribed the entire new issue. Between us, Van Bibb, his friends and I now hold a commanding majority—"

He pressed the tips of his gloved fingers together.

"You want Kent's very much, don't you? I never cared for that idea once I learned of your—ah—democratic philosophies. Now I have an even more compelling reason for keeping the firm out of your hands. I assure you, my dear—it's never going to be yours."

"Mr. Stovall, you're exhausting my patience. You've made it clear that you've defeated m—"

"But I haven't! Not completely! You overlooked one additional possibility—"

Her hands pressed against the desk, she whispered:

"What possibility?"

"Why—the mortality of human flesh. I am older than you by several years. Suppose I were to be struck by a sudden illness. Suppose I were to die. My estate—to be handled by my future wife and my two cousins who sit on the board—might very well accept any reasonable offer for Kent and Son. But it will never happen now. I intend to issue explicit instructions to Miss Van Bibb—to my cousins—and to my attorneys—that you never be permitted to purchase the company. Never as long as you live. Nor any of your heirs, for that matter. Ah, that hurts, doesn't it? Well, suffer with it. Till the moment you die, suffer with the knowledge that even tens of millions of dollars will never give your family what you've striven so desperately to acquire—"

Amanda absorbed the words almost as if they were physical blows. She knew he meant every one. He'd out-pointed her again; she'd never thought of the contingency he'd described—

"That's what you came to tell me, Mr. Stovall?"

"That and one thing more. I want to learn a little more about you—"

The teasing smile twisted his lips. She was frightened again, trying to decipher his intent.

"That's correct—I want to know more about your background. Your life in California—and wherever else you've been. I plan to dispatch a pair of trusted investigators to the gold fields. I'm sure a woman as—determined as you can't have survived merely by the exercise of piety and the performance of good works. I'd like to know how checkered your past really is—"

Amanda shook her head, still unable to fathom his purpose. What could he possibly learn that would hurt her? That she'd shot a man? That she'd run a brothel in Bexar? Neither fact would be to her credit if it were made public. But scandal couldn't prevent her from continuing her business affairs, any more than it had prevented him. And she had no hope of being accepted in the higher echelons of society. Unearthing the past seemed a wholly futile exercise—

Or so she believed until she asked, "Why?"

She turned icy when he said, "You have a son, do you not?"

Oh God, no, she thought. Of course that was the reason.

"An heir to the name of your pretentious family?"

"I—"

"Come, I know you do! And I'm sure you have high ambitions for him. Commendable. Let's hope *his* reputation isn't blackened too terribly by whatever I might discover. Because I'll make it public, I assure you. Any shame which attaches to you will attach to him. In short, I'll do everything in my power to make his life difficult—to prevent him from rising in the world—I will smear and stain your name—and his—until any aspirations you may have had for your son achieving respectability will be quite gone. No one attacks me with impunity, my dear woman—"

The skull smile widened.

"No one."

"Stovall—" She could barely speak.

"Ah! I've touched a genuinely sensitive spot at last!"

"Don't do anything to harm my boy. This is only between us."

"Indeed it is not. And I'm encouraged by your reaction. There must be something you don't care to have aired about—" Abruptly, he seemed nonplussed for the first time. "I fail to understand why you're smiling."

It was a smile bordering on tears:

"Do you? I'll tell you. I once had a plan to use much the same strategy on you."

"What do you mean?"

"Your affairs in the Five Points—with a young man and woman named Joseph and Aggie Phelan—"

Stovall's gloved hands clenched. His cane slid off his knees to the floor.

"I know about them. At one time I thought of informing Van Bibb's daughter."

Warily: "But you didn't—"

"No, I didn't."

He breathed loudly, relieved. "Scruples. That, of course, is the difference between us."

"I didn't do it, Stovall—and I ask you to be decent enough to act with similar restraint. I don't care what kind of filth you spread about me. Just don't hurt my son—"

Almost weeping, she bent across the desk:

"Let's call a truce. You have the company. Isn't that enough?"

She was desperate now. If his inquiry agents followed the trail of her past from San Francisco to Los Angeles, then back to Texas, every chance Louis had for a respectable life could be wiped out—

His mother murdered a man.

His mother kept a whorehouse.

His mother was scum—

Humiliated and hating the man smiling at her beside the hearth, she did the hardest thing she'd ever done.

She begged:

"*Please*, Stovall! A truce!"

He laughed in a merry way. "A truce?" He raised a glove to the white silk. "With a family who did this—?"

The glove lifted the silk. She pressed her knuckles to her mouth as sour vomit climbed into her throat. She averted her head; squeezed her eyes shut—

When she looked again, he had let the silk fall back into place.

"No, my dear Mrs. Kent, a truce is out of the question." His voice grew steadily louder. "If it's humanly possible—and one or two of your inadvertent reactions make me think it is—I'm going to see that your boy is never welcomed in the kind of home where I'm sure you'd wish him welcomed. Let him live with your money. Let him derive what satisfaction he can from that, because he'll never have the satisfaction of being called a gentleman—nor the satisfaction of owning Kent and So—"

The rest of the sentence was blurred by the explosive sound of shattering glass.

v

Hamilton Stovall grabbed up his hat and cane, leaped to his feet, spun toward the library doors. Another window broke. The front sitting room—

She heard the scream of a frightened horse; Michael shouting from the kitchen—

Stovall loped toward the doors. He was two steps from them when Louis burst in.

The boy stopped in the doorway, glanced briefly at Stovall, then at his mother. Amanda saw the panic on his face:

"Ma, there are men out front! Twenty or thirty—come from nowhere—"

She heard shouting; cursing; the heavy thud of fists pounding the front door.

Rynders' thugs. Waiting until dark to strike—

Stovall realized the danger, even though he didn't understand its source or cause. With a shrill yell—"Get out of the way!"—he bolted for the hall.

Louis didn't react quickly enough; didn't step aside. Stovall's cane slashed wildly. The gold knob struck the boy's temple.

Louis fell sideways, his head slamming the heavy woodwork of the door frame. He cried out; tumbled to the carpet as fists beat harder on the front door—

He's killed him, Amanda thought, all the hatred bursting loose within her. *HE'S KILLED LOUIS—*

Screaming for his carriage driver, Stovall stepped over the still form sprawled in the library entrance. Amanda wasn't even conscious of tearing open the drawer of her desk, pulling out the old Colt and firing.

A red splotch appeared on the dark fabric of Hamilton Stovall's coat, between his shoulders. He pitched forward, his hat rolling in one direction, his cane in the other. He fell at the feet of Michael Boyle, who had appeared suddenly from the rear of the hall.

Unable to speak, Michael stared at the woman behind the desk. Her right arm was extended to its full length. The gun in her hand showed no sign of motion. A tiny wisp of smoke curled out of the foot-long barrel.

vi

Abruptly, Amanda came back to life. She ran to the fallen boy, flinging the Colt on the carpet as she knelt between Louis in the doorway and Stovall's body in the hall. She touched the boy's lips—

"He's breathing!"

"What in God's name did Stovall—?"

"Hit him," she said. "With his cane—"

"There she is!" someone outside yelled. "That's the one who hid the nigger!"

She twisted around; saw white, distorted faces pressed against the narrow windows on either side of the front door.

Another voice: "Where's Mickey? Mickey has the pistol—"

A third: "Don't wait for Mickey! Break the goddamn door!"

Mr. Mayor miaowed at the noise of shoulders battering the wood. The door gave off an ominous crack. The cat arched his back and crept away from the shouting; the thudding; the fist that suddenly smashed window-glass and reached around for the bolt—

Amanda jumped up. "Take Brigid out the back. Brigid and Louis."

Michael scowled, pointing at the darkening skin just below the boy's hairline:

"It could be dangerous to move him—"

"It'll be a lot more dangerous if he stays here! Get him to a doctor! *Now!*"

"I can't leave you to face—"

"Michael, I'm not going! You can carry Louis better and faster than I. There are things here I have to protect—"

The front door splintered. Scraps of wood fell inward. The disembodied hand, bloodied by the broken glass, was still groping for the bolt. Michael's face showed his agony as he tried to decide what to do.

"I'll be all right!" She held up the revolver, turned the cylinder. "I've four more shots—and I'm sure the neighbors have already summoned the police—"

From the portico came another strident yell:

"Shoot the fuckin' horse, Mickey!"

An explosion. A wild scream of animal pain.

"There goes the driver! *Catch him—!"*

With a grind and crash, the carriage was overturned. Michael and Amanda heard the driver's shrieks—

"Damn you, Michael, *go!"*

The young Irishman rushed to Louis, lifted him in both arms. With one last look at his employer, he hurried toward the dining room. He moved swiftly; yet Amanda was conscious of the extreme care with which he held the still figure of the boy—

Let him get away, she prayed. *Let my son live—*

The red hand found the bolt at last. As she retreated toward the library, the already-ruined front door swung inward, wrenched off its top hinge by the force of the men crowding against it. In the drive, the coachman was still screaming.

Just as she started to close the library doors, she glimpsed a lick of flame. The carriage set afire—

Burly, oafish, the men spilled into the long front hall. One who was faster than the rest leaped at Mr. Mayor. The frightened tom started to run. The thug caught him by the tail.

The white cat yowled, claws slashing. The thug swung him hard. The cat's head broke open, spattering the wall—

Amanda saw that an instant before she locked the doors. She closed her eyes and leaned her forehead against the wood, listening to the sounds of the carnage: shouts; filthy language; furniture breaking; windows smashing; draperies being ripped down—

She stumbled around behind the desk. She put the Colt on a pile of papers; picked up the display case containing Jared's medallion. She carried it to the mantel and set it up beside the tea bottle. She retrieved the Colt, returned to the mantel and stood there, waiting—

Bart said it would come to this. Take up the sword—perish with the sword.

Perhaps if I hadn't hated Stovall so much—or wanted Kent's so badly—Louis wouldn't have attacked Kathleen—

Nor this mob come—

And Stovall wouldn't have hit my son—

If, IF!—the complexities of cause and effect tormented her as she waited for the first onslaught against the library doors—

Shoulders slammed the outside of the panels. Her heart beat frantically as she positioned herself two steps out from the mantel.

The bolt housing tore loose.

The doors swayed.

Buckled—

"There's the bitch!"

"Give her what-for—"

"For Kathleen McCreery!"

She had a wild glimpse of half a dozen men milling in the hall. One had his penis in his hand, urinating on the carpet—

The men charged her across the wreckage of the doors. She shot the first one in the chest.

He screamed and slapped his frayed jacket, slammed backwards into the arms of his companions. While she revolved the cylinder, the thugs retreated into the hall again, yelling and cursing as they tried to free themselves from the weight of the dead man. One thug stepped on Stovall's head.

"Mickey, damn ye, where are ye, boy?"

"Mickey, bring your gun—!"

The whole house thundered: heavy boots slammed the ceiling; glass crashed and tinkled; great thumps and thuds and splintering sounds built to a deafening din.

The thugs advanced cautiously outside the library doorway, using the walls to hide themselves from Amanda. One bearded face suddenly peered around the splintered frame. She aimed the Colt. The face disappeared. In the distance, bells clanged. Police wagons. Blocks away, but coming fast. Distracted by the sound, she failed to see the hand that snaked around the doorframe clasping a small, shiny-plated pistol. The moment she did see it, the pistol gave off a loud pop.

She started to duck behind Michael's favorite chair. Something struck her below her left breast. She glanced down, faint all at once. Her dress was stained dark red.

She dropped to her knees, one hand on the chair so she wouldn't fall. The wound began to hurt.

"You got 'er, Mickey!" a man howled, charging into the room. "Let's tear the fuckin' place apar—"

She shot him between the legs. The bullet lifted him off his feet and hurled him on top of the man she'd shot in the chest.

The library was smoky now. She gasped for breath; stood up despite the pain; stretched out her left hand, groping for the mantel—

The pain was constant; hard to bear. But she wouldn't let them reach her. She wouldn't let them pull down the sword or the rifle. Wouldn't let them smash the green bottle or the case with Jared's medallion—

Another man tried. He almost had his hands on her before she blew away half his face.

That sent the attackers fleeing back into the hall, out of the line of fire.

The bells clanged louder. Hoofs rattled on concrete. Iron-tired wheels screeched. Under the portico, someone yelled:

"*Police—!*"

There were panicked cries; the sound of pounding feet; a last crash of glass from somewhere at the rear of the house—

Amanda held onto the mantel with all her strength. The left side of her dress was soaked red from breast to hip—

I killed Stovall, she thought, gazing down at the blood. *And what did Jephtha say—?*

Without blood there is no remission of sin—

Her blurring eyes moved to the wall clock.

Fifteen until ten.

Fifteen minutes more and the steamer would put out from North River bound for Canada—

She almost smiled.

She let go of the mantel and the Colt revolver at the same time, unconscious before she struck the carpet.

CHAPTER 11

Judgment

AMANDA KENT DE LA GURA lived seventeen days after the attack on her home. She lay in her bedroom on the second floor, conscious for short periods, and in relatively little pain at first. During one of the brief periods of wakefulness, Michael Boyle told her eight men had been caught and arrested by the police; the rest had escaped. No connection between any of the eight prisoners and Isaiah Rynders could be established, he informed her somewhat cynically.

Occasionally Amanda heard unfamiliar voices; the faint rasp of saws on the first floor; the rap of hammers. Workmen had already begun repairing the damage, estimated at eighty thousand dollars.

In Amanda's room, there was no evidence of the attack. The draperies had been replaced. The damaged furniture had been removed. The thugs had destroyed furnishings throughout the house; smashed great holes in the plaster; ripped up carpeting and defecated on the floors. But while Amanda slept, Michael supervised the quiet work of making it seem as though her bedchamber hadn't been touched.

Sometime on the second or third day, a doctor bent over her. She didn't recognize him. Since moving to New York City, neither she nor her son had ever required a doctor's care. In fact she couldn't remember the last time she'd been seriously ill.

Now, however, it was a different matter. The doctor told her the pistol ball had lodged in or near her left lung, and couldn't be removed. She knew from his expression she was going to die.

"I've also been attending your son," he said.

"Where—" At times, speaking even a few words was difficult. "Where is—?"

"Mrs. Ludwig's home. We'll move him here as quickly as we can.

Young Mr. Boyle got him to me in time. He suffered a wicked concussion but I believe he'll pull through."

She fell asleep weeping.

ii

On the fourth day, Michael brought her a *Tribune* with the account of Hamilton Stovall's funeral, and a letter postmarked in the nation's capital. She could barely find strength to hold the envelope:

"I can't read it, Michael. The hand seems familiar—"

"I opened it, Mrs. A. It's from your cousin's son."

"Jephtha? He's alive—?"

"In Washington. He doesn't think he can go back to his family."

"Is—is there an address?"

Michael pointed it out. "A Methodist parsonage."

"Write him. Tell him—to come here. Shelter—"

"What, Mrs. A?" He bent close to her.

"*Shelter him,*" she whispered as her eyes closed. "Help him—start again—"

iii

On the sixth day, Theo Payne arrived from Boston in response to a telegraph message Michael had sent. Amanda smelled the whiskey on Payne's breath the moment he entered the bedroom, turning his hat brim nervously in his hands.

He sat on a chair at the bedside, listening attentively:

"Downstairs—there's a manuscript. I want—Kent's to publish it. I want—you to stay on as—the editor."

"Stay on?"

"Mr. Benbow—has approached the Stovall estate. They are—willing to sell. The executors have no—have no—" She struggled to get the words out. "—objections to my politics, and—and my money is as good as—anyone's. I want you to teach my son all you know, Theo. I want the firm to—to stand for something again."

"You know my position. I am strongly in favor of abolitionism. I would even propose starting a newspaper similar to the one Kent and Son once published." Eagerness livened his voice. "I've had experience in that line, you know—"

"If you do start a paper," she whispered, "it must do more than—than support freedom for the slaves. It must—it must stand for that and—preserving the Union too—"

Payne looked downcast. "I'm not sure both can be done together—"

A moment later he leaned forward. "What did you say?"

Silently, her lips formed two words:

"*Must be.*"

After several minutes had passed, he assumed she wasn't going to waken again soon. He began to tiptoe out.

"Theo—"

He started, unnerved by the unexpected loudness of her voice. He turned back. Her eyes were open; clear and alert.

"Theo," she said, "clean the sign."

"The sign? Oh—the one in front of the firm—"

"Better still, have—a new one painted. It's a goddamn disgrace."

He watched her eyes close again, then continued to the door, vaguely ashamed because he wanted to whoop with joy.

iv

Rose visited on the seventh day. It was a tiring experience for Amanda, because Rose seemed all bluster and profanity:

"Damn it, Amanda, you've got to—to get out of that bed—I don't have—another friend who'll tolerate my cigars or—or go out with me in public wearing—trousers—Jesus Christ, how horridly I'm behaving! I can't help it. *I can't help it—*"

She hid her face with both hands.

v

On the ninth day, summoned at Amanda's request, William Benbow, Junior arrived from Boston. With the door of the bedroom closed, the attorney showed her the papers transferring legal guardianship of Louis Kent de la Gura to Michael Boyle.

"Only one—mistake," she said. "Scratch out—de la Gura. His name is Louis—Kent."

Old Benbow helped guide her hand so she could write her signature. It was all but illegible.

vi

On the eleventh day, Amanda felt sufficiently alert to hold another short conversation with Michael. She wore a lavender bed gown that Brigid had helped her put on. Her hair, unpinned, lay fanned on the pillow, so nearly white that it was almost indistinguishable from the linen. From time to time, her wrinkled face constricted with pain.

"Michael—?"

"I'm here."

She clutched his extended hand, treasuring its warmth.

"Louis is—?"

"Perfectly fine, though still sleeping a good deal."

"I wish I could see him."

"Why, you will, Mrs. A. You'll be up and ab—"

"No, I—" She coughed. "—won't and you know it. I think I—forgot to ask before. Did anyone—find Tunworth—?"

"The night of the attack? No. I expect he was safely in the Astor House when it took place. He's gone home minus one nigger."

"About Jephtha—"

"I wrote him. I invited him here to live."

"Good. Remember, all the Ophir money—is his—along with the profits of the issues I bought with part of that money—"

"I'll see he gets every penny."

"You—mustn't—say that word again, either."

"What word?"

"Nigger. I—don't like it. You're not a slum boy any longer, Michael, you're—part of my family now. You are all I have to depend on—the only one who—can take Louis in hand—see that he grows up to be—straight and decent—and learns the business under Theo Payne—"

"I won't say the word again, Mrs. A," Michael whispered. "I don't think I'm fit for the responsibility you've laid on me. But I'll try to be worthy of it."

She sighed, a faint, reedy sound. "I did so much that was wrong—"

"And so much that was right."

"But—" She seemed not to hear. "At least Kent's will be back in the family."

"Yes. Benbow says all's proceeding smoothly."

"Michael—" Frantic pressure from her feeble fingers. "You must promise me—"

"What?"

"Never tell—Louis how—Stovall died."

"I had already decided I wouldn't. One of the mobsters was found dead with a pistol on his body. A copper whacked the fellow too hard with his stick. So the story is, the dead chap's the one who shot Mr. Stovall. The press has already printed it that way. The ball from your Colt was of much larger caliber. But the police overlooked that. I—I'm afraid I bribed them to do so. There's little point in them prosecuting a woman who—"

He stopped abruptly.

"Who is going to die?"

A long silence.

"Michael—?"

"Yes?"

"When you put up a headstone—in Watertown—"

"Oh, Mrs. A, what's this morbid talk of headstones?"

"Listen to me. Along with my husband's name, I want the name Kent on it. Amanda Kent de la Gura—"

She began to drift off, murmuring it over and over:

"Kent. Kent—"

Crying silently, Michael Boyle held her hand long after she was unconscious.

vii

On the fifteenth day, she thought she had begun to hallucinate. She saw a familiar face; gray eyes; hair whiter than she remembered it—

"Bart?"

"Yes, sweet, it's me."

"How—how is it possible?"

"Why, the story of the mob's attack has been telegraphed to papers all over the country. Along with the account of how you probably helped a nigra girl escape to Canada. You should hear them cuss you in Charleston! That's where I read about it—"

"Charleston! I—tried to write you in London—"

He shook his head. "I went home. Damned if I can altogether explain why—unless it was the feeling of starting to grow old among people I didn't know very well. The folk in Britain are marvelous. Polite. Hospitable—and the Royal Sceptre captaincy paid far better than I'd expected, once I added in the primage. But after I lost you, somehow I came to feel I—I didn't have anything. Not even a home. If a man doesn't have a woman—and I swore I'd never fuss with another until I met you—I suppose he should at least have a home. I never figured I'd do it, but one day I gave notice to Royal Sceptre and walked out. I confess I damn near bawled when the steamer sailed in past Fort Sumter and Fort Moultrie and I saw the Battery in Charleston again. I'm running a little cotton packet up and down the coast—"

She tried to laugh; it came out as a faint rasp:

"You—took sides after all."

"Guess I did, in a way."

"So did I—" An image of Jared's medallion drifted into her mind. "You were right, no—no one can stay out of it."

"Listen, you'll never get me to a political meeting, sweet! I'm content to savor the southern climate as is—I stay far away from platforms where Yancey and Rhett and some of the other secessionist fire-eaters puff out their sulphurous rhetoric—"

"There's—so much hate on both sides now—"

"Yes, there is." He looked at her with forlorn eyes. "It'll tear this country apart."

"The Union has to survive. The *country* has to survive—"

"Not certain it can, sweet."

"There's too much that's good at stake. Too much that was hard-won—"

"But it's a matter of principle on both sides. And the voices keep getting louder—"

"There are other voices. Kent's will be one soon. Against slavery—"

"Well, there you go!"

"But against bloodshed too—"

"Amanda," he said, "it's an impossible problem. The north will never countenance slavery, and the south will never give it up. Each wants its own way. That always leads to but one conclusion. 'Perish with—'"

Abruptly, he cut off the sentence, realizing it had a closer and more painful meaning.

She recognized his discomfort:

"You were right about that too. Stovall's dead. I shot him. He attacked Louis—might have killed him—"

"Yes, the Irish lad informed me."

After a moment, she said:

"Bart—I wish you'd bend down and kiss me. That—that's a frightful thing for an old lady to ask, isn't it?"

He put his face near hers.

"No."

"I expect I should have married you—"

"I know you should have, sweet."

"I did what I had to do. But I love you."

"Yes, I love you too. More than I can begin to tell y—"

Silence.

"Amanda? Did you hear—?"

In panic, he felt for her pulse—

Thin. But it was there. She was only sleeping.

                                      viii

On the morning of the seventeenth day, with the draperies open to admit the sun of another bright winter morning, she felt unusually lethargic. Breathing was difficult. She was struck by the certainty that she wouldn't live much longer.

One hand rested on a blue-covered legal document. The agreement of the Stovall estate to sell Kent and Son. It had arrived by messenger from Boston late the preceding night. Michael had brought it up and laid it at her bedside so she saw it the first thing when she awoke.

She wished she could have spoken to Louis. But he was still recuperating; still sleeping a good deal, Michael said.

All at once she heard a faraway melody.

The piano. The piano in the music room; the piano no one had ever played—

And now familiar, melancholy notes rose upward through the house—

Bart. The Chopin piece.

Somehow the music soothed her. Seemed not melancholy but full of sweet promise and healing. She let her mind range peacefully back across all the years, from the tepee of the young Sioux, Plenty Coups, to her marriage to Jaimie de la Gura—the turmoil in Texas—Cordoba and the birth of her son—Bart in California—

And the end of her life here in New York.

It was time for an accounting.

On the credit side, she'd preserved the family. Put it in trustworthy hands. With Joshua Rothman and old Benbow and Theo Payne to assist him, Michael Boyle—a Kent in spirit now, if not in name—would serve well until Louis achieved his majority. She only prayed she hadn't warped her son's character too severely; prayed Michael would be able to mold him into an honorable man. At least there was a hope of it—

Perhaps Jephtha would help when he came to the city. On Jephtha's side too, the family had heirs; his sons. Whatever their position on the divisive issues tormenting the country, they were Kents. With the proceeds of the Ophir claim in Hopeful, and with the promising reports from the Sierras, they would be wealthy men—

If there were no war to destroy them; to destroy the nation—

On the debit side, she knew she had at times been ruthless in order to survive; ruthless in obtaining her ends. So ruthless, Louis had very nearly been sacrificed. Yet from her ruthlessness had come the restoration of the Kent fortune. Perhaps that entry had a place on both sides of the ledger.

And the company. The company belonged to its rightful owners again. Her hand moved over the blue-covered document; a kind of caress—

All at once she felt quite sleepy. The sunlight burned her eyes. Details of the room melted away in the glare—

The appearance of that intense light told her the end was very near. She was terrified of dying alone. Bart and Michael had gone downstairs for breakfast with Rose, who had sat with her through the night. She tried to grasp the bell pull—

She was too feeble to reach it.

Weary and frightened, she gave up trying to assess her own life. She remembered the Mandan legend of the vine; the great womanly hands left the vine alone, or tore it, denying paradise. The meaning of the legend brought a certain comfort. Only a Divine intelligence could fully and accurately judge a human life, and find it worthy or wanting—

She'd taken lives. The man in Hopeful—and Hamilton Stovall—lingered most acutely in her mind. Those acts would weigh heavily in the judgment, she knew.

But the judgment itself was beyond her.

I am a Kent.
I did what I had to.
Let the verdict come down.

An almost child-like expression of pleasure came onto her face. Settling her head more comfortably on the pillow, she turned toward the intense light. She'd quite forgotten the light shone through a window in a specific house in a specific city in America—

Or did it?

She felt her strength waning. She was suddenly ashamed of her own fear.

Guilty she might be. But what human being was not? There were things in her past she needn't be ashamed of; things to be proud of; she wouldn't surrender so meekly to a condemning judgment—

That's not what grandfather would have done.

Slowly, her eyes closed.

It was puzzling. The light remained.

Growing steadily brighter—

Suddenly, clear and sharp, she saw the vine to paradise.

She spit on her hands and began to climb.

Afterword

The Kent Chronicles have produced an immense and positive response from readers. One question is frequently asked: "What's true and what isn't?" A short comment may be in order.

The Kent family, of course, is fictitious—but at all times, an effort has been made to make each of the Kents *representative* of a certain type of person living in a particular era in American history. For instance:

The grim circumstances faced by several of the family members in Volume 3, THE SEEKERS, reflect the reality of the period: life on the cutting edge of western expansion was stark; brutal. Many were defeated by it; many others persevered. (But to romanticize or prettify the historical realities of such a period, it seems to me, would diminish the courage and determination of those who endured and overcame its hardships.)

Factual details have helped shape the lives of the fictional characters. A good example from this volume is the escaped slave in the packing box. (What author would have the nerve to invent such a device?) In the period described, a man named Henry "Box" Brown actually made his escape to the north in this fashion.

As to actual events and people, I made a mental pledge at the beginning of the series that I would never deliberately or knowingly distort the record, whether of a battle, or the character of an historical figure as I saw him or her through the lens of research. One or two small liberties with chronology have been taken in the first four novels, but that is the only sort of deviation I feel is defensible in books which attempt to relate the story of our common past.

I must admit to one compromise. Before I undertook the writing, I acknowledged it would probably be impossible to cover so much history without committing errors; hopefully, careful research would keep them minor—as in Volume 1, THE BASTARD, which originally included a sequence in which a match was struck—long before matches of that sort were available. That one, mercifully, was caught in the galley proofs.

Accepting the probability of unintentional error was the price of seeing the work reach readers in a reasonable time; I either had to run the risk or face taking a lifetime to do the writing.

Happily, the approach, with all its hazards, seems to have been the right one. A great number of men and women have written to say the series has re-kindled a desire to delve deeper into American history. No writer or publisher could ask for a greater reward.

JOHN JAKES